LEGACY OF THE VALIANT
A TALE FROM NORVEGR

EDALE LANE

Legacy of the Valiant; A Tale from Norvegr

By Edale Lane

Published by Past and Prologue Press

Edited by Jessica Hatch

Cover art by Enggar Adirasa

First Edition , April 2023

CONTENTS

FORWARD AND ACKNOWLEDGEMENTS

M yths and legends come from somewhere. I don't believe one day some guy in Europe and some other guy in China spontaneously came up with the images and stories for dragons out of the blue. Something they encountered that was strange and unfamiliar inspired the similar winged serpentine pictures, the shape of the heads, the long, lethal tails. Then embellishments were added, the stories told more exciting, the artwork more detailed. I'm not proposing there were real fire-breathing dragons and Saint George gained his fame by killing one... and I'm not saying there weren't. Yet I'm convinced from a historian's point of view that once upon a time, long ago, people in different parts of the world saw a scary creature they never had before, and the tale of the dragon was born.

The same is true of Norse, Roman, or Greek mythology. Fantastic tales of gods and heroes, imaginary creatures and horrifying monsters all had a basis in some actual person, animal, or event. In this book, you will read of fantastic adventures and extraordinary beings told by skalds and storytellers; you will also come to understand where such stories may have gained their origins. Could the greatest power on earth truly be human imagination?

I would like to acknowledge the hard work and valuable input of my proofreader Aimée. Thank you also to my dedicated partner, Johanna White, and my facilitators, Stephen Zimmer, and J. Scott Coatsworth. I didn't get this out to my regular team soon enough to receive beta input, but there will be ARC readers, and I appreciate you so much. Of course, I wouldn't be still happily engaged in my new career if not for you, the readers, and I thank you most of all for taking this journey with me. And to everyone out there who ever thought you were too short, too tall, too big, too small, too infirmed, too flawed, or too unimportant to ever be of great worth, think again. I challenge you to dig down and find your inner hero.

I

Bàtrgørð, shipbuilding camp in Yeats, land of the Swedes, 690 A.D.

"Tell us the story of Sigrid and Elyn," Leiknir urged. Eager, round eyes peered up at his father Torsten, as he added another log to the fire. Its flames danced just far enough away to avoid catching the twig roof of their lean-to ablaze.

Kai nestled close to her girlfriend, Tove, under the shelter of the shed. Spring marked longer days, thawing snows, and the beginning of boatbuilding season in Bàtrgørð, a small seasonal seaside village a short way north of Lagarfjord where King Freyrdan Finebeard and most of his people lived. However, temperatures still dipped after dark and body heat was especially welcomed.

Powerful men who could swing axes to down trees and assist Torsten with constructing the vessels composed most of the sparse camp's population, although women had important roles to play as well. Kai and Tove's jobs were to prepare food, wash and mend clothing, take care of anyone who got injured or sick, and run errands as required. A few wives and older women also inhabited tents or crude huts thrown together for the season. Everyone would return to Lagarfjord for the next winter.

"Aye, son, tales you never tire of hearing," Torsten replied in good humor.

A robust man with bark-brown hair, a braided beard, and talented hands, Torsten had a knack for storytelling. He was also Kai's adopted father, whom she loved, and she shared his affection for Leiknir as if he was her blood kin. Eight years ago, when she'd been Leiknir's age, she had wandered down from the piedmont, where her family had once taken goats and sheep to graze during the summer months. Kai had been half-starved and grieving over the fever that had claimed her parents and brother, leaving her to fend for herself.

She never understood what had gone wrong, why her family had been cursed with the disease after they had gladly observed the practice of hospitality by welcoming in a weary traveler. The traveler had been the first to fall ill, and the rest had followed. It made no sense that her brawny father, strong mother, and lively big brother had all succumbed while she, the scrawny, too-small girl, had never fallen sick at all. It was a great mystery, which often prompted Kai to wonder if the gods may have had something important in mind for her to accomplish one day. She had spent years blaming them, but as she'd matured into a young woman, Kai realized sicknesses and accidents happened to the good and bad alike. Maybe no one was to blame.

"To the west, in the misty land of Norvegr, arose twin heroes Sigurd and Sigrid, as tall and blonde as Swedes, and almost as brave," Torsten added with a wink, which prompted Leiknir to giggle. The boy squeezed in between Kai and his father and pulled up a woolen blanket.

Kai felt a sense of contentment in her life as Tove wrapped an arm around her shoulders. She pulled her closer and twirled Kai's long flaxen braid impishly. With a grin, Kai glanced up into Tove's playful eyes, set in a square face framed by light-brown tresses. Her lips were full and inviting, and Kai reveled in kissing them, but this was not the time. She loved stories about Sigrid and Elyn even more than Leiknir did.

In mesmerizing fashion, Torsten recounted story after story: how Sigrid had wrestled the great brown bear, ridden on a whale's back, rescued a princess, and fought courageously on the battlefield. Then the mighty Elyn was introduced to the narrative, which included the stories of how she and Sigrid had been trapped in and later escaped from a troll cave, uncovered a malicious plot, and made peace between warring factions. The saga continued with the two magnificent shieldmaidens' voyage to the Russ, where they discovered a priceless treasure sealed in an underwater cavern. To show their good will, they shared the spoils with the native inhabitants of the region, thereby gaining loyal allies. Torsten added their adopted daughter, Ingrid, to the tale. She had grown up to become the most beautiful woman in Sogn and had married the king's son, Asbjorn Bloodaxe, who had recently assumed his father's title.

Torsten related one incredible adventure after another, even an unbelievable tale of a voyage west to a green island, where the women discovered strange musical instruments and battled a tribe of men who wore skirts. When the moon was high in the star-studded sky, Torsten moved on to the newest part of the story—the portion that tugged at Kai's heartstrings.

"Sigrid and Elyn shared a love as fierce as their swords, and neither man nor beast could defeat either valiant shieldmaiden," he recounted. "Alas, 'twas a sickness that brought the beautiful, flame haired Elyn to her grave. The older of the pair, Sigrid, was heartbroken at the thought her beloved may not share the same world as her in the afterlife, so at fifty-five years of age, the hero set out on a quest to find *Bifröst*, the rainbow which bridges the realm of Miðgarðr to Ásgarðr and the court of the gods."

Kai twined her fingers with Tove's, wishing for the connection to carry her through the end of the tale.

"Sigrid consulted a *völva*, who told her the gods move the bridge daily to keep mortals and *jötnar* from using it. At Sigrid's urging, she employed her *seiðr* to part the veil between worlds and see where Bifröst would be in one moon's time. Acting on the vision, the hero traveled far to the north, past the line where no trees grow, and did battle with a colossal white bear to access a cave, where she came upon the foot of the legendary pathway to the dwelling of the gods. Though Bifröst's red stripe burned as fire, Sigrid pressed on. Yet once she had crossed the rainbow bridge, she found the god Himinbjorg standing guard lest anyone pass uninvited."

"Sigrid would not be turned away," Leiknir announced with confidence. "She told Himinbjorg who she was and demanded to make her case before Odin."

Torsten smiled and ran a rough-skinned hand over his son's head, mussing his hair. "Indeed. Nothing would stand in her way. Sigrid made a plea before all the gods to place Elyn with the slain warriors because, even though she had not died in battle, she had earned the same right as anyone who had. They agreed on one condition." He held up a finger and scanned his small audience. "Who recalls what she must do?"

All three cried out, "Kill Jabbar the Giant!"

"Hey!" Torsten mocked dismay. "If everyone knows this story, why do I bother telling it?"

They laughed and Kai responded, "Because we love to hear your version best."

Torsten winked and touched her soul with his smile. "Jabbar was the meanest, nastiest *jötunn* in all the nine worlds, and he happened to be hiding out in ours. He had been causing a lot of trouble and none wished to fight him. However, no reports of the disasters this biggest of giants had caused could quench Sigrid's zeal. She battled him for three days and three nights, creating rumblings throughout the earth. At last, she defeated the monster, but not before he had delivered to her a mortal wound. The Valkyries came for her and when they brought her to Odin's Hall, Elyn was already there waiting for her."

"Did all that really happen, Father?" Leiknir asked in disbelief. "And if she and Jabbar killed each other, who was there to bring back the report?"

Torsten stirred the fire with a stick and gazed upward at the multitude of shining stars. "Many are the things we have not seen with our eyes, yet we know them to be true," he said. "Can you see the air, or merely its effects? Can you see love, or is it something invisible you feel inside? Have you visited the far-away lands the travelers tell of, or do you accept their word about scorching deserts of sand and strange animals who dwell not in our forests? Who can say if Sigrid really crossed Bifröst and reasoned with the gods? We know Elyn died, and Sigrid would not rest until she secured a way their souls could remain together until the fateful day of Ragnarok. Is this not how you would like to believe the story ends?"

"I suppose so," he answered and bowed his head.

Kai's gaze followed Torsten's heavenward, and she pondered the twinkling lights above. The thickest mass of them seemed to form a road—no, a bridge—stretching to some faraway place. Could this ribbon of stars be Bifröst, and were Sigrid and Elyn up there somewhere feasting at Odin's table, enjoying rousing battles each day, exchanging stories with Thor and Tyr? She wagered they could teach the Valkyries a thing or two.

"I wish they were still alive so I could meet them," Tove said. "I've met women who have taken up a spear or an axe to defend their village, but never a real shieldmaiden or a woman jarl."

"Me too, but I know what a fearsome foe illness can be," Kai murmured. "At least Sigrid could use her sword against the giant; what chance did Elyn have to defeat an unseen enemy inside her own body? I like to believe they are up there together even now."

Torsten considered her with a compassionate face. "Only the gods know why one is taken, and another spared, Kai. We were fortunate to have you join our family. You recall my wife died in childbirth, along with the infant who would have been my daughter. But Freya, in her mercy, sent you to us to take the lost child's place and help me care for Leiknir when he was little. It is coming time for you to marry and start your own family."

"I don't wish to marry," Kai admitted, reclining into Tove's arms once more. "I wish to be a hero, like Sigrid and Elyn."

Tove kissed her forehead when Leiknir laughed. "Kai, you are too small!" he cried. "I am only ten and already am taller than you. What would you do—strike at your enemies' knees with a tiny knife?"

"Badgers and foxes are not big, but can be fierce fighters," Kai retorted. "I've heard of great warriors being brought to the grave by bee stings. No one wants to mess with those."

"Kai, you do not have to carry a sword to accomplish great things," Tove consoled her. "Look at Torsten. Have you ever seen him fight? And yet he has won more victories for Yeats than a hundred warriors because he is the best shipbuilder in the region. Our longboats weather the roughest storms carrying our raiders, fishermen, traders, and explorers safely to their destinations and home again. Do not be troubled about paths that are not yours to follow. I will stay with you until one of us finds the ideal man to marry. I have never thought less of you for being a woman who helps in the camp, for even the helpers share in our triumphs."

Kai buried her head in Tove's shoulder and nodded against it. "I am good at helping." She knew her family was right; who was a petite orphan to dream of becoming a mighty shieldmaiden? Still, she was troubled by Tove's vow of fidelity. It came with an expiration date. Tove may love her, but she would choose a traditional life once she found a husband. Kai, however, had no desire to marry or even lie with a man. She wished she and Tove could remain together their whole lives. Unfortunately, such arrangements were rare and criticized—unless one was a legendary warrior or nobility and free to do as she pleased.

"We should all go to sleep now," Torsten advised. "Tomorrow will be a busy day. Tove, you are welcome to stay with us unless your parents require you to return to their hut."

"They do not mind," she replied. "I think Kai would prefer I keep her company here tonight."

Tove wasn't wrong, and Kai whispered, "Thanks."

They all lay close together, covered in blankets and furs with their feet toward the fire. Kai turned on her side, rested her head on Tove's shoulder, and wrapped an arm around her, fingers finding skin under her girlfriend's layers to caress. She fell asleep happy, having decided to live one day at a time. At this moment, all was right with the world, so why not embrace it? Yet in her dreams, Kai carried a sword, performed valiant deeds, and was hailed as a hero. The dream, too, made her heart smile.

2

Gnóttdalr, primary town in Sogn, Norvegr, 690 A.D.

"Stay." Solveig refused to release Ragna's hand, tethering the lanky shieldmaiden with steel muscles and a will to match, to the cushioned bed in her private chamber. The princess never forgot this room had once belonged to her grandmother—great aunt by birth—Sigrid the Valiant.

"I am expected at the practice field," Ragna replied, regarding Solveig with impatience.

"It's not yet dawn," Solveig protested. "At least stay until the cock crows." She slid her body over Ragna's and pushed up onto her hands and knees, hovering above her lover like a well-rounded bumblebee seeking nectar from a succulent flower. Silky brunette tresses cascaded over her bare shoulders as she gazed at Ragna through beguiling, chestnut eyes. "If you wish for a workout while it is yet dark, I can oblige you, my dear."

Ragna, whose ginger-gold hair remained in her braids from the day before, laughed. Without warning, she flipped Solveig, claiming the high ground for herself. A gasp escaped Solveig's lush lips as pulses worked their way through her thighs and core. "I should take you now just to quiet your pleas, but in case you don't remember, your brother's wedding is today. You have to help your mother and sister with the preparations."

Solveig had not forgotten the marriage ceremony. It was not every day an heir to the throne of Sogn was wed. She reached out with slender fingers to trace

Ragna's warrior tattoos, having memorized each line and swirl. She had coaxed their meaning out of her lover months ago, as well as the story behind each scar. Ragna was a few years older and acclaimed as an elite among the kingdom's warriors. To Solveig, the scar that marred Ragna's cheek was her most beautiful feature. She had received it a year before, protecting a group of children from a fisherman who had gone mad. He had attacked her with a pole hook used to grapple large fish. Ragna had hoped to subdue him without injury, but after having her face sliced open, she abandoned the plan and ran him through with her sword. The children's parents praised her, the fisherman's wife cursed her, and Solveig's father, King Asbjorn Bloodaxe, promoted her to guardian of his household.

Ragna lowered her lips to claim Solveig's, and the princess exulted in the kiss with delirious pleasure. "There's time for us," Solveig cooed. Ragna smirked, nipped at her nose, and rolled off, taking most of the blanket with her.

"Tempting, but I have security to put in place. My pleasures—and yours," she stressed, pinning Solveig with a commanding stare, "must wait. I swear, my honey, you may struggle to lift a full vessel of mead, but you have more stamina in bed than a stallion in a corral filled with mares!"

Her jest made Solveig laugh. "Will you dance with me at the celebration tonight?"

Ragna wiggled into her under tunic before tossing a pillow at Solveig. "I might be able to squeeze you in."

"I command you to be safe."

"I answer to your father," Ragna reminded her, then she relented with a warm smile. "But I'll take your order under advisement. When will you marry and leave me to my less voracious lovers?"

"Me marry?" Solveig laughed. "That's what I have brothers and a sister for. Luckily for me, Herlief was born first, relieving me of such burdensome responsibilities as producing heirs." She considered uttering a remark about Ragna's other lovers, then thought better of it. She didn't wish to appear needy or jealous, and everyone knew Ragna enjoyed the company of both men and women. The shieldmaiden had never promised to be exclusive in her coupling, only that she would give her life to protect Solveig and her family from harm. Solveig rested in confidence, knowing Ragna's word was as pure as gold.

What the princess had not revealed to anyone was how she truly felt about Ragna. To her, the sun rose and set in the magnificent warrior woman's luminous green eyes. Each time Ragna left the safety of the city, Solveig sensed a tight anxiety in her chest and fretted through her routine until the shieldmaiden returned. She had tended to Ragna after the fishhook incident, nursing her back to mental as well as physical health. It seemed this past year Ragna had seldom strayed from her to romp with another, although Solveig supposed it was only because she was self-conscious about her scar. She sensed Ragna thought of their relationship as a friendship with shared pleasure, rather than a lasting love. Therefore, Solveig strove to keep her heart in check and not allow her emotions to run away with her.

"All Gnóttdalr knows by now I shan't marry," Ragna confirmed as she sat on the side of the bed and pulled on her boots. "I won't be forced to obey a husband, nor would I be caught dead with a man who wasn't robust enough to make me. I have remained unmarried for thirty years and as long as my sword arm stays strong, I can continue as I am. But you, little dove, are a princess."

She pivoted and stroked Solveig's cheek in a tender caress, meeting her gaze with sincerity. "It may be impossible for you to avoid matrimony much longer. You are already twenty-two, a grown woman past the age most are wed. Your father is king, and though he dotes on you, indulging all your desires, a diplomatic marriage could prove inevitable. You are not Sigrid, my sweetness, and I am not Elyn."

But oh, how Solveig wished they were! *If only I had the power to rule. Then no one could tell me what to do.* She wanted to throw her arms around Ragna, to profess her love, to pour out her heart, but such a display would not do. She was indeed the daughter of a king and must behave accordingly. It was her brother's wedding day, and she was happy for him. She would be the best oldest daughter a king could wish for, and mayhap she would not be forced into a treaty-marriage or some such travesty.

Solveig turned her face into Ragna's hand and kissed her palm. "Don't make your soldiers wait on you," she said. "I'll see you at the feast."

"There you are, dear."

Ingrid's countenance lit up at the sight of her lovely older daughter entering the great hall. It seemed it had not been so long ago that she and Asbjorn had celebrated their marriage in this very chamber. Ingrid had lived here as a small child with her adoptive parents—her aunt Sigrid and her partner Elyn—until the king and jarls in charge decided it should become the capital of their newly reunited kingdom; after all, the town lay nearest the old border and was the most centrally located. Her family then moved to Hafrafell to join Jarl Siegfried's household when her Uncle Sigurd married Siegfried's younger sister, Birgitta. The twins and their mother were compensated with a fabulous new ship for donating their property, and Sigurd assumed Siegfried's jarldom upon his death. Ingrid had returned to Gnóttdalr when she married Asbjorn to become princess and eventually queen. Through all the moves and travels, these timbers and planks, this longhouse were what she would always call home. Her four children were born here and now Herlief would be wed within these walls.

"Yes, I'm here," Solveig responded with mischief dancing on her countenance. "Did you think I would sleep the day away?" She greeted her mother with a hug and kiss on the cheek.

"Never. I sent Baldr to the alehouse to secure enough drinks for the celebration," Ingrid said, "and Sylvi is out gathering flowers for the arrangements."

"What do you need me to do?"

Solveig's sweet smile delighted Ingrid's heart. Of all her children, Solveig looked the most like her mother, besides her hair being an unusually deep brown. They had the same brown eyes, straight nose, square chin, dimples, and curvy figures. They were of an identical and average height and enjoyed the same favorite foods. Solveig exhibited the qualities of temperance, wisdom, and courage important for an effective leader, and she had a loving nature. Ingrid recalled how, as a child, her daughter would become attached to animals—cats, dogs, goats, or cows—and relish their company for hours each day, then be inconsolable when the pet died. Ingrid had tried to explain to her about the circle of life and how animals did not live as long as people. Solveig would recover her good cheer and fall in love with another fur-child, thus repeating the cycle.

"Bodil and Fiske will take care of the cooking and cleaning," Ingrid relayed. "I need you to help me decorate the hall with banners, candles, ribbons, and boughs of evergreen, then arrange the flowers with Sylvi when she returns." She smiled at her daughter. "Nothing is fresher than a spring wedding. The musicians will require a place to set up, and we'll need extra chairs and tables outside to leave room for dancing in here. But first, go remind your father I need canopy tents set on the lawn in case of a shower. We don't want our guests to be rained on."

Solveig's cheerful laugh tinkled in Ingrid's ears. "Don't worry, Mother. Everything will be perfect. Where is the grumpy old man?" she asked, peering around the great hall. "He should be eating his morning meal by now."

"I think he went out to the stables with Herlief to select the best mare to give Karina for a marriage gift. Of course, he has a ring and silks for her, but you know Herlief—nothing is as valuable as a fine steed."

"I'll find him, relay the order, and return to help you."

Ingrid watched her daughter stroll through the open front double doors, the hem of her yellow day dress brushing the floor. Her heart was full of so many emotions—joy over her son's marriage, pride in all her children, and yet concern for Solveig. She was a beautiful woman who had shown no interest in a man. Ingrid wished for nothing more than her daughter's happiness, though she wondered if the life Solveig longed for would be possible. Even when she was a small child, it had been apparent she had inherited her great-aunt Sigrid's spirit. She wanted to play swords with the boys, to run on the trails and fish in the streams. Problems had appeared when Solveig's body refused to keep pace with her nature. She suffered frequent mishaps, such as breaking an arm, tripping over roots, and running into low-hanging branches, and the girl couldn't hit the broad side of a cowbarn with a bow and arrow.

Asbjorn had called in the town's *grædari* to determine what was wrong and if he could help their daughter, who was also susceptible to coughs, colds, and stomach-aches. The healer had performed many tests and rituals, anointed her, and prescribed a tonic to bolster her strength, but he could not improve her eyesight or magically fortify her constitution, nor cure her lack of coordination. Ingrid recalled the day she and Asbjorn had sat down with Solveig and conveyed to her the reality that she would never be a warrior. Only on the day Elyn had succumbed to the raging fever that laid her once powerful body low had Ingrid otherwise experienced such sorrow. She was proud of the woman Solveig had become; however, she still worried about her future happiness.

3

Solveig lengthened her stride across the yard toward the stables as the morning light filtered through the mountains in the east up the fjord, sparkling on sprouting chartreuse leaves and pink buds laden with dew. She pulled her buff wrap snug over her shoulders as a breeze rushed uphill from the harbor waters below. To her right, gardeners had turned the ground in preparation for vegetables to be planted while on her left Ragna led the king's guard through their drills. Though she was unable to distinguish details like facial features at more than a few feet, Solveig had learned to identify people by their voices, body shape, gait, clothing, and other unique characteristics. Solveig's soul swelled with pride at the sound of Ragna's commanding alto barking out instructions.

Hearing more familiar voices ahead, she entered the stable and spotted her tall older brother and ruddy, brawny father discussing the horses. "This ten-year-old red dun gelding is trained for a variety of roles," Asbjorn suggested, giving the short, sturdy pony a pat. "He could pull her wagon or serve as a mount for riding."

"Yes, but look at this creamy dun mare." Herlief stepped across the aisle motioning to a stunning Nordic Fjord horse, or Fjording as the breed specific to the region was commonly called. "She is gentle and surefooted, and at three years old, eligible to be bred."

Herlief was an attractive enough fellow, Solveig supposed, with characteristic straw-blond hair hanging loose to his shoulders and a splotchy beard that would never be as thick or as long as his father's. Three years his junior, she had always looked up to him, and for a while had attempted to be his equal; there had also been a time he had wished to stay as far away as possible from his annoying, odd little sister. As adults, however, the two had become close friends.

"Choose Cress," Solveig suggested as she joined them. The cream pony, named for a popular type of white flower, nodded as if in agreement. "Horses may live twenty-five or more years, longer than any animals under our care. You want a companion Karina can enjoy for a long time. Besides, most of our stock are brown duns; Cress stands out from among the rest, as does your lovely bride, Herlief."

Their father frowned and crossed his arms over his barrel chest, knitting bushy, burnished brows together. "Since when did you become an expert in horseflesh? Who has selectively bred Fjordings since before you were born? Do you not think I know best?"

Solveig offered him an adoring smile. "Certainly, you know best, Papa... about most things. But which of us is a young woman like Karina? Who knows what Herlief's bride will be most thrilled to receive—a practical wagon cob, or a distinctive, gorgeous young pony she can train and bond with over half a lifetime?"

Asbjorn pursed his lips and scratched his beard. "It would appear I'm out-numbered. The two of you are always teaming up against me for something or another," he grumbled.

Steadying herself on his arms, Solveig stretched on tiptoes to brush a kiss to his fuzzy cheek. "Mother wants you to come set up canopy tents outside the great hall to accommodate the overflow crowd."

"Why do they need tents?" he complained. "Karina's family and the visiting jarls will all have a seat at my table. What do I care about some moochers who are only attending for free food?"

"I have many friends, Father," Herlief acknowledged. "They will not all fit in the feast hall."

"And Mother doesn't want anyone getting wet. You know how showers pop up in the spring."

"My son, Herlief the Popular." Asbjorn pointed a thick finger at him, catching his gaze with matching blue eyes. "You would do better to keep three or four companions close to your side than allow dozens of tag-a-longs clamoring for your attention. Notice how wise your sister is to be selective in the company she keeps. You don't see her wasting her money buying drinks for everyone in the alehouse."

Herlief wrapped a wiry arm around her shoulders and gave her a squeeze. "Solveig is dearer to me than a hundred friends, but we are very different people. She is content to be a homebody, while I crave adventure." He kissed her cheek before fixing his father with a good-natured challenge. "A man can never have too many friends, especially when he will one day be king."

Her brother was misguided to assume working in the home satisfied Solveig, yet what other choice did she have? She yearned for exciting experiences as much as he did, except she had not been blessed with his strength and dexterity. Not only had she been born a woman, but a fragile one at that. Solveig was determined to secure her position by making her presence indispensable to the household so her parents would not rush to marry her off. Her relationship with Ragna brought her happiness, as did being a capable leader in her father's kingdom.

Asbjorn just shook his head. "Do not let time spent with your fellows come between you and your bride," he warned. "If Karina is an ounce like Ingrid, she can make your life a blessing or a Helheim. I may administer a kingdom, son, but your mother administers me! It seems I must now go erect tents, an extremely pressing matter for a king to attend to."

Brother and sister laughed as their father lumbered out. "He protests, but he is as thrilled as the rest of us over your marriage," Solveig assured Herlief.

"I know. Do you really think she'll like Cress?" He returned his attention to the fair pony and rubbed a hand down her neck.

"I do. In fact, I recall Karina pointing at her when the herd was out to pasture last fall before the snows came. 'Look at the pretty pony whose color stands out from the rest,' she said, with an aspect of wonder on her face." She thought for a moment, then added, "You do also have jewelry and clothes for her, right?"

"Mother picked them out," he admitted, rolling his eyes.

Solveig snickered. "I suppose all that remains is to get you presentable, then."

Herlief glanced down at himself inquisitively. "What's wrong with how I look?"

With a groan, Solveig replied, "You must bathe, trim and comb your hair, put on your best tunic. What kind of king will you make when you don't even know how to present yourself?"

"I will make a powerful king by the might of my spear, axe, and sword," he declared, "by my courage at sea and my wisdom at court. What does my appearance matter?"

Solveig took his arm to lead him back to the longhouse. "Believe me, it matters."

I ngrid wore her finest silk and stood beside her husband, brimming with joy and pride to behold her firstborn wed Jarl Njord's granddaughter. She wished the old man had lived to see this day, although he had celebrated Karina's tenth birthday before he'd died with a sword in his hand. His son, Jarl Bjorn, father of the bride, occupied the spot across from them with his petite wife, Zigge.

They assembled on the front porch of the longhouse since the guests were too numerous to all fit inside at once, and she wished for no one to be excluded. Thankfully, the clouds still held on to their droplets, though Asbjorn had set the tents in place with tables and chairs for the feast just in case.

Her charming son had donned a new, purple tunic trimmed in gold, and Karina wore a lovely pink-and-white gown embroidered with runic designs, her golden hair braided intricately and encircled by a finely spun silver crown. As she gazed at them, it dawned on her that Karina was her youngest daughter Sylvi's age—seventeen. *Will Sylvi marry soon?* Ingrid wondered.

The betrothed couple stood in the center of the assembly with Gothi Osmin administering the rites. A respected older man with a bald top and gray beard,

Osmin finished reciting the proper verses and moved on to the next tradition. "What swords have you brought to hereby exchange?"

Herlief spoke, holding up an ornate silver blade embossed with a wolf motif. "Karina, my beloved, I present to you the sword of King Tyrulf, my grandfather, so one day you may bestow it upon our firstborn son as an heirloom. Guard and protect it, even as I vow to safeguard and defend you from all dangers." He passed the sword to Karina, who kissed the pommel before handing it to Sylvi, who stood as her bridesmaid.

Ingrid had promised herself she would not cry, though she was struggling. Sylvi was now a woman, a lovely woman who favored her father's looks, with burnished hair and glistening blue eyes. Thankfully, she had not inherited his stocky build but was rather the slenderest member of their family.

Karina then offered a weighty weapon, longer by several inches than the one she'd received. "Herlief, my beloved, I present to you the sword of Jarl Njord, my grandfather, as a symbol. From this day forward, you will stand as my protector in place of my father. May this proven blade serve you without fail."

"Do you have the rings?" Osmin asked. Herlief handed his gifted sword to his younger brother, Baldr, who acted as his groomsman.

Ingrid considered her younger son equally handsome, with his fawn mane waving about his shoulders and his face sprouting a wispy beard. He almost matched Herlief in size, though his serious nature mirrored their father's. The age gap between the boys hindered a close relationship from forming; but Ingrid trusted Baldr would remain loyal to his brother. She had raised them to be family first, nobility second. "Power does not lie with a title, nor do riches follow a crown," she had taught them since infancy. "Rather, worthiness inhabits a character that remains true to our values, regardless of what circumstances may present themselves."

Herlief and Karina held up simple gold bands, which Osmin had cast for them. Serving as a *gothi* was not a paid position, but an honored calling. Those who answered it entered an apprenticeship to learn to read the runes and perform religious rites and sacrifices, and most gothi engaged in a craft or profitable occupation, alongside the attention they took to pleasing the gods. Osmin was thus also a goldsmith and crafter of jewelry.

With a nod from the officiant, Karina slid her ring on Herlief's finger. "As this ring has no end, neither will my devotion to you. I give it as my pledge of fidelity and trust."

Herlief took a smaller band and placed it on Karina's finger. "As this ring forms an unbroken circle, I surround you with my faithfulness. You shall bear my sons and daughters, and I shall be your husband."

Ingrid's first tear of joy could no longer be contained. She understood the sentiment of the ceremony and the reality that couples sometimes developed problems and divorced for various reasons. The gods did not hold the breaking of the marriage vow against them unless it had been taken frivolously. Even Odin and Frigga had not remained married forever, though their bond of friendship had endured. However, it was exceedingly rare for a woman to leave a king for any reason beyond cruelty, just as rare as it was for a king to dismiss his wife save for infidelity. If they could not work out common troubles between themselves, how could they hope to administer a kingdom? She and Asbjorn had issues and disagreements like any couple, yet they were now a stronger unit for having weathered such storms. She prayed the same for Herlief and Karina.

Osmin dipped a fir twig into a bowl of thick, dark liquid and sprinkled drops of it over the pair. "With the blood of an unblemished goat sacrificed to Frigga, goddess of hearth and home, I bless this union between Herlief Asbjornson and Karina Bjornsdottir on this Freya's Day. May you have many children and your home overflow with joy and laughter. Honor the gods and each other, so that your days may be long in the land. Now prosper together as husband and wife."

A cheer arose from the gathering as the two kissed beneath a canopy of delicate flowers.

4

Bàtrgørð, Yeats

A westerly breeze whisked across the forests and plains on a sunny spring day, and the sea lapped gingerly at the shore. Kai and Tove engaged in their chores of helping prepare the midday meal and hanging the laundry while goats and chickens wandered freely, nibbling at weeds and pecking at seeds. The occasional bleating and clucking made such a common backdrop, Kai seldom noticed it at all. When the sun beamed high overhead, Tove's mother, Anika, charged them with another assignment.

"Kai, Tove," the sturdy woman called. Kai responded quickly, with Tove trailing after her.

"Yes, camp mother?" Kai halted in front of Anika, who ran the outfit with rewards from one hand and punishments from the other. Kai admired her, not only because she was a physically formidable woman, but because under her steel exterior, beat a generous heart.

She piled baskets filled with fish, berries, and bread into Kai's arms and handed Tove a dozen water bags dangling from their leather cords. "Take food and drink to the men and tell them I said no ale or mead until they are done for the day. I'll not have one chopping off his hand or foot because of strong drink."

"Yes, Mother," Tove replied. "Then Kai and I are going to collect more berries in the meadow."

"No, you aren't." Anika slapped her hands to her amble hips and stared critically at the pair. "You use that excuse to lie in the grass together away from camp. Don't think I don't know it. You can waste time when it's raining. There is too much work to be finished on a pleasant day like this. You will check the fish traps, collect the eggs, milk the goats, then return here with haste. We're planting the vegetable garden this afternoon and it is much easier for you two to reach the ground than for Thora and me."

"Don't worry, Anika," Kai assured her. She poked an elbow into Tove's ribs when she rolled her eyes. "We'll get everything done and come help with the garden, won't we, Tove?"

"For Freya's sake! Now I have two of you giving me orders," Tove exclaimed in good humor. "Let's go deliver these before my arms fall off."

Kai and Tove took sixty long strides from the cook fire and clay oven to the spot on the beach where Torsten labored with several boatbuilding apprentices. "Anika sends her blessings," Kai sang out as they approached.

"And lunch," Tove joined in.

"Many thanks to Anika and you girls," Torsten answered. He lay aside his axe and wiped the sweat from his brow. "Stigr, take a break. We'll secure the next plank after we eat."

"Hey, Kai, Tove, my two favorite people in all the nine worlds," Stigr greeted them. "What have you brought to fill my stomach today?"

The lean young man with bouncing ginger curls lay aside his tools and swaggered up to them with a broad smile on his freckled face. He took a full skin from Tove as Kai passed him a basket. "The usual fare," she replied. "And for you, Torsten."

The master stem-smith took his food and drink and sat on a fat piece of left-over tree trunk. "How is Anika today?"

"A bossy taskmaster, like always," Tove complained.

"Hey, this bag has water in it." Stigr frowned and shook the skin at them. "Where's my ale?"

Kai answered him as she passed lunch trays to the other workers. "Anika says no strong drink until you have finished work for the day."

"I told you," Tove affirmed.

Two burly men led a team of ponies dragging a massive tree trunk to the site. They stopped, allowing the ponies to rest, and collected their food. "Fish again?" one grumbled.

"I should go hunting," Kai suggested. "I'm a decent hunter, both with traps and a bow. Torsten, tell Anika to let me go hunting."

"You can't go alone," he declared, "and I need all the men here working on the boats. King Freyrdan has commissioned five longboats he needs ready by the summer solstice. As you can see, we have three in various stages of construction and two more to begin. Everyone will have to be content to with the food on hand."

"But Torsten, you know I can find my way and am an excellent shot, and certainly not afraid of the woods. I could bring us a deer or a mess of rabbits," Kai insisted. Though she was eager to contribute to the camp's needs, she was tired of simple, dull tasks anyone could accomplish, and wished for a greater challenge. "Tove and Thora can help Anika with the garden this afternoon, and I shall make everyone cheer by bringing meat back to the village."

"Kai can indeed bring down a big buck with her bow," Stigr declared, bolstering Kai's confidence—until he added, "but how will she ever get it back here for us to eat?"

Always jests about my size. She glared at her friend as he and the others laughed. Then she shifted her attention to the ponies with the tree trunk lying behind their tails. "I'll take a pony. You oversized oafs are always teasing me. The lot of you are worse than Loki."

"Why not let her go?" Kjell, Tove's father, joined the group. Bàtrgørð's blacksmith, renowned for his weapons-forging, set down a box of rivets he had brought from his forge, which sat stood on a small rise overlooking a stream near the circle of dwellings. "She is a grown woman, despite her small stature. A dagger may not have the heft of a sword or the reach of a spear, but it can kill just as well."

"Thank you, Kjell!" Kai grinned at him, glistening with approval.

"Let her go hunt," Stigr repeated. "We'll work better when we're satisfied with roasted meat."

"All right," Torsten relented. "But Kjell, you must inform your wife she is down one helper to plant her garden. Crew, eat your fill now. We must labor until it is too dark to see on a fair day such as this. King Freyrdan needs these ships to take his raiding party east. Gaining a plentiful bounty will see all of us through the winter."

"Kai shan't embark on her hunt alone," a youthful voice declared. Torsten twisted over his shoulder to spy Leiknir standing with a quiver and a bow in his hands. "I'll go with her to keep her safe."

Kai and Torsten both stifled the laughter about to bubble forth from their lips. "You are a worthy son, Leiknir," Torsten stated with approval, "but Kai is a more experienced hunter, and well acquainted with the land in this region. You must promise to listen to her and heed her instructions."

"I will," he groaned impatiently.

With a nod to Leiknir, Kai placed a hand on Tove's shoulder. "Pass my apologies to your mother and let her know we'll bring back the best meat we can find. That will please her, too."

A silent exchange passed through their gazes, warmed with affection and mutual admiration. "May the god Ullr guide your aim and grant you much success," Tove bade her. "I'll explain to Mother."

Kai climbed onto the brown pony with its black stockings, mane, and tail and pulled Leiknir up behind her. Away they went at a gentle lope, armed with their bows and arrows. Midday was not the best time to hunt. Dawn or dusk would have been preferable, but Kai was determined to prove herself regardless of the hour. They rode until they could no longer see or hear sounds from Bàtrgørð, then continued some more.

Apart from the occasional rolling hill, the terrain was mostly flat, and evenly divided between grassy meadows and deciduous forests. Torsten had chosen this area to build ships for its readily available oak, the preferred wood for his craft, and because of the protected beach with its gentle tides; however, the timbers and grasslands teemed with wildlife for hunting, making it ideal in every regard.

Pulling the small horse to a halt under a broadleaf oak at the rounded top of a knoll, Kai pressed a finger to her lips, motioning for Leiknir to remain quiet as they dismounted. She tied their pony to a nearby tree. Before them lay a lush valley cut with a gurgling brook, hemmed in on tree sides by forest. It was a perfect location for roe deer to graze.

She crouched low in the tall grass and the boy followed her lead. Scanning the lea, Kai spotted a pair of roe deer grazing in a golden field of wildflowers. A doe who still bore her grayish-brown winter coat shot a wary glance around without noticing them. When the larger deer beside her raised its head, Kai spied the six-pointed antlers he had yet to shed. It was still early spring, and she knew he would lose his rack any day to make way for a fresh one to grow.

Every part of the deer was important—the meat for eating, skins for tanning, bones and antlers for crafting and toolmaking, and hooves for glue. The small roe were plentiful in the region; however, unlike reindeer or moose, a single kill would not suffice for the entire camp. They would need to bag them both.

Kai scooped up a handful of soil and released it into the air, testing the wind's direction. Silently, she motioned for Leiknir to follow her downwind, and they circled close enough to get a shot. Both hunters held children's yew bows, which were smaller than standard ones, with only a fifty-pound draw rather than a warrior's ninety pounds of force. With slow and steady movements, they crept to within two hundred paces of their prey and stopped. Kai readied her bow, nocking an iron-tipped arrow against the string.

"Take the doe," she whispered to Leiknir. "Aim for the center of her body, then raise your point to compensate for the distance. I know you can do this."

With a serious expression, the boy nodded and cocked his bow. As Kai aimed for the buck, she murmured, "On three. One, two, three."

Both arrows flew swift and true. The startled, wounded deer barked out their cries and darted for the trees. Kai and Leiknir ran after them, pumping their arms and legs with all their might. Kai knew the roe could run many lengths before falling dead and they needed to reach them quickly so wolves or a bear wouldn't claim their kills.

Once in the thick of the woods, Kai relied on her tracking skills, pointing out signs such as a blood drop, hoof print, or broken twig to Leiknir as they went. Before long, they came upon the buck lying on the ground, its tongue protruding from its mouth and its eyes glassy in death.

"That was a good hit, Kai," the boy praised her. "It almost struck his heart. I know my arrow landed, but I think it was more in the middle. Why did you tell me to aim there instead of her chest?"

"Because mid-body is a larger target and easier to land an arrow," she explained, "even if it won't kill the deer as fast. We can track her, but if you had missed, someone would complain he didn't get enough meat at dinner tonight."

"I suppose any strike is better than none," he agreed. "I'll go find her."

"No, Leiknir. I need you to stay with the buck. Find a sturdy sapling and cut it with your axe to make a pole. Then tie his feet together so we can carry him to the pony. I'll track down the doe."

Leiknir gave her an irritated look, sighing in obedience. "Papa said I have to do what you say."

"That's right," Kai confirmed. "You are turning out to be a fine hunter, little man." She patted his shoulder in a big-sisterly manner. "Now let me find your kill and I'll boast of you when we return to camp."

Together, the lad and Kai carried both deer to the spot where they had left the pony and hoisted their carcasses over its back. As they neared the camp, Tove ran to meet them. "You did it!" She exclaimed. "Look, Mother, meat for roasting!"

Anika glanced up from her work and leaned on her hoe handle with an irritated expression. "Kai, you are always finding an excuse to run off and do men's work, leaving Thora and me shorthanded."

Even so, Anika's helper, Thora smiled. "I'd be delighted to help you prepare the deer for dinner," she admitted.

Tove hugged Kai with glee. "I'll help too."

"No," her mother retorted. "You and I have to finish planting. Let Kai teach Leiknir how to dress the deer. She is more of a big brother than sister to him, anyway."

Kai's blue eyes sparkled at Tove. "Go finish the garden," she said with a grin. "I'll need your help with a matter later when it gets dark."

With a bemused smile, Tove turned back to the garden patch, though she shot a devilish glance over her shoulder at Kai. "You better need me," she quipped.

"You two play too much," Leiknir protested.

At dusk, when the roasting venison filled the air with a savory aroma, Torsten, Kjell, Stigr, and the other workers trudged up the hill from the beach, bringing with them a wagon and a small group of travelers.

"Look who we found," Stigr announced.

"And they bring a troubling report," Kjell added.

An older man with a gray beard spoke. "We bring word of raiders from the south moving up the coastline attacking villages and towns," he declared gravely. "You should be prepared in case they strike here too."

5

Gnóttdalr, in Norvegr

Solveig and Ragna sat aside from the others at a small table in King Asbjorn's great hall, with cups of mead and a Hnefatafl board between them. The warm fire crackled, and they could hear the rest of Solveig's family talking and laughing from the expansive dinner table across the room. It had rained outside all day, the dampness adversely affecting Solveig's breathing, yet she did her best to pretend all was well. She wore a simple linen dress with a red bib-apron corded at the waist while Ragna was still in her tan leggings and rusty-brown gambeson from her day's duties.

"Are you certain you wish to move your piece there?" Solveig asked.

Ragna shot her a narrowed glance, briefly re-evaluated the board, then removed her finger from her piece and sat back. "Yes. It is a good enough move." She took a swallow of her mead and pulled the band from her red-gold hair, allowing it to flow freely about her shoulders. "Don't you think I know what I'm doing?"

Solveig raised a brow at her amazing shieldmaiden, drawing back one corner of her mouth in a crooked grin. "I am quite certain you do indeed." Solveig's dark hair hung loose except for two narrow braids pulled away from the sides of her face and fastened behind with a beaded cord. "Papa spent many winters instructing me in the finer points of Hnefatafl. I only wish you to have a fair chance."

"You already took the more difficult position of defending," Ragna confessed. "I know you usually win, so I don't understand why I continue to play with you."

"Because deep down you can't stand to lose, and even though it makes you angry, you want me to teach you to win."

Ragna crossed her arms and scowled, her emerald eyes glaring and stirring Solveig's heart with their intensity. Although her attention was focused on their game—and her opponent—she overheard other voices in the hall. "Herlief, at last," boomed her father's gruff baritone. "It has been three days since your marriage ceremony. I was beginning to worry we'd never see you again."

"Oh, don't badger your son," Ingrid chided. "Herlief, Karina, please join us for roasted duck and cabbage soup. We still have some of the imported wine left from the feast as well."

"You may have my seat," Baldr offered. "Geirfinnr has challenged me to an axe throwing game."

"Not inside my hall, you won't," Asbjorn bellowed.

Solveig moved her playing piece, then glanced over her shoulder to see what her family would do next. Baldr heaved up the round bottom of an old barrel painted with concentric red and yellow circles, bearing a red one in the middle. He carried it across the room and hung it on a peg at about shoulder height above a row of vacant sleeping benches. Then he gathered three hand axes and marched ten paces to the other side of the central hearth.

"Geirfinnr and I will stand at this mark," Baldr stated, "and take turns throwing axes at the target. The object is to land as close to the center as possible on each throw."

"And if you miss and hit my wall?" Asbjorn thundered.

Herlief laughed. "Then they should never be allowed to carry a weapon in your defense, Papa! That is so easy. Give me some meat, for I am famished, and I'll show those two how to hurl an axe!"

Solveig was amused by her father and brothers and suspected the muscular arm of their leading warrior Geirfinnr would prevail. Returning her attention to the checkered board, her good humor deflated like a ruptured air bladder.

Ragna had moved, leaving a piece vulnerable to capture, and now her focus was directed at the men's throwing match.

Giving her extra chances would not help Ragna excel at the strategy game of Hnefatafl, though it was with regret she captured her lover's pawn. "It is your turn, Ragna."

It did not take the divination of a völva to determine Ragna's interest had pivoted to a contest where she could really shine. Baldr let loose his throws to cheers from the other warriors who occupied the hall. All three attempts hit the target, yet only one nipped the edge of the middle circle.

"Step aside, lad," the tall, broad-shouldered Geirfinnr said with a look of confidence. Proven in battle, Geirfinnr was Herlief's peer, a good six years older than Solveig's little brother, with tawny hair and a full beard. He took a stance and heaved his pitches.

"Not bad," Baldr allowed as he went to retrieve the axes.

"My turn now," Herlief demanded, and he hurried over with a goose leg in one hand to join them.

Ragna had not wavered her gaze since the contest began. Solveig felt the tug as well. She would give anything to play target games with her brothers; however, she could barely see the big, round barrel end, bright paint and all, where it hung on the wall across the center aisle from her table. And for her arm to hurl an axe such a distance would be ridiculous. Perhaps that was why she concentrated on learning botany, geography, and strategy, why she had joined her mother in embroidering and memorized as many skald's songs as she could. Solveig's body may not cooperate to her satisfaction, but there was nothing weak about her brain... or her intuition.

"Ragna." At hearing her name, the shieldmaiden glanced back at Solveig.

"Oh, I'm sorry, my dove. Is it my turn again?"

"It is indeed," Solveig proclaimed. "You march over there, take the axes from my brothers, and show them how to land all three in the center of the barrelhead. We can finish this game another time."

Enthusiasm flashed across Ragna's features as she balled her hand into a fist. "You know me so well. I will beat them for you, Solveig; just watch me!"

And she did. A pang of loneliness wiggled into Solveig's soul when, after an hour, Ragna was still engaged in revelry with the men. She abandoned the gaming table to join her mother, Karina, and Sylvi.

"I am amazed at how Ragna has won the most throwing bouts," Karina commented.

"That is because you are new to our hall," Sylvi explained. "Ragna is one of our finest warriors. Papa even named her guardian of the household, although she spends much more time protecting Solveig than the rest of us," she added as a tease, grinning at her sister.

"Oh?" Karina asked and blinked her lashes. "Why is that?"

Sylvi just laughed and Solveig suddenly felt embarrassed. As was typical, her mother came to her rescue.

"Solveig and Ragna are close companions," Ingrid said. "They are both un-married women, though with distinctive skills that balance one another, and they both have a flair for adventure."

"I enjoy adventure, too," Karina replied. The green gown from her dowry wardrobe complemented her honey-gold hair, and her countenance glowed the way one would expect from a newlywed bride. "Once I traveled on a ship with my parents around the end of the peninsula to Borre. The city had a gigantic market where my mother and I bought silks and Father sold ivory and furs. We attended a festival with dancing, music, and storytelling. On the journey home, we saw a pod of whales, and it was all quite exciting."

"It sounds like a wonderful adventure, Karina." Solveig's smile was bitter-sweet. Her parents had tried taking her on voyages several times, but always ended up bringing her back home. She had become seasick, and the ventures proved unpleasant for everyone. Each time she would plead to come along, insisting since she was older, she could tolerate the ship's movement on the water, and yet each time she became violently ill. Her last attempt had been six years ago when she was sixteen.

Her gaze was drawn by Ragna's laughter from where the shieldmaiden stood with Herlief, Baldr, and the other warriors. Solveig understood everyone else could distinguish them clearly at this distance, yet they were all fuzzy to her.

Still, she recognized Ragna was enjoying herself, so she smiled in their direction. Although Solveig had no problem seeing close things, such as handwork and game boards, the span of the great hall may as well have been the width of a fjord.

Feeling a brush against her leg, Solveig glanced down to spy a gray, white, and black elkhound peering up at her with a hopeful expression. Her spirits lightened, and she sank her fingers into the dog's rich, thick ruff.

"Mist, where have you been?" Solveig chided. She had been worried by Mist's absence over the past several days.

In an instant, all four women's interests had been captured by the family pet. The dog didn't answer, only licked Solveig's wrist and wagged her tail.

"Mist, we are so relieved to have you back," Ingrid avowed and joined in awarding pats to the dog.

"I'll bet she's been out on a hunt," Sylvi suggested. "Or she was shy about all the crowds coming for the wedding."

"You're probably right," Solveig admitted. She caught the elkhound's cheerful face between her palms and issued a direct order. "Don't you go exploring without me ever again."

Ingrid laughed and shook her head at her daughter's antics.

"You are sleeping in my room tonight," Solveig decreed. With a wistful glance at Ragna chugging ale in a race with her fellows, she thought, *Because I don't think anyone else will be.*

6

The next day, bright with sunshine, Solveig and Baldr mounted their favorite Fjordings from Asbjorn's stables and set out to survey their farmers' fields. Some tenants tended to be slow to begin the massive chore of plowing their plots while others had, on occasions, experienced legitimate issues that set them behind, such as broken equipment, illness, or a lame horse. Her mother, who learned from Sigrid, had taught Solveig the importance of maintaining both an excellent, supportive rapport with the farmers and an overseeing, critical eye to ensure the region would produce enough grain and other foodstuffs to feed the population through the winter. Solveig's compassionate encouragement and Baldr's serious demands created an effective balance in dealing with landowners and tenant farmers alike. Despite their youth, the king's children commanded respect among the citizenry.

Their rounds confirmed most farmers were operating their tasks on an optimal schedule, with only a few needing aid or a kick in the rear to get them up to speed. With the likelihood of another hard freeze behind them, oats, barley, and rye should be sown this week, followed by beans and peas within a fortnight. While each family was responsible for their own herbs, greens, and root vegetables, foodstuffs that could be dried and stored for community distribution were supervised by the crown.

When the pair returned to the longhouse in the afternoon, their father and mother were holding court in the great hall. Baldr was keen to attend, but Solveig was tired from an active day and planned to retire to her room to work on her current embroidery project—a silk sash embossed with runes for good fortune for Ragna to wear under her armor. However, the moment she and her younger brother passed through the entry, she sensed something was amiss.

"I didn't witness the attack, my lord," a middle-aged man unfamiliar to Solveig was saying. "However, I saw the results. Blood was everywhere. Some of the livestock had been carried off while cows, goats, and a pony lay dead on the ground. The farmer's hut had been smashed as if giant boulders had rained down on it, thick timbers snapped like twigs."

"What did the farmer say happened?" Ingrid asked.

She and Asbjorn sat on twin thrones on a small rise at one end of the hall, with tapestries and wall sconces behind them. The regular crowd had gathered. Not counting those who resided in the great hall, there were fewer than twenty bored souls who wished to be entertained by others' disputes, as well as the citizens who had brought them before the throne. King Asbjorn's shoulders were draped in his rare white wolf's pelt, which he wore over a thick, leather jerkin with bare arms, displaying his impressive warrior tattoos and engraved silver armbands. A silver headband above his furrowed brow partly tamed his burnished mane as he considered the stranger with an intense gaze.

"I found Snori, my neighbor, shaking in his yard house," the fellow continued. "At first he was incoherent, muttering about Ragnarök and the end of the world, so I took him home to my house, which is closer to the edge of town."

Solveig, engrossed in his story, realized she had visited every farm in their oversight and had not seen this man. She stepped closer for a better view of him.

"He wouldn't eat, but eventually I got him to speak. He said his farm was attacked by a jötunn."

"A jötunn?" King Asbjorn's voice and brows raised in disbelief. "In my kingdom? Nothing such as this has been reported in my lifetime, nor is it repeated by the *skalds* in their tales. Surely your friend was mistaken."

"Our farms lay on the outskirts," the stranger continued. "Nestled on a plateau up the mountains near the southern border with Sygnafylke. I rode to the coast and begged transport on a fisherman's boat to get here, and it took me two days. I knew I had to bring this report to King Asbjorn and Queen Ingrid at once. It's too important a matter to ignore."

"Olag," Ingrid addressed him, leaning forward in her seat with a concerned gaze. "Did your neighbor describe the jötunn? Since no one has seen one in generations, how did he recognize it?"

The farmer Olag replied, "Snori told me the creature was as tall as a house with hands like shovels and feet like small boats. He said it had a hideous face, a hump on its back, and it tossed a wagon like it was a shoe."

"Why didn't he accompany you to give this account himself?" Asbjorn asked suspiciously.

"He was too distraught, too afraid to leave my house. My lord, you must do something. I sent my wife and children to her mother's in Skalavik, on the coast, but I can't return to plant my fields until I know the monster has been killed."

Solveig had been drawn into the conversation and did not hesitate to ask her own question. "Jarl Anders administers your *fylke*, doesn't he?" Olag whipped his head around to her and nodded. "Then why didn't you go to him for help? It would seem this is a local matter."

A few of those in the hall motioned their agreement. Olag's shoulders slumped, and he slowly turned back to the king and queen. "He didn't believe my account, my lord. He laughed me out of his great hall. But I prayed to Odin you would realize this great threat and act to save us all."

Asbjorn's frown deepened, and he scratched his chin through an expanse of beard. He exchanged a look with Ingrid and another with Solveig before regarding Olag with a somber expression. "I agree with Princess Solveig; this matter does not lie in my jurisdiction. Only if Jarl Anders seeks my support, will I send soldiers to investigate this... this giant," he declared, waving his hand dismissively. "Crushing houses, killing livestock, tossing wagons. Your neighbor's cattle were more likely attacked by wolves, his house collapsed from disrepair, and he drank so much he thought he saw a jötunn. Go home and plant your fields, Olag, and have a safe journey."

"But, my lord!" he protested, displaying fear in both his tone and visage.

"You heard the king," Baldr stated. "Go home and don't spread rumors, which may give rise to baseless unease in the kingdom." He laid hold on Olag's arm with a respectful yet unyielding grip and escorted him from the hall.

A whirlwind of banter arose, and it took Asbjorn some time to put an end to it. Finally, he stood and announced, "Court is dismissed for today. Please show yourselves out."

Two hours later, Solveig's family, along with Ragna and Geirfinnr, gathered at the king's table. The other table for the garrisoned soldiers and their guests had been moved to the far end of the chamber to afford the family privacy to discuss the unsettling events. A thrall named Bodil served the king's table while another called Fiske poured ale and presented food to the warriors. Asbjorn had shut himself away to think after hearing Olag's tale and now joined his wife, sons, daughters, and key military advisors to eat. It seemed to Solveig, though, that he only brooded, withdrawing further from his family.

"Ragna, did you hear about the farmer's testimony in court today?" Solveig asked. Ragna sat at her right hand, next to Geirfinnr, and Baldr on her left. Her father and mother occupied the ends of the table while Herlief, Karina, and Sylvi sat across from her.

Ragna sopped her bread in the flavorful dip the cook had provided and took a bite, giving Solveig a considering gaze. "Indeed. It is all anyone has been talking about. It is nonsense—pure and utter babble. There are no such things as jötnar... at least none which dwell on our earth."

"But the sagas and lore of our ancestors—" Baldr began in rebuttal.

"Have you ever seen one?" Ragna interrupted. "Do you know anyone who has? Maybe once generations ago, giants and dwarves shared our world, but no longer. Oh, people blame them for their troubles. A boulder rolls down a hill; a jötunn did it. A cow dies prematurely; it was an angry spirit. The earth shakes, and dwarves must be playing their drums under the mountain. But they are all merely stories. Such creatures do not exist."

"Just because you've never seen one doesn't mean they aren't real," Sylvi said. "They shan't be seen if they don't wish to be."

"Mother?" Solveig waited for Ingrid's full attention. "Skalds tell stories about Sigrid battling a giant named Jabbar and how they killed each other, so Odin would bring Elyn to Valhalla to be with her."

Ingrid poked at the turnip, beans, and pork on her plate, but said nothing, prompting Solveig to push her for confirmation.

"We need to know what really happened to Grandmama," she declared in a solemn hush. Although she perceived the sorrow that choked her mother like a chain around her neck, her demand was not unreasonable.

In a voice much smaller than was fit for a queen, Ingrid responded, "I don't know."

"You must know," Herlief interjected. "It was only ten years ago. Solveig and I remember it, only we were never given a straight answer. Did Sigrid fight a jötunn?"

"You all recall how she was when Elyn was sick and even worse after she died," Ingrid reminded them. "She was devastated, brokenhearted beyond repair. She moved like one of the undead through Elyn's funeral and sat about in silence for days. After about two weeks, she returned from visiting Great-Grandfather Olaf's grave and announced she was leaving on a quest."

"I remember," Baldr said. "Papa suggested she take a troop of soldiers with her, and she refused."

"She declared she must find Bifröst," Solveig supplied thoughtfully. "Then she never returned. But do we even know for certain she died? She could have lost her mind and still be wandering about Norvegr searching for a legendary bridge that doesn't exit."

"It exists," Asbjorn spoke at last. "We frequently see the arch of colors in the sky, yet I've heard of none who ever discovered the spot it touches the earth. Storytellers from the north arrived that winter, proclaiming the battle between Sigrid and the giant and the happy ending she secured. How would such travelers know about Sigrid's quest if they hadn't met her?"

"I told your father we should not dispute the skald's tale," Ingrid confessed. "True or not, your grandmama earned her place in the sagas alongside Hagbard and Signe, Gunnar and Brynhild, Sigmund, Beowulf, Hervor, and other heroes of legend. If the skalds want to say she slew the meanest giant in all the nine realms, I would rather it be so than to believe she froze to death in the northern wastelands chasing a myth."

Silence fell over the family, and they ate without speaking for a while. Then Geirfinnr made an offer. "My lord, if you wish, I could travel south to investigate this farfetched yet troublesome report. I could speak to the farmer who saw the monster, interview others in the area to discover what they know. There is no reason to commit your troops when a mere inquiry is all you require."

"I thank you, Geirfinnr." Asbjorn cast his gaze down the table at his mighty, loyal fighter. "However, we shall wait. If we hear no more about this matter, it was nothing except one man's delusion. I'll not insult Jarl Anders by behaving in a way that would undermine the authority he holds over his fylke. If he sends an envoy because more evidence and testimony are presented, then I would be glad to give you the mission. Now, let's not lose sleep over a fable."

That evening, Solveig retired early, and Ragna joined her. She sat on the side of the bed, in only a thin, white under-slip, brushing her long, dark strands in silence. Ragna shed all her clothes and washed with soap and water from the basin.

"I didn't mean to discount the story about Sigrid and the giant," Ragna said at last. "I just don't believe in monsters and creatures nobody has ever seen."

"You believe in the gods, don't you?" Solveig swung a questioning gaze to Ragna as she slid under the covers at her side.

Her damp, strawberry-blonde hair draped the pillows as her lips parted in innocent astonishment. "Of course I believe in the gods," she said. "I talk to them, and sometimes, I swear they give me signs. I identify closely with Tyr. Not only is he the god of warfare, but of order and justice, which I value. He sacrificed his own hand to capture the dangerous Fenrir to keep all the gods and people safe. But the gods do not inhabit the realm of men. I just..."

Solveig set aside her brush and snuggled under the blanket with Ragna, leaving one candle lit. Turning toward the shieldmaiden, she reached for her, sliding a smooth hand over her taut skin.

"I understand how much Sigrid means to you," Ragna confessed, "and I didn't want you to think I was making light of the legend. Maybe she did fight a jötunn at the northern end of the world, and if I'm wrong and there is a monster, I'll slay it to safeguard you. I just found the man's story preposterous."

Solveig leaned in and kissed her lips. "I know you weren't dismissing Sigrid's saga; thank you for saying so."

"You seem more tired than usual today, little dove." Ragna stroked Solveig's cheek, pushing back a strand of hair.

"Baldr and I rode to all the farms, and then with the additional worries about monsters... I suppose I am more tired than usual."

"You must pace yourself, Solveig. We can't have you falling ill."

She managed the energy for a smile. "You are sweet to me. Thank you for protecting me from the imaginary creature threatening our land," she teased. "I'll sleep better knowing I'm safe in your arms." She brushed another kiss to Ragna's lips with an impish grin. Then, feeling fatigue weigh heavy on her limbs, Solveig released a sigh. "Will you just hold me tonight?" she implored.

"It will be my pleasure to do so, honey with the dark brown eyes. It's funny," she remarked. "You don't resemble Sigrid at all."

"Not physically," Solveig admitted with a yawn. "But I've still got a piece of her spirit in here." Ragna laid her hand on Solveig's breast, feeling her heartbeat against her palm.

"Yes, there it is," she cooed and kissed her mouth. "Now sleep, princess, so you will have strength for tomorrow. All is well, for I'm right here with you."

In the safety of Ragna's embrace, Solveig drifted into slumber, half-hoping jötnar were real, and half-hoping they were not.

7

Bàtrgørð, Yeats

"Kai!" rang out a cheerful greeting. An athletic man in his prime leaped out from behind the travelers' wagon with a broad grin and open arms. He was dressed as a warrior with a studded gambeson, arm bracers, and shin greaves. A sword in its scabbard hung from his belt, and a *rönd* was slung over his back. Kai recognized him at once.

"Uncle Jerrik!" She raced to embrace Torsten's brother, her heart leaping for joy. As the most acclaimed warrior in Yeats, Jerrik always had stories to tell her about his adventures.

"Uncle Jerrik!" Leiknir bounded over to the fellow, who shared his sandy hair and lively eyes. "I bet you can't still play the game."

Torsten propped a hand to his hip and shook his head at his brother's antics as he stood beside the stranger with the gray beard, who kept a hand on the cart-horse's reins.

"What do you mean, little man?" Jerrik laughed and held out his arms as straight as tree branches, his hands balled into tight fists. "Give it a try."

Leiknir grabbed hold of an arm and pulled until his chin raised above it and his feet dangled in the air. "Come on, Kai," Jerrik encouraged her with a charming grin. "Take the other one."

She snorted out a laugh and shook her head. Without warning, she hopped up, grabbed his sturdy arm, and hauled her chin up before plopping back to the earth. "I got a sway out of it this time," she declared.

"Only because you jumped." Jerrik enveloped Kai and Leiknir in those same powerful arms and smacked scratchy kisses to their cheeks from lips buried in his straw beard.

"The travelers shall join us for dinner and spend the night in our camp," Torsten announced. "And we will hear their tidings."

"And we appreciate you, my brother," Jerrik replied, shifting his arm to drape over Torsten's shoulders. "I am cheerful to see you all, yet the news is no laughing matter. First, Kai, I hear you and Leiknir here have supplied us with a scrumptious repast. Ale?"

"Certainly." Tove placed a full horn in Jerrik's hand. "Anything for the fiercest warrior in the land of the Swedes." Kai didn't care for the sparkle Tove directed at Jerrik, but she also realized he was twice her age with two wives already. He would not return her flirtations.

"Come and make yourselves at home around our fire," Anika said to the travelers. Kai blinked at her sudden display of friendliness and supposed it was for the sake of the strangers. She noticed some sheep wearing collars and bells with the caravan, nibbling the grass beside their cart. Two young women exited the wagon and flanked the sides of a third woman wearing a many-colored dress. Kai paid attention to this woman, whose head and face were obscured by a thin, foggy veil.

"You are kind," the gray-haired traveler with the walking staff said, inclining his head to the matron in charge. "I am Haldor, Gothi of Birka, and this is Frigg, the völva, and her attendants. We are enroute to Uppsala to make a sacrifice and entreat Freyr to provide a fertile growing season for our crops and to increase our flocks and herds. Jerrik and his three warrior companions have agreed to escort us in case of trouble."

Torsten offered the company prime seats near the crackling fire and lit a few torches on their poles for extra light as the sun sank beyond the horizon. Kai and Tove helped the older women pass out baskets of fresh meat, bowls of soup, and berries with honey-sweetened cream on top. Stigr made sure everyone had enough ale, including himself.

Kai sat with Tove two rows behind the travelers while the men took the better seats to engage in conversation with the guests. Despite a canopy of stars shining on an inky canvass above, the smell of smoke and good food in the air, and the dancing orange and yellow flames of the firepit, Kai's attention was drawn to Frigg, who still had not removed her veil, thereby maintaining an aura of mystery. *How old is she? What does she look like?* Kai had not even heard her speak, and her curiosity was stirred.

"You mentioned danger." Kjell turned the conversation back to where it had begun an hour before.

"Yes," Haldor replied, and a hush fell over the camp so all could hear. "Raiders have been conducting attacks along the coast south of here," he reported. "They have not reached Lagarfjord, and I doubt they will attempt such a grand target. The king's town is well fortified, and our information counts a single ship, though it is said to be large, like a trading vessel with a hold beneath the deck. One report cited twenty fighting men with spears, swords, axes, and bows wearing armor and helmets. They strike swiftly, hacking off arms and legs, and steal what valuables they can gather, and then they are back on their ship."

"I don't know what they could grab here," Torsten opined. "We have no silver or valuables."

"You have weapons," Jerrik noted. His gaze scanned the circle until it rested on Kai and Tove. "And young women."

"We've no money to pay ransoms," Kjell retorted in an angry huff.

"I don't think they are seeking ransoms." Jerrik lowered his gaze and set his empty plate on the ground by his feet. "Slaves will fetch a good price this time of year. Especially attractive young women." He drained the remaining ale from his horn.

Everyone sitting around the fire directed their gazes at Kai and Tove.

"I won't let raiders get near my friends," Stigr declared in a convincing tone. "Let the treacherous bastards try!" He steeled his jaw in determination.

"I see you are loyal and steeped in courage," Jerrik praised him, "but it will not be enough to save the girls."

Torsten locked eyes with his brother. "They should go with you to Uppsala. We have nothing of value here besides the girls, unless they wish to take off with an unfinished longboat. Stigr, men," he said to his crew of workers, "we will focus on laying down the last two keels and carving the headpieces. None of the vessels should be finished until all are ready for the final planks to be riveted in place. We'll have nothing for them to steal."

"I will travel with you, gothi," Kjell declared, "to protect my daughter and Kai. I'll not burden you with the task, but Torsten is right. They'll be safer with you, Frigg, and your escort. Tove is my baby, my youngest child and the only one not yet wed. I'll cut out the throat of any foreigner who would make her a slave."

Seeing the expression the muscular blacksmith bore, Kai believed he could do it. In support of his friend, Torsten added, "We've enough rivets, augers, and axe heads to see us through until Kjell returns. However, when you do," he said to Kjell, "I'll need my anchors. Keep watch over our girls."

"You are sending us to Uppsala?" Kai was not surprised the men were making plans without her input, though it still upset her. "If you would allow me to train to fight, I would not be a burden on others to protect me. Jerrik, I am as good a shot with a bow as any man in this camp," she announced.

"True, yet you must sleep sometime," Torsten replied, fixing her with a steadfast glare.

"We will take the young women to Uppsala." It was the first time Frigg had spoken since the party's arrival, and all attention shifted to the völva. Her voice had an accent that sounded foreign to Kai. While she was completely unafraid to stand up to raiders in the camp, an idea emerged in her mind. Maybe traveling with the seer would be fortuitous. She had never been to Uppsala, yet people always talked about the temple there, the statues of the gods, the rituals, and the sense of the gods' presence in the holy place.

Kai squeezed Tove's hand, and her girlfriend looked at her. "We should go with them," Tove agreed. "I've never been to Uppsala. We can be helpers for Haldor and Frigg. And maybe Mother won't worry if she knows we are safe."

"We'll manage without you two for a few weeks," Anika professed. "Your big oaf of a father too. Even if there is no danger at all, everyone should make a pilgrimage to the holy site at least once."

"It is settled then," Haldor stated. "The young women should be ready to leave with us at first light."

"I'll pack a bag," Tove said to Kai, "and you do the same. I'll stay in Mother and Papa's hut tonight, as I am certain she will wish to give me instructions."

Kai nodded with a serious expression. "While I agree we should go, I don't like the idea of leaving Torsten and Leiknir behind."

"I will watch out for them." Kai glanced up to see Stigr standing tall and tough. He reached out a hand and pulled first Kai, then Tove, to their feet before catching them both in his strong embrace. "You can tell me all about your adventure when you return. And if raiders attack our camp, I'll aim for the biggest, ugliest one." He placed kisses onto each of their cheeks before releasing his hold.

Camp members took turns wishing the young women well, giving them good luck tokens and words of advice. Thora, whose husband and sons helped Torsten with the boatbuilding, put a bronze Valkyrie figure in Kai's hand. "She has always kept us safe."

Kai studied the small statue, no bigger than the size of her palm. The maiden's hair was pulled back with a band, and she carried a sword in one hand and a shield in the other. The artist's details were amazing, and Kai traced the fine lines of her face, helmet, and the pleats of her skirt. "Thora, this is too precious of an item. I cannot possibly—"

"Do not insult me, child," Thora chided her. "Didn't Torsten teach you how to accept a gift?"

Thrilled by the woman warrior that rested in her hand, Kai nodded. "Thank you very much, Thora. I shall treasure it always." She hugged the older woman, brushing kisses to her face.

Thora smiled and winked at her. "Off with you now. Tomorrow, a new adventure awaits."

Kai headed for her lean-to. She didn't own much and would have to decide what to bring with her. Away from the group, who still murmured about the possibility of attack and how they must prepare a defense, she spied Frigg, who appeared to be watching her. It was hard to tell, though, since she remained veiled.

What is that about? Why does she not wish for anyone to see her face? Will she have a prophecy for me? Kai wondered. Shaking her head, she continued to her abode. *Doubtful. Who am I to think the gods would speak to me?* Although... She had been spared when the sickness claimed her first family and blessed with a second one, so there could be grounds for hope.

8

Two warriors marched ahead of the holy travelers' wagon and two behind. Kai, Tove, and Kjell trekked alongside, guiding the nine sheep the pilgrims had brought to sacrifice in Uppsala. She had defied conventions and worn a pair of Leiknir's trousers under her hunting tunic, determining the attire to be more practical for travel than a dress. She had an axe tucked into her belt and carried a knife in its sheath; such tools were always needed, whether one was traveling or not. And she went nowhere without her bow and quiver of arrows. Kai felt better having the weapons within her reach while embarking into the unknown.

Frigg and her two blonde acolytes kept to themselves, though Haldor interacted with the others to a small degree. Sometimes Kai would peer at the völva, trying to get a peek behind her veil; other times when she ventured a glance, she caught the woman's shrouded head facing in her direction. There were so many things she wished to ask, so much she wanted to learn.

Kai and Tove slept on furs covered with a blanket under the wagon and, being deprived of privacy, refrained from sharing pleasures... at least any that might draw attention. Kai derived plenty of delight from merely touching Tove, tracing silent kisses down her neck, and from the comfort of her nearness. If Tove's father held any objections to their relationship, he kept them to himself. It was not so unusual for two young women to form a close bond or even engage in sexual activity; it was all but unheard of, though, for them to never marry.

On the third day of their journey, a soft rain fell, and Kai ran ahead to hunt, scoring two geese and three rabbits. The landscape had leveled out to a broad plain with the path taking them through a meadow. The sea to their east was near enough for Kai to notice the salty breeze, while to the west stood a vast forest, with the shadowy silhouette of mountains rising in the distance beyond it.

When Kai returned from hunting, she caught Tove talking with a red-haired warrior who had accompanied Jerrik as they walked together. Kai felt a pang of jealousy, wondering if this was the man Tove would abandon her for.

"You're back!" Tove's countenance brightened, sending relief coursing through Kai. "Gorm was telling me about the time he helped Jerrik fight off a gang of thugs."

"Nice mess of game you've got there," Gorm praised with a friendly smile.

"Thanks," Kai answered and hoisted them into the back of the wagon out of the rain. *She has a right to talk to other people,* she chided herself for being too sensitive. *All is well.*

By the fourth night, when they were able to gather dry wood for a fire after a sunny day, Kai and Tove roasted the geese and boiled the rabbits in a stew with wild onions, carrots, and garlic.

The company sat around the fire enjoying their meal and praising Kai's bow for providing a welcome change from traveling cakes and dried strips of meat. Emboldened, Kai dared to ask something she had long wanted to. "Kjell, would you craft a sword for me?"

Her odd request quieted everyone as they all stared at her. Jerrik responded, "What do you need with a sword? Many warriors do not even own one."

"Because I wish to become a shieldmaiden." Though she had voiced this desire in the past, she exhibited more conviction this time. "I want to protect others, not require my own armed guard. No one believes I can fight because I'm small, but they are wrong. Völva Frigg, Gothi Haldor, what do the runes say? Do you have a word from the gods about me? Kjell is the finest weaponsmith in the land, and Jerrik is the greatest fighter. Tove is happy with a woman's traditional role, but I... is there even a chance? Holy mother, if you order me to abandon this dream, I will put it away and seek meaning elsewhere."

Frigg inclined her head, and Kai glimpsed the side of her face for an instant. She couldn't discern if her skin bore an unusually dark tint or if it only fell in shadow. *Could she hail from a faraway land? Does she hide her face to conceal a foreign heritage?*

Then Frigg spoke in her distinctive manner. "Every person is given a destiny by the gods upon his or her birth. Few are those daring enough to follow them. Therefore, do not say only kings or elite warriors have destinies. From a tiny acorn grows the mighty oak. We will ask the gods about you in Uppsala, my dear."

"I will also pray on the matter," Haldor said. "We'll arrive at the temple in two more days. There the presence of the gods is strong. You may even receive your own sign."

Hope leapt in Kai's heart, higher and brighter than any flame.

That night under the wagon, Tove asked, "Is it so important for you to learn to fight? Can't you be content being a huntress? There is honor in it, and few women hunt. Please, Kai. The life of a shieldmaiden is perilous."

"I know, my sweet," she responded and kissed the center of Tove's palm. "But there is more to me than what everyone sees. Who knows what the future holds?"

"Exactly." Tove cradled Kai's face between her hands and gazed at her with concern. "I don't want to lose you. There are other ways to show your importance. Being my friend, sharing what we share, isn't that important?"

Kai pulled her close and burrowed into Tove's neck beneath her flowing light-brown hair. "You are the most important person in my life, yet... I know if I sacrificed my future to please you, it would one day break my heart and cause me to feel bitterness toward you. You've made it clear that you'll choose to marry. If I abandon my dream and then you abandon me, what will I have left?"

"Oh, Kai," Tove sighed. "If I marry a man so I can have a family, children of my own, I will not stop loving you. We will still be best friends, even still share intimacy. But if you get yourself killed trying to accomplish a feat you are not suited for, it will break my heart."

Feeling moist kisses sweetened with Tove's tears against her throat, Kai replied, "Then let us try not to break each other's hearts."

She slid a hand beneath Tove's sleeping tunic, reveling in her smooth skin. Tove responded warmly and guided Kai's lips to touch hers. "I hope never to hurt you, my dear one," Tove vowed. She slipped a leg between Kai's thighs spurring her pulse to race. As their kiss deepened, Kai tugged the blanket over their heads. The fire had dwindled to glowing embers, and the camp had grown quiet except for the occasional cough. In private tenderness, the couple sealed their devotion to one another.

On the fifth day since leaving Bàtrgørð, Haldor announced, "Watch now; we are entering Uppsala. Listen for voices on the wind; be aware of sensations in your hands and feet, for this is holy ground."

Glancing about the meadow clothed in wildflowers, Kai spotted immense oval-shaped mounds. "Those are the ship burial sites of kings," Kjell said as he pointed to them. Birds chirped in the scattered tree branches and Kai kept a sharp eye out for ravens, Odin's messengers.

The wagon rolled along past many spectacular mounds until they crested a small rise. Ahead lay a wide plain in a lovely expanse of valley with hills to the east and mountains to the west. A river flowed through the hollow, and beyond, a towering *hof* glimmered like gold in the sunlight. As she took in the curious, multiple layers of roofing, which rose to a cupola, its spire's needle pointing skyward, Kai also noticed an immense tree on one side of the temple and what appeared to be a longhouse on the other. Her gaze passed to a grove of oaks, which framed the temple grounds on the other three sides.

Excitement built in her chest as they neared the fabled site. They strode across a bridge over the river with the wagon rumbling behind. Jerrik insisted on leading the way to ensure the safety of all. Then Kai spotted a well beneath the spectacular tree and her lips parted in wonder. When they stopped in the temple yard, she leaned her head back and stared up at a structure unlike any she had ever seen.

"It looks like Ásgarðr," Tove voiced in wonder.

Haldor leaned on his staff with one hand and motioned with the other. "Our sacred place was designed at least two hundred years ago to mirror the invisible realm on the physical plane. This tree represents the World Tree, Yggdrasil, and the well exemplifies Urd's Well, the well of fate from whose waters Yggdrasil grows. The longhouse is a recreation of Odin's banquet hall, where we will feast tonight and sleep in warmth and comfort. The sacred grove of oaks is where the sacrificed animals will hang and where Frigg and I will go to seek the voice of the gods. Come," he instructed. Frigg and her assistants had already climbed out of the wagon and stood with the others now. "I will show you the inside."

Jerrik and another soldier flanked Haldor so he would not enter the temple unprotected. Kai could not imagine anyone would attack them on this ground, which was holy to all the Norse tribes and kingdoms; however, Jerrik was performing his due diligence. Frigg and her attendants followed, then Kjell, Tove, and Kai, leaving the other two guards for last. Eleven Swedes paraded into the building of cut timbers and thatch, each moving with reverent awe.

Their feet echoed inside the walls, and the flapping of a dove's wings drew Kai's gaze upward. High windows let in sunlight whose beams seemed to concentrate on three larger-than-life statues carved of oak in seated positions. Closest to the front, Thor held watch, gripping his mace or hammer. Then came Odin dressed in war armor and Freyr projecting an immense phallus. Pedestals bearing silver bowls stood beside each god, and red, white, and black banners hung from the rafters.

Kai turned in a circle, taking in the runic texts and carved markings over the door, at the bases of the statues, and in various places around the spacious chamber. Haldor set about lighting the candles that rested in iron holders, which sprang up like small trees.

"This is amazing," Tove exclaimed in a whisper. Kai was too enthralled for words.

"Are there no priests here?" Jerrik asked. "No one to stand watch?"

"Do you think Thor requires a human to stand guard? Cannot the gods protect their own?" Frigg asked rhetorically. "The central area of Uppsala is host to hundreds during the nine-year festival. Then priests attend to each of the three gods represented here, cooks prepare the meals, and gothi perform the *blóts*. Musicians play, mead pours, and men and women sleep with whomever they like. Ours is only a seasonal request, though important enough to be worth the journey. Tonight, we will make a sacrifice of the male sheep we brought, offer their blood to bless our soil, and their bodies to sustain our crops. We will eat and drink in the banquet hall and stroll through the grove of the gods."

Everything proceeded as the völva had decreed. Kai and Tove prepared a meal at the hearth in the banquet hall. They found grain, mead, and dried fruits stored in the pantry to combine with staples the party had brought and fresh greens they picked in the meadow. Haldor performed the sacrifices on an outdoor stone altar and collected the sheep's blood in a silver bowl. One of Jerrik's companions tied a cord around the dead sheep's feet and hoisted each one onto a different oak branch near the altar.

Frigg carried the bowl of blood into the temple, singing a song of praise and thanksgiving to the gods, and everyone else followed. She placed it on the pedestal beside Freyr. Haldor dipped a fir twig into the bowl and sprinkled the blood on the statue, the völva, her attendants, and then on all others present. Both he and Frigg recited prayers and lifted open palms in supplication for fertile fields and a bounteous fall harvest. They banned evil spirits and pronounced blessings over the people's flocks and herds. Kai found it all fascinating.

Afterward, they washed in water from the well and filed into the banquet hall to eat the meager feast Kai and Tove had prepared. They all drank, sang songs, and told funny stories—that is, all but Frigg, who remained veiled and quiet. Kai noticed when Frigg and Haldor slipped out.

"Tove, I am going to follow them," she whispered. "I need direction from the gods. Perhaps Thor or Odin will give me a sign."

Tove pursed her lips in disapproval. "Well, Gorm, the young warrior with the red hair, has been noticing me. Perhaps he would like to enjoy my company tonight," she quipped and threw her gaze at the brawny young man with ginger curls.

"Why do you take pleasure in tormenting me?" Kai scowled, then huffed out a breath. "Do what you believe is right; I must do the same. If you are not entangled with a man when I return, I will come to you."

Without awaiting a response, Kai pushed up from the table and hurried out the door. She realized Tove would use any ploy to ensure she stayed put. *She won't really lie with the warrior, will she?* Kai shook off her apprehension.

Lazy streaks of cloud drifted in front of a large full moon overhead, which cast the grove in an unearthly glow. It was easy to follow the religious leaders, so Kai stayed far enough back to avoid detection… or at least she thought she had.

"Girl, come forth." Frigg, seated with Haldor on a fallen log under a canopy of boughs and leaves, called to her. Startled, Kai eased her way meekly to their spot. "We suspected you would come."

"I do not mean to intrude, holy mother." Kai lowered her chin and plopped onto the ground in front of them.

"You seek a sign," Haldor stated in an understanding tone. "I will cast the runes and see what they have to say."

Kai sat up straight and watched with intense interest. The old gothi poured small, square stones carved with symbols out of a pouch and into his hand. Shaking them like dice, he released them on the soil in a spot illuminated by moonbeams passing through the branches. He scrutinized them before gathering them up and tossing them a second time.

Nerves wrestled in Kai's stomach as tingling vibrations of anticipation flowed over her skin. "What do they say?" She was almost afraid to ask, but she required an answer as surely as she needed to breathe.

"It is possible, though not by ordinary means." Haldor exchanged a look with Frigg before catching Kai's gaze.

"What do you mean?"

"To become a hero requires trials and sacrifices," Frigg explained. "Few can endure them. The key lies in your desire and your belief. Lose one, and you have lost all."

"What must I do?" Kai asked. Her heart thumped so loudly in her chest, she was certain they could hear it.

"To forge a hero's blade, Kjell will need the proper ore. You must prove your strength of will by retrieving a shard of Damascus steel and returning it to him. This ore is not found in our lands, only in the south across the sea. Some markets on the peninsula may have a blank or two, but the price would be so high only a king could pay it."

"Then how can I—"

"Your second task is more difficult."

Kai's heart sank at his words. *More difficult?*

"You must prove your strength of heart by giving your life for another," Haldor proclaimed. "And last, you must prove the favor of the gods by returning from the dead. Those are the three conditions I read in the runes."

"Return from the dead?" All hope vanished and Kai felt the weight of defeat drag her into a well of despair. "Not even Sigrid could return from the dead. You ask the impossible."

"Nothing is impossible for one who believes," Frigg responded. "Would you prefer to endure my trial?" Kai raised her gaze to the völva. Slowly, the seer lowered her veil. Leathery red skin etched with unnatural dark creases covered the left half of her face, her forehead, and encircled both gray eyes, which held Kai's unapologetically. The vicious burn scars continued onto a portion of her scalp and left ear; however, the rest of her head bore lovely wheaten strands like Kai's. The right half of her face displayed the natural beauty of a woman in her mid-thirties.

Compassion wrenched Kai's soul at the sight, yet she did not shrink from it, nor did she allow pity to show in her expression. She sensed a calm strength flowing from Frigg with the same intensity as the full moon glowing in the night sky.

"I asked the gods for a gift without realizing the price. It was only after my family's home burned that I received my prophetic sight," she recounted. "My parents and brothers were spared, but a burning beam fell on me in my sleep. I do not wear the veil because I am ashamed of my appearance, but for the benefit of those around me and because I do not desire sympathy. Blessed are you, Kai Torstensdottir; you see me for who I am. Know that I see you, too." She lifted her opaque scarf and draped it over her head and face once more.

"Though I would not wish it, I could pass your trial. Yet I cannot give my life for another and return from the dead," Kai repeated in despair. "Should I forsake my dream?"

"No. Helheim is paved with forsaken dreams. However, you should not always take the words of the gods literally. There are different kinds of death," Frigg explained. "Be of strong courage and continue to follow the path where your heart leads you. Heroes come in all sizes."

Haldor added, "Complete the three conditions set forth by the gods, and Kjell will forge you an unbreakable sword. I will then emboss it with runes and Frigg will infuse it with her seiðr. Such is the destiny that lies before you. You may walk its path or not as you choose."

"I'll do my best."

Kai left the holy leaders deep in thought as she puzzled over how to fulfill the tests dictated by the gods. When she entered the longhouse, everyone had settled onto sleeping benches lining the walls, some passed out from drinking. She heard Tove's giggle coming from a fur occupied by the red-haired warrior, and her spirits sank further into the depths. She trudged past them without a word, lay on her own bench, and covered herself with her blanket. In the low firelight, she picked up the bronze Valkyrie figure Thora had given her and focused all her attention on it. Valkyries didn't die. Would she join their ranks?

Soon, Tove slipped in beside her. "Don't be angry," she implored Kai in a contrite tone. She brushed a gentle kiss to her cheek. "It didn't mean anything. You were curious about your matter; I was curious, too. I've never been with a man, so how would I know if I would enjoy it or not?"

She took Kai's hand, interlacing their fingers, and brought her knuckles to her lips. "It is you I love. But you left me to chase your destiny, and I had too much mead."

"So, how was it?" Kai's tone remained stiff and indifferent, not letting on how much seeing her girlfriend with another tore at her heart.

Tove grimaced. "It kind of hurt. I suppose if I wanted a baby, I'd have to get used to it. Oh, Kai, please don't be angry with me. Tell me what the gods said." Tove cuddled close and slid a hand across her belly under her tunic, her touch tantalizing Kai's skin, pushing her deeper into despair.

Kai closed her eyes, wishing she could block out the whirlwind spinning so fast it made her dizzy. "I must believe and do the impossible."

9

Gnóttdalr, Sogn, one week later

The gardens and fields had all been planted and more lambs, kids, calves, and piglets were added to the herds daily. Birds twittered joyful songs as the sun warmed the earth with longer days. Solveig tingled with the magical freshness of spring as she flitted about the longhouse. She was also happy no more tales of destructive giants had arrived at her father's hearth.

"What are you doing, Papa?" Solveig stopped in mid-stride to stare at her father, who had donned his armor and weapons. "Is there trouble?"

"No trouble," he rebuffed her with a stern frown. "Can't your father go out to spar in the yard with his warriors without you looking at him like he was a two-headed ox?"

Solveig laughed and breezed to his side. "You haven't sparred in a while, so take care."

"That's why I need to practice, to keep my sword arm strong," he answered, flexing his biceps. "And it's your warrior friends who must be careful!"

Solveig kissed his furry cheek. "In that case, don't accidentally chop off one of our soldier's arms."

He responded with a rare grin and a deep belly laugh, then paraded out the open entryway.

Enticed by a fragrant breeze and the bright sunshine, Solveig sashayed across the hall and stepped out into a paradise. Down the hill from the king's citadel lay the vibrant town of Gnóttdalr, built in terraces that tapered to the docks on the fjord. While she could not see individual houses, the princess made out a tapestry of rooftops, gardens, pens, and the deep blue of the water beyond. What Solveig could easily see was the crown of majestic mountains rising from beyond the palisade and rolling fields. The forest green of pines and firs melded with gray stone climbing up to the snow-capped peaks that cut a jagged line against the light blue sky. She smiled at the eagle's cry and wished she could spot the regal bird. Having seen one up close before, she brought its image to her mind's eye.

"Who will stand me to a round today?" she heard Asbjorn boom.

"None but I, my lord." She recognized Geirfinnr's voice as a warrior stepped out to meet him with a rönd and, she presumed, some sort of weapon. The others started a cadence of beating axes or swords against their shields as they cheered. Closing her eyes, she pictured each one, her thoughts lingering on Ragna. She would not spar with the king, Solveig was certain. She would consider herself unworthy of such an honor, although it wasn't true. Though Ragna may have come from humble beginnings, she had earned the admiration of her peers—and her princess.

Solveig felt a familiar presence beside her; the sound of her footsteps, the smell of the scent-grass and heather oil she dabbed on told her who it was without needing to look. "Good day, Mother. Papa is flexing his muscles in the yard, but I think he just wants to enjoy the lovely day."

"Spring has made him frisky," she replied. "I shooed him out so I could get some weaving done, but now nature calls me. Would you care to go for a walk into town?"

Just then, a sentry atop the compound watchtower clanged on a hollow brass pipe. "A ship approaches flying Jarl Anders' flag."

A sudden dread leapt into Solveig's throat, and she took Ingrid's arm. "Yes. I would very much like to escort you to town to see who has arrived and what they want."

"Do not fret," Ingrid consoled her daughter. "They probably have goods to trade in the market. We'll go find out."

They did not make it to the gate before a dozen others, including Herlief and Karina, strode out ahead of them. Baldr broke into a run, dashing down the hill with Mist barking after him, running to keep pace.

"Save it, Geirfinnr," Asbjorn grumbled. "Let's see who is paying us a visit."

The two joined Solveig and Ingrid while Ragna stayed behind with the other soldiers, making ready for whatever the situation might require. Solveig took Geirfinnr's arm and strode down the path. By the time they had all arrived, an envoy and several warriors had disembarked from the vessel while a half-dozen men and women in ordinary attire unloaded bags and barrels of goods.

"Greetings, King Asbjorn!" called a man who seemed to be her father's age. From what Solveig could make out, he was dressed in a bright yellow tunic with red trim.

"Bjarni, welcome." Asbjorn reached out, and the men clasped wrists. "I notice you have brought items to trade. Let my boys help you carry them up to our market and we'll see what we have that is suitable to exchange."

"No need, my lord." Bjarni's tone remained solemn, and Solveig's chest tightened. "They are a gift from Jarl Anders: ivory from our walrus hunt, whale oil for your lamps, mead and ale for your soldiers, and colorful cloth for your women."

"It is most generous of Jarl Anders," Ingrid replied, though her countenance showed concern. "For what occasion? Does he wish for something in return?"

"The gifts are yours," Bjarni declared. "Yet is there somewhere we may speak of an important matter?"

"Come to my hall, friend," Asbjorn invited him, worry now clouding his former cheer. "Bring your guard if you like."

"They should stay with the vessel," Jarl Anders' ambassador advised. "We will be returning south to Skalavik soon."

Solveig's dread only grew on the way back to her longhouse on the hill. Geirfinnr remained silent at her side, offering his arm to steady her climb. Shortly, her family members, Geirfinnr, and Ragna sat at the king's table with Bjarni while a servant set flatbread and ale before them.

"Is this about the report of a jötunn?" It may have been out of place for her to speak first, but Solveig was not one to tiptoe around a problem.

With a grave nod, Bjarni replied, "Aye. We did not believe it when the farmer rushed into the great hall, frantically jabbering about a giant. It was preposterous. Then, a few days later, others whose herds graze outside of town arrived in with the same story. So, to settle everyone's fears, Jarl Anders sent a patrol to look for the creature, supposing it was most likely a big brown bear starved after a winter's hibernation. Six men on horseback with spears, bows, axes, and swords, led by one of our most elite warriors..." Bjarni took a swallow of his ale and passed a mournful glance around the table. "They didn't return."

Solveig could have heard a dove's heartbeat in the silence.

"They could have gotten lost," Herlief at last supposed with a shrug. "It hasn't been that long. If they went high where the snow is still melting, they could have been cut off by rushing waters."

"It's possible," Bjarni acknowledged, "and Jarl Anders considered it. He sent a second patrol out. Yesterday, one man returned. He was covered in dried blood and was in such shock that he remains unable to speak. Jarl Anders held council last night and the freemen of Skalavik voted to ask for your aid. We rowed here overnight to bring the request."

"Then Jarl Anders believes there is a jötunn in his fylke?" Asbjorn asked in a skeptical voice.

"He is convinced a real danger prowls the southlands," Bjarni concurred. "Whether it is a giant remains to be seen."

Asbjorn narrowed his brows. "Why didn't Jarl Anders come himself? Or send his son?"

Bjarni's composure wavered. Solveig detected terrible grief in his eyes before he mustered a response. "His son is one of the missing."

The words struck Solveig like an arrow. She knew Anders' son. He was her age, and they had socialized at least once a year on some occasion or another, since they both were children.

"I shall lead an investigation into Randolf's disappearance," Herlief declared with iron conviction. "He is my friend and may still be alive, trapped somewhere. Volunteers will flock to my side, Father, so you need send none who do not wish to come."

"Herlief!" Karina exclaimed, fear whitening her face to snow. She grabbed her husband's hand.

"Stay calm, woman," Herlief rebuked her softly. "I must lead the expedition. I'll call for our finest tracker."

"Then you need look no further," Ragna said, sending a wave of panic through Solveig's soul. "You know I am the best, and I am not afraid. I do not believe in giants and am certain we'll find a reasonable explanation for what's shooting terror through the southlands like a flaming arrow."

Herlief nodded at her. "I didn't want to assume without asking you first."

"I will stand at Herlief's right hand," Geirfinnr proclaimed.

"And I'll go, too," Baldr volunteered.

"You'll do no such thing!" Ingrid was a soft-spoken woman, strong behind the scenes, and invariably in control of her emotions. But in that instant, her shout was as shrill as the bleat of a lamb being chased by a wolf.

"Your mother is right, Baldr," Asbjorn agreed. "It is foolish for both my sons to engage in any dangerous mission together. One of you should always remain far from the fray to protect our kingdom's security and my lineage. Herlief is more experienced, and men will eagerly follow him to their deaths. You may indeed be capable, son, but this is not your time."

"Someone must stay here to protect your sisters," Ragna proposed. "What if these attacks are a ruse to call warriors away from Gnóttdalr so an enemy can attack the king's fortress? I will assign soldiers to stay behind under your command—with the king's permission, of course."

"I hereby grant permission," Asbjorn declared. "Baldr, you take charge of the army while Herlief leads a party of twelve to investigate."

"Nine soldiers and our three—Herlief, Ragna, and Geirfinnr," Ingrid concurred. "Three and nine are lucky numbers. They will bring good fortune to the expedition."

"We can accommodate twelve on our ship," Bjarni said.

"They shall take one of my longboats," Asbjorn decreed. "They may need it to find the monster, and they won't need to trouble you for a ride when it's time to return home."

Bjarni nodded. "Jarl Anders is forever in your debt."

"A threat ignored is a threat that grows." The king recited the proverb as a bleak warning. "It is in our kingdom's best interest to eliminate the menace before it spreads."

"Will your crew be ready to leave in an hour?"

Herlief replied, "Give us two. I still must select nine volunteers from among the fighting men and women."

"Thank you, wise king," Bjarni said and bowed his head. "I'll wait for them at the docks."

While Herlief left to assemble the volunteers, Solveig watched Ragna cross the great hall to the trunk where she stored her belongings. With apprehension roiling in her gut, Solveig scurried off to her room and returned in all haste. She stopped beside the shieldmaiden and waited for her to glance up. In her hands, she fingered a red silk sash embossed with golden threaded runes.

"I want you to wear this under your armor," Solveig said when she caught Ragna's attention. She handed her the favor and explained, "I asked the gothi to help me select the right runes."

Ragna held the wide ribbon and took time to examine it. Solveig pointed to each embroidered rune as she spoke. "□ is Odin's symbol to lead you into wisdom, truth, and inspiration." She slid her finger to the next bit of gold stitching. "□ is for leadership and victory. This one, □, will grant you the divine protection of the Valkyries. And the □..." Solveig paused, peering with uncertainty into Ragna's leaf-green eyes.

"I know what it stands for, my dove. It is Gebo, the gift rune, and represents partnership and love." In an uncharacteristic manner, Ragna displayed her affection toward Solveig in a public space. Reaching a hand behind Solveig's neck, she drew her close and covered her lips in an affirming kiss. "Thank you, princess. I am honored by your favor and the protection it will bring me."

She draped the sash over one shoulder and tied it at her waist before pulling on her chainmail. "And thank your father for this," she added, motioning to the mail shirt. The heavy, armored tunic had been hand-riveted from hundreds of tiny, metal rings. It had been expensive and had taken many hours to fashion. Its sleeves extended to her elbows and its hem to her hips.

Solveig took Ragna's cheeks in her palms and fixed her with a sincere gaze. "I hope you are right. I pray there is no vicious giant for you to confront, only a grouchy old bear like my father. Be safe and come back to me." Solveig sealed her order with a kiss.

"Do not be afraid, Solveig. Encourage Baldr. He wishes to lead, yet he isn't completely sure of himself. And don't let your dog chew on my extra pair of boots while I'm gone," Ragna added with a laughing smirk.

"Mist would never." She pressed her lips together to hold back a smile. She was too nervous to make jokes.

Solveig assisted Ragna in buckling her sword belt and collecting her weapons before she said, "I need to wish my brother luck as well. Ragna, I..." The words she wished to say pounded like a battering ram against her lips, desperate to get out, but this was not the time or place, not with her lover leaving any minute. Ragna needed to be focused on her mission, not thinking about a love-sick princess. "I know you will succeed."

"With you cheering me on, how could I fail?" Ragna's eyes sparkled with her reply, and she waved Solveig away. "Go bid Herlief farewell. We will return before you know it."

Tearing herself from her beloved shieldmaiden, Solveig strode to where Karina stood beside Herlief, struggling unsuccessfully to hold back her own tears.

"Karina," her brother chided his wife with good cheer. "Why is your face wet? Is it raining inside the hall?"

"Oh, stop, you!" She wiped her cheek and sniffed. "You must swear that if you find an actual jötunn that you will not challenge it, do you hear me? Everyone knows how strong and brave you are; do not prove to them that your stupidity is even greater."

Herlief laughed and turned to Solveig. "Am I a fool, sister?"

She flashed him a smug grin. "You have been known to behave foolishly on occasions. Now, mind your wife's admonishment, or you'll have Hel to pay!" Solveig wrapped her arms around her brother's neck and kissed him. "You, Ragna, and Geirfinnr look out for each other," she pronounced seriously. "Karina is right; there is strength in numbers, and you are the king's son. You have nothing to prove."

Baldr stood by stoically, his face etched with lines of disappointment as much as concern.

"Listen to Solveig," Karina implored her husband. "We have babies to make, which will prove difficult to do if you are laid up with injuries."

"Yes, big brother," Sylvi concurred as she took her turn to hug Herlief. "I want nieces and nephews to practice on so I can be a good mother. Don't be like a sheep that wades in water too deep and drowns itself. Come home to us."

Herlief laughed, flipped Sylvi's hair, and tweaked her nose. "I'll return if only to tease you."

Solveig and Sylvi stepped aside as their mother and father approached. Ingrid hugged Herlief and kissed his cheeks. "You can fight and lead. But do your feet know their way home?"

"Yes, Mother," he groaned impatiently.

"I love you, son. Kill the monster and be done with it."

"The women have offered sound advice, Herlief," Asbjorn said. "There are twelve of you—twelve of the bravest warriors in all Norvegr. Together, you can defeat the giant. Then think of the songs and stories people will share!" He clasped his hands behind his son's neck and brought their foreheads together. "You are my son, and I am proud of you." He embraced Herlief in a brief hug, slapping his back, then stepped away.

"Karina, help my mother and sisters while I'm gone," he charged before diving into a honeymoon kiss so deeply intimate that Solveig rolled her eyes, and their father groaned.

"Get out of here, boy!" the king laughed. "Don't forget your spear. A spear has better reach than a sword. And bring my longboat back in one piece."

Solveig and her family accompanied them to the docks, along with the whole town, to see the prince and his warriors off. Some sang songs and others recited prayers. Young men cheered while old men made jokes. Solveig fixed her focus on Ragna and waved cheerfully as the longboat pushed away and the oars lowered. She continued to stare and wave as the craft became a fuzzy blob of brown on the waves and she could no longer distinguish the people aboard. A sick feeling gnawed in her gut, and she feared she may faint from the stress. She took a slow, deep breath and steadied herself on Ingrid's arm.

"This is a glorious day," Asbjorn proclaimed. "Herlief's name will always be remembered as the warrior who saved Sogn from a rampaging jötunn."

I hope, Solveig added silently.

10

South of Uppsala, in the land of the Swedes

Kai was troubled on the return trip from the temple at Uppsala. The first two days she remained quiet, although she hunted in the forest ahead of the wagon so everyone would have fresh meat to eat. The most expedient path took them along the coastline, a route which was flat and void of thickets.

At first, she wondered if the gothi and völva were mocking her desires, yet they had seemed sincere. Perhaps it was the gods who enjoyed a laugh at her expense. Nobody could return from the dead except as a ghost. Was that the riddle? Must she become a *vættir*, a spirit of the land, to achieve her destiny? It made no sense. *Frigg said the words of the gods may not be literal,* she pondered. *Mayhap I would only be dead for a moment, then regain my breath. I once witnessed such when a fisherman fell into the river. His friends dragged him out and beat on his back and chest; then he breathed again. Once an old woman hit her head and lay unconscious for four days. People were sure she was walking the land of the dead and forgot to completely leave her body first, yet she awoke and went about her business. Something like this must be what Haldor meant.*

Rain fell their entire third day of travel until Kai's every step splashed in a puddle and her hooded cloak was soaked through. "I suppose we will not be able to build a fire tonight," Tove remarked as she trudged beside Kai.

"I don't think so."

"I wonder how everyone is doing back at the camp?" Tove tried to engage her in conversation. "I wonder if the raiders ever came?"

She shrugged.

"Kai." Tove reached for her hand and Kai let her have it. "I am so sorry. I feel you have been avoiding speaking to me because of the night of the fertility ceremony. The way Gorm explained it, engaging in sexual relations was part of the ritual, but ever since, you have been so distant. Please forgive me."

"It would be a lie if I said it didn't matter," Kai admitted. "However, that is not what burdens me, sucking away every cheerful thought." She raised her gaze from the mud to glance at Tove's distraught expression. "Of course I forgive you. From what I've heard, the fellow's words were true. I should have stayed and shared pleasures with you instead of going into the grove."

"What Haldor and Frigg told you?" Tove guessed. "Is it what has plunged you into brooding? You still have not explained what they said."

Kai kept Tove's hand in hers as they swerved to avoid a deep puddle, rain droplets rolling down her face like tears. "I'm not sure how to explain it," she confessed. "I hope they can find a dry spot to halt the wagon tonight, so we do not have to lie in mud. I wish to hold you and feel you near me."

"If the ground is wet, I will gather pine needles to form a mat for us," Tove promised. "I want to be close to you, too. You will feel better once we get back to Bàtrgørð and return to our normal activities. Maybe Torsten will teach you how to speak to the trees and listen, to choose the right ones for each part of the longboat. You could become a stem-smith like him. That would be a fabulous destiny."

Kai smiled for the first time since receiving her prophesy. She was soaked through, sloshing in puddles, with no chance for a fire, yet Tove's encouragement shone more light on her soul than the sun at the summer solstice. "You know I love you, right?"

Tove diverted her gaze with a bashful blush and a squeeze of her hand. "Yes, I know, and am joyful in the knowing."

The rain had slowed to a drizzle by the time the party made camp. They chose a sandy portion of beach where the water had seeped away, making it more comfortable to lie on. Kai, Tove, and the others dined on traveling cakes and salted herring. Though cold, it satisfied Kai's hunger. She fell asleep snuggled together with Tove under a damp blanket to the steady sound of waves crashing and the rhythm of her lover's breathing.

She awoke to the clang of steel.

"We're under attack!" Jerrik shouted.

Kai scrambled out from under the wagon. First light glowed over the vast waters of the sea. The rain had stopped, but everything was wet—too wet to burn, she thought, until a torch tossed by a pitch-haired raider lit up the wagon. Jerrik and two other guards engaged in battling their attackers while Gorm lay facedown in the soggy sand with a spear shaft rising from his back. Kjell swung an axe in an effort to ward off two raiders with swords. Smoke billowed from the wagon and battle cries filled the air.

"Tove!" Kai yelled with eyes wide as she reached down to yank her out from under the burning wagon.

"Oh, *skitr*!" Tove screamed. Covering her mouth in horror, she spun in a circle, taking in the scene.

A raider clutched one of Frigg's acolytes in a mighty grip while a second man chased after the other attendant. Haldor drew Frigg away from the burning wagon toward the road, but their path was blocked by two assailants bearing spears and shields.

Kai snatched up the only weapon near at hand—a short piece of driftwood as thick as her forearm. A tall, wiry man with a shaved head and sandy beard lunged for Tove; Kai brought down the full force of her stick on his forearm, resulting in a loud curse and shocked expression from the raider. He took a step back, rubbing his injured arm and giving her an assessing gaze.

With determination, Kai tightened her grip on the length of branch and charged her foe. His eyes widened as she neared him, and by Odin's beard, if he didn't laugh at her! Filled with fury, she pitched backward, sliding the last few feet between the tall man's legs, and smacked her rod upward, slamming it into his groin with all her might.

"That will teach you to laugh at me!" she raged and pushed between his legs to her feet while he doubled over, holding himself.

It was then she caught sight of an aggressor grabbing Frigg's wrist and pulling her from Haldor. She was too far away to reach him, and her bow was... probably burning in the wagon.

"Hey, you she-troll's hairy ass!" she yelled at him. When he glanced over his shoulder, she hurled the stick, which landed fat end first in his face, bloodying his nose, and inducing him to let go of the völva.

"Leave her be!" The sharp command came from a mature man in the raiding party. His straight, bay-brown hair was cut above his shoulders, and he bore a long horseshoe mustache. From his higher-quality leather armor and his bearing, Kai presumed him to be their leader. He spoke the Norse language, although with an accent foreign to her ears. "Do not touch the seer or the gothi. Have you no sense? They hold the ear of the gods and can curse us all."

"We have nothing to steal," Haldor proclaimed in anguish as he guided Frigg to stand behind him.

Kai spun back to the action on the beach to see where she could be of help, but her spirits sank. The raiders outnumbered her small party two to one, and they had been taken by surprise. Jerrik lay motionless, bleeding from his head, along with their other three guards. To the fighting men's credit, their enemies had suffered losses, too. Blood tainted the puddles and soaked into the thirsty ground while the wagon burned, and the ponies pulled against their tethers, which were tied to an outlying tree. Their fearful whinnies filled the air while their hooves danced as if they were on hot coals. A beefy raider with a deep scar and a deeper scowl held a sharp blade to Kjell's throat. Both of Frigg's acolytes had been captured and the tall, bald man with the throbbing balls held Tove in a solid grip. Kai was the only one left to drive away their attackers.

Thoughts blurred in her mind. *If only I had my bow!* Now she didn't even have the makeshift club. *I'm fast. I could run, and they might not catch me. But to whom would I go for help? It is two more days' journey to our camp.* She spied an axe dropped by one of the injured or dead foes who lay nearby. With a quick calculation, she considered, *If I can lay a blade at the leaders' throat, they will have to do as I say.*

Without further hesitation, she made a dash for it. She detected movement from the corner of her eye and dived for the handle, wrapping her fingers around it just as a large boot smashed over the weapon, barely missing her knuckles. Kai groaned, and the raider laughed.

"The old man is right, Einar," called a man in a warrior's gambeson from the back of their smoldering wagon. It had been too wet for a strong blaze but suffered damage all the same. "There's nothing back here but some worthless rubbish."

"We can still turn a profit from the ponies and the women," replied Einar, the short-haired man Kai had pegged as the leader. "Take the blonde women and the pretty young one," he directed, "only don't *take* them. They are worth more unscathed."

"I ask you, man from the southern shores," Frigg said in a gentle tone. "Do not take my attendants. They are training to serve the gods. Your people must believe in the gods and their power."

Einar tromped toward her and studied her with cruel eyes. Without warning, he yanked the veil from her head. Gasps ascended from some of his soldiers as he threw the cloth into the mud. "I know you are a witch. If we have your apprentices on board our ship, you cannot curse us without damning them as well. If you have the ear of the gods, you can beseech them, and perhaps good men will buy your acolytes when we reach the market in Bilhyryn."

Kai's heart raced. She wanted to do something; she *had* to do something. A glance up informed her that the man whose colossal foot was pinning the axe to the ground had a knife loosely stuffed in his belt. She bolted up, whipped it from his girth, and brandished it at the entire troop of foreigners.

Every one of them laughed—except the stern Einar, who focused an icy glare at her. She shifted her attention to the tall fellow gripping Tove's arm.

"What about her?" he asked, pointing at Kai.

"She is not worth the bother," Einar replied as he marched away from Haldor and Frigg toward the center of the group. "She's too small for labor and too feisty to sell as a wife. I don't want to waste space in our hold on her. Leave the runt and load the other three and the ponies on the ship."

"No!" Kjell struggled against the brute who held him, getting the skin of his neck nicked for his troubles. "Don't take my little daughter!"

"She looks like a grown woman to me," Einar stated.

This couldn't be happening. Kai could not be left behind as too insignificant to matter while these ruffians carried Tove away to be sold into slavery. There had to be something she could do to save the woman she loved.

"You are wrong, Einar," she proclaimed in her most commanding tone. Fire lit her eyes as she tightened all her muscles like a deer about to spring. "I am worth ten times what Tove is," she said, motioning to her girlfriend. Fear and dread consumed Tove's countenance, and she trembled in the bald man's hands. "I am a warrior, more skilled than any of you!" Kai turned a tight circle, holding out the blade she had snatched.

Another uproar of laughter erupted.

"See?" Kai declared. "Think of the gambling odds you would get. Place bets on me to win at what, five to one, ten to one? Then you will rake in profits when I defeat all challengers."

"More like a hundred to one!" a raider called out.

"But there isn't a bunny league," teased another. "Who would agree to fight you?"

"Let's go," Einar instructed, and started for the small dinghy they had come ashore in.

"You cannot take Tove!" Kai yelled in fury. "Take me instead."

"I have made my decision," Einar snapped, shooting her an irritated glare.

Kai stormed toward the tall, bald man with her small blade at the ready. "Let her go," she hissed.

A raider standing a few yards away hurled his shield at her. It spun with a wobbly motion and struck her with enough force to knock her to the ground at Tove's feet. Rolling on her back, she looked up with a hopeless, mournful expression.

"Please," she whispered so only Tove and the marauder who clutched her could hear. "Leave her with her father, who needs her. I am an orphan whom no one will miss. Test me in a fair fight against any of your men. If I win, promise you'll let Tove go."

"Kai, you can't." Tears streamed from Tove's eyes as she gazed down to where Kai lay pleading for the chance to lose either her life or her freedom.

The man whose balls she had busted seemed moved by her plea. "What would it hurt, Einar? The men could use some entertainment," he suggested. "Let her fight Bozidar. If she wins, we take her to bet on as a fighter. If she loses, we leave her and take this young woman for the slave market. What say you?"

"I say it is an insult to Bozidar to match him up with a little girl," answered another of the raiders with a serious frown.

"Oh, come on," joshed a third with a humorous grin. "It will give us all a laugh."

Kai rocked forward and pushed to her feet, steadier from being smacked by the shield and emboldened by her inspired idea. Of course, she had no notion of how she might defeat a seasoned warrior twice her size or more, but she had to try.

"Yes, Einar," she repeated with passion. "You aren't afraid a little girl will best one of your big, powerful warriors, are you?"

He marched to her and looked down his nose with a sneer. "Would you really fight Bozidar to the death rather than say farewell to your friend?" He motioned to the tallest, brawniest warrior in the bunch. "You realize you could go free. Either way, you'll never see this woman again. You must be the smallest fool I've ever come across—or the biggest."

"I will fight, I will win, and you'll let Tove go," Kai stated, as if it were fact.

"Don't, Kai!" Tove beseeched. "He'll kill you."

Kai turned a doleful gaze to her girlfriend. "Do you have such little faith in me? Isn't it enough I must convince our enemies?" Before she could allow self-pity to take root, she turned her stare back to the pirate leader with fierce resolve.

"So be it," he consented. "Bozidar, what say you?"

The burly warrior in the charcoal gambeson stepped forward with an amused grin. "I will squash her like an ant. It isn't sporting."

"Then let me have a weapon," Kai suggested.

"Aren't you holding a little knife?" a raider hollered. "Anything else would be too heavy for you to lift." More laughter.

Dagger in hand, Kai moved away from Tove and her captor to face Bozidar. His neck was as thick as an ox's, his mane of brown hair like a bear's, and his arms as solid as oak branches. The Slav held a spear two feet longer than Kai was tall, with both a sword and an axe in his belt. He was to her like a giant.

My days of being a hero could be short-lived, she thought as she assessed him. *But at least today, for the next few minutes, I will step into my destiny. I shall not allow them to take Tove without a fight.*

II

Kai realized she only stood a fool's chance of winning. Nobody had ever heeded her requests to be trained to fight, but she had watched the warriors practice, and she knew which end of a blade was the sharp one.

'Desire and belief' is what Frigg said. I need both. Well, I sure have the desire part flowing, she thought as she tried to plan an approach. *I can't risk throwing the knife, for if I miss, I'll have no weapon at all. If I can just get close enough...*

The walking mountain the raiders called Bozidar spun his spear as he marched near, amusement playing over his features. Kai zigged and zagged as she maneuvered into a position to strike. He was easily over six feet tall to her five and must have weighed at least twice as much; neither fact dissuaded her. Her hope rested in the assumption that she would be quicker and more agile.

She crouched under a jab from his weapon, feinted left, then committed right, leading with the tip of her short blade. Bozidar whipped the butt end of his spear shaft around and caught her under the chin, sending her flipping through the air to land face-first in the sandy mud with an oof.

Once Kai had been kicked by a horse; this hurt far worse. With her head spinning and heart pounding, she guessed her jaw might be broken. The sting of humiliation made her angry, causing her desire to swell in intensity.

"That was easy!" Bozidar declared to the cheers of his fellows. Kai pushed up and struggled to get her feet under her wobbling body. She still gripped the knife, but through her blurred vision, she caught sight of a short length of chain lying a yard away, part of the harness that hitched the team of ponies to the cart. The wagon smoldered behind her opponent, but the wet wood no longer supported the flames. Thinking the chain could be useful, she staggered toward it through the ringing in her ears and snatched it up in her left hand.

"Look!" called out the raider with his bloody blade pressed to Kjell's throat. "The mouse is going to try again."

Uncertain her mouth would work, she answered to herself, *I am indeed!*

Perhaps because he considered it unsporting, or maybe out of boredom, Bozidar tossed his spear to another foreigner and drew his axe. "You can still run," he jeered.

Kai wound the chain around her arm like a bracer, shook her head, and faced him with her dagger. All her focus centered on her opponent and how she might bring him down. She recalled the leader, Einar, saying it was a fight to the death, yet she feared if she killed their biggest warrior, they would not hesitate to execute her in retaliation.

Bozidar flung a chop at her, which she dodged. She took a swipe at him and missed. Planning where her feet should go, Kai worked her way closer to the side of the damaged wagon. Her opponent's next swing came within a hair of slicing her modest breast, but she jumped back in time, stretching with her knife to rip a piece of his sleeve.

Oohs and cackles erupted from the attackers' ranks, and she heard Tove's voice pleading, "Stop this, Kai! Run away." It was a directive she refused to obey.

Swift and decisive, she commanded herself and dashed into the move. In an instant, Kai sprang, landing her first foot on the wagon wheel, her second on its seat, and then leaping onto Bozidar's back before he had time to twist around. As she executed her dive, Kai popped the loose end of the chain off her forearm and into her knife hand, so when she crashed onto the big man's back, she snapped it across his throat and pulled, leaning all her scant hundred pounds into the action.

Immediately, Bozidar's free hand shot up to tug at the chain, yet he could not squeeze his fingers between it and the flesh of his neck. She heaved with all her meager might, praying to whichever gods may be listening for strength. Seeing the giant's right arm make a preparatory move, she shifted her head and shoulders to his left before the axe iron could strike her. He shook and contorted, and she hung on.

A dozen voices shouted a din of instructions at Bozidar, although she could distinguish none individually. She just had to keep the chain tight until he passed out. He must not have been as dull-witted as he appeared, for he dropped his axe and reached both hands across his shoulders, plucked her off, and tossed her over his head to the ground in front of him, where she landed with a painful thud.

It would have been a good idea had it worked. Kai glanced up in time to see the backswing of her foe's sword. She rolled away from the blow—and that's when she spotted her bow. It lay on the sand with a heap of items the thieves had pulled from the back of the smoking wagon. Surely her quiver of arrows would be there too. If so, maybe she'd have a chance.

Kai scrambled up in time to avoid another strike. Spinning on one foot toward the big man, she at last landed a cut to his arm. "The mouse bites!" he hollered, shaking it off.

Pushing past him, she zoomed the short span to the rear of the cart.

"Look, she's running away!" someone yelled. "Pay up."

Taking bets, she murmured to herself and skidded into the pile of supplies scattered at the back of the wagon. She thrust the knife into her belt and grabbed up her bow and quiver before speeding around the vehicle, staying ahead of her pursuer while she strung it on the run. Chest heaving with ragged breath, still half in a daze, Kai spun around to face her enemy with her weapon cocked. A bluff wouldn't do; he'd run her down. Neither could she risk killing him.

Kai let the first arrow fly at the edge of his stocky girth. Bozidar cried out in fury when it sank in, and he halted his forward movement. Her second shot also landed where she had intended—the toe end of his boot, pinning his foot to the wooden shield it rested on.

"You *sorðinn veslingr*!" he bellowed at her in fury. He ripped the shaft from his side and reached to snatch the one that might have cut off a toe.

"Halt and live." Kai's words were forceful and direct as she stared down the sight of her arrow, aimed at a chest so massive a child couldn't miss it. Suddenly, the crowd was silent and the morning air thick with tension. "We had a bargain." Though she could not risk glancing away from Bozidar, she perceived Einar in her peripheral vision.

"You are worthless as a fighter," the leader stated. "Yet you have displayed courage and resourcefulness, and if my guess is correct, you have some skill with the bow."

"Aye, I have," she answered steadily. "I hit what I aimed at."

"You are the strangest woman I've ever encountered," Einar declared, shaking his head. "Lower your weapon and place it on the ground. Bratmir," he directed to the tall, bald crewman who held Tove. "Release the girl and take the little one instead." He brushed a hand through his hair. "Thor's hammer! I've never witnessed such a display."

Kai slowly set her bow and arrows in front of her, and Tove rushed into her arms. "I don't believe it, none of it," she sobbed. "Thank Freya you are alright."

Realizing it would be for the last time, Kai hugged her in return. She squeezed her eyes shut and breathed in Tove's sweet honeysuckle scent.

"Take care of Torsten for me," she asked Tove.

Bratmir took her by the arm then, pulling her away. "Why would you ever do such a stupid thing?" he asked.

She glanced up at her captor, perceiving his bewilderment, an expression less harsh than curious.

"Tove is my best friend," she answered him in honesty. "I made a vow to protect her. Your people understand about vows, don't they?"

He nodded, a serious curtain falling over his rugged visage. "'Tis rare even an honorable man keeps them," he admitted.

"Kai!" she heard Tove's voice cry out in agony yet did not look back. If she did, she may start crying, too, and such would simply not do. "I love you," Tove vowed, "and I won't forget."

Kai trudged on, keeping her eyes on the ground. It touched her heart to hear Tove's confession, and it made her sacrifice well worth it.

She watched the man who had been restraining Kjell march by, collecting scattered weapons. A few raiders picked up their fallen comrades and placed them in the dinghy. To Kai's relief, she saw Jerrik stir from the spot where he lay, though he was still too weak to help. She put a finger to her lips to quiet him as they passed.

"Raiders from the southern land!" Frigg's distinctive voice rang out. "Njǫrd, god of the sea, will not be pleased with you."

Einar laughed and threw a reply over his shoulder. "Njǫrd is exceedingly pleased with me, witch. Why do you think our raids meet with so much success?"

Bratmir loaded Kai into the small craft with Frigg's two attendants. She had not yet learned their names, but they were exceedingly more attractive than she was with their long legs and womanly figures. "Let us stay close together," Kai suggested in a hush. "Everything will be all right."

She wasn't sure why she felt compelled to comfort the holy women. Shouldn't they be comforting her? They appeared so frightened and sorrowful. One looked as though she had been weeping, and the other was doing so now.

"You two, bring those ponies," Einar commanded to a couple of his crew. "Bratmir, take half of the men and the women to the ship and come back for the ponies and the rest of us."

"Aye," he replied, and shoved the bow off the shore.

Kai gazed at the scene on the beach. Haldor stood beside Frigg, steadying her with kind hands. Kjell hugged Tove close, and Jerrik propped himself up on an elbow, blood still gushing from his head wound. The other three warriors remained motionless, the wagon smoldered, and Kai's hopes and dreams for the future lay shattered in the wet sand.

It seemed surreal, as if she would awaken from a bad dream at any moment. They were halfway to the ship when the irony hit her with the impact of Bozidar's spear shaft. Torsten had sent them to Uppsala to protect them from harm, yet the plan everyone believed to be wise had backfired. *I wonder if the raiders attacked Bàtrgǫrð too. Will I find captives I know on the ship? Are Torsten and Leiknir safe? Shall I ever see them again?* The oars slapped the water in rhythm as Kai pondered her situation.

"Kai?" She glanced over at the tall, bald man. "Is that your name?"

She nodded grimly and cast a despondent gaze to the floor of the boat.

"I'm Bratmir, first mate under Einar's command. You made an impression on me today," he confessed. "I still think you have sawdust for brains, but I will instruct the crew to leave all three of you untouched on the voyage home. I expect there might be a short man who will buy you for a wife when we get to Bilhyryn. Don't cause trouble, you hear?" he warned. "Einar would just as soon throw you overboard, I suspect, even though I judge you to have potential."

Kai nodded in silence and shot one more glance at her companions on the beach—at her first love. Only time would tell if Tove would also be her last.

12

Gnóttdalr, ten days later

Although her nerves remained on edge, her emotions never far from the surface, Solveig continued to perform her role as a leader. She and Baldr paid another visit to the farms, pleased to spy green sprigs sprouting over all the grain fields. Kids and lambs had been born and soon more berry varieties would ripen. With the equinox passed, the daylight hours lengthened and shepherds from pastures on distant hills brought wool to trade at the market.

Down at the docks, men were preparing their boats for a whaling expedition. "A fellow spotted some gray whales and sea wolves a few days north of here near the coastline," an excited fisherman reported.

"I wish I could come with you," Baldr admitted, "but I must wait here until my brother returns. When do you think you'll sail?"

"We're planning to leave at first light tomorrow," the man said as he loaded an armful of spears and harpoons onto the vessel. "We don't want to get up there and find they've taken out to sea."

"Understandable," Baldr replied with a nod. "May the god Njorn and goddess Gefion grant you good fortune." As they rode away, Baldr turned to Solveig and vowed, "One day, I'll have an adventure of my own."

"I'm sure you will, little brother," she concurred with a smile. "You have many years of voyages ahead of you, but right now you are stuck with me. I wish

Herlief and Ragna would get home soon. Are they chasing this creature to the ends of the earth?"

"I agree. It is taking entirely too long, which could only mean two things." Letting his pony find its own way, Baldr fixed her with a serious gaze. "Either they are enjoying feasting in Jarl Anders' hall too much, or something has gone wrong."

Solveig snapped her focus back to the trail, a frown forming on her face. "Do not suggest such things, Baldr," she ordered. "And do not dare mention your concerns in front of Mother."

"I won't," he muttered. "Although you realize she is thinking the same."

They rode through the gates to find Asbjorn and a stable hand leaning on a corral, watching the king's prized black stallion engaged in a courting ritual with a dun-bay mare. She spread her hind legs, lifted her tail, peed a little, and whinnied. The stud, who had been strutting about, stopped by her rump to sniff her scent. Then he stretched his neck high and curled his upper lip before letting out his own squeal.

"Catching a good show?" Solveig asked. She waltzed over to greet their father while Baldr took their horses to the stable.

Asbjorn afforded her a serious look. "Proper breeding is not entertainment; it's an art. I need to pace Midnight if he is to cover the leading mares this season. The others will go to Ramrod, as we don't want all the offspring to be related."

"I'm certain you must consider many factors to maintain the most excellent herd in Sogn," she conceded with a smile.

His mouth dropped, and he suddenly looked appalled. "Best herd in Sogn? Do you take me for second rate?" he thundered as he slapped fists to his ample waist. "My Fjordings are the finest in all Norvegr as surely as you are standing here!"

Laughter bubbled from Solveig's lips, and she stretched up to kiss his cheek. "Certainly, Papa. Whatever was I thinking? I must be exhausted from our rounds today."

He wrapped her in a beefy arm and peered down with concern. "You didn't overtax yourself by riding around with Baldr, did you?"

"No, Papa. The fresh air does me good. I just came over to offer you a slight diversion before going in to see if Mother needs anything."

A smile escaped his grizzled face, and Asbjorn kissed Solveig's forehead. "Run along then; I'll see you at dinner."

She had made it to the longhouse door when the tower guard sounded the hollow brass pipe, signaling all present of an approaching ship. "It's Herlief's longboat!" he shouted between clangs.

Ingrid appeared in the doorway and breezed past Solveig. "Mother, wait for me," she called. Karina and Sylvi were right behind her.

Baldr caught up with them from the stable while Asbjorn bellowed, "Slow down, you crazy fools! You'll fall on the path and break a leg. The ship hasn't even docked yet."

Solveig waited a beat for her father to catch up and took hold of his arm. "I'll walk with you, Papa." She understood his old bones ached from injuries sustained long ago. He was not as surefooted as he had once been, yet he still could fell a tree with a few whacks of an axe. They made a solid pair as Solveig could steady him and he could see where they were going.

"There now," he said, patting her hand. "You're a good girl. Let's hear what Herlief has to say about what took him so long."

Eagerness to embrace her brother and her lover tightened in Solveig's chest, along with apprehension. *What* has *taken them so long?* The nearer they got to the docks, the tighter the knot in her stomach grew.

It seemed everybody in Gnóttdalr bunched in between them and the pier, all talking at once. Solveig's eyesight may have been poor, yet she wasn't blind. There were not enough people on the boat. Her grip tightened around her father's arm, and she felt him tense.

"Make way!" His gruff voice boomed over the din. "I must welcome our warriors home. You folks wait your turn." Villagers moved aside, allowing for Ingrid to pass through, followed by the rest of the family. Several on-board pulled up the oars and laid them over the keel in the belly of the short-draft vessel as it glided up to the landing. Geirfinnr put a hand on the gunwale and leaped over onto the planks to secure a rope around a dock piling.

"Herlief!" Ingrid yelled in an anxious tone. Solveig watched her mother's head bob about as she searched for her son.

The king abandoned Solveig and dashed ahead of his wife and other children to climb into the moored longboat. "Herlief!" he demanded, as he stomped the length of the craft.

Catching sight of Ragna, Solveig's apprehension eased a measure. Still, she scurried into the huddle of her family members, unable to breathe until she saw her brother safe and sound.

With the boat docked and its sail lowered, Solveig counted only four people on board—and one lay on the planks with severe injuries. Panic erupted from her core. She glanced at her mother to find Baldr holding her securely. Karina and Sylvi clutched each other's hands while King Asbjorn paced back from the stern.

"Where is my son?" he demanded.

"I'm sorry," Geirfinnr said remorsefully, though it was all he was capable of uttering.

"We would have returned his body if it had been at all possible." Ragna's words fell with regret. She had suffered a gash to her head. Her brow was still bloody, and she had one arm in a makeshift sling. Solveig wanted to rush to her, to hug and kiss her, to ask what had happened, to tend her wounds; however, she felt lightheaded and woozy, and feared she would never make it over the railing of the ship, so heavy was her grief over her missing brother.

"What happened? How can this be? How dare you return without Herlief?" Solveig had never seen her father so distraught. He slapped his hands on his face and drew them down his beard with wide eyes searching the almost empty longboat. "I demand an explanation. My son!" His voice cracked, and he had to catch himself on the mast to keep from toppling over.

The crowd had become strangely silent, other than a few whispers and murmurs. "Herlief!" Karina's wailing cry cut through Solveig's soul. Was her brother truly lost? Dead? Something had gone woefully wrong on the expedition, and they all needed answers, but standing out on the pier surrounded by the entire town was not an ideal setting to receive the report.

Swallowing her tears, Ingrid supported her family by taking charge of the situation. "You men," the queen called, pointing to two bystanders on the dock. "Carry the injured warrior up to the great hall in our longhouse, and you"—she laid a hand on a young woman's arm—"fetch the grædari and bring him up the hill at once."

"My lord," Geirfinnr said to the king. "I'll tell you all, though it is a tale you will scarce believe."

"We want to know!" a man from the crowd shouted. "What happened to Prince Herlief?"

"Is he coming back?" asked another.

"Let us assess the situation," Solveig announced in a robust voice, which required almost all her remaining stamina. "And tomorrow we will provide the details. Please, give us time to hear what our returning warriors have to say."

"I want to see my son!" Asbjorn snarled.

Ragna dared to touch him, laying a gentle hand on his shoulder. "My lord, come to the longhouse with us so we may relay the account. Herlief fought with more courage and skill than I have ever seen. You should be proud of him."

"Proud of him?" Asbjorn's voice cracked, and Geirfinnr and Ragna guided him over the gunwale of the boat onto the dock. Ingrid took him by the arm, wiping at her tears, while Baldr escorted Karina and Sylvi. Without a word, Solveig took Ragna's arm, and the crowd parted to let the procession trudge gravely up the path to the king's great hall.

Ingrid helped settle her husband into his seat at the head of their table with considerable difficulty. Though her own heart was shattered by the dismal news and her brain foggy from the shock, her first duty was to Asbjorn, who was agitated and grief-stricken to a greater degree. When the servants brought out trays of food, as it was near dinnertime, he sent them away, instead demanding a full chalice of wine and a bowl of mead for the table.

When she gazed at him, she could hardly recognize her husband behind the wild look of one who had lost his soul. He downed half his goblet before staring out at the solemn lot. A somber Baldr sat on the king's right and a stunned Geirfinnr on his left. Between the king's seat and hers huddled Karina and Sylvi on one side and Solveig, Ragna, and Knud, the surviving warrior, on the other. Every face lay veiled in shadow, every tongue mute with sorrow.

"Geirfinnr, Knud, Ragna." Asbjorn called their names with a forlorn timbre. "Speak."

Knud shook his head, lowered his chin, and stared blankly into the full cup of mead resting between his grimy, war-hardened hands. In his mid-thirties, the battle-scarred veteran could form no words.

Ingrid shifted her gaze to Ragna, spying Solveig's tender fingers atop her hand on table. The shieldmaiden's other arm appeared to have suffered an injury, and she had yet to care for the wound on her head. "I cannot even believe the encounter myself, my lord," she uttered. Solveig stroked her hand in a tender caress.

"We set out the morning after we arrived," Geirfinnr began. "The first night we rested in Jarl Anders' hall, ate his food, and listened to witness accounts; then we embarked overland in search of the jötunn. Ragna tracked him; still, it took us three days to discover his lair."

"But what happened to Herlief?" Asbjorn threw back the rest of his wine. "Fiske, more!" he bellowed.

"My lord," Ingrid addressed her husband. "It is difficult for us to receive such ill tidings, yet we need to understand what happened. Please allow your warriors, Herlief's friends, to relate the story."

Ingrid's heart ached too. Wasn't it she who had given birth to Herlief, who had suckled him at her breast, who had overseen his early education, who had tended his scratches and skinned knees? She loved her little boy and the charming, courageous man he had grown into. Who had tucked him into bed at night? Who had sung him songs? Yes, Ingrid loved Herlief with a mother's fierce passion, and yet she understood the world in which they lived. The values of her people were etched into every fiber of her being, every crevice of her soul.

Even as she mourned the loss of her firstborn, she had never been prouder of him. Though she did not yet have the details, it seemed her Herlief had died a hero's death, protecting others from a grave danger, with a sword in his hand, with bold tenacity and the strength of his beliefs. Didn't her husband recognize as much?

"They sit here at my table with scratches! Why did they not protect their prince, their future king?" Asbjorn hurled his empty chalice across the chamber, where it clattered and rolled across the floor. Their servant Bodil scurried to pick it up with fearful eyes drowned in tears.

Ingrid understood her husband's outburst of temper was to cover his true feelings. He did not wish to be seen weeping in front of underlings, or even his remaining children. The king must not succumb to such weak sentiment in public, so he thundered with bluster. She was about to suggest they retire for a brief period under the guise of needing to change clothes or wash or some other excuse, so he may have a private moment to grieve, when Ragna spoke in a meek tone.

"Would you prefer we had disobeyed his orders? My lord, I wish more than any 'twere I who had perished, so that Herlief might be sitting with you tonight. He insisted on leading the charge against the creature."

Asbjorn ran his fingers through his thick mane and shook his head. "I do not wish you to have died in Herlief's stead," he uttered, "but only for all my warriors and my son to have returned triumphant. It is not for me to rebuke his heroism nor to diminish his valor, yet my heart is broken. For twenty-four years, I groomed him to take my place one day, and now he is gone. Baldr will be a fine king in time." He lifted a weary gaze to meet his younger son's and Ingrid read the pain that passed between them.

He is in shock, she realized. *He loves Baldr just as much as Herlief. Asbjorn only needs time to grieve and process it all. He'll be back to himself in a day r two.*

"Yet we will always love and feel the absence of my brother, Herlief," Baldr completed the thought. No one spoke for a moment, and Fiske set another cup of wine before the king.

Ingrid shifted her attention to Geirfinnr. "Tell us what happened. Does the creature exist? Does it still live?"

13

Solveig glanced at her father. His chest heaved and his hands could not remain still. He picked up his cup, drank, set it down, brushed the table, scratched behind his ear ... She was devastated over the loss of her brother too, as she was certain the whole family grieved; however, Asbjorn seemed ... different.

Mist lay at her feet, the dog's head on her paws, casting gloomy glances about the crowd. Solveig had learned long ago how animals could sense humans' moods and emotions. It was clear her pet understood Herlief's absence was a cause for concern.

Ragna turned forlorn eyes to her and confessed, "I didn't believe it ... until I saw him. I cannot state as a fact the madman was some jötunn from the sagas, for who has ever seen one? But he was taller than any human, with enormous hands and feet, and so incredibly strong. He didn't talk, only vocalized in grunts and screams. He wore clothes fashioned from hides, tanned leather, and wool cloth. His face ..." Ragna couldn't go on. She lowered her gaze and shook her head.

"The giant, or whatever he was," Geirfinnr continued, "had a hideous face, all red and black, like a demon. We couldn't see the rest of his body. As Ragna said, he was clothed and used weapons. His hair was wild and matted, as if he had never bathed, and he possessed a pungent odor, yet his misshapen jaw grew no beard and he had a hump on his back, making him lean forward. I can't fathom how tall he would have been had he stood erect."

When Asbjorn failed to respond, Ingrid spoke. "You said you joined with Jarl Anders and his soldiers and tracked the giant, we'll say, for lack of another term, to a cave. How many of you were there? How many giants?"

"Our twelve warriors and twenty more, including Jarl Anders and his men," Ragna replied. "He wished to search for his son who had not returned, so he came himself."

"And did he find him?" the king inquired in a loud voice tinged with bitterness. "Did Jarl Anders recover his lost boy?"

"His head." Knud's reply was terse and shaky, and his gaze remained fixed on the table. "While we waited, the monster made sport of tossing out the heads."

Asbjorn gulped his wine, then with slurred speech bellowed, "Fiske! Why's my cup empty?" The servant dashed to fill it as Solveig's soul plunged into a dark place. She could understand why her father would wish to dull his senses, but it wasn't like him to do so.

"Please, continue with your report," Ingrid prodded.

Ragna squeezed Solveig's hand and glanced away from the king in his despair. *She loved and admired my brother as I did,* she recognized. *We all grieve for him and the others who perished. She loves and honors my father. Or is it shame that will not allow her to look at him? Ragna has nothing to feel guilty about.*

"It took three days for Ragna to find the cave where his tracks ended," Geirfinnr said. "Our troop formed a shield wall, and we called for him to come out. At first, we heard banging noises from inside, yet no one ventured forth. Jarl Anders sent two scouts into the cave. After a short while, we heard a man's terrified cry, then silence. Neither of them returned. We tried taunting the giant to entice him to come out." The warrior shook his head. "Night was falling, so we moved to a clearing not far away to set camp and a watch."

"The next morning, one of our warriors, Ulfvaldr, was gone," Ragna recalled. "He was on the last guard shift before dawn."

"Herlief talked about launching an attack," Geirfinnr said. "Jarl Anders declared it was too risky, as none of us had ever been inside the cavern and had no clue how to navigate it. This went on for two more days, each time with another sentry missing."

"We were at a standstill," Ragna offered in frustration. "He wouldn't come out and we couldn't go in. Jarl Anders went on a tirade, shouting obscenities at the cave entrance, calling the giant every insulting name he could think of."

"That's when the heads were hurled out," Knud uttered in disbelief. "Old, sallow ones, partly decayed from the group Jarl Anders' son had taken in search of him earlier."

"When the jarl recognized the one belonging to his son, he drew his sword and charged in with a torch in his other hand," Geirfinnr said.

"Herlief would not let him go alone," Ragna added, "so we all readied our weapons and rushed in after him."

"There was colored smoke, fog, I don't know," Geirfinnr reported. "And strange noises the likes of which I've never heard."

"Something must have been in the red and orange smoke, because it made us cough and feel odd, like being drunk to the point of passing out," Ragna recalled. "I remember stepping on bones—human ones, I think. We couldn't breathe, had to retreat, and Herlief pulled Jarl Anders out of the cave against his protests. Later, he expressed his gratitude."

Geirfinnr resumed testimony. "A few days later, during a downpour of rain, the giant emerged, carrying a barrel in one hand to fill with fresh water. Immediately, we mounted an attack. I admit, his size and strength were intimidating—frightening, even—but it was his leathery, twisted face, the inhuman parts of him, that were downright terrifying."

"So, in your estimation, the creature wasn't a bear, nor was it human?" Ingrid inquired.

"I don't know what it was," Knud replied with a shudder. He finished his horn of mead.

"I hit him with several arrows," Ragna said, "and he batted them off like toothpicks. He flew into a rage, snatched up a spear, and swung it about, knocking back anyone who got near. The fight only lasted a few minutes before he retreated into his cave with the water, but he had killed two of our men and seriously injured five more."

Across the hall, the grædari tended to the wounds of the fourth warrior, while the other men and women who occupied the chamber keep their distance and silently absorbed the troubling story.

"Jarl Anders and Herlief devised a plan." Geirfinnr held every ear. "Herlief would lead a team of four into the maw of the grotto, engage the creature, then rush back out, hoping he would chase them. The rest of us had prepared a huge net to throw over him so we could get close enough with our weapons to do damage. They marched in carrying shields and spears, one man with a bow to shoot needling arrows at him. They shouted and taunted, and we heard the giant's voice. Herlief and the others drew him out, and we attacked."

"The net only worked for an instant," Ragna admitted. "As I thrust at him with my sword, he struck we with the back of his hand, sending me flying yards through the air where I came down hard on a rocky spot. I lost consciousness for part of the fight. When my vision cleared, I saw him, free of the net. He grabbed Herlief." The battle-hardened shieldmaiden swallowed and lifted a questioning gaze to Ingrid.

"It's all right, Ragna," the queen replied with steel in her tone.

"Herlief did not flinch nor try to flee," Ragna said. "He chopped at the giant's arm with his axe, but it ..." Her voice trailed off, and she had to look away.

"The monster killed Herlief," Geirfinnr stated without detail, "and tossed his body into the cave. By the time he tired of the fight and retreated, only the four of us, Jarl Anders, and three of his warriors still breathed. If over thirty men could not defeat him, what could eight do?"

"Arne and two of Jarl Anders' men were unable to walk, much less fight," Knud added in regret.

"If this beast stays local to his cave, the people of Gnóttdalr will all remain safe," Ingrid noted in a robust voice so all in the hall could hear, "yet we cannot allow it to terrorize even a small corner of our kingdom. King Asbjorn and I shall discuss the matter and devise a solution."

"We can't even bury him!" The king's eruption startled Solveig and the others, who had become accustomed to his quiet drinking. He tried to pitch his goblet again, but it got no further than the end of the table. In response to his outburst, Mist knotted herself into a tighter ball pressed to Solveig's foot.

"Herlief should have a royal funeral, be buried in a mound with his ancestors. This giant denies him his rightful place!" Asbjorn could barely get the words out.

"Father," Baldr said in tender censure. "My brother feasts in Valhalla with Odin and Thor and the kings and heroes of old this very night. What does it matter about his mortal flesh? His body may lie in a smoky cave, but his spirit will live until the end of the age in Ásgarðr. We mourn while he celebrates. I say we lift a drink in Herlief's honor." He raised his horn of mead and all at the table and around the hall did the same. "Skoll!" he shouted.

"Skoll!" The others in the chamber followed suit, though Karina and Ingrid's cheers were not so vigorous. Solveig took a moment to feel Karina's pain. She and Herlief had only recently married and already she had become a widow. She'd find no better husband, though she would eventually need another. The young woman would be welcome to live in their longhouse as long as she wished, but she was too young to remain unmarried. The uneasy reminder of her own age and precarious position of an unwed woman gnawed at Solveig's gut, along with all the other poisonous vermin eating her from the inside out.

Herlief was supposed to marry, produce heirs, and become king when Papa dies, she recalled. *I was of no consequence, and now I am the oldest. Baldr will no doubt be named heir; yet will this create more pressure for me to take a husband? Will Papa insist on it?*

"To my heroic son!"

Solveig snapped her attention to her father, who pushed up from the table on wobbly legs. He frowned, swayed, and reached for Baldr's mead horn; he gave it to him, and the king raised it high.

"He was brave, but where did it get him?" He jutted up his chin, and Baldr and Geirfinnr steadied him. "Valhalla gains another warrior—so what? Doesn't Odin have ample of them already? I should've gone. I'm old. It should have been me, not my son, who perished. What am I supposed to do now, huh?"

He tossed back the sweet drink, streams trickling down the edges of his beard, and would have toppled to the floor if not for the loyal men at his side. "Come, Ingrid. Let's retire to our chamber. I've heard enough."

Solveig had relinquished Ragna's hand so she could toast her brother. She missed the contact. Sorrow descended over her like a thick fog, and her heart broke for her parents. Then she felt the comforting warmth of her lover's fingers in hers and breathed.

"Ragna, I am taking you to see the grædari now," she stated with authority, "and then it is off to my chamber to get you washed and fed. You have been through a harrowing ordeal, but we must be ready for whatever tomorrow brings. The giant still lives, and as long as it does, it threatens the normal state of affairs. You and Geirfinnr are now the leading experts on the monster, and I fear you will be called upon to face it again." She stared into Ragna's haunted eyes and asked, "Can you?"

The firm jaw of her shieldmaiden raised up and down. "I can, and I will."

After having Ragna's wounds tended to and getting some food into her, Solveig led the shaken woman into her private room, where she had instructed the servants to fill her bathing tub with hot water. "Off with those clothes," Solveig commanded. "It'll be a wonder if they can be salvaged."

"No one is discarding my chainmail," Ragna declared, raising a challenging brow. She had already taken it off for the healer to set her broken arm and now allowed Solveig to help her out of the rest of her clothing.

The princess handed her into the tub, thinking, *No goddess in any of the nine worlds could possess a more fabulous body than hers.* Her long legs toned with lean muscles, her buttocks' perfect roundness, her tight tummy, powerful arms and shoulders, and her perfect, pert breasts...

Of course, there were too many scars, but they came with the territory. Lowering Ragna into the water, Solveig shifted her gaze to her face. She almost didn't notice the prominent fishhook scar anymore, and anyway, it did nothing to detract from the woman's bold features and stunning eyes. The sound of Ragna's sigh as she settled into the heated water sent a stream of relief trickling through the rocky fragments of Solveig's heart. She set about washing the shieldmaiden's hair, face, neck, and body—gently, so as not to cause pain, but with enough energy to scrub away the blood, sweat, and grime.

"Why are you so good to me?" Ragna sounded baffled.

"Because." Solveig wasn't certain how to answer. This was not the time to be making confessions of love. "You fought valiantly at my brother's side, you serve my father and the kingdom with honor, and you are my dear friend. You are always watching out for everyone else, so someone must take care of you." She poured a bucket of water over Ragna's head to rinse off the soap.

Ragna let it flow over her strawberry-blonde hair; then Solveig parted the strands to examine the gash along her scalp. The healer had put some stitches in it and given her a salve to apply. Solveig gently patted the area with a dry cloth and applied the herb-infused ointment.

"I don't deserve your attention," Ragna responded in remorse. "I returned home while Herlief—"

"Hush now." Solveig sat on the stool beside the tub. She leaned over and kissed Ragna's forehead. "I know you are feeling guilt, but there is no reason to. I have witnessed it before in sailors who were the only ones to survive a shipwreck or a mother whose child died of an illness. You suffered two substantial injuries, Ragna; there is nothing else you could have done. You are not to blame."

Color flashed in her face, and Ragna turned to her. "I could have—"

Solveig would not allow her to finish the phrase. Catching the woman's cheeks between her palms, she claimed her lips in a life-affirming kiss, savoring it for longer than she should have. Even though Herlief was gone, leaving her in a state of uncertainty, Ragna was still with her—alive, if not well.

"Come," she instructed. "Let me dry you and get you into bed. You are staying with me tonight so we may find comfort in each other's arms ... just lying in one another's embrace, nothing more. You must be exhausted and in pain, and we share heartaches. Tomorrow, the sun will rise, and life will continue. Papa shall develop a plan for us to act on, but your arm must heal before you can fight again. I'll offer prayers for you."

Solveig detected a sliver of gratitude shining through the shame in Ragna's expression, and she held out a wool bath sheet for the woman to step into. As she wrapped it around her, Ragna whispered, "Thank you." She was barely dry when she threw her good arm around Solveig, the broken one hugged between them, and pulled her into a firm embrace. "I am so sorry."

The princess held her, listening to her sob, feeling the warm tears fall onto her own face as they pressed together. It was the first time Ragna had shown any vulnerability in her presence, which Solveig welcomed as a sign of closeness their relationship had not yet known. Despite the heaviness of loss weighing on her heart, holding Ragna in her arms, providing her as much comfort as she gave, made Solveig feel like she was the strong one for once.

14

Onboard the Dreki in the south Baltic Sea, two weeks after her capture

"Hurry it up, mouse," growled a rough deckhand on Einar's bulky cargo ship, *Dreki*. It was a stupid name, since it wasn't a Norseman's vessel and had no dragon headpiece adorning its bow. Still, it was a deep, fat boat, so perhaps it represented a corpulent serpent that did nothing other than eat and sleep.

The first day at sea, Einar had taken Kai by her flaxen braid and chopped it off with his knife. "So everyone will know you are a slave," he explained. He had done the same to all the women in the hold. She had counted twenty-three when she arrived, and they had added six more since then, along with some older girls and boys, making the space, which was already shared with ponies, unbearably crowded. Einar stashed the silver, weapons, jewelry, and other valuable loot in chests in his cabin. Now they traveled south to the Slavs' market port of Bilhyryn so the captain could cash in his prizes.

The sunlight blasting in from the open hatch above her was blinding, as Kai, the other hostages, and the stolen livestock had been locked away in the hold for most of the voyage. Because it amused the raiding crew, they shackled Kai with the most distasteful chores available. She struggled to ascend the rickety ladder with her hands bound by a leather cord, carrying a waste bucket to be tossed over the gunwale. She had to hoist the full container to catch each rung above her as she climbed, and the urine and floating bits of excrement sloshed over the rim of the pail, washing her in their offensive odors.

Pushing her head above the edge of the deck, she heaved the bucket up and plopped it in front of her. Bozidar, the hulk whom she had embarrassed during their fight on the beach, strolled by and kicked over the pail, spilling its contents mostly on her.

"Why are you such a clumsy mouse?" the callous warrior scolded her with a laugh. "Get up here and scrub this deck clean," he ordered. The crewmen standing around laughed with him.

Kai was beyond being angered by anything they did; however, being soaked in raw sewage had plunged her spirits to a new depth. She couldn't retaliate; it only resulted in beatings. She couldn't jump overboard either, as no land was in sight, so she slogged up onto the deck.

"I'll clean it, but I need a mop or rag," she answered.

"Use your tunic," the man with the scarred face suggested, raising more laughter. "It's already soiled anyway."

"Aye," Bozidar agreed. "Since we aren't allowed to have you, we should at least get to look at your tits."

"Hey, if we're goin' to get to look at tits, bring up those bigger women," the other man proposed. "The little warrior's are so small and puny."

Kai felt herself sliding into a puddle of despair, yet she refused to cry in front of them. It was all they wanted her to do—to act the part of a desperate victim, to suffer from their humiliation—and she refused. Though she had never possessed much pride, she would not forfeit what little she had to entertain her captors.

In a sudden burst of bold energy, she pushed to her feet, her chin raised in defiance, and whipped her smelly tunic off over her head. What difference did it make if she mopped the deck with it? It was already saturated with crap. In only her trousers and shoes, she squatted and mopped the planks with her garment, keeping her steely blue eyes trained on Bozidar.

The crewmen's laughter grew so raucous, it attracted the attention of the first mate, who strode over to investigate.

"What is this?" Bratmir demanded. He sucked in a breath when his gaze fell on Kai and fury filled his face. "Rostik," he barked to a cabin boy who was enjoying the show as much as the rest. "Give me your tunic—now!"

The lad yanked it off and handed it to his superior with a fearful look.

Bratmir's icy glare passed over the crewmen and their laughter withered. "Don't you men have work to do?"

Kai, still busy with her mopping, heard their footsteps shuffle away.

"Just havin' a bit of fun," the one with the scar grumbled, lowering a sour face.

"Put this on." Bratmir cut her bindings and dropped the tan shirt onto Kai's bare shoulder. She slithered into it, then glanced up, holding a hand to her brow to shade her eyes.

"Thank you, sir," she replied.

"Did they hurt you?" If Kai did not know better, she would have sworn she detected concern in his tone.

"No, sir. Just the usual."

This incident had been nothing. Last week, the ruffians had decided to play a game of catch and used Kai as the stone. They had tied her wrists and ankles; one man took her hands while the other held her feet. Then they swung her back and forth until they had created momentum and tossed her across the open deck hatch like a sack of grain for two others to "catch," which they only sometimes did. Bratmir had reprimanded a pair of them with a whip when they'd purposely shortened their throw to let her fall through the hole and crash to the bottom of the hold ten feet below, knocking the wind from her chest. The first mate had berated them for the potential damage to the merchandise and threatened to lash them to the mast for the rest of the voyage if he caught them endangering the life of a captive again. Still, it had not stopped them from harassing and mocking her at every opportunity.

"I'm sorry for spilling the bucket, Bratmir," she apologized, though she knew it was not her fault. "It is difficult for me to climb the ladder with a full pail and my wrists bound, but I will try to do better."

He crossed his arms and gazed down at her, shaking his head. "I saw what they did, little one. You have done everything right. Don't worry. We'll be to Bilhyryn soon." He reached a hand down and she took it. He pulled her up to stand in front of him. "Go wash in the rain barrel there." He pointed to a wooden drum tied in place outside the captain's cabin. "I don't want you spreading a sickness to the others. Einar would skin us all alive if the lot of you were to die."

Bratmir's ounce of kindness renewed Kai's hope. Mayhap the gods had not forgotten her. She hopped to the barrel and splashed clean water over her face and shorn hair.

Taking advantage of a few minutes in the fresh air, she glanced around the vessel. It looked nothing like the sleek, low-draft longboats Torsten constructed. Its deep hold below the surface restricted it from coming in close to shore or up shallow rivers; however, it created an expanse for cargo that their small attack crafts lacked. Above the center of the ship rose a single mast with a square sail rigging similar to Torsten's, but much taller and made up of a larger, heavier fabric. This vessel's sides weren't clinker built, with the planks overlapped at one edge and riveted together. Instead, it was of the carvel style, with sawn timbers attached to a frame above each other, presenting a flat-sided hull.

A sudden wind whipped across Kai, and she turned her attention to the sky. Clouds rolled in from the west and she could sense the ship rocking with the choppy swells.

Relieved to have the muck washed off, she returned to Bratmir. "Is there anything else you need me to do?" If the possibility even existed of making a friend out of this tall, bald fellow, she would cultivate it.

He shook his head. "Do you want it back?" he asked, pointing to her soiled tunic, where it lay in a pile on the deck.

Kai shrugged. "I can wash it ... eventually. Bratmir, did you notice the change in the weather? It could mean a squall is coming."

The man cocked his head, considering her with interest. "You are an odd woman, such a jumble of knowledge, grit, and humility. If I could ..." He cast his gaze away from her to the dark clouds in the western sky. "You might be right.

Go below and make sure everything is secure. We may well be in for a rough ride. I need to consult the captain."

Kai sensed a moment of connection with the man. No, she did not wish him to buy her to be his thrall or wife; she had no intention of belonging to anyone and would surely escape the first time a chance arose. Yet, unlike everyone else, she felt he saw her, and because of it, she liked him.

"Yes, sir." She picked up her bucket and reeking tunic, then climbed back down the ladder. A shadow fell over the opening as Bratmir closed the hatch, and his face was the last thing she beheld. The latch snapped locked above, and Kai's eyes had to readjust to the murky dark of the hold.

"I have returned with an empty waste pail, if anyone needs to use it," she announced.

A few of the others murmured, but most remained quiet. A woman from a village farther down the coast from Kai's paced nervously, muttering to herself. She did this frequently, but Kai didn't let it bother her. Everybody dealt with confinement in the hold in their own way. Whenever Kai fell into melancholy, she thought of Tove, and how grateful she was to be the one here in captivity instead of her lover and friend. *It is so much better I am here to have skitr spilled on me and be the butt of every joke than my sweet Tove.* Kai may have been plucked from her people and carried across the sea to a foreign land to be sold into servitude, but Tove was safe. This was her triumph, her one heroic deed, and it made her feel awesome pride in herself. *Heroes come in all sizes, Frigg said.*

As less and less light filtered through the cracks in the planks above them, Kai deduced more time must have passed than she thought—or the dark clouds had caught up with them.

The hatch raised, and a bearded face appeared. "Your food." A sack was dropped down from above, and the wooden door slammed shut. Women and young boys and girls scurried over. Kai had taken over the job of ration distribution to ensure everyone got something to eat. This time when she opened the bag, there were small, rock-hard loaves of bread, cheese that smelled as if it was far past its prime, some smoked fish, and a few heads of cabbage. She doled out their rations to each of the prisoners, saving some for herself as well.

No one disputed her system anymore, as most had all but given up. Kai, however, devoted as much time as possible to dreaming of her future as a hero... Kjell crafting her sword, Haldor inscribing the runes, Frigg pronouncing enchantments over it. She saw herself victorious in combat and reveled in the cheers of crowds. She dreamed of lying with Tove, sharing intimate moments of passionate bliss.

Kai must have dropped off to sleep because she was awakened when the roll of the vessel on the rough sea slammed her head against the hull. Thunder sounded from a distance, and she could hear rain pelting the deck above their heads.

Yrsa, one of Frigg's blonde-haired acolytes, scrunched in beside her. "I'm frightened," she admitted.

Scanning their dim surroundings, Kai sensed that everything was wet. Still, it was only seeping rainwater; the ship remained sound. "It'll be all right, Yrsa. I'm sure the captain has sailed through storms before."

Despite her words of encouragement, Kai was concerned. Torsten built his longboats of axe-cut timber from carefully selected oaks, so that each plank naturally bent the way it should. King Freyrdan had praised his ships for being light and like flexible sea serpents, bending with the waves. This monstrosity they depended on to save them may not be such a formidable craft.

Madlen, the second acolyte, plopped down on Kai's other side and stared at her with frantic eyes. "What if the ship breaks up?"

Remaining calm, Kai quipped, "Then grab something that floats and hang onto it."

"We are all going to die!" cried the woman who constantly paced the hold.

"Watch your tongue," Kai commanded. "We are certainly not all going to die. I, for one, intend to live."

"So you can fulfill your destiny," Madlen mocked her. "The gods have forsaken us. What makes you think they care about your fate?"

"I committed my life to Freya's service," Yrsa bemoaned. "Still, she abandoned me, left me to raiders who will sell me as a thrall if I don't perish at sea."

"Our futures have not yet been revealed," Kai declared. "How do we know being sent south is not part of a grand plan? Don't lose courage."

"Look!" exclaimed a boy on the cusp of manhood as he pointed toward the hull. A streak of lighting from above allowed the others to see what agitated him—a trickle of water was leaking through the planks.

All around them, thunder roared, waves crashed, and the carvel pitched up and down, back and forth like a leaf in a whirlwind.

"My mothers, my fathers," Yrsa cried, her face tilted upward. "Ancestors of my people, I come to join you. Make room for me at your table now."

Kai's heart skipped a beat as the thought that it could all be over soon raced through her mind. "No," she pronounced with fierce determination. "It is not my time to die."

15

The pounding scuffle of feet overhead caught Kai's attention. She needed to discover what was going on, how bad their situation was. Rising from between the two timorous acolytes, she staggered to the ladder as the craft rocked on the sea. She caught the rungs in a death grip, easing her way up, and lost her footing only once. Dangling from the grasp in her bound hands, she struggled to catch the rung with her foot again, then continued until she pressed her head against the hatch door. It was still sealed from the outside.

"Hey, can you hear me?" she yelled against the clamor of torrential rain, crashing billows, and thumping boots on deck. "What's happening up there?"

Kai wasn't sure if gaining the truth of the situation would make it any better, but she despised being locked in dark oblivion.

"Somebody up there!" she screamed at the top of her lungs. "We're taking on water!"

She detected the metallic clink of the latch sliding. The lid opened, and a slough of water descended on her as she recognized Bratmir's ashen face. A wave slapped the hull, tipping the caravel to one side and throwing Bratmir to the deck. Kai hung on tight. Blinking the stinging, cold liquid from her eyes, she spotted him on his hands and knees, reaching toward her with a dagger.

A sudden fear raced through her as she overheard shouts from above. "Throw the cargo overboard so perhaps we'll be spared!"

Einar's demand rang back in opposition. "Are you crazy? The weight in the hold is all that keeps us from capsizing!"

Kai gazed up at Bratmir with trust and submission, and he cut her bindings. "It's only fair we should each have an equal chance of survival."

Relief flooded her heart, even though they all remained in peril. "What can I do to help?" she beseeched him.

A corner of his mouth pulled up briefly before another crashing whitecap smacked the half smile away. He placed the knife handle in her hand. "Free the others but stay below where it is safer. Several crewmen have already been washed overboard. It's bad, Kai; I can't promise we'll make it."

"Do what is required, Bratmir," she responded. "Can you swim?"

"Aye, although we are still days from shore. We must endeavour to keep the ship aright, yet I know not how. The swells have broken our oars, and the sail had to be taken down. We are at the mercy of the sea and the gods. I believe you are good luck, little one. Perhaps we'll have a grand story to tell our children one day. Stay safe," he ordered.

As he lowered the door, she called back, "You too!" Kai didn't know if he heard her, yet she didn't hear the lock slide in its groove. *He doesn't want us to die.*

Kai clenched the blade between her teeth, loosely held the rails, and slid quickly to the bottom. "Everyone!" she hailed. "I am coming to cut your restraints. Our captors do not wish us to perish, but we are required to stay below."

A jumble of words and phrases spilled from many mouths at once, so that Kai couldn't distinguish who said what.

"They must think we are doomed!" a woman cried as she freed one person after the next.

Once her ropes were cut, the nervous woman glanced toward the ladder. "I have to get out of here!" she cried and dashed for it. A powerful jolt to the hull knocked her off her feet, and she careened into it, smashing the ramshackle pathway to the outside into rails and rungs which collapsed in a pile on the floor.

"Merciful Freya, now we're trapped!" Yrsa's voice cut through the din.

"Now what do we do?" Madlen shrieked as she sloshed about. "The surge is above my ankles. It will keep rising, and we won't be able to get out."

"Do not be afraid," Kai encouraged them. "Bratmir said it is safer down here than on deck, where men are being swept overboard. He did not lock us in. If the water rises, we shall rise with it until we can reach the hatch and climb out. There is no need to panic."

"But I can't swim," one of the older women in the group moaned.

"Nor I," chimed in several others.

Kai wobbled to them across the swaying timbers and gripped the first woman's arm. "It doesn't matter. You can float. Everyone can." Raising her voice, she yelled, "Find something made of wood to hold on to. Arik," she called to a boy whose name she had learned. "Break apart the benches and crates into planks so everyone may have one." The lad nodded and set about his task.

As each captive received a board to clutch, the panic subsided slightly. Kai had to think of what would come next, though. When streaks of lighting flashed shooting light through the cracks in the decking, she watched; when they were plunged back into near darkness, she listened. She placed a hand on the side of the hull, feeling the vibrations in the wood. *If only we were on one of Torsten's longboats*, she thought with longing. The timbers creaked and groaned, opening more gaps for water to trickle through.

Then she heard collective shouts and screams from the deck above, curses and exclamations of dread accompanied by scrambling noises. An urging in her gut, an intuition, compelled her to secure herself. Kai rushed to a large beam near the middle of the chamber, part of the ship's framework, and clamped her arms around it, still gripping the knife Bratmir had given her. The ponies danced, their nervous hooves tapping on the floorboards, accompanied by anxious whinnies. This was it.

"Hold on!" she yelled to the others.

She hadn't seen the giant swell, which had terrified the men on deck so, but she knew the moment it enveloped the cargo vessel. The *Dreki* pitched to port and continued to lean, throwing most of the people and horses belowdecks off their feet and into a desperate slide; however, rather than tilting back to center as it had before, it kept going. Kai squeezed her legs around the post, hugging it like a long-lost lover, and whispered a soft prayer.

The screams of the ponies, cries of the women and youths, and the overpowering sound of the massive wave howled in her ears. She heard the terrible crack of the mast breaking and other timbers being smashed. Her stomach lurched into her throat as she was turned completely upside down.

When the horrible thrashing subsided, Kai righted herself to discover she stared up at the keel and down at the sea pouring in through the deck hatch beneath her. People and horses fought to claw and kick their way through the churning water. Madlen wore a mask of shock and horror as she clung to the upturned waste bucket, probably holding a pocket of air to support her weight. Kai couldn't see Yrsa anywhere.

Kai had only minutes to devise an escape plan, or they were all doomed. "Arik!" she called to the lanky boy, who bobbed nearby. He whipped wide eyes to her, desperate hope on his youthful face. She showed him her knife. "We must open a hole in the hull large enough to climb out before the water fills the chamber. You will help me do it."

He nodded in agreement and swam over to the support. Kai pushed up as far as she could, giving herself four feet of air between the surface and the ship's bottom, then wedged the blade in a crack. "Get up here and help pry these planks apart," she instructed her helper.

The boy, who was about Kai's size, slithered up the pole and clasped his hands over hers. Together they pressed with all their might against the knife's handle, working it back and forth, struggling to rend asunder construction intended to resist such efforts. As they widened the gap, a flash of lightning shined through, bolstering Kai with hope. She slid the blade a few inches over and they forced their weight into the action again. This was slow work, and the deluge kept rising. Kai blocked out the horrified cries and miserable screams to focus on her task.

Arik grinned when they wobbled the knife sideways, opening a small gap. There was air above them, though whenever the surf crashed, water poured in. With another tug, they reached their fingers through and pulled. The weakened board broke, and their lifesaving hole was born.

Kai quickly pushed the steel into the crack between the next two planks to repeat the process.

"It's working!" Arik exclaimed. In his excitement, he pulled even harder with her to loosen the boards. Then a sudden clinking sound shattered Kai's enthusiasm. The weapon's blade snapped at the handle and fell, sinking into the water, which now reached her chest, leaving a mere two feet's worth of air. The weapon was not designed to be a pry bar. She recalled the völva's prophecy: *Kjell will craft for you an unbreakable sword. All I must do is believe,* Kai thought, *yet how can I do so when death is upon me?* She summoned her will and buried her trepidation. Though she couldn't dispel all doubt, she could still grasp firm to hope.

Kai cast a mournful glance around. Only a handful of the more than thirty souls still kept their heads above the surface. Demoralized from their kidnapping, weakened by their captivity, despondent at the dreadful prospect of being sold as slaves in a foreign land, never to see their families and loved ones again, the others had given up.

Arik's pitiful cry of failure stung her ears. *Think, Kai!* she ordered herself. In the dark, wet gloom, permeated with defeat, inspiration sprang to life.

"We still have a chance!" she proclaimed. "All we have to do is swim out the open hatch at the bottom, then up to the surface. We can climb on top of the overturned ship or into the dingy."

Madlen fixed her with a sorrow-filled gaze as she clung to the bucket. "I can't swim."

"Then take in a deep breath and hold on to my belt," she suggested. "Torsten taught me to dive for kelp. It will be easy." She reached a hand toward Madlen.

The woman trembled and shook her head. "I can't. I'm afraid," she protested. "You and Arik go. Who knows? The water may have stopped rising. See? It isn't coming is as quickly anymore."

While it was possible the flooding was subsiding, Kai understood the ship could not remain buoyant with only this small pocket of air to keep it afloat. "No, Madlen. You have to come with us. All of you," she hollered out to the six or seven who could hear her. "Our only chance is to swim down and exit the hatch. This vessel will sink."

Shocked, horror-filled eyes stared at her, yet nobody agreed to her idea. "I can't," one said.

"I won't," declared another.

"I'll take my chances in here," echoed a third. Kai turned to Arik, who nodded.

"I'll come with you," the lad said.

"Are you sure you won't try, Madlen?" Kai pleaded with the acolyte. "I know I can pull you through."

"I will only drag you down. You are the one with the destiny, Kai," she said. "My fate lies in Ran, where I will meet the reward reserved for those who die at sea."

Kai realized she couldn't make the others follow her. After a nod of understanding for Madlen, she turned to Arik. "Take a deep breath and follow me. When we get free of the hatch, work your way along the sunken deck to the railing, then kick for the surface. You can do this."

With his acknowledgment, they both took generous breaths and dove.

The frigid water felt like pins and needles pricking Kai's chest. Accounting for the warming of spring, she supposed they wouldn't quickly freeze to death, yet determined the faster she and the boy could climb onto the overturned keel out of the icy depths, the better. She pulled through the brine like a shark diving for prey and swam through the opening with ease. With the salt stinging her eyes, she looked back for Arik, who was right behind her.

Kai crawled along the submerged deck to the railing, and over she went, kicking and paddling for the air waiting above. When she thrust her head out into the rainy air, she sucked in a breath of relief, brushing her arms to and fro over rolling billows while she treaded water.

The thunder had ceased, and the rain slackened but choppy waves with towering swells still plagued the sea. Keeping her chin up, Kai scanned her surroundings. Only the sternmost portion of the keel remained visible. Climbing on now would be a waste of energy, and if the caravel was to be sucked under, it could take them with it. She needed something else.

"Arik!" she called. No response. A sick tension gripped her chest, and she pushed through the foam, bobbing up and down with each surge. "Arik!"

As Kai searched for him, she came upon the paddle portion of a broken oar about five feet long. She latched onto it even as she grasped her surroundings. Picking up voices, she swam in their direction, hoping to find Arik. As an upsurge lifted her, she spied the dinghy in a nearby trough. Several men inside were straining at oars while others still in the sea tugging at its sides.

Einar's shout rang out. "Stop! You'll swamp the boat!"

"Then help us in!" The frantic plea came from Bozidar, who must have been in the water. Einar was right; if he attempted to haul his bulk over the rail, the small craft would tip over.

"Just hold there," Bratmir ordered the larger man. "When the storm calms, we'll pull you in."

They may have been her captors, but they were alive, and they had a boat. In truth, she could bear no bitterness toward them; didn't Swedes also conduct raids against foreign lands? It was the way of things. Raiding was what men did to survive or to better their situations; it wasn't personal. With a clean heart, Kai swam in their direction, the length of wood in her hand gripped with fingers so icy she no longer felt them.

When she hit the next crest, the scene had changed. Now, the men bobbing in the churning expanse grappled with those in the dinghy in a life-and-death struggle that tore at her soul. Those in the craft whacked at their comrades with oars while the frenzied, half-drowned raiders tugged for purchase, even pulling some fellows overboard in a primal fight to survive.

Because their attention was focused on each other, the Slavs didn't see the enormous curl, rising from the deep, looming over their precarious vessel like the gigantic hand of some angry god. "Bratmir!" she screamed as loud as she could. "Look out!"

He must have heard her, for he stopped battling his crewmen and peered around to spot the swell, as great as a longhouse. Grabbing the rudder, he steered their bow into the impending wall of water. Kai held her breath. It was the best move he could have made, granting them the possibility of cutting through it rather than being flipped as the *Dreki* had been.

Her heart sank when the dinghy rose to stand on its tail, vertical to the upsurge. Men tumbled out, and the wave devoured the small craft, chomping it into splinters under the force of its power.

"Bratmir!" she called out. She took a deep breath and wrapped her arms and legs around her portion of paddle and rode the massive crest like a swan. Once it had passed, the blue returned to the choppy four- and five-foot rises produced by the storm. She presumed just such a monstrous swell had flipped the ship.

Still struggling to push her way through the rough water toward the spot where the dinghy had broken up, Kai shouted again. "Bratmir!"

"Kai, is it you?"

Her heart leapt at his response. A whitecap lifted the first mate into her line of sight, grasping for a piece of wood as he struggled to keep his head above the curls.

"Bratmir, we must find something larger to hold onto," she hollered as she kicked toward him.

When she reached him, she discovered he had missed the plank, which had been washed in another direction. With great pants and efforts, he flapped his arms across the surface of the water, kicking with his feet.

"Here," she instructed. "Grab my paddle."

Raising his chin to keep the water out of his mouth, he laughed at her—again. All these people ever did was laugh at her! Didn't he know she was trying to save his life?

"That twig can barely help you stay afloat. What good would it do me?" Well, he had a point. "I'm tired and cold, little one. My ship and mates are all at the bottom of the sea. It is time for me to abandon the struggle and allow death's arms to embrace me."

"No, Bratmir," she pleaded. "We'll find a larger piece of wood, a portion of mast or a barrel—the door from Einar's cabin. There is wreckage all around here. You mustn't give up."

He gazed at her with a mixture of admiration and resignation. "You'll make it," he said. "I have confidence you will. When you recount this tale, remember me kindly. At one time, we all aspired to be heroes; then circumstances got in the way, tempting us, causing us to stumble and fall. A hard life forms hard men. The moment you hit me with that silly stick, I knew you were different. Go find your sturdy flotsam and ride it to safety, Kai. And thank you for the surprising delight of your company."

"Please don't give up," she urged him, agony spreading through her at the thought of being alone. "Don't you want to see how I turn out?"

With an amused laugh, he replied, "I'll be watching from Ran." It was silly for tears to stream down her face as she watched him sink into the brine, but she had held them back for an hour. They fell for Yrsa and Madlen, Arik, and all the souls who were lost. She wondered for a moment if she would perish here, too. After all, this narrow piece of oar couldn't keep her afloat on its own; she had to continue to kick her feet.

There'll be time for mourning later, she decided, scanning the wreckage for something better. The entire ship had sunk out of view as the rain slowed to a sprinkle, yet she detected some noticeable pieces of debris. As she swam toward them alone in the dark, the cold hit her again. Even breathing was a struggle, and her numb limbs were exhausted from fighting the choppy billows.

In a trough between crests, Kai caught sight of her salvation. There floated the larger portion of the broken mast with a crossbeam attached. Her energy renewed, she surged for it with resolve and climbed on. Afraid the chill and exhaustion may send her into sleep, she took a length of rope still affixed to the long post and tied it around herself. She propped her hands and feet on the shaft so they would rest above the icy water and rode the choppy waves, hoping they would bring her to a friendly shore.

16

S olveig sat on a bench behind the longhouse, watching Ragna train with
Baldr, Geirfinnr, and the other warriors. The shieldmaiden had insisted
on keeping up with her training despite having her splinted arm in a sling, and
Solveig supposed she was right. Why should her healthy bones and muscles
fall into neglect simply because one required time to mend? It also allowed
the woman an outlet for her emotions, which she was reluctant to share. Just
when she thought they had reached a milestone in their relationship, Ragna had
retreated into her shell of imperviousness, shielding herself with resolve to slay
the giant who had humiliated them.

However, Ragna's bravado, which Solveig had expected anyway, was not the
chief reason for her concern. Her father wasn't handling Herlief's death well,
much less the threat this jötunn presented to their lands. She grieved for his
personal battle with melancholy, yet it was Sogn for which she feared. A fog of
dread had descended over the kingdom. Herlief had been more than popular;
citizens far and wide had loved him as a man and respected him as a warrior.
A foe who could defeat him along with a troop of thirty at his side gripped
them in the icy claw of terror. Herders refused to take their flocks up to the
mountainside pastures, and villagers along the southeast border abandoned
their houses to move north or to the coast. Traders' and market vendors' prices
had increased in the precarious climate. People even postponed weddings and

festivals because they were wary of traveling the roads. To make matters worse, Solveig had heard the rumor King Rundrandr the Wolf of Sygnafylke, the kingdom across their southern border, had gone to war with his neighbor, King Geirmund of Hördaland. Such a conflict could easily last beyond the summer and interfere with Sogn's trade routes.

At least summer had warmed into bloom, and the longer days meant it would be easier for sentries to spot a rampaging jötunn. Still, Solveig wore a fur-trimmed shawl about her shoulders as she sat outdoors in the mild weather. She was just getting over a bout of illness. Nothing unusual for her—three days of fever accompanied by muscle aches, weakness, difficulty breathing, and a throbbing head. However, the timing of her semi-annual sick spell could have been better.

"Take it easy, Ragna!" Baldr said with a laugh. "We don't want your other arm broken."

"Here, let's go for a run to strengthen our stamina," Geirfinnr suggested. "I will be the first up to the grassy knoll and back." As he struck off, axe in hand, the rest of the warriors in training followed out the back gate, including Ragna.

"In your dreams!" Her voice echoed through the palisade; then they were beyond Solveig's sight. If her calculations were correct, it would take them less than half an hour to reach the top of the knoll and come back. Geirfinnr would indeed be first; however, whether 'twould be Baldr or Ragna in second was up for grabs. A lanky youth, Erik Bjornsson, sometimes passed them, but he would likely finish fourth, followed by the balance.

Solveig knew she should go back inside to join Karina and Sylvi in weaving a tapestry in Herlief's honor. Ingrid had secured the expertise of a local artisan known for her stunning tapestries to design and oversee the project, yet it would take all of them months to complete, so intricate was the detail required. Though sewing and weaving held no interest to Solveig, they were activities in which she could excel despite her poor eyesight. The major cause for her reluctance was the depressing atmosphere in the longhouse.

Asbjorn had not devised a plan to defeat the monster. He slept, woke up and drank until he passed out, slept some more, then awoke to repeat the cycle. He had appeared at only a few meals and avoided his children. Ingrid had taken over the administrations of her husband's kingdom, and Solveig was so impressed by her ease in doing so that she wondered how much of the work she had done behind the scenes all along. When the jarls all came to pay their respects, it was her mother who received them and their gifts of condolence. Asbjorn wandered into the meeting they held to discuss the emergency, pointed a finger around the table, demanding they send their sons to face the menace next, and then stomped away.

News of King Rundrandr on the warpath disturbed Solveig the most. What if his attacks on the south went poorly? Might he turn his attention to Sogn, a land beset by its own troubles?

Blowing out a breath, she closed her eyes for a moment and listened to her surroundings. Someone scratched with a hoe in the vegetable garden. A light breeze rustled the broad, green leaves of a nearby maple, and a duet of common chaffinches drifted down from its branches. It was a lovely day, and the fresh air was easier for her to breathe than that of the smoky longhouse; she could take another moment to herself before heading inside.

Solveig pictured herself lying with Ragna in a field of clover with yellow dandelions and purple heather all around, the air filled with the sweet aroma of honeysuckle. It made her smile. In the daydream, Ragna curled her long, lean body near to her and stroked her cheek and lips with a red clover blossom. The vision was so real Solveig could almost taste the flower she had nibbled on as a child and with which her mother still brewed a flavorful tea. Just as her imaginings took a turn toward the intimate side, Geirfinnr and others from the city guard tromped into her daydream uninvited.

"We are all going down to the alehouse. Reinvaldr has challenged Floki to an honor fight over an insult, and everyone is placing wagers," he announced to Ragna. "We knew you wouldn't want to miss out. Also, I was hoping you and the pretty serving girl, Erika, would join me for a private party, if you get my drift. She's been asking about you since you haven't been around much. She and I have a good time occasionally, and I know it would be better with you."

It was as if Dream Geirfinnr hadn't even noticed Solveig lying there, caressing Ragna's silky leg. And there went the confounded imaginary Ragna, getting up and leaving her behind. "What an excellent suggestion," she said. "Solveig won't mind, will you, my dove?" She cast a whimsical look over her shoulder, which was suddenly bare as her clothing had changed into the revealing neckline of a tavern wench's blouse.

Solveig's dream had not turned out the way she had hoped, but it didn't mean she couldn't devise a way for it to manifest into the real world. After all, wasn't she the clever one, the strategist, the scholar? She needed to think of a way around all the obstacles so she and Ragna could live together as partners, like her grandmothers had done. Until she did, Solveig decided she should help work on the tapestry with her sisters. After all, it was more imperative than ever she remain an essential member of the household.

She had just reached the front entry when two men unexpectedly rode through the gates to the estate. The guards on duty stopped them, and she waited, watching, until the exchange concluded. Then one of her father's soldiers took their horses' reins while the other escorted the men toward the longhouse.

As they came into view, Solveig was struck by what an odd pair they made. Though both were of average height, one looked like a warrior in his prime while the other looked like something the cat might drag to the doorstep. The first man's sandy hair brushed his shoulders, and his full beard appeared well-groomed. His clothing mimicked a jarl's, though Solveig recognized he was not one of theirs. He was all lean muscle and arrogance as he marched up to her with a vibration of self-importance as obvious as the scent of the sea on a fisherman.

"Good day, princess," he greeted her with a smug expression, his hands clasped regally behind his back. He offered her a slight bow while raking her with a lascivious gaze. "I am Troels the Bold, and this is my companion, the gothi Arvid."

Inspecting Arvid, she saw in him something both more and less than she did in Osmin, the gothi with whom she was familiar. The stooped man was old—though how ancient she couldn't surmise. Dressed in robes with a pouch tied around his waist and carrying a gnarled staff, he displayed an aspect of mystery instead of conceit. His head was completely bald, and he bore a long river of chin beard, which reminded Solveig of a white fox tail. She regarded them both with suspicion.

"I am Solveig, daughter of King Asbjorn," she introduced herself as a genteel woman should. "What do you require? Lodging for the night? Provisions for your travels?" Those were the typical requests.

"My lady, we are here to see the king on a most urgent matter of the greatest consequence," Troels stated grandly.

"The king is in mourning for the loss of his son," she replied. "He is not receiving visitors, even his own friends. I'm afraid you have chosen a poor time to call. Please come back in a fortnight to state your business." *Surely Papa will be better by then*, she hoped.

"But you see, my dear, that is the very reason for our presence at your great hall," he explained. "I am a champion in the land from which I hail and have heard you have a giant that needs to be slain. Arvid and I are here to offer our services to your kingdom."

She narrowed her eyes. *Where does this insolent man find the audacity to call me 'my dear'?* But no one had even sighted the creature since Herlief's fatal incident. Ragna was not back to full strength, and Asbjorn sorely lacked volunteers to launch a new hunt. Baldr and Geirfinnr had been planning another mission, but Ingrid had forbidden Baldr to leave Gnóttdalr until the king had recovered from his depression. If he were to drink himself to death or fall and break some important body part, the responsibility of leadership may have to be passed to his only remaining son at a moment's notice.

Reluctantly, Solveig motioned to the open doorway. "Please, come in. You are welcome in our hall. My mother and brother will receive you. I'll need to check with the king and see if he is up to a discussion. Either way, someone with authority will listen to what you offer."

17

S olveig glared at the pompous stranger from across the great hall. An hour had passed since his arrival with the old magician in tow and everyone who was anyone had crowded in to satisfy their curiosity. Asbjorn had pulled himself together enough to wash his face, dress, and settle on his seat of judgment with Ingrid at his side. While Solveig was overjoyed to see her father getting out of his chamber and interacting with people, she did not trust Troels or his dubious companion.

Ragna leaned in close toward Solveig, where she had propped herself against a support post. "Who are they?" She smelled like the woods and meadows and her own sweet sweat. Even that did nothing to calm Solveig's apprehension.

"Trouble," she replied.

The lean-muscled man strutted forward before making a grand show of humility, bowing to the king with a sweep of his arm. "King Asbjorn, lord of Sogn, thank you for your gracious hospitality. I am Troels the Bold, and this wise old wizard is Arvid, a reader of runes and master of seiðr. We are Danes from Vendill in the south. When tales of the savage jötunn reached our peninsula, at once, I said to Arvid, 'I must journey to Sogn and see for myself. Would you accompany me on this adventure?' So, we set out on the next trading vessel for Norvegr. Perhaps you have heard of my exploits, how I defeated a vicious troll in Ribe, or how I sailed west to Britannia and returned with a vast treasure."

The stranger struck a pose standing with his feet apart, his right hand over his heart, and his chin lifted in triumph, like heroes on tapestries or statues. Solveig had never heard these tales, but she had met a longboat of Danish explorers once.

This man's speech did not sound like theirs had. She suspected he was making up the entire story. "A troll? Do you believe this dung heap?" she whispered in Ragna's ear.

"A month ago, I would have scoffed at him," Ragna admitted. "Though I am still not convinced the giant we battled was a creature of legend, I no longer discount the possibility. He was big with obvious deformities, but a troll? What will it be next? Did he encounter Jörmungandr, the Serpent of Miðgarðrdr?"

Maintaining physical contact with Ragna, Solveig fixed her attention on the king's response.

"I can't say I've heard your name mentioned by our skalds," Asbjorn said. "I suppose you want something in return for your aid." He displayed only vague interest in the self-proclaimed hero, but at least he was lucid, for which Solveig was immensely thankful.

"Only if I am successful," Troels replied. "I have a powerful arm and a keen wit. Arvid has the ability to locate otherworldly beings, and I possess the skill to subdue, capture, or kill it as circumstances demand."

"Is that so?" Asbjorn asked in a skeptical tone.

"Good," Solveig whispered to Ragna. "Don't be taken in by this fraud."

Ragna replied, "Asbjorn is no fool," and stared at the strangers with a stern expression.

"I see you are unconvinced," Troels observed, his manner still light and jovial. "Perhaps a demonstration?"

The king raised a brow. "I hope you do not propose to slay one of my warriors to prove your worth. I need them all to protect us from the giant."

"Nothing of the sort, my lord," he responded with a smile. "Do you have a local gothi who could act as a learned observer? Arvid shall ask the gods questions on my behalf, then consult the runes to read their reply. Your holy man is invited to watch to ensure the answers are interpreted correctly."

Asbjorn leaned toward Ingrid and discussed the proposal privately with her for several minutes.

"Something about his plan sounds amiss," Solveig murmured to Ragna. "I can read runes. I'll verify them myself."

"And if he wants to test his skill against someone..." the shieldmaiden began in a challenging tone.

"No. Your arm has not healed." Solveig kept her tone light when she added, "You can always kill him later if he cheats us."

"Troels of the Danes," Asbjorn then announced, "we will observe your demonstration. Geirfinnr, please go fetch Osmin and ask him to come here. We may continue at my table when my gothi arrives." He stood, took the queen's hand, and left the platform to consult with Baldr.

Solveig felt excitement in the air and overheard various townspeople making exclamations of hope. Several, including a few star-struck young women, gathered around the foreigner to fawn over him. It made Solveig's stomach turn when she witnessed him flirting with them as if he were in an alehouse rather than the king's great hall.

"Don't worry, princess," Ragna consoled her. "The monster will probably rip him in half."

"You're right," Solveig agreed, "if in fact he has any intention of facing it. Come, let's secure our seats at the table. I mean to watch this demonstration."

A bowl of mead graced the center of the table, and everyone had filled their cups by the time Asbjorn and Ingrid re-appeared. Osmin sat beside Arvid while Solveig and Ragna occupied seats on the foreign gothi's other side. Across from them, Baldr and Geirfinnr flanked Troels, engaging him in tales of adventure. *Do they take him seriously?* Solveig wondered.

Once Asbjorn settled into his seat of prominence, he motioned to Troels. "Convince me you can defeat the monster."

With a nod, Troels picked up pieces of wood and iron he had brought into the hall during the recess. Standing, he assembled them into a device that occupied half the table. "This, King Asbjorn, is the recreation of a Roman weapon. Do you recall hearing of the Romans?"

"I've heard them mentioned in ancient tales," Ingrid replied. "They came from a land far to the south and had at one time many kingdoms across the sea along with Britannia, but not Norvegr."

"Correct," Troels said as he adjusted the oversized crossbow. "See the bolt this weapon fires?" He held up an arrow the length of a child's spear with a long, iron head sharpened to a thin edge. "The *scorpio* is a type of ballista, small enough to be portable yet three or four times the size of a crossbow with an immensely greater draw strength. Notice this lever." He laid his fingers on a cogwheel and rolled it, making the butt of the weapon raise and lower. "It adjusts the firing angle. And here—" He worked a crank, which pulled back the tight bowstring until he pressed it into a pocket. "I lay the bolt in the groove, which I'll not demonstrate indoors lest anyone be injured," he added with a smile and a wink. "I adjust the angle if needed, and when I'm ready, I pull the trigger to release the powerful thrust the weapon employs to launch the projectile. While I feel certain a bolt of this size, with a four-hundred-pound draw weight would be sufficient to bring down a jötunn, there is more."

He held up the massive arrow and pointed at the tip. "Arvid is a master of the brewing and application of poisons. He knows the deadliest mixtures of toxic plants and will apply a lethal potion to the arrowhead to ensure the monster can't survive."

Everyone leaned in to study the scorpio with interest and amazement. She did not want to admit it, but even Solveig was impressed by the braggart's plan.

"Would you mount this in the back of a cart?" Baldr asked as he smoothed a hand over the taut, curved limb of the miniature ballista.

"That is one way," Troels affirmed as he worked to charm the king's son. "It could also be mounted on a stone if we laid a trap to lure the monster out. With a craftsman's help, I could construct more of them, so if one was not in the proper range, another could be. Once Arvid has located the creature, I propose to scout the area to plan the ideal location for the weapon."

"I hate to say it," Ragna whispered to Solveig, "but this could work. The small arrows I hit him with were ineffective, but that bolt... and with poison? The best part of Troels' plan is that the warriors could stay clear of the giant's reach. Trying to fight him up close proved fatal."

A lump formed in Solveig's stomach. Could it be that she was only put off by the man's manner? Might he truly be able to slay the foe threatening the kingdom?

"It is impressive," Asbjorn said, "but it will take more than a clever weapon to defeat a jötunn."

"Indeed." Troels took his seat as the warriors continued to admire the scorpio. "Arvid, do you have your runes?"

The old man, who had yet to utter a word, withdrew a cloth bag from the pouch at his waist and shook it. "Gothi," he addressed Osmin in an unusual accent. "Would you care to examine my runes?"

Osmin opened the bag and emptied its contents onto the table. They were ordinary-looking runes, but rather than being carved of stone or wood like a common set, they were fashioned from fine ivory. Solveig noticed Osmin's expression of awe as he touched them.

"These seem to be in order," Osmin reported with a glance to the king. Asbjorn nodded and motioned for his visitors to proceed.

"Arvid, ask the gods if I come to King Asbjorn's hall with true intentions or false," Troels directed.

The old man's bony fingers were steady as they returned each piece to the bag. He held it up and uttered words in a language foreign to Solveig. She frowned, as she was fully aware the gods understood the common tongue of all the northern kingdoms. When he lowered the pouch, Arvid reached in with his eyes closed, withdrew a rune, and laid it on the table.

Solveig recognized it at once: □. Osmin pronounced, "*Óss*, Odin's sign of wisdom, inspiration, and communication. It may be interpreted as truth."

He drew out another: □. "*Kaun*, the torch," Arvid stated this time. "The beacon of truth."

Did this mean the arrogant, devious, lecher was none of those things but an actual hero? Oh, he was a lecher, alright, but still...

"Can I defeat the beast?" Troels asked.

Arvid reached in once more and pulled out a rune. This one was ▢, *Purs*, the thorn. "See, the symbol of the giant or danger." The next he withdrew, Solveig recognized as ▢, *Týr*.

"Týr," Osmin declared in wonder. "The emblem for victory."

Solveig was dumbfounded. It must be a trick, some sleight of hand. Arvid was a magician, and somehow, he had made everyone believe that the gods were speaking through the runes. Yet she had seen the complete set laid upon the table and watched while he returned them to the bag. Even Osmin had inspected them. She didn't know how Arvid had done it, but surely these signs were not true.

"King Asbjorn." Troels rose from his seat and paraded around the room. "I have come a long way in hopes of another adventure for our bards back home to sing about. I have brought a unique weapon, not used in two hundred years, that can kill the giant, and a gothi with the ear of the gods, who through rituals and runes can learn the whereabouts of the monster threatening Sogn. What's more, I have the courage, skill, and determination to track it down and destroy it, saving your kingdom from further fear and calamities. My demands are not unreasonable, nor do I expect payment until the deed is done."

Every eye in the hall was upon him, each ear enraptured by his claims. Faces shone with anticipation and the mood had transformed into one of hope and expectation.

"What are these reasonable demands?" Asbjorn asked.

Troels lifted his palms. "Only a single chest of silver," he declared, then turned his gaze to Asbjorn's oldest daughter. "And the hand of the beautiful Princess Solveig in marriage."

Shock hit Solveig like a wooden beam. All color drained from her cheeks, and she gripped Ragna's hand so hard her knuckles turned white. Swallowing the lump in her throat, she waited on the edge of a sword for her father's reply.

The king sighed and rubbed the back of his neck with a wide hand. A pained expression on his face, he exchanged a helpless look with Ingrid before he answered. "If you bring me the jötunn's head on a pike, then you may have your silver and your bride."

"Father!" Solveig shot to her feet in outrage while Troels regarded her with a smug visage.

Ragna grabbed her arm and pulled her down into her seat, hissing quietly, "Not here. Not now."

Asbjorn's brow narrowed, and he scowled in disapproval. "Do you not wish to do your part to save our kingdom from danger?"

Solveig bowed her head in front of the crowd of witnesses. "I indeed wish to do my part to save the kingdom from danger, Father."

"Then it is settled!" Troels announced in triumph, leering at her with a wolfish gaze. "Have you musicians? Let us celebrate with drink and dancing."

Without joviality, Asbjorn waved for the performers and cheers arose from the gathering.

"This is some sort of trick," Solveig swore to Ragna.

"I agree," Ragna said in hushed tones, "but you can't contradict the king in public. Speak to him afterward and make your concerns known."

"I shall indeed," she swore. How could he? Offer her up to a total stranger, a foreigner? Would the rake take her away to Vendill, never to see her family—much less her lover—again?

Solveig remained seated at the table, her arms crossed defiantly over her chest, watching Troels laugh and drink and dance. *What is your scheme, Dane?* The men toasted him, the women threw themselves at him, and Solveig brooded. Then a dark thought crept into her mind, and her eyes shot to her parents.

"Ragna, watch him," she instructed and rose from the table.

As she made her way around to where they sat, the blond Dane spotted her and whirled in to block her path. "A man would challenge even worse monsters than a giant to gain a wife of your exquisite beauty, Solveig." His voice dripped with honey while he surveyed her with the eyes of a snake.

She shot him an icy glare. "You must defeat it first, my lord. If you will excuse me." She moved to step around him, but he caught her about her waist, his hands inching lower than they should have. "You will take your hands off me," she seethed in a low, dangerous hiss.

"I only wish to dance with you," he replied, innocently lifting his palms.

"I believe there is a line of women who wish to dance with you," she quipped. "The events of the day have tired me, so I will say good night." Not awaiting his response, she scurried to her mother and father.

"Papa, I request a moment to speak with you both in private."

Asbjorn sighed in defeat. "Dear sweet one, what's done is done."

"Nothing is done yet," Solveig stated with conviction. "All he has accomplished is boast and bluster. Please, Mother, Father, you need to hear my concerns."

"Asbjorn, my heart isn't settled in this matter either," Ingrid admitted. "Let us listen to Solveig."

The king grumbled, downed his cup, and staggered to his feet. "Come on, then." Mother and daughter followed him to her parents' private chamber in the family's residence at the end of the longhouse. Once inside, Asbjorn's legs seemed to give out, and he plopped onto the bed.

"We all must make sacrifices for the good of the kingdom, Solveig," he began. "I won't listen to your pleas to remain unwed."

"That's not the issue," Solveig explained. She sat beside him and gave him a hug. Ingrid settled on Asbjorn's other side. "Papa, I believe these strangers are trying to fool us with clever lies. Think of how this marriage would threaten Baldr. Isn't it obvious? This braggart is an ambitious enemy. He seeks to gain a claim to the Kingdom of Sogn through a marriage to your oldest child, and once you pass on, he plans to fight Baldr for your crown, if not murder him outright. Don't you see? If you must marry me off to someone, let it be one of our jarls or an allied king's son, not a total stranger."

"Sweet Solveig, we face a crisis now," he retorted. "We can deal with conspiracies once Herlief's death has been avenged, and the giant is no more. Besides, what if Troels is telling the truth? How can he fake killing the jötunn?"

"You haven't seen the evil intent in his eyes, Papa. And the stunt with Arvid and the runes? Surely some trick. Please reconsider."

"Solveig, you saw his new weapon and how he encouraged the people," Ingrid said. "Yet I agree with our daughter, Asbjorn. This foreigner only arrived today, and we haven't had a chance to verify his honesty or purpose. We must observe him and his gothi closely, always have one of our loyal men watch them in case they are trying to trick us. They could be spies sent by enemies of whom we aren't aware. Or they could be dupers here to rob us."

"Or they could be who they claim to be," he offered.

"Listen to Mother." Solveig took hold of her father's arm and peered at him with an earnest gaze. "Troels' speech does not even sound like that of a Dane. Don't trust them."

"I'm disheartened, drunk, and miserable with grief and remorse, but I have not lost all my senses." He patted Solveig's hand and kissed her cheek. "Either he will slay the creature, or he will not. Maybe you'll get lucky and the jötunn shall rend him asunder. Right now, I welcome any warrior willing to face it. Don't be angry with me, my child. It is the weight of leadership. The kingdom's best interests must come first, even before the desires of my beloved daughter's heart. Now, let me drink myself to sleep, wretched man that I am. I am losing children by the handfuls. What other tests can the gods throw at me?"

"Leave us, Solveig," Ingrid said gently. "Have faith everything will turn out as it should."

Solveig lowered her gaze and nodded. "I will try."

18

Kai lay on the floating mast, her feet dangling in the water as the waves rocked her gently back and forth. The rays of the sun were warm, although they had blistered her exposed skin, which flaked and peeled from dehydration. She had collected rainwater from showers following the big storm in a fragment of the sail which had clung to the mast, but she had drunk it all by the previous morning.

She brushed her fingers through the sea and used her parched tongue to lick chapped lips. Kai understood she could not drink the salty liquid as it would dry her out faster, but it tempted her. *Maybe I can just swish it in my mouth and spit it out,* she considered. She scooped a cupped hand into the brine; however, when she raised it to her lips, the salt burned so badly, she poured it out and abandoned the idea.

I am so glad it is me drifting out here alone, parched with thirst instead of Tove. It would crush my heart to think of her enduring such hardship. She will be home in Bàtrgørð by now, safe with her family and the others. Torsten and Leiknir must be wondering what has become of me. At least I am free now. I only need to find a boat traveling north and convince them to take me along. I can row to earn my passage.

A sound overhead caught Kai's attention, and she sat up. Gulls glided by, screeching out their calls. One dove close to her and swiped a tiny fish from near the surface. Two more landed and perched on the far end of the mast, eying her as if she may make a suitable meal. At first, she regarded the birds as a nuisance, but then it dawned on her sunbaked brain she must be nearing land. Popping up with a jolt, Kai whipped her head around, seeking a shoreline. Still, all she saw was the vast expanse of sea sparkling with white lights reflected from the sun. "Soon." She struggled to croak out the word, but her throat was too dry to form proper sounds.

The appearance of the gulls renewed Kai's hope, and she tried to stay alert to watch for land. She thought she saw a beach several times, only to be disappointed by the vibrating, shimmering waves. After a few hours of watchfulness, she became weary, her smidgeon of energy sapped by the radiating ball of light in the sky. Kai lay on the mast pole again and wondered what time it was. As the days continued to lengthen, she couldn't be certain if it was the dinner hour or not. She had given up the desire for food now, wishing only for water and shade. At least the temperature remained mild. Light or not, Kai closed her eyes and fell into sleep.

She awoke to screams and the sound of a scuffle. As she lurched out of an intimate dream in which she exchanged kisses and caresses with Tove, Kai suddenly became aware of firm earth beneath her. Her senses shot wide. *Land! I've washed ashore!*

Dusk had fallen, yet plenty of daylight remained. As she pushed to her hands and knees, blessing all the gods for their providence, a woman's shrieks and men's laughing jeers caught her attention once more. She blinked and concentrated on focusing her scratchy eyes. Fifty yards down the coast, she glimpsed a woman struggling with two, maybe three men; she appeared to be in distress.

Kai pushed herself up but was so wobbly she almost toppled over. Purposefully planting her feet on solid ground, she gained her balance and glanced around. There, a few steps away, a short piece of wood from the wreckage swirled in the surf, half caught on the sand; she snatched it up.

There were two problems with her rescue attempt: how to cross the distance unnoticed by the woman's assailants, and how in her present condition she might disable them. *Maybe they will be too busy trying to rip her clothes off to notice me.* With no coherent plan in her befuddled mind, Kai launched into an uncoordinated charge, gripping her waterlogged club and hoping for the best.

At first, they didn't spot her. Once they did, one man restrained the distressed woman while the other two trotted to meet her, grinning at their good fortune, no doubt. Kai tried to think of effective fighting moves she had seen others use; however, as the men rushed up to her, she merely dodged to the side, slamming her board as hard as she could into one of their knees. The wiry fellow grabbed his injured limb and cried out in pain, hopping on one foot.

The other shot her a glare, spun, and started after her. When he reached for her, she ducked his grasp and struck him in the knee, too. This time she pivoted and followed through with a bash to his head, dropping him to the ground.

Kai was getting dizzy as she whirled around again to get a fix on her first attacker. He limped, but advanced on her, shouting angry words in a foreign tongue. She acted as though she was going to strike him in the face and when he flung his arms up to block the attack, she swapped the angle of her thrust and crushed her make-shift club into his groin. The move had been effective against Bratmir, so she presumed it would work on this smaller fellow. She was right.

When he hugged himself, doubling over in agony, she hammered the plank to the side of his head. With both men dazed in the sand, Kai sucked in dry, painful breaths and lurched toward the last attacker, who held the frightened woman in front of him with a knife to her throat. He glared and shouted words Kai didn't comprehend, but she didn't need the words to understand what he meant.

She slowed and lowered the piece of wood, looking as faint as she felt. Then partly from fatigue and partly as a ruse, she dropped to her knees, appearing as harmless as a limp kitten. He lowered the knife, clenched the woman's wrist, and dragged her along as he closed in on Kai. White lights danced in front of her eyes, and she tried to think. She blinked and panted, bracing herself with her hands on her thighs as she peered up. A hand axe was loosely tucked in the brigand's belt. Just as he reached for her, Kai sprang up from her toes, lunged forward, and yanked the weapon from his strap, losing her balance and rolling across the sand in the process. He yelled at her again and lifted his leg to kick her. When he did, she struck, the axe head slicing through his boot and wedging itself into his foot. He screamed in agony, grabbing for his wound.

Despite her spinning head, Kai knew this was the moment to make their escape. She thrashed to her feet, grabbed the terrified young woman's wrist, and motioned for them to run.

The slender dark-haired woman with dusky skin said something in return that sounded agreeable, and they scurried away from the rogues. Kai tried to blink away the lights flashing before her eyes and remained on her feet for a few minutes until she tripped. She would have fallen if the maiden hadn't caught her.

"Thank you," Kai croaked out, steadying herself on the girl's shoulders.

Without warning, the woman cried out in amazement, hugged Kai, and kissed both her cheeks. She then shot off a string of conversation in a language foreign to Kai.

"I don't understand what you're saying," she interrupted.

"Oh." The young woman took a nervous glance behind them, probably checking if they were being followed. "You from north, ja?"

Kai nodded. "Yes, I'm from Yates in the land of the Swedes. I do not speak your language."

"You are girl!" she exclaimed with a look of admiring surprise. "Come. Papa talk." She took Kai's hand and led her along at a brisk walk. "Water, ja?"

Kai nodded fervently. "Yes, please!"

They soon entered a seaside village where they were met by curious looks. A few of the villagers asked the young woman questions, to which she rattled off brief answers to without stopping until they reached a well. Kai collapsed beside its stone wall while the young woman drew out a bucket of water. She scooped out a ladle full and handed it to Kai, who swallowed quickly, allowing little streams to trickle out along the edges of the dipper.

Kai was aware of a black-haired man standing over her conversing with the young woman, and she recognized the word "papa."

"Not too fast," he admonished her. "I realize you are thirsty, but you don't want to make yourself sick."

"You're right," Kai said, with more clarity now. "But I've been adrift for days with nothing to drink."

"That I can see for myself," he observed. "You must come to our house, eat, bathe, rest. My Danika told me how you saved her from the good-for-nothing ruffians on the beach. I told her do not go to gather clams and mussels alone, but does she listen? *Nemaye*, she does not!"

Danika lowered her chin, swished her skirt around her hips, and appeared repentant.

"She will listen to my instructions now, yes?" Her father pinned her with a stern expression, and Danika nodded.

"I am Gavril, a merchant trader, which is why I know your language. I deal with many Danes and Swedes in my business. And you, little brave one, you are?"

"Kai, from Yeats in the land of the Swedes," she replied and held out the empty dipper. Gavril smiled and filled it halfway for her. She returned his smile and sipped. "You are kind, and I appreciate your hospitality."

"You, blonde girl with short hair," he stated, indicating her out-of-place appearance. "Gavril shall award you the greatest prize for saving my *durnyy* daughter. But first, we clean you up, yes?" He stretched out a hand and Kai grabbed it, allowing him to pull her to her feet.

"Yes," she agreed.

Gavril's plank house was like houses in Kai's town of Lagarfjord, only without the embellished gables or decoratively carved doorposts. It was a simple structure: a long, rectangular room with a central hearth and sleeping benches along the walls. Chests and a table comprised its other furnishings, and a few embroidered wall hangings served as decorations. A woman who resembled Danika, only older, scurried over to meet them while two twiggy boys bounced in and out, jabbering excitedly.

"This is Kai," Gavril introduced their guest in the Slavic tongue. "She saved Danika from those troublemakers we chased out of town yesterday."

"O, *myla dytyna*!" The woman wrapped Kai in a colorfully woven blanket before planting kisses on both her cheeks. Then she pinned Danika with a reprimanding *tsk* and shook her head.

"Thank you," Kai responded. "Can you tell me where I am?"

"You are in my home," Gavril said, "and you will sit over here on a cushion and eat the stew my wife Katja has prepared."

It wasn't what Kai had meant, as she could see that for herself; however, she allowed him to seat her in the visitor's spot, where she graciously accepted the bowl of fresh food.

Danika and her mother were clearly having a discussion about why the young woman had been on the beach away from town alone, and about how foolish she had been.

"Gavril, what place is this? What town and land?" Kai specified after savoring her first several bites of stew. She wouldn't make him scold her for eating too fast as well, though she was so famished she could have swallowed it all at once.

"Our town, Truso, is a center for trading and fishing, situated in the land of Varni where the Vistula River meets the sea. We are on the Amber Road, where furs, ivory, and amber from your people in the north meet silk and various metals coming from the south. This is a vital trade route, yes? Good for my business. But the fishermen, they are here too, and farmers, craftsmen, and the rest. It is not as big a center as Bilhyryn, but important enough."

"You are Slavic people?" she asked.

"Mostly, though you will see other fair-skinned, blonde-haired folks like you around," he mentioned. "Some Saxons, Danes, and Swedes have settled here in friendship. I speak all three languages." Pride shone in his bright smile.

Danika brought her own bowl over and sat beside Kai, gazing at her with curiosity. She asked her father something, and he gave her a brief reply before returning to their guest. "My daughter wanted to know what you were saying, and she asks you to tell us how you appeared magically from the sea to save her."

Katja kneeled in front of Kai and swathed some sort of odorous cream on her face, then across her raw wrists, where her bindings had rubbed, and over the cracked skin of her hands, talking to her in the Slavic tongue the entire time.

Gavril laughed. "And my wife wishes to tend to you, like she does."

"Please tell her thank you, and the food is delicious." Kai smiled at the woman, who grinned in return.

After Gavril spoke to her, he nodded to Kai, who recounted the story of the raiders, the shipwreck, and the timing of when she washed ashore.

"It is the providence of the gods," Gavril proclaimed. "There can be no other explanation. Katja, our faithfulness has been rewarded for the gods to deposit Kai onto the beach at the exact time Danika needed her. But tell me, Kai," he said, returning his gaze to her. "You come to us half-drowned and delirious with thirst. Are the warriors of your tribe so fierce that even a little girl can fight off three mature men?"

Kai's embarrassment must have been obvious to them because Danika reached an arm around her waist to hug her. "I am a grown woman, not a little girl. I just didn't grow as big as everyone else. But, yes, the Northmen are indeed fearsome fighters."

Danika said something, and Gavril translated. "My daughter says you were matchless and bold, yet you did not have to intervene on behalf of a stranger. You could have laid on the beach and remained safe."

Kai shook her head. "No, I could not have. It's in my nature to help anyone in need. I could never have lain on the sand and watch her be assaulted." Danika hugged her and brushed a kiss to her cheek. Katja beamed, and the two boys bounded back in, grabbing bowls of stew and chattering to everyone.

"And now comes the matter of your reward," Gavril announced. "What can we do to help you, Kai of the Swedes?"

19

K ai spooned the last morsel of the stew into her mouth, giving his words careful consideration before answering. She was warm and dry, her belly satisfied, and her cracked skin soothed by these kind people. Would they have done the same for her had she not liberated their daughter from brigands? Kai had a feeling they would have, and it made her smile.

"I didn't come to Danika's aid to gain a reward," she said with honest humility. "Nor do I require one, and yet..." Kai chanced a glance at Gavril, hoping, that as a trade merchant, he had use of a ship. "I would very much like to secure passage on the next trading vessel sailing for Birka." It was the most prominent trading center near her home, so surely someone would be traveling there soon. "I can row an oar or do other work to earn my passage."

"But of course!" A big grin encompassed the man's wide, tan face, forming wrinkles in the corners of his brown eyes. "Our captains have already embarked on their spring venture, but they will be returning north when the leaves change in the fall. You will spend the summer with us, yes? We will learn from each other, and I can practice my Norse speech. Maybe I can teach you some of our language."

Although fall was later than Kai had hoped for, her spirits lifted at the thought she would see her home and family again. "I don't wish to intrude or be a burden," she admitted.

"Nonsense! What are your skills?" Gavril sat forward, inspecting her.

"I can hunt," Kai answered with pride in her voice. "However, I would need a bow, as mine was lost."

"A hunter!" he exclaimed before translating for his family. The two lads lit up with excitement, and Katja and Danika seemed amazed. "A bow is easier to come by than fresh goose or venison. I have never been successful at hunting and must rely on trade for meat. You will be an asset to our home."

His declaration eased Kai's mind, and her tired, achy body relaxed. Gavril rattled off a series of sentences, and Danika jumped at the chance to volunteer for something. He turned back to Kai.

"Truso has a bathhouse," he said. "It is not a hot spring, like what sailors talk about in their tales. The water is heated with great stones from a firepit, though. Danika will take you now, yes? Then you come back and sleep."

"I appreciate your thoughtfulness." Kai set her empty bowl aside and hugged the older man.

"And I appreciate your courage," he answered.

Danika jumped to her feet and held out a hand. Kai took it, and the young woman led her through town to a large community building across from the forge. It was dark at this hour, yet some villagers were still out, coming and going from the alehouse or the wharf. They regarded her with curiosity, and Danika chirped out a cheery explanation.

Once inside the bathhouse, Danika led her to a curtained-off section with a large, oval tub filled with water. While not clear, the liquid did not appear to be dirty either. Kai supposed they didn't change the water between each patron, or even every day.

"Clothes off," Danika instructed her as she used oversized tongs to move hot rocks from the firepit into the tub.

Kai folded the striped blanket Katja had wrapped around her and carefully peeled out of her salty shoes, trousers, and tunic, which Danika gathered and dropped into a second tub. Kai recognized a look of appreciation in the young woman's gaze as she looked at her nude body. Although she had never considered herself attractive, with her compact frame and slight features, she supposed she sported firm muscles, and her light skin tone might be a novelty to the Slav. There was certainly nothing more to read into her response. Stepping over the rim, she eased into the warm liquid and relaxed.

Danika scurried back and poured oil from a bottle over Kai's shoulders, rubbing it all over her arms and back. "Too dry," she uttered with a grimace. She added more in her language, probably expounding on her brief observation. The woman's touch was soothing, and it seemed to Kai she had done this before, perhaps for her mother or father. Lover? It was none of her business. Yet Danika was attractive, with a pleasant voice and disposition. *No. I'm with Tove, and I'll be going home soon. There is no reason to think of another woman. Besides, I am a guest in her home. It would be inappropriate.* Still, she could appreciate the blissful sensations.

As Danika worked soap through Kai's hair, she frowned. "They cut off hair."

"Yes. It used to be long like yours."

She muttered angry words and shook her head. "You still *harnyy...* pretty."

Kai blushed. "Thank you, but I am plain among my people. I just look different to you."

Danika shook her head. "Strong, not afraid." She added more in her language as she bathed Kai, clearly admiring her courage and her actions on the beach. She had just chosen the wrong word at first. Still, it made Kai feel good. Praise was praise, no matter what it was for.

Once Kai had been scrubbed and oiled, Danika held up a blanket to wrap her in it. Danika was only a little taller and more filled out than she was. Maybe Kai wasn't so tiny compared to the women of Varni.

Her host showed her to a bench by the firepit to dry off while she set to washing her sea-soaked clothes. Danika held up the trousers and turned to Kai. "No dress?"

She shook her head. "I prefer men's clothes," she explained. "Especially while being locked in the hold of those raiders' ship. It's easier to move in to hunt, to ride a pony, or do all the chores I usually do. I may not look as pretty as you in your dress, but my clothes are practical."

Danika squeezed a stream of droplets from the woolen breeches and narrowed her eyes at Kai. "You pretty, even if no dress." She snapped the pants, sending more drops flying, and laid them over a rack by the fire. Then she returned to scrub the tan tunic Kai had received from the cabin boy, who was probably now serving in the halls of Ran. They were all gone, her captors. In the safety and warmth, Kai was struck with wonder at how she alone had survived the vicious storm and crushing billows.

"Sorry others die." Danika offered her a sorrowful glance, as if she had read her mind. "Glad you live," she added cheerily.

With a little laugh, Kai agreed.

Danika hung the tunic on a nearby rack and fished Kai's shoes from the tub, frowning at them. With a sigh, she uttered, "Need new *choboty*... for feet." Kai could see that her worn, soft-leather ankle boots were stiff and cracked from being saturated in the brine. Danika dropped them and shook her head before dragging hole-infested, woolen socks from the laundry tub. After wringing them out, she held them up and made tutting sounds.

Kai laughed. "They are all I have. Don't throw them out."

With a mischievous expression, the young woman replied, "Danika give you, ja?" Then she tossed the ragged footwear into the fire. "Sit." She motioned for Kai to stay, left the bathhouse, and returned with socks, shoes, and a clean garment for Kai to put on.

"Is my *plattya*," she declared, handing it to Kai. "Put on, yes?"

Kai smiled in gratitude and slipped the dress over her head. "Thank you. My clothes will be dry in the morning, and I can give this back to you. You have been very kind to me."

Danika's dark eyes danced at her from a beaming, round face. "Kai help Danika. Danika help Kai." She collected Kai's damp clothes and took her hand to lead her home.

The next day, Kai had regained a measure of strength and asked Gavril for a bow. He brought her one and a quiver of arrows, which she took hunting. She returned with four rabbits and a goose, feeling helpful rather than like an invalid. Kai may have suffered misfortune, but she was no victim; she would never see herself as one.

Days turned into weeks. Kai and Danika improved at communication, which was useful for the times when Gavril was out of town conducting trades. In his absence, the family looked to Kai for provision and protection, and for repairing broken items. One day, a man of low reputation dared to harass Danika while she was at the well collecting water, and Kai put him in his place. Danika expressed her gratitude, explaining how important it was for her to be presented pure for a prospective husband. She had her eye on a sweet, shy fellow, and wished he'd hurry up and approach her father with a proposal.

Whenever Gavril returned from a day or two away trading, Kai eagerly inspected everything he'd brought back. She had not forgotten about the Damascus steel she had to acquire for Kjell to forge her special warrior sword, but she had not yet spied it among his goods.

Three weeks after she'd washed up on the Varni shore, Gavril was summarizing his latest trip, which had been to Bilhyryn. "The word they received about your shipwreck was that all perished," he told her. "They were expecting great spoils from the northland, and I suppose you were to be part of it. I did not mention you to them, in case some of the raiders' friends came looking, wishing to recoup a portion of their losses."

She nodded. "Thank you. I also think all the others perished at sea. Gavril, may I ask you a question about trading?"

"Certainly." They were sitting together on a bench outside his dwelling, and he turned to face her. The door stood ajar to allow air in, though the family spent more time outdoors than in the stuffy heat of the house. The boys had run off with friends and Danika and Katja were engaged with other village women in an open-air work structure, weaving at the looms. It seemed to Kai all the other women did was spin, weave, sew, cook, and clean—all important tasks that did not interest her in the least. Did they hold no interest to the other women, who simply made themselves do them because the work had to be done? Was she being selfish, engaging in activities she found more satisfying instead of performing her duty as a woman? Kai shook off those thoughts to focus on the vision she had latched onto in Uppsala.

"Have you in your trading business come across an ore called Damascus steel?"

He nodded. "It is a rare and costly ore, highly valued for crafting swords. What interest does a young huntress have in such a metal?"

Kai didn't want to seem foolish to her benefactor, yet she needed to know. "Where might I purchase a bar of it, and how much would it cost me?"

His eyes widened with surprise, and he ran fingers through his black hair as he thought. "I have seen it in the weaponsmith's shop in Bilhyryn. Warriors and hrafy—jarls—seek weapons crafted with the ore. It is much lighter than iron, yet stronger. I cannot imagine what they trade for it. Horses or silver, I expect. Not the simple merchandise I deal in. Why do you ask?"

Kai stared at the dirt. Did she dare share her vision? What difference would it make if this man thought she was a foolish dreamer? He would honor his word to secure her passage on the fall trading ship to Birka, regardless of what foolishness she uttered.

"I need it for a hero's sword," she confessed. "A seer and a holy man of my tribe told me if I completed three quests, I could step into the destiny I most desire—to become a warrior hero, those most revered in my country. I know I am too small, but Frigg said heroes come in all sizes." She dared glance at Gavril and was encouraged to see he hadn't broken into laughter. "I must bring a shard of Damascus steel from which to craft a champion's sword. The other two conditions are much more difficult to fulfill, but one thing at a time." *To give my life for another, and to return from the dead,* she recalled, though she feared to reveal those stipulations. Gavril would think she had gone mad.

"Please keep watch for the ore, Gavril, and let me know if you see any. I will worry about how to buy it when the time comes. If it is indeed my fate to acquire the metal, the gods will provide a way."

"You are already a hero, Kai," he said. "A sword does not define one's character; only their actions can do so. I will be on watch for a shard of Damascus steel and will let you know if I see one. The gods saved you from the disaster at sea and guided you to our shore. If it is meant for you to obtain the metal, I feel certain they will provide the means."

Kai considered him with appreciation. *I am no hero yet. All I do is help people when I can. I haven't accomplished anything extraordinary, such as the sagas proclaim. All I did was hang onto a floating piece of flotsam. Anyone would have chased attackers away from a woman in distress. Anyone would have traded places with her best friend to keep her from danger. Tove.* She closed her eyes and pictured her girlfriend in her mind, smiling to find she had not forgotten her fair face. Joyful anticipation stirred in her core at the thought of going home to Torsten, Leiknir, and her sweet Tove. *Won't they be surprised to see me? And if I can obtain the ore, I'll be one step closer to my destiny.*

"Thank you, Gavril. You are a good father and a good friend. I am fortunate indeed the gods led me to you."

With a smile and a wink, he replied, "I believe we are both fortunate in that regard."

20

Gnóttdalr, three weeks after Troels' arrival

Solveig inspected Ragna's arm in the privacy of her bedchamber. It was the first time in over a week she had convinced the shieldmaiden to join her. Before then, she had claimed she was needed by Baldr, the warriors, and every other excuse she could offer the princess.

"See?" Ragna proclaimed, her lush tresses flowing about her bare shoulders. "Good as new." The gash in her head had healed, too, and Solveig could no longer hold her back from the action.

Troels, who continued to dine and sleep in their great hall, had guided Asbjorn's craftsmen in constructing three scorpiones, which Ragna could not stop gushing about. Arvid had performed a ritual and declared the gods had revealed to him the giant's new hiding place. Only a few scattered reports had made it to Gnóttdalr regarding jötunn attacks, and even those were suspect. A traveling merchant claimed the creature had stolen his wagon and horse, along with all his merchandise, and a hunter reported he had shot a moose that the giant carried off into the woods. These incidents had occurred farther northwest than the monster's last sighting, as if he were slowly moving in their direction, yet no more houses had been destroyed. No stories of people being ripped limb from limb and devoured had emerged.

"I suppose," Solveig admitted. "You seem quite fit indeed." She turned an amorous gaze to the warrior woman and brushed her fingers through her flowing tresses. With concern knotting in her gut, she dared ask what weighed on her mind. "Have you been avoiding me?"

"No." Ragna pulled her tunic back on, wearing a defensive, evasive expression. "I have had much to do. I came to see you because tomorrow we strike out in search of the giant. Troels says he knows where to find him and Baldr has helped him devise a plan to destroy it. I will join the team."

Anxiety clenched in Solveig's throat. "I have missed your company, and now you are to leave again, riding into great danger."

"I didn't think it appropriate to come to you," Ragna began with regret in her tone.

Solveig caught her in a passionate embrace. "I don't want him; I want you."

Ragna's powerful arms wrapped around her, and she nuzzled her face into Solveig's neck. "But you are promised to him." The shieldmaiden's reminder tore at her core.

"Only if he kills the jötunn," she declared with resolve. Ragna's kisses brushed her skin, filling her with a swirl of relief and longing. "But if you kill it..." Solveig shifted her chin to catch Ragna's mouth in a searing kiss of promise.

Ragna stepped back, shaking her head. "Even if I pull the trigger of the scorpio, Troels will claim victory, for it was his weapon and his idea. His gothi divined its location. Do you think I enjoy the idea of losing you to him? In truth, you were never mine. You are a princess, and I am—"

"The woman I love." Solveig blurted out the desperate words, as if holding them in a moment longer would be like throwing herself on a pyre. "I understand you may not feel the same depth of passion or devotion as I, and it's all right. I'm not asking it of you, Ragna. I just... wanted you to know. I love you, and no fulfillment of my father's bargain will change that. The last time you hunted this beast, Herlief and our other warriors didn't return. If you should meet with ill fate..." Her heart thumped fearfully against her chest, and Solveig felt as if an anvil rested on it. "I couldn't live with myself if I didn't at least confess my heart to you."

Then she was once again safe in Ragna's arms, feeling her heartbeat, encompassed by her energy and strength. They remained holding each other in silence for what seemed to Solveig like hours, though it was probably only minutes. Then Ragna's kisses rained over her, and she sighed with desire, seeking her lips, her mouth, her tongue. Without resistance, Solveig guided her lover onto the bed, her hands finding purchase over her lean, firm body.

"We at least have tonight," Ragna finally admitted. "I can never deny you, my dove. I fear I'll have to move far away when you and Troels have wed. Never could I be the cause of gossip to fall from jealous lips to accuse you."

"Shh." Solveig quieted Ragna with a kiss. "Let's live one day at a time. The future will take care of itself."

As she reveled in Ragna's touch, Solveig relaxed. Ragna had not replied with mad declarations of reciprocal affection, nor had she brushed Solveig aside as silly. The woman instead made love to her with her customary vigor and something more—more emotion, maybe, added tenderness, something deeper beyond description.

Did her warrior sense the need to protect her own heart? Surely she did. Ragna was in a much more precarious situation. She was the one who must step aside, who must endure in tacit resignation when Solveig married whomever. She had said as much before.

Am I foolish to have ever thought I could avoid the fate of a king's daughter? Ragna is older and wiser, and still I believed I could resist the inevitable. Yet even if it must be, Freya, I beseech you, provide for me one who is at least worthy. I may never be completely satisfied, but I could be content with a w rthy man.

Solveig drank the life-sustaining rapture Ragna offered and gave all her ardent energy in return, filling her with bitter-sweet pleasure long into the night, until her lover drifted to sleep on her. Still, in the silent darkness, she craved Ragna's caress, and to enjoy rendering the mighty warrior weak as a kitten. She could only pray this would not be their last night together; she wished for it to never end.

"Men and women of Sogn," Troels announced with a grand gesture outside Asbjorn's hall the next morning. "You have nothing to fear! Your fine warriors and I shall return with the head of the beast to prove to you the danger has passed." He stepped up to Solveig and wrapped an arm around her. "Then I shall make your beautiful princess my bride in a hearty celebration!"

He grinned and gave her waist a squeeze.

"Smile," he hissed between teeth clenched in a grin.

Solveig shot him a heated glare before turning a plastered smile to the crowd. She had yet to understand his game. It was beginning to seem his plan would succeed. What had happened to the deception? She was sure he would have stolen as much loot as he could carry and been gone by now, yet here he was about to lead her little brother and their warriors in a mission to end the terror that had gripped Sogn for months.

Asbjorn and Ingrid stood behind them in support, while Ragna and Baldr already sat upon their mounts with their weapons and supplies. When Solveig dared a glance at Ragna, she found the shieldmaiden staring stoically toward the gate. *It's for the best*, she told herself. They had said their goodbyes earlier that morning. Ragna wore the sash Solveig had given her, declaring it had kept her safe on their first mission and would do so again. She had kissed Solveig and bade her not to worry before leaving the bedchamber. Despite her directive, Solveig almost drowned in anxiety to watch them depart. If they were successful in their quest, she would have to marry a man she detested; if they failed... it was unthinkable.

"Baldr," their father called, catching his son's attention. "You are in charge of this expedition," he declared for all to hear. "Assist Troels, but don't let things go awry. Your first duty is the safety of all; killing the beast is second. Accomplish both goals, and we shall enjoy a feast such as Gnóttdalr has never known. Troels, may Odin's eye be upon you, his wisdom whisper in your ear, and may Thor's mighty arm grant you strength."

"I will accept your blessing, worthy king," Troels replied and smacked an unrequested kiss to Solveig's lips. She reddened but could hardly rebuke him while the entire assembly cheered—well, all but Ragna and Ingrid, the two women in the world who understood her.

The drummers beat a rhythm, and flutes lifted a cheery tune as the procession of two wagons bearing the scorpiones and twenty warriors on Fjordings from her father's stable exited the palisade gates. They expected to be gone a week, though it could be longer. Solveig's spirits sank as Ragna and Baldr became too fuzzy for her eyes to make out. It was then that she felt a compassionate lick from her faithful dog, Mist.

She lowered her chin, greeting her with a smile. "So, you have come to comfort me, have you?" She sank her fingers into Mist's fur while a pink tongue lolled from the dog's gaping jaws. She could swear her pet was smiling at her.

Feeling a hand on her shoulder, Solveig turned to see her mother's eyes glistening with tears. She hugged the older woman with affection. "Don't worry, Mother. Baldr will come back safely. Geirfinnr and Ragna know what to expect. They're not going into the venture blind this time."

"I know you are right," Ingrid agreed, then slid to arm's length to look Solveig in the eye. "But can you honestly profess you harbor no fear?"

Lowering her gaze, Solveig shook her head. "Let us keep busy so we'll have no time to imagine the worst."

Asbjorn stepped near to his wife and daughter, worry deepening his frown. He rubbed the back of his neck and shook his head. "It isn't grief alone I wrestle with, but guilt as well. Every night I keep thinking, 'what should I have done different?' If Baldr doesn't return..." He lowered his head, uttered a curse, and turned away.

Ingrid caught her husband's arm and gazed at him with compassion.

Solveig hugged him close and kissed his beard. "We love you, Papa. Losing Herlief was hard for us, too. Baldr will return; just wait and see."

He kissed her forehead. "You are a gem, Solveig. I love you very much. I know you don't care for Troels," he added in a whisper, "and I regret the distress it has caused you. Maybe you will grow to like him in time."

Solveig didn't answer. She knew he was acting in the best interest of the kingdom, yet he still didn't understand what a snake Troels was. Best-case scenario, the giant would kill only one member of the team—the sleazy rake she was supposed to marry.

The week passed slowly, and Solveig spent a lot of time with her mother, sister, and sister-in-law. She rode around to the farms, checking crops and inspecting granaries for leaks or repairs that may be needed before harvest time. In town, she exchanged news with traders, learned the war to the south raged on unresolved, and prices continued to climb.

However, there was no way around lonely nights, when her thoughts drifted to Ragna, and she wondered how things were going. The third night, she disobeyed an instruction her mother had given her as a child, scooped up her dog, and plopped her in bed with her. She didn't care if Mist started to feel entitled; she craved warm company.

Eight days after Baldr and the warriors had left, Solveig was engaged in weaving the honorary tapestry with her sisters under the old craftswoman's tutorage, when she heard the clanging of the brass pipe atop the watchtower. She, Karina, and Sylvi leaped up and dashed for the gate. In no time, her mother and father had joined them.

The day was bright with bluebird skies; still, Solveig couldn't see the party approaching. "Can you see them?" she asked frantically. "Are they all there? How many?"

"It's hard to count," Sylvi answered, "but there are many. Both wagons are intact."

Encouraged and unable to contain herself, Solveig started down the path with a troop of friends and family members accompanying her.

"Baldr?" Ingrid called out hopefully. As they neared the caravan, her mother's relieved cry sounded. "Baldr! You look well, my son!"

"Hear, hear!" Asbjorn didn't run. He never ran; it was unbecoming to a reserved king, but he took long strides toward his returning son.

Relief further poured into Solveig's heart as the red-haired shieldmaiden's form came into focus. "Ragna!"

"How did you fare?" a man in the crowd shouted excitedly.

"Where is the jötunn's head?" asked another.

Troels pulled up beside Baldr's lead position and shook his head. Now that they were close, Solveig spied an unfamiliar look on his typically arrogant face. Frustration, disappointment, even confusion bore in his features.

"He wasn't there," Troels growled, hanging his head in embarrassment.

"We arrived at the cave," Baldr explained, "right where Arvid had said it would be. Only the giant had moved on. We found a dormant fire and cooked bones along with a pile of boughs and straw the creature used for a bed. I don't know if he discovered we were coming or moved in search of better prey."

"Some local hunters in the area said they spotted him a month ago," Geirfinnr added. "And the nearest village reported missing cattle at the beginning of summer, but no trouble since."

"He should have been there." Troels spat out the words in ire, as if the creature had no means or right to move to a new location. His humiliated scowl deepened. The man flashed a glare over his shoulder at Arvid, who rode in the seat of a cart. The gothi shrugged, offering him an apologetic look.

Solveig would have given their reactions more consideration, except she was suddenly overwhelmed with joy. Her brother and Ragna were home safe, and she didn't have to marry Troels! A celebration was truly in order!

21

Over the summer months, Asbjorn sent scouting parties to scour the countryside for the jötunn each time a sighting was reported. Troels did not slink away in shame, as Solveig had wished he would, but rather he became bolder with her, insisting she dance with him in the great hall and sit beside him at feasts. Whenever she made an excuse to avoid his company, he spent his evenings with another young woman in her stead.

Good, she thought. *Let him seek his pleasure with those who would reciprocate them.* She was perfectly happy to invite Ragna to her bed. However, under Troels' scrutiny, their rendezvous weren't as frequent as Solveig would have liked. Ragna had become hypervigilant about ensuring no flapping tongues disgraced the princess. While Solveig was not officially betrothed, many in the town who admired Troels considered her to be.

With the solstice behind them, the brief nights lengthened. Vegetables and beans were harvested, the grain was not far behind, and still the creature eluded them.

One evening after dinner, Solveig sat with Baldr, engaged in a game of Hnefatafl. She had been trying to teach him the finer nuances of the game, as he would need more than a strong sword arm and courageous attitude to lead the kingdom. "You must consider not only your present move, but the next, and the one after it," she explained. "You need to pay close attention to my strategy and anticipate what I may do next."

"I'm trying, but who can fathom what goes on in your mind?" he complained. "Ragna knows you better than anyone, and she has only beaten you twice in as many years. She told me she's convinced you let her win."

Solveig drew her brows together, discontented by his words. Maybe she had been distracted by Ragna's shapely form or powerful air, but she hadn't lost those matches on purpose. As she considered her Hnefatafl fascination, it dawned on her that only her father had ever truly beaten her, and it had been years ago. She had indeed mastered the skill and now began to wonder how she might transfer her knowledge of strategy to other areas of her life. After all, such was the point. Hnefatafl was only a game, yet its purpose was to develop leadership skills, to force the player to look ahead and prepare for every contingency. How might she plan a countermove if Troels ever did kill the giant?

"Look at the pieces on the board, Baldr," she instructed her brother. "You are playing the aggressor. Plot out how you might work your pawns to flank one of mine and capture it." Even as she drilled him, Solveig arrived at an epiphany. She almost always took the defending position because it was the more difficult one. The attacker had more pieces and, therefore, could afford to lose more. Yet in doing so, she had become accustomed to defense strategies. In dealing with Troels, she must practice offensive moves. *I will have to convince Papa to play with me again so I can take the offensive position.*

Baldr scowled at her. "I understand in theory this game can sharpen my mind, but it seems like merely a way to pass time. What would really help me become a leader would be to conquer the giant... if we could find it."

Just then, Ragna and Geirfinnr burst into the great hall, excitement dancing in their features. "There's been a jötunn sighting!" Geirfinnr cried. "Back near the original spot where we fought it."

"Only along the cliffs overlooking the fjord," Ragna added in breathless eagerness. "A fisherman swears the jötunn ambled down the cliff and stole his entire catch—nets and all."

"And it didn't attack him?" Baldr asked in astonishment.

Ragna and Geirfinnr exchanged a curious glance. Geirfinnr replied, "No. He said he was afraid and ran away down the beach. It scooped up all his fish in their nets and hauled them up the bluff."

"When he was sure it was gone, he got into his boat, rowed to Skalavik, and reported to Jarl Anders," Ragna added. "The jarl sent a longboat with ten oarsmen to bring the word as swiftly as possible."

"We ran ahead while they stopped to refresh themselves at the alehouse," Geirfinnr said.

Asbjorn, having heard the commotion, entered the hall and talked with his warriors and Baldr. "Where is Troels?" he asked once they had rehashed the testimony.

They all shrugged. "I didn't see him at the alehouse," Geirfinnr admitted.

"I will find him." Arvid, who had been lounging nearby, stepped forward. "I do not know why the gods forgot to answer me this past month, but this sighting is welcome news. Good king, your patience with us will soon be rewarded. I suspect Troels has wandered into the meadow to pray for guidance. I will find him and bring him here at once."

Praying in the meadow, my ass, Solveig thought with disgust. *He's in some eager young woman's bed, as sure as I'm standing here.* She didn't care. Better there than in hers.

She shot Ragna a determined look before approaching her father. "Papa, this time I wish to travel with the party on the expedition. I should see this creature for myself. Mayhap my skill with strategy will prove useful."

His mouth dropped in utter astonishment. "Absolutely not! Do not dribble foolishness, daughter."

"It is all right, Solveig," Baldr said as he moved to her side. "I will keep a tight rein on the group. The lessons you have taught me, I'll not forget. I know your spirit is strong." He leaned into her ear. "You do not wish to slow us down. I will watch out for Ragna for your sake."

The brutal truth of his words stung. She didn't want to slow them down. She wanted a body like Ragna's, but alas, such was not her fate. With sadness and regret, she nodded and turned away.

A few hours later, Ragna slipped into her bedchamber, and Solveig's heart leaped. "What are the plans?"

The shieldmaiden settled on the side of her bed. "We embark at dawn, which is soon now. We are taking the longboats, as they will be faster. Do not be afraid, my sweet." She stroked Solveig's cheek. "We are ready this time. We have Troels' weapons and Baldr's leadership. I know you asked to go, but Solveig, I do not wish it. I want you here in the garrison's safety, not out chasing giants. No one doubts your courage." She touched her lips to Solveig's before continuing. Ragna's voice cracked then, and the unfamiliar moisture of tears glittered in her eyes. "*I* do not doubt your courage. Remember, it also requires valor to stay behind."

"I would rather be with you," Solveig confessed, "fighting at your side. I would spend my life with you, yet it seems the gods do not take my desires into account." She cupped Ragna's face in her palms and traced her scar with her thumb. "Don't forget my love for you. Even if I have to marry Troels, knowing you are safe will help me to endure. Take care with your life, Ragna."

"Anything for you, princess." She dove into a deep, thirsty kiss, spiced with passion, smothered in regret. "Don't you know I love you too?"

The words Solveig had so yearned to hear rung in her ears long after Ragna was gone. The ships sailed away, and she had once again been left behind.

The summer had been the worst Ingrid could recall living through. She had lost her firstborn child without regaining his body for a proper burial. The tragedy had reduced her robust husband to a drunken sluggard, although he was slowly recovering. Her sweet daughter was being cornered into marriage to a man she detested while the kingdom quivered in fear of a legendary monster. And now her younger son sailed away with a self-proclaimed hero Solveig insisted was a fraud. Though she had spent much time with her eldest daughter over the months since Herlief's death, she felt a chasm between them, such as had never existed before. She longed to gather her into her arms and assure her everything would be all right, but she didn't want to lie. Ingrid had a sick feeling things were far from all right.

Thoughts turned over in her mind as she considered everything that had happened. First the giant appeared, attacking farms and killing people. Jarl Anders sent a team to investigate, and they were all slaughtered, including his son, so he reached out for help. Herlief took Gnóttdalr's finest warriors, joined with Jarl Anders' army, and they got ripped apart, all but a few. Then Troels showed up promising to save the day with his special weapon and amazing gothi, whose prophecies Solveig believed to be tricks. Yet when they struck out to kill the jötunn, it was no longer there.

Newer sightings of the once fearsome man-killer had given accounts of it stealing cattle and fish, yet no one else had been injured. Why would it suddenly change its pattern of behavior? Before, it was easy to track, and now it avoided being sighted. The giant was real, as both Geirfinnr and Ragna had testified to its size and strength. Did it have an agenda other than mayhem?

Then there was the shift in Troels' manner after he had first failed to slay it. Was he merely embarrassed to have missed his opportunity to gloat over his victory? Her daughter suspected he only sought a way to claim Asbjorn's crown and would deceive Baldr—or worse. Surely he did not intend to offer her son up to the monster to put himself in line for the throne as Solveig's husband. No, Geirfinnr, Ragna, and their other loyal warriors would never allow it. Still, the pieces of information did not line up coherently.

Now summer had ended. Farmers were harvesting their hay and grain. Woodcutters stockpiled kindling in covered sheds to carry through the coming winter, and hunters took to the forests to secure meat for salting and drying into chewy strips. The whalers had just brought back their prize and were down at the wharf, stripping it of blubber for oil lamps and meat to trade for wool and cheese. Tanners hurried to finish turning pelts into leather while the temperatures were warm enough to process the skins. Men labored to fill the storehouses even without Asbjorn's usual supervision. If Baldr and Troels did not defeat the threat on this venture, they might have to wait until spring to try again.

Her son and his troop had been away three days as Ingrid sat with her daughters, weaving the final threads into the hem of Herlief's tapestry. Ingrid took a moment to sit back and admire it. A blond warrior with a scant beard struck a valiant pose upon his favorite bay pony, a sword lifted in his right hand. In the background was a longboat with a serpent head stem post. It would make a fitting tribute for generations to admire; Herlief would not be forgotten.

Suddenly, a potter from the town burst into the great hall with a terrified look on his face, gulping for air. "We're under attack! All the able-bodied men have rushed to the fore, and I've come to warn the king." Even as he spoke, the signal bell clanged from the tower.

Ingrid bolted up in realization. "King Asbjorn is in the stable."

"I'll get him, Mother," Solveig cried as she raced out.

"Who? Where?" Sylvi asked as she and Karina clasped shaky hands.

"They bear Sygnafylke's colors," he said, shifting nervously from one foot to the other, wringing his cap in his fists. "They came in longboats, and I think they are after our granaries."

Of course, Ingrid surmised. *Their war with Hördaland has exhausted their supplies, and they seek to steal from us. But why so far north? There are other fylkes nearer the border.* At once her heart was stricken with a terrible possibility; had they already attacked the southern fylkes of Sogn? *What about Baldr and the others?*

Ingrid rushed to the longhouse entrance and spotted Asbjorn and Solveig racing out the gate on horseback toward town. Clutching the doorpost, she swallowed her fear and prayed for their safety.

She wasn't certain she breathed again until she saw her husband and daughter trotting back up the path. Ingrid ran to meet them at the gate.

"We chased the intruders away," Asbjorn huffed, "but not until they had made off with most of our stores. Sorðinn Rundrandr the Wolf." He spat on the ground. "Weasel is more like it!"

"We lost two men, and a half dozen were injured," Solveig reported. "It seems they were not trying to kill people—probably did not want to incur Papa's wrath. Opening a two-front war would be the height of stupidity."

"Bloody bastard could have asked instead of sending thieves," Asbjorn raged.

"I am more concerned about Baldr," Ingrid confessed.

"Baldr?" Her husband slid from his horse and approached her with a confused expression. "What do you mean?"

"They were making for Jarl Anders' fylke on our border with Sygnafylke," she reminded him. "If they are raiding us, surely they went after our southern fylkes first. Baldr may be facing more than one foe. And if they were caught unaware..." Ingrid embraced Asbjorn, not wishing to consider the possibilities.

"Do not worry needlessly, my love," he soothed. "They have only been gone three days. I must take an inventory of the damage."

"I will go with you, Papa," Solveig, who had not dismounted, declared. "I have been monitoring the harvest and will know how much we lost. At least a few farmers still have crops in the field, but I'm certain there will not be sufficient grain to last the winter."

Ingrid released Asbjorn with a nod. "I'll organize gatherers to bring in nuts, pine needles, and edible bark and leaves from the forests. I know what we can survive on. If we pull together, no one will starve."

It wouldn't be easy, but with what her husband and daughter counted that day, Ingrid felt she might yet devise a rationing plan to see them through. She worked on it for two days with Sylvi and Solveig's help, but the third day brought an even more devastating blow.

The posted sentry banged on his brass pipe. "Baldr's ship!"

Did he say ship? Alarm lurched into Ingrid's heart. They had departed with two. The entire household rushed down the road, past garden patches and hog pens, past houses and businesses to the docks to meet the longboat. All the while Ingrid's nerves were on edge as she imagined horrible scenes of death and destruction.

"Baldr!" she exclaimed in relief as she recognized him at the bow of the vessel pulling up to the pier. His step over the gunwale was labored and solemn.

"Mother." He stood still as she threw her arms around him and kissed his cheeks.

"You are home safe, and it is all that concerns me," she declared in relief.

"The jötunn?" the king asked as he tied the line to a piling.

Baldr shook his head. "We got caught up fighting raiders from Sygnafylke, never made it to the cliff cave the fisherman had directed us to."

"Where's Ragna?" At the sound of Solveig's frantic voice, an arrow pierced Ingrid's heart.

"Geirfinnr?" Asbjorn called his best warrior's name. His rugged face appeared over Baldr's shoulder, but he was looking worse for wear. A bloody bandage encircled his middle, and he leaned on a spear for support.

"I'm here, my lord," he answered in a heavy tone. "We lost half our number, engaged in several battles. Jarl Anders also suffered casualties."

"Ragna?" Solveig hiked her skirts and leaped over the edge of the longboat to check each injured warrior's face. Ingrid's spirits sank like a millstone into fathomless depths.

"Solveig." Baldr's voice was full of sympathy. "Ragna feasts in Valhalla with Herlief, though I cannot testify to Troels' fate."

"Troels was killed, too?" Asbjorn seemed surprised by the news.

Geirfinnr's expression hardened. "He took an axe to the back, fleeing the first skirmish we encountered. Arvid lies in our boat, gravely injured. At least the old man did not turn tail and run like a cowardly skunk."

The anguish in Solveig's cry tore at Ingrid's soul. She left Baldr to gather her daughter in her arms. "Sweet girl, I am so sorry."

"How can this be?" Solveig shook in her embrace, and Ingrid worried for a moment she might faint from the shock.

"Sister, you would have been so proud to see her battle our enemies," Baldr declared. "Even the Valkyries must have envied her valor and might. She took down five foes in a row, suffered two spear strikes, and still saved Geirfinnr's life."

"It's true," Geirfinnr attested. "I was gashed in my side and moving slowly. I didn't see the attacker behind me, and Ragna rushed in, hacking off his axe arm before he could land the fatal blow. She distinguished herself as much as any warrior, and I'm certain Thor raises his cup to her at Odin's table this very night."

While their testimony rang with inspiring praise, Ingrid understood full well it would be of little comfort to her daughter.

She held her close, the boat gently rocking on its mooring, and let Solveig grieve.

While the others carried the wounded out to be tended, Solveig found her voice through her sorrow. "Ragna." She peered at her mother through anguished eyes. "What will I do? She was everything I always wanted to be."

Ingrid stroked her hair and kissed tears from Solveig's cheek. With tender compassion, she answered, "Perhaps that is why you loved her so."

22

Land of Varni, beginning of fall

With Danika and her family for company, the summer had moved by quickly for Kai. She went hunting several times a week, bringing back an impressive variety of game for Katja to cook or Gavril to sell. She had been most excited about bagging a pair of hard-to-find Eurasian lynxes, whose fur was prized for capes and vests.

"Do you think the weaponsmith will trade me the ore for these?" she had asked Gavril hopefully.

He had studied the pelts and taken them to the best tanner in Truso, who had done a marvelous job of dressing them out, all soft and pliant to the touch, before consulting a smith friend. "They are exquisite," the big man had admitted. "If you had four more, he might consider it a fair trade."

Kai's spirits had sunk, and Gavril gave the pelts to his wife, who beautifully adorned two woolen cloaks with the furs—one for Kai and the other for Danika. While Kai cherished the unique, spotted garment, which drew admiring gazes all over town, she would rather have had the steel. Fall had arrived, and she hadn't a clue how she might pay for it.

When the first dry leaves began to fall, Gavril told her it was time. "The trade ship to Birka departs from Bilhyryn in three days. The captain is a friend of mine, and we have done business together many times. I will go with you, bring him my chests of goods to trade with the Swedes, and see you off."

Both Danika and Katja teared up at their goodbyes. Even the boys said they would miss Kai's funny way of talking and the meat and furs she brought home; they had a collection of tails to prove it.

"I never had a sister," Danika gushed. Kai had learned enough of their language to understand as the young woman hugged her tight. "I would like to keep you, except I know how you miss your family." She pressed sloppy kisses to both of Kai's cheeks, then caught them between her palms. "I will not forget you, Kai. Because of you, I can present myself to Milenko unspoiled." Danika had become engaged over the summer. She wanted to hold the marriage ceremony before Kai set sail, but Milenko's grandparents had to travel all the way from Estland.

Katja hugged and kissed her next. "I will miss you, Kai with the short, straw hair, and not just the meat you give me to cook, yes? Your bright blue eyes and your stories, too."

"Thank you all for taking me in, for making me so welcome." Kai was sincerely grateful and would miss the family as well, yet she was as excited as a fox in a henhouse to be going home. She threw her lynx wrap about her shoulders and picked up a bag that contained her old set of clothes and some food for the trip to Bilhyryn. Then she collected the bow Gavril had given her. "I guess this is goodbye. I will remember you all fondly. And Danika, don't make Milenko have to save you from ne'er-do-wells too often." They all laughed, and she and Gavril were on their way.

The journey was a full day's walk, but Gavril wanted an extra day in case anything slowed their travel.

They chatted as they marched along, Gavril pulling a small cart with his merchandise and Kai asking questions about the land and the city they traveled to. She wondered if she would see a slave market. Kai was aware that some of the wealthier men and women of Lagarfjord kept thralls who had been captured in battles or who had ended up in a bad way through debt or misdeeds. King Freyrdan had several house servants who tended his great hall; however, she had never seen humans being bought and sold. She shuddered just thinking that such would have been her fate if not for the horrific storm.

"And over there is another fishing village." Unaware of Kai's inner turmoil, Gavril was pointing in the direction of the seacoast.

"Everything is so beautiful," she commented. "And not all the same. Some stretches of the beach are long expanses of white sand while others are covered in dunes. And look! The forest up ahead extends all the way to the water. Torsten, my father, would like that—if they were oaks. Then his workers wouldn't have to haul the trunks such a distance to the water's edge, where he builds his longboats."

"By late afternoon, we'll pass a rocky area where you can stand high and look out over the sea. It's a breathtaking view shortly before we reach our destination."

"Is it near the road?" Kai asked hopefully. "I may never be back here, and I don't want to miss something special."

He laughed and shook his head. "Not far off the road, which follows the coastline. You are a curious one."

"I like to learn new things," Kai answered.

A few hours later, she noticed they traipsed up a steeper incline than they had been on before, and anticipation of the view rose in her chest. Her land overflowed with beauty as well, but one could never have too many lovely vistas in her estimation.

"Here's a trail that takes us to the best spot." Gavril pointed to a narrow footpath leading off the main road. Kai followed, checking out trees and interesting rock formations. "Now watch your step," he cautioned. "Danika got a foot caught one time and twisted her ankle. You may be small, but I don't want to carry you the rest of the way."

Placing each foot deliberately in front of the other, Kai determined she would not be a burden to one who had been so kind to her. Then sounds in the distance caught her attention. "There's other people out here," she declared.

Gavril frowned and held out his arm to block her way forward. "This is not the time of year visitors come to the cliffs. Let me see who it is before we continue."

Kai wasn't about to stand around while Gavril could be walking into danger. She waited for him to take the lead, then followed a few paces behind. He shot a disapproving scowl over his shoulder, though it did nothing to dissuade her.

As they neared the voices, Kai could tell they were loud and frenzied. They were accompanied by boots running back and forth—and a woman's cry. Being quicker and lighter on her feet, Kai gripped her bow and sprinted ahead of Gavril, though she still watched where her steps landed.

"What shall we do now?" The woman's shriek sounded above the lower voices. "Someone must do something!"

Slowing to a trot, Kai saw a small crowd gathered in a circle, each man or woman more distressed than the next. One man was tall and broad-shoul-dered, with wavy brown hair, fine clothing, and a sword dangling from his belt.

"I don't know what else we can try," the striking man hissed out in frustration. "I can't fit in the crevice. I've tried a dozen times."

"We should get hammers and axes and chop our way in," another, even larger, suggested.

"Can't do that." An older, thin fellow with a gray beard contradicted him. "Do you want to crush the poor lad to death?"

"Bojko!" the woman cried. "Can you hear me?"

"I'm here, Mama!" The return call was weak and sounded far away.

By the time Kai had joined the assembly, she had surmised a child must have fallen through a crevice and become stuck.

"I suppose you already tried lowering a rope?" she asked in the language Gavril had been teaching her. She hoped she got all the words right.

The circle of six men and two women stared at her like she had just dropped out of Álfheim. One woman stood about her height yet bore far more breadth; everyone else was normal size except the two larger men.

"Of course we tried a rope, you stupid girl," the warrior type with the fine clothes and sword at his waist chided her. "You are a girl, right? Hard to tell with the short hair."

Kai was an outsider, and this was none of her affair. They didn't seem to like or trust her, and the wise thing to do would be to wish them luck and be on her way.

Gavril caught up to her and talked briefly with the gathering while Kai studied the narrow hole between the rocks.

"It is Bojko's birthday," the shorter woman explained. "He's six. He wanted to come out to the cliffs to look at the sea."

"We brought him once before," the tall, brawny man answered. "I had no idea there was a crack large enough for him to fall through."

"I ran back to town for help," a lanky, beardless youth attested. "Our friends and Zlatan, Bilhyryn's champion, came to help." Kai flicked her gaze back to the stately warrior who had insulted her.

"Do not worry," Zlatan said in a calm tone. "I will think of something."

"I can do it," Kai stated. She unpinned her lynx cape and laid it aside with her bow and travel bag.

"Can do what?" Zlatan crossed his arms over his muscled chest and eyed her suspiciously.

"Fit in the crack. I can get the child out."

The people murmured, speculating, already making wagers.

"Kai, you can't," Gavril insisted. "You'll get stuck, too."

"Even if you can fit," the tall, brawny man countered, "how will you get Bojko out? The rocks are jagged and will cut you. And he is at the bottom. Will you then step on him? There is no room to reach down."

"He's right!" the boy's mother concurred, nervously wringing her hands. "We tried to send a rope down. My Bojko tied it around his waist, but when we started to tug, the rope got cut on the rocks, and he fell back in."

Kai lay flat and peered into the stony fissure. The inside was dark, and the bottom was too far down for her to see, given the angle of the afternoon sun. "Does anyone know how deep it is?"

"Pretty deep," came a small voice from below. "But I can see your funny head." His words prompted a smile.

"What are you thinking, Kai?" Gavril asked as he dropped into a crouch at her side.

She swiveled to a seated position and started unlacing the new boots Danika had given her. "Does anyone have any oil?"

"Yes!" The excited mother raised her hand. "But only one lamp full. I brought it in case it got dark before we made it back to town. Why do you want oil?" She gave Kai a puzzled expression.

"I will rub it on to make me slide easier." She reached up, and the baffled woman handed her the clay lamp.

"But like they said," Gavril argued, "how will you get him out?"

"Easy," Kai explained. "You'll lower me into the crack headfirst. I'll stretch down and grab him; then you'll pull me out by my feet."

"You aren't very tall," Zlatan observed. "What if you can't reach his hands?"

Kai gazed up at the impressive man. He looked like a real champion with a gleaming sword and noble bearing. He had arrived to rescue the child, only to discover he was too big to get to him. Could Frigg's observation have been right? Did heroes really come in all sizes?

She grinned. "We shall tie a cord around my ankle, and I'll crawl down until I reach him."

"And if you get stuck?" The big man Kai supposed was the boy's father asked in concern.

"Then you will drag me out." Throwing modesty to the wind, she yanked off her tunic and trousers so all she wore were her well-worn, linen under-breeches. Kai offered a silent prayer of thanks to Freya she was not enduring her courses that day, then rubbed oil all over her skin.

"You trust these strangers to pull you from a tiny crack in the rocks?" Gavril stared at her in amazement.

"I trust you," she replied in sincerity. "And I believe the child's father and mother are anxious enough to get him out that they would lend a hand. Then there's Zlatan's reputation as a hero to consider." She winked at him while sloshing oil over her legs. "He wouldn't want word to get out he left a Swedish girl stuck upside down in a jagged crevice, am I right?"

Zlatan rubbed his chin as he frowned at her, then relaxed his posture with a hearty laugh. "What a saucy little minx you are! And bold too. All right, I'll help."

Gavril and Zlatan collected a baldric and several belts from the group and fastened them securely together. Then Gavril buckled the strap around Kai's ankle, testing various movements of her foot to be sure it would not slide off. This was perhaps the first time Kai was thankful for her small breasts, though they had also made it easier for her the day she'd bared them in front of the *Dreki's* crew.

"Bojko," the boy's father called. "Someone is coming down to get you."

"When I reach for you, grab my wrists and hold on tight," Kai instructed the boy. She hadn't slathered the oil that far down her arms and had thoroughly wiped and scrubbed her hands with sand to be sure they were dry.

Peering into the narrow darkness of the fissure, she took a deep breath, then began her headlong crawl. Her racing heart was reassured by the powerful grip the men clamped to her ankles as she picked her way between sharp edges of stone. It was indeed a tight squeeze that required her to take shallow breaths.

"I can see you coming," the small voice sounded.

Kai felt the skin on her shoulder tear. Then there was a scrape to her breast and a cut on her thigh, which caused her to wonder how many lacerations the boy had.

When her feet cleared the opening, Gavril called down, "We're holding you by the strap now. Don't worry, Kai. I won't let it rub against the side."

His words were comforting, as she did not wish to die caught in a crack in the rock from blood pooling in her head. She knew being upside down would kill her before thirst or hunger could. Then she hit a snag as her hips seemed to be stuck. A mild panic flew through her as she realized she was being squeezed within an inch of her life. It was dark, the air hard to draw in, and she couldn't move.

No, Kai, don't do this! she scolded herself. *You've been in worse situations. You didn't give in to fear when the ship's hold was filling up with water, so don't do it now! Heroes don't panic—they think and act.* Wiggling her hips, Kai sucked in her abdomen a bit more and pushed out of the vise. Relief flowed through her as she hit a space wide enough to take in a full breath. Then she felt Bojko's hands in hers.

"Get my wrists, not my hands, sweet boy," she directed. He worked his fingers higher, and they latched onto each other. "Pull us out!" Kai yelled, hoping they could hear her.

Brimming with anxious nerves and joyful celebration, Kai held on tight while the men hauled her up by a strap around one foot. There were more scrapes and cuts, as she could not help guide her ascent and was at the mercy of tugs from above. At last, she sensed the rush of cool air over her feet and a powerful hand grasping her ankle.

23

The satisfaction of facing the danger and retrieving the little boy, of accomplishing a feat the bigger, stronger men could not, was a feeling like none Kai had ever experienced. The rush soared through her veins as she watched the mother clutch the child to her breast and kiss him all over. A tear of joy rolled down his brawny father's cheek as he hugged them both. *I did that—me! I've always wanted to really help people, to truly make a difference.* Sure, she felt proud, but beyond it rose a more intense emotion she couldn't quite identify.

"Now we should take you to a bathhouse and find a healer to tend your cuts," Gavril stated in pseudo-complaint. "I'm glad we'll arrive in Bilhyryn with a day to spare."

"Bilhyryn is where we live," the boy's mother announced. "You shall stay with us tonight and I'll take care of you, brave little woman."

Kai sat on the rock and beamed up at her; Gavril dropped her clothes on her, and they all laughed.

Kai quickly dressed so they could get back to town before the pitch of darkness. Bojko's parents introduced themselves as Vladislav and Jana, and said they had another son named Stanko. On the way to their house, Zlatan recounted his sundry adventures, and Kai described the temple of Uppsala. Before she knew it, they were at a dwelling much like Gavril's.

"I'll heat some fish soup to go with this morning's bread," Jana offered. "Then I'll put salve on Kai and Bojko's scrapes and cuts."

"Most kind," Gavril answered, and they took seats on the benches along the wall.

"So, Gavril, you are a merchant? I noticed your cart," Vladislav inquired. "And haven't I seen you in town before?"

"Indeed," he replied. "I come to Bilhyryn several times a year. And if I am not mistaken ..." Gavril tilted his head to the side and waved a finger in his direction. "You are a highly acclaimed weaponsmith; am I right?"

Vladislav beamed at him and puffed out his broad chest. "I run a forge and have been known to craft weapons."

Gavril nudged Kai and winked at her. "This little one is seeking a rare ore, Damascus steel. She is required to bring a blank shard to Yeats with her when she goes home, but we have been unable to find a single scrap of the metal. You wouldn't happen to know where she could get some, would you?"

Vladislav gave them a bashful grin and leaned forward on his elbows, casting a wary glance around the room. When he opened his mouth to speak, Kai cut him off.

"No. I did not crawl into the rock for a costly reward," she stated emphatically. "I did it to help Bojko. Anyone else would have done the same, except I was the only one small enough to fit. I cannot ask anything of you."

Kai caught his gaze and recognized the look of astonished bewilderment. His brows furrowed, and he sat back, assessing her with a critical eye. "Merchant, does she tell the truth?"

Gavril nodded. "It is what she does. She fought off three ruffians to defend my daughter not five minutes after she washed up onshore, half drowned and failing from thirst."

Jana, who could clearly hear everything from the other side of the room, pinned Vladislav with a sharp stare and slammed her hands to her hips. "Our son is worth far more to us than some silly metal, be it steel or gold," she announced. "The young woman could demand any price, and it would not be too high. Yet she asked for nothing and shimmied into a crevice no wider than your foot, without regard to her own safety, to pluck my precious Bojko from jaws of stone. She did not say, 'How much silver will you pay me to plummet headfirst into a dark hole.' No." The sturdy woman sliced the air with a stiff hand. "Give her what she needs, husband."

Vladislav offered Kai an apologetic expression. "I would never deny a benefactor fair compensation. And you, bossy woman"—he raised his gaze and pointed at her—"should know better than try to accuse me of being cheap and holding back from giving Kai what she requires. Did you not marry an honorable man? Or are you a foolish goose?"

She smirked at him with twinkling eyes and returned to stirring the soup. "That's what I thought," she replied.

"Kai, while the ore is sold or commissioned to be fashioned into a sword the moment I get my hands on some, I received a small shipment just this morning," he explained. "I haven't even had time to open the crate. It is over here by the fire, so nobody could steal it from my forge." Vladislav stood, took two steps, and ranted in dismay. "Jana, one would think you were daft from the day your mother discovered you lying under a cabbage leaf!" He motioned toward the box she had set the bowls and bread plate on.

"Why are you howling like an ogre?" she countered. "How was I to know 'twas not an empty crate? You keep promising me a proper table. You have two of them in your forge, but for our home? Bah! Everything for work; nothing for the family. Come now and eat. You can look at metals later, ja?"

Vladislav laughed, swept his wife into his arms, and smacked her on the lips. "You shall have a table," he declared, "before winter. Now," he pronounced, beckoning Kai and Gavril with a hand. "My Jana is a loud woman, but a fabulous cook."

"Who are you calling loud?" she countered playfully. "You should get a job standing at the pier hailing ships in from the fog."

Kai felt warm and fuzzy all over as she recalled her parents' similar banter from when she was a child. It made her wistful, and she wondered if one day she and Tove might act as this couple did.

"Can't you two behave while we have company?" their older son, Stanko scowled. "You are embarrassing me with your silly bickering." He picked up a bowl his mother had just filled and a hunk of bread to go with it.

"I want to hear more stories from the northland," Bojko chimed in as he nibbled from a tray of nuts and dried fruit as an appetizer.

Vladislav reached out a hand to muss Stanko's hair, but his son wiggled out from under it, looking at him with displeasure. His father only laughed.

"Do not be embarrassed of your parents, Stanko," Jana scolded him. "One day you will be a father and have sons who want nothing to do with you. Then what? Eat your dinner and be happy your brother is not still crushed in the earth."

Stanko plopped onto a bench and focused his attention on eating, as Jana passed wooden bowls to Kai and Gavril.

The soup was delicious, the salve soothing to Kai's broken skin, and the company delightful. While Jana was tucking Bojko into his blankets and furs to sleep, Vladislav pried open the crate. He pulled out a dozen bars of iron, some tin, copper, and phosphorous, and three blank rods of Damascus steel.

"Well, well, what have we here?" Vladislav lifted one from the straw filler in the crate and held up a gleaming length of the prize metal. "This is what you need—for a sword, perhaps?"

Kai's gaze caught the glint of firelight flash across the shiny surface of the alloy and she almost salivated. She held out a tentative hand, and Vladislav passed it to her. The long bar fit in her hands but weighed no more than a few pounds. She wrapped her grip around its end as if it was a hilt and extended the rod, slicing the air with it. She sensed an otherworldly glow lighting in her core as she handled the steel, imagining what it was destined to become.

She could hear the men's laughter as her eyes made love to a glorified piece of ore. "Alright then," Vladislav concluded. "A sword indeed. If you weren't leaving the day after tomorrow, I'd make you one, but it takes longer to craft a proper blade."

"Thank you, but I have someone to forge it," Kai answered without looking up from the steel bar.

"And I have two other blanks here to produce swords for the locals," he added. "None need know there was ever a third, which reminds me." He held out his empty hand.

Noticing what he was about, Kai returned the length of steel, regret tugging at her soul as she released it. "We don't want some opportunist to club you over the head, take this from you, and toss you overboard, now do we?"

"Oh." Kai hadn't thought of that. She had owned nothing of value before. "No."

Vladislav examined the bar. "Tomorrow I shall heat one end red hot and punch a hole through. When it has cooled, I'll fasten a cord to it so you can wear it underneath your tunic and cape, away from prying eyes."

"Which means you can't go around whipping off your clothes," Gavril added with a laugh. Kai blushed.

"I cannot thank you enough," she confessed. "This is a dream coming to pass for me. I never thought I would find it. I must have somehow gained the favor of the gods."

"It is interesting to watch how things play out," Gavril mused. "There is a word I have heard, kismet—what will be. Some say, 'One hand washes the other'."

"Exactly," Vladislav concurred. "You did me a great service, and now I try to do the same for you."

A tingle played all along Kai's battered skin. She couldn't wait to get home and show everyone. *The Damascus steel for my sword, one light enough I can wield it. Jerrik will train me, and everyone shall see my potential.* Though how Kai would manage to give her life for another and return from the dead, she hadn't a clue.

This voyage across the wide sea transpired without incident, and Gavril's captain friend saw to it that Kai wasn't bothered. Their arrival was met with excitement in the bustling trade center of Birka, where Kai found a fishing boat heading north. An icy wind chilled the evening air when it deposited her on the dock at Lagarfjord, where she expected to find Torsten in their winter home. No one had paid much attention to the fisherman and his small craft or his passenger.

The sun sat like an orange ball on the calm surface of the sea beyond the mouth of the fjord, before sinking out of view. It left in its wake a pale, iridescent light for Kai to find her way. Lagarfjord was a good-sized town with hundreds of residents, as it served as King Freyrdan's seat of power; however, few roamed the streets as it was presently dinner time. Kjell's forge was closed, as were the fish market, the potters', the tanners', and other craftsmen's shops.

Kai weaved through the wooden structures, making a stop by a yard house. A well-packed road led to the king's longhouse, with side paths splintering off to dwellings, garden plots, and storehouses. Several chickens not yet settled on their roosts pecked at seeds along the path, and a curious cat regarded her with faint interest as it groomed its paws. Someone's dog bayed at her passing, prompting its owner to scold it from behind a cracked door. Nervous to see everyone after so long and excited about the stories she had to tell, Kai stopped in at the one place bustling with activity—the alehouse.

A fellow sang and played the lyre while his comrade plucked the metal tongue on a jaw harp, vibrating its unique tone from inside his mouth while folks drank, laughed, or danced to their tune.

As she reacquainted herself with the familiar hall, an excited voice rang out. "Kai, is it really you?"

She pivoted to spot Rurik, a worker from Torsten's shipbuilding crew. The sandy-haired man, now sporting foam on his beard, sloshed half his ale from its cup as he bolted up and ran to her, stopping to stare in disbelief so he wouldn't knock her over.

"And I'm glad to see you, too, Rurik." Her grin lit up with enthusiasm. "Is the whole company back from Bàtrgørð? Are Torsten and Leiknir at our winter house?"

His mouth dropping like a fish's having a hook wriggled from its jaw, Rurik blinked, then ventured a finger to her shoulder. "Does everybody see her?" he asked. The crowd concurred. "So, you're alive!"

"Well, yes!" Kai chuckled. "Last time I checked."

"I have to tell everyone," he blurted. He offered her a one-armed hug while trying not to spill the rest of his drink. "They won't believe it—I don't!"

As he rushed past her, Kai grabbed his sleeve. "Where's Torsten?"

"Probably at your winter house, like you said. I'll bring the others. Wow, this is … incredible!"

Rurik having bounced away, Kai waved to the merrymakers, who gaped at her from around the room. "Hi. I'm home," she offered hesitantly, then she exited the establishment before the crowd descended on her to find out if she was real or a figment of their imaginations.

A silvery moon shed its light on her walk to Torsten's modest plank house. While he was an important man in their community and a regular guest in the king's great hall, they had always maintained a private residence in town. It was not rich or ornate, since such wasn't the stem-smith's style, and they spent half the year away at Bàtrgørð, yet it was a sound structure with a sod roof for added insulation. A plume of smoke wriggled skyward from the smokestack, warming Kai's soul with the pleasure of home.

She opened the door and strolled in as she had done hundreds of times in the past. Torsten and Leiknir glanced up from their plates where they sat at a small table at the far end of the dwelling; the food never made it to their mouths. For an instant, neither of them moved or made a sound, only stared at her in disbelief.

Kai felt suddenly insecure and gave them an apologetic look as if she was late to supper. "I'm home."

Leiknir sprang up and raced to greet her with an energetic hug. "You're alive! How can you be alive?"

She was struck at once by how he had grown. While still skin and bones, the lad was noticeably taller.

She hugged him back. "I suppose I have a story to tell you." When her gaze shifted to Torsten, she saw the tears rolling down his face. He rose more slowly, meandering his way across the room until his comforting arms enfolded her.

"Kai." He kissed her cheek and forehead with a sentiment she had seldom observed in her adopted father. "We mourned your death," he said. "We had a ceremony. How can it be? Then again, I don't care—the gods have given you back to us!"

"Oh, Torsten, Leiknir, I was never dead," she stated with assurance. "The raiders you sought to keep us safe from caught up with our party anyway, but they didn't kill me."

The door opened behind her, and a group of people burst in. Gasps and astonished expressions followed. Within moments, the small house was filled with friends and neighbors. Kai stepped back, deposited her bow and travel bag on the floor, and slipped off her luxurious, fur-lapeled cloak.

"Kai!" Tove covered her mouth as tears fell from her stunned eyes. Her parents and Stigr stood with her, and they all looked as though they'd seen a phantom.

Without hesitation, Kai threw her arms around Tove, pulling her body against her chest with unmatched ardor and relief. She showered her face with kisses, drinking in the scent and feel of her with a thirst like she had known the day she'd washed ashore in Varni. Remembering to not gulp in too much at once, she eased back and caught Tove's cheeks between her palms.

"I am so happy to see you, again, all of you," she added, casting a misty gaze around. "What?" she asked as they all stared. She lowered her hands as she tried to read the room.

Stigr was the first to find his voice. "We understood what a selfless and courageous thing you did to fight for Tove's freedom, and we sang songs of praise to honor you, but shortly afterward, a whaling craft stopped in and reported the terrible storm at sea."

"They discovered wreckage from the raiders' vessel," Kjell said. He swallowed a lump in his throat and took his turn to hug Kai. "They searched for survivors and found none. They brought us word all aboard had perished, and we were exceedingly sorrowful. I cried and offered your departed spirit thanks because, if not for you, 'twould have been Tove at the bottom of the sea."

"They did all drown when the ship broke apart," Kai confirmed, "but I grabbed a piece of the broken mast and rode it to a foreign shore." Her bright eyes dimmed as they all still stood about in shock. "I didn't die, everyone!" she reassured them. "I'm not a ghost."

"But we thought you had," Tove replied, haunted by an expression Kai couldn't quite interpret. "We were sure of it."

"Tove was beside herself with grief," Stigr explained. "As was I—as were all of us." He motioned to Kjell, Anika, Thora, Rurik, and the others squeezed into Torsten's plank house.

"Stigr and I comforted each other," Tove said. She took a step back and slipped an arm around his waist. "We were wed last week."

The blow was like a harpoon to her chest, yet Kai did her best to hide her disappointment. She had always known Tove would eventually marry, but she hadn't expected this to be her welcome home.

24

Gnóttdalr, three weeks after Baldr's return

Solveig took her time wandering from the yard house. Although an icy rain fell accompanied by swirling gusts, she invited the stinging sensations.

"What are you doing out here?" Ingrid bellowed from the back doorway. "Come inside this instant!"

Plodding through mud toward her mother, Solveig responded innocently, "I'm wearing a cloak." This was true, even if soggy wool didn't provide the best protection against the elements.

Ingrid bundled a blanket around her shoulders as she tugged her daughter into the family's area of the longhouse, away from those keeping warm in the great hall. "You should have just used your chamber pot. What were you thinking?"

Solveig shrugged. "Then a servant would have to get cold and wet taking it out."

Her mother shot her an impatient look. "Bodil and Fiske possess greater resistance to illnesses than you, my treasure. Are you trying to catch your death? You know it is not what Ragna would have wanted."

She let out a sigh and pulled the blanket her mother had draped her in tighter. "I suppose."

Inside the residence, Mist rubbed against Solveig's shin and peered up at her with an adoring gaze. Solveig chose to ignore the devoted expression, though a part of her longed to invite her pet behind her defenses.

"Come out and join other people," her mother encouraged. "Sit by the fire and dry yourself. Baldr needs more Hnefatafl practice."

"Baldr doesn't want to learn. He loses interest quickly, for his mind is on other things," Solveig answered. "As is mine."

They stopped in front of her bedchamber door. Ingrid unwrapped the blanket, removed Solveig's wet cloak, and hung it on a peg. Then she straightened the dry cover back around her shoulders. "You are spending too much time alone, just as your father did after Herlief. It isn't healthy. The kingdom needs you. *I* need you."

Solveig winced, then took a stabilizing breath. "I realize I have been shirking my responsibilities, and for that, I am sorry. I simply don't feel like doing anything. Can't everyone get along for a few weeks without me? It isn't as if I accomplish important tasks, anyway. Sylvi returned with Karina to spend the winter in Jarl Bjorn's longhouse, so I don't have to entertain her. It is good my sister has a close friend and mayhap she'll find a husband there. But my best friend is gone, and I have no interest in finding another. Give me an assignment and I will perform it, but don't ask me to be sociable."

"Oh, sweet child." Ingrid hugged her and kissed her cheeks. "You are like your grandmother in so many ways, yet so different in others. I wish I knew how to console you. I wish so many things."

The look of desperate longing in her mother's eyes was almost powerful enough to dissolve the fortress Solveig had constructed around herself. She realized Ingrid loved her with an unyielding fervor, and she wished she could be and do and give her what she wanted, if only to light a smile where anxiety now reigned, but she couldn't. Solveig had determined this was the last time her heart would be broken.

Asbjorn, dismayed over the mission's failure, had gotten drunk the night they returned and had staggered to his feet to announce to the entire kingdom that whoever could slay the giant would win his daughter's hand in marriage. Solveig was sickened by the idea that the best she could offer Sogn was to act as a prize for the warrior who displayed the skill and bravery to rid them of the looming menace. She'd drunk to excess herself after hearing his proclamation.

As usual, he had come to her the next day to apologize and explain how vital solving this issue was to the security and well-being of all. She quickly pointed out to him how she had been right about Troels, and he conceded the matter. Solveig could now only pray someone worthy would slay the monster. Love was far beyond the point now; she only needed a husband she could tolerate.

Why can't I wield a sword and spear and fight the jötunn *myself? Why does my body betray my spirit? Do the gods take pleasure in laughing at me?*

In her darkest moments of despair, Solveig had considered taking her own life. She was as knowledgeable with herbs and plants as any grædari and was certain she could make her death appear to have been from natural causes, given how often she battled sickness. But she and the gods would know; such was a coward's way out, and the descendant of Sigrid the Valiant was no coward.

"I wish many things, too, Mama," she answered and kissed Ingrid's cheek. "I suppose what is to be will be. I saw Vidar up and around this morning. I'm glad he has recovered from his injuries. How are the others faring?"

"Gafdan is adjusting to the loss of his arm, though I fear his spirits are no more vital than yours."

"I should visit him," Solveig realized. "Perhaps I can inspire him despite my melancholy."

"You could indeed. Osmin has taken Arvid into his home to care for him and manage his progress. He still suffers from a great fever as often follows deep wounds and Osmin doesn't know if he will survive, though we are hoping for a full recovery." Something gleamed in Ingrid's expression as she stared past Solveig. "I want answers."

Her mother's resolve and her line of thinking sparked the slightest sensation of interest in Solveig's grief-weary soul. "So do I," she realized. *I do want to uncover exactly what those two were up to and why it went so wrong for them.*

"There is much to do before the snows set in," Ingrid announced, returning to a more formal matter. "When this awful freezing rain stops—if it ever does—I'll need your aid and expertise with plants. In fact, the people I sent out gathering have filled one of the pantries already. Are you up to coming with me to sort through the leaves, berries, mushrooms, and others to cull those which aren't good to eat? Then we must devise a way to preserve them. It will be odd not relying on grains and porridge this winter, and the raiders took all the meat we had preserved. Baldr has been overseeing a team of hunters, but I worry it will be impossible to restock as many pounds of meat as were lost. Praise all the gods they didn't take the hay. It's one thing to scrape and scrounge and concoct a change of diet for the people, but without the hay, our cattle and flocks would surely starve."

Her mother had valid points as always. "Certainly, Mother. I can help." At least she was being asked to use her knowledge rather than her ability to bear children as a means to protect and preserve the kingdom. Queen Ingrid was right: too much sulking about alone only made her feel worse. Mist wagged her tail in hopes of a smile Solveig could not yet bestow. While Solveig wasn't ready to feel good, and even wondered if she ever would again, she could settle for feeling useful.

That night the temperatures dropped, and all the wintery mix of the day turned to ice. Solveig dined with her family in a hall filled with warriors, their wives and lovers, and several indigents who had no other warm place to go. Farmers and herders had gathered their cows, pigs, goats, sheep, and chickens into barns and lean-tos while craftsmen and townspeople who owned but a few animals brought them into their houses. Cleaning up after a goat was far better than losing years of its milk and cheese. Fortunately, their great hall merely overflowed with humans and a few dogs to tidy the scraps and crumbs from the meal.

Geirfinnr tried to engage Solveig in light conversation and lively banter, and she appreciated him for it. However, every time she gazed into the face of her friend—Ragna and Herlief's friend, too—a pitiful ball of sadness formed in her stomach. He had returned alive from both battles while her big brother and her lover had not. It wasn't Geirfinnr's fault, and he had done nothing wrong to make her feel this way. He had even been slashed in the side in the clash with King Rundrandr's raiders, and she was exceedingly relieved he had recovered. Still, seeing him made her think of Herlief and Ragna and miss them even more. She excused herself far earlier than he or her mother would have liked and shut herself in her chamber.

Solveig stirred the embers of her hearth to life and laid on several pieces of kindling and a fat log to last through the night. Hanging her dress on a wall peg, she sat and brushed her hair, as was her habit. She should be washing her face and hands, picking her teeth and rinsing her mouth with mint water, observing all her beauty rituals. After only a few strokes, she set the brush aside, too dismal to continue. An eerie light from the fire danced around the room and Solveig settled under her covers, feeling utterly alone. Ragna was gone, and Solveig saw no path to ever reach her again. A princess who'd never seen battle would not be ushered into Valhalla to sit at Odin's table, and Solveig could not fathom the possibility of trying to drag Ragna away from the reward she deserved and surely took such pleasure in.

"She is lost to me forever," she whispered to the shadowy, flickering lights. "Grandma Sigrid, is this how you felt when you lost Elyn?" After a silent pause, Solveig considered the question. "No. You were partners for decades, raised my mother, experienced countless adventures at each other's sides. You grew old together, like Mother and Papa, while I was only with Ragna less than three years. She only confessed her love for me right before—"

Her eyes clenched shut, and Solveig fought back the nightly tears. "Ragna, can you see me, hear me?" she ventured. "Do you know how I miss you? But... I don't wish to make you sad. No. You are with Odin and Thor now, with Herlief and all the elite warriors. You feast with Great-Grandpa Olaf and many ancestors. You should not be looking down at Miðgarðr to be burdened with woe. Somehow, I must find a way to let you go—not to forget you, but to release the loss I feel each time I picture your face or hear your laugh. I long be able to remember you with joy, not like this."

A subtle word formed in her mind. *Time*. While no voice was attached to it, she remembered when she was a little girl, excitedly chasing after Grandma

Sigrid with a tiny wooden sword, calling, "Let me come with you! I am ready for an adventure."

Sigrid would scoop her up, toss her in the air, and catch her with a grin. "In time, little beauty. But not yet. Everything in its time."

Solveig imagined it may take more than time to heal her crushed spirits. It may take a miracle.

As she drifted into sleep, Solveig found herself in a strange dream. A blacksmith laid a red-hot length of metal on an anvil and hammered it with powerful strokes. He was no one she knew, nor did Solveig recognize his shop or the town. The clanging of iron striking steel reverberated through her, and she could sense the heat from the forge. The vision shifted, and a gray-bearded man in a wolf-skin mantle used an etching tool to carve runes into the finished sword. He passed it to a woman whose face was hidden, and she pronounced a blessing over the shining blade. "For an unexpected hero," she said. "What everyone claimed to be impossible is now manifested in our presence." When she saw a woman's hand grip the hilt, Solveig burst awake.

She sprang up in bed, breathing hard, excitement building through her core. *It's me! There is still a chance I can do what everyone insists I cannot!* But who were these people in her dream? She never saw herself take the sword, only a woman's hand. "My eyes!" Solveig blinked and rubbed her eyes before glancing around her bedchamber. Nothing had changed. In the dim light of the embers' glow, she could easily distinguish her hands, her blankets, the items on the little stand beside her bed, yet across the room, the walls and what hung on them remained blurry and unfocussed.

Never mind, she told herself, still brimming with hope. *It could happen later with time. I should try to increase my physical strength. For years everyone has said, 'Let me do that for you,' and, 'I will carry the heavy basket,' but no more. I'll practice lifting weighty things, slowly at first, then increasing the load little by little. Time. I must make time my friend rather than my enemy. No one will hunt the jötunn during winter, and by spring I could have developed muscular arms. If I kill the giant, I need wed no man, for I will have won my ow n marriage rights!*

Solveig didn't bother with the details, such as the fact that most women of Norvegr already possessed such rights. Certain duties were expected of women in noble houses, though, and marriage to an equally important family was among them.

Invigorated by the revelation of her dream, Solveig could not fall back asleep. *I must stop listening to what everyone tells me I cannot do and start believing in my vision. It will not be easy, and with winter I may fall ill again. No—see how I already slip back into my old way of thinking? I must repeat, 'I am strong' over and over until I believe it myself.*

25

Ingrid awoke to banging noises coming through the wall from Solveig's room. Alarmed and fearing the worst, she threw off her blanket, snatched a cloak to cover her sleeping shift, and rushed out. Asbjorn called after her, "What's wrong?"

"I'm going to find out," she replied from the hallway. She barged into her daughter's room with a harried look of confusion. "What in Miðgarðr are you doing in here?"

Solveig looked nothing like a princess at the moment. She wore a pair of Baldr's trousers, cinched around her smaller waist with a piece of rope, and a moss-green tunic Ingrid never recalled seeing anyone in the household wear. Her daughter's lovely, brunette hair tied back more closely resembled a horse's tail than her trademark tresses. Her arms were piled high with baskets spilling half their contents to the planks beneath her feet, yet she replied innocently, "I am rearranging my room."

A glance around confirmed the entire chamber stood in a state of disarray; nothing was where it had been and hopefully not where it was intended to end up either. "You're... but... Here, put that down and—" Ingrid's gaze shot to the bed, now piled with clothing and wall hangings, as well as a big bundle of smiling fur. "I told you not to let that dog on your bed!"

"Well, she has to be there, so she'll be out of my way," Solveig said, as if it were the most logical of statements.

"Honey, let me get some help for you." Ingrid moved in to take the baskets from her arms. "You shouldn't exert—"

"No!" Solveig whirled the bundle away from Ingrid's reach. "This is my project, and I'll conduct it my way."

"But Solveig, how will you move the heavy dressing table or the bed? This trunk? Or—good Odin's beard, the bathing tub!" Ingrid was thrilled her daughter seemed to be pulling out of her despondency, yet she did not want her to strain a muscle or crush her foot dropping something on it.

Setting down her bundle on the immovable-looking trunk, Solveig pivoted to her with a devilish smile. "You must learn not to worry so much, Mama. I am, after all, a grown woman. And if you hadn't noticed, I'm no invalid. I intend to build up my strength over the winter, so you may as well become accustomed to me doing things for myself."

Ingrid eyed her suspiciously. This fresh burst of energy lifted her spirits, yet it also gave her cause for concern. Just what was going on in her daughter's unpredictable brain? There was a reason she beat everyone at the strategy game of Hnefatafl. She could ask her directly but supposed she wouldn't receive a truthful answer. No. Ingrid would have to figure out this new scheme of Solveig's on her own.

"If you are planning to do more for yourself to keep occupied, perhaps you will give some thought to your personal appearance," she quipped. "It wouldn't kill you to brush your hair."

Solveig laughed and brushed a kiss to Ingrid's cheek. "What good would it do until I have completed my project? Don't worry; I'll be presentable by dinnertime."

"Just promise you'll ask for help if you need it," Ingrid insisted. "There's no shame in accepting a helping hand."

"I promise," Solveig said and turned her mother's shoulders toward the door. "But it may take me all day."

Having been bustled out of her daughter's room, a warm sensation lit Ingrid's heart. *She laughed!* For the first time since Baldr had returned with word of Ragna's death, Solveig had laughed. Ingrid didn't care what had gotten into her; she was simply overjoyed her daughter showed a sign of life returning to her spirit. *And she promised to join us for dinner tonight. I must make a few arrangements.*

Ingrid whisked back into her chamber to find her husband contemplating getting up. "What was the banging about?"

"Solveig is alive again," Ingrid beamed, selecting a dress from the wall peg. "She has embarked on a project to rearrange her room."

"By herself?" he frowned.

"Yes, and we shall indulge her as I indulged your drinking," Ingrid declared. "But now you are king again, and there is much to be done before we are snowed in up to the eaves."

"Yes," he concurred. "I am going with Baldr today to see our longboats lifted from their moorings and secured in dry dock. A few fishermen plan to overturn their vessels on the shore in case fair weather allows them a few more days to fish. While our harbor is not beset by storms every winter, I would rather have to take a boat down if we need it than have it damaged."

"Wise planning," she said and selected a tunic and clean gambeson for him to wear. "Now I have some planning of my own. No feast tonight, as we are conserving rations, although I want some entertainment. I'll let it be a surprise for when you and Baldr return."

"I love Baldr," Asbjorn stated as he pulled off his white sleeping tunic, revealing a broad, hairy chest rife with scars and muscles alike, along with an expanding belly. "I am proud of him and believe he will be a fine king one day. And I don't want him to think my months of lamenting Herlief's death indicated otherwise."

"Oh, Asbjorn," she sighed. "Not at all. Baldr loved Herlief, too. He understands, yet it would be good if you said these words to him as well."

The king pulled the tunic she had given him over his head and then wrapped on the red-and-yellow gambeson displaying the colors of Sogn. "You are right, and I shall. But he isn't Herlief—jovial, funny, charming in his manner. Baldr may even make a better king, and yet..."

"It is all right to miss and still love the son you lost, husband; I do. The key, and what I hope for you and Solveig, is to remember those we lost with joy rather than sorrow. You still have three admirable children, while some poor fathers have only worthless offspring," she added with a chuckle.

"Yes, well, with your help, mayhap we can rise to the occasion." Asbjorn took Ingrid's hands and touched a kiss to her lips. "By Odin's eye, if you aren't still the most beautiful woman in the kingdom!" Ingrid blushed, always pleased by his praise, yet in her estimation, Solveig had indeed surpassed her.

Solveig hurt in places she hadn't known she had after a day of physical labor, and still, she felt exhilarated. She would not mention her dream to anyone—not yet. To please her mother, and keep secret what she was doing, she chose her finest winter dress for the evening. Her hair was properly brushed and styled, her earrings and necklace proclaiming her station as much as the quality of her gracious manners as she glided into the great hall to take a seat at her father's table. It didn't matter that Geirfinnr occupied Ragna's place or Baldr had moved to Herlief's. She would not be concerned with who was missing or which new people ascended to their table; Solveig's focus was now set on her future, one she was determined to create for herself regardless of what others believed.

She smiled as a troupe of musicians played; Bodil and Fiske served wild-leaf salad and roasted boar. There was no bread to sop in sauces or sweet pastries for dessert, but it was a break from soups high in liquid and low in solid components. "What's the occasion?" she asked.

"I just thought a change of pace was in order," Ingrid responded, a twinkle in her eye. "I'd like to see your room when you've completed the makeover."

"I've finished. You're welcome to take a look after dinner."

The music stopped and Ivarolf, a local skald with flame-red curly hair and a trim beard, a man slight of frame yet with a thunderous voice, took the floor. All eyes turned to him in anticipation. Children in the hall bounced and beamed, and even Solveig felt an almost forgotten eagerness at the prospect of a tale.

"Ivarolf," Asbjorn addressed the popular storyteller. "Please share a tale with us."

"Aye, my lord." Ivarolf assumed a position on the dais from where all in the hall could see him. He placed a regal hand over his heart and bowed to Asbjorn and Ingrid. "What you are about to hear is as true a tale as any, filled with treachery, intrigue, action, humor, and a satisfying end. Listen now to the Theft of Thor's Hammer—and how he got it back," he added with a wink and a grin. The children bubbled, and Solveig settled in to enjoy.

"Mighty Thor, defender of the realms of both men and the gods, had a penchant for smashing in the skulls of giants with his legendary hammer, Mjölnir. One day, his weapon went missing—a terrible problem for Thor. The god of thunder searched high and low." Ivarolf added to his storytelling by pretending to search the hall for the missing magical weapon, even lifting a wide-eyed child to look under him, drawing laughs from the assembly.

"Then Thor received word Mjölnir wasn't lost but had been stolen... by a fearsome jötunn named Thrymr. This was unsettling news for all in Ásgarðr, for it was the magic hammer which granted Thor the ability to kill jötnar."

Solveig wished she had a magic hammer to kill their giant. *Could such a weapon exist in our world?* she wondered. *Why doesn't Thor come to our aid? Did Papa not make enough sacrifices to him?*

"The situation was so desperate, Thor beseeched both his trickster brother, Loki, and Freya of the Vanir for help to get it back. Freya owned many magical possessions, and one of them was a cloak of falcon feathers that gave its wearer the ability to fly. She lent it to Thor and Loki." Ivarolf lifted a cape from a wall peg near the door and flung it about his shoulders. "Loki volunteered to use it to fly off to *Jötunheimr* on Thor's behalf, for the inhabitants would all be driven to kill the giant-slayer on the spot."

After twirling about the central hearth, Ivarolf returned the cloak to its peg and continued his tale. "Loki found Thrymr, who admitted to stealing Thor's hammer. The jötunn agreed to return it on one condition: he wished to have the beautiful Freya brought to him to become his wife," he pronounced in dramatic fashion.

Praise Odin's eye our giant doesn't seem interested in gaining a human wife, or Papa would probably offer me up to him, too! Solveig's imagination conjured even more horrendous ways she could save the kingdom; no, slaying the monster was still her best option.

"Loki returned with Thyrmr's demands and he and Thor shared the proposition with Freya, who was so put off by the mere suggestion she wed some ugly brute from Jötunheimr, she flew into a fit of rage. I mean, really," Ivarolf extended his question to the women in the chamber. "Would you want to marry a foul smelling, ill-mannered, dotard of a jötunn?" They laughed, with disgusted faces and shook their heads. Solveig was feeling quite entertained.

"In fact, she was so furious, her anger rocked the halls of Ásgarðr, causing her illustrious necklace Brísingamen to fall the floor, and she stormed off. Then all the gods and goddesses of the Æsir joined in planning a way to retrieve Mjölnir, for without it, the jötnar may well invade their land. The guardian god Heimdallr proposed an idea so ridiculous, so preposterous, so outrageous—" pausing for effect, Ivarolf turned in a circle with a finger raised in anticipation—"that it just might work!"

"What was it?" asked a fully engaged young woman nestled on a bench between others.

"He proposed Thor should dress in a bride's clothing, wear Freya's necklace Brísingamen, which the giants would recognize, and pretend to be her. He could then attend the wedding ceremony, and at its conclusion receive the prize of Mjölnir. Well, at first, Thor completely rejected the plan, as you may suppose. 'I'll not put on a wedding dress and prance about the halls of Jötunheimr pretending to be Freya!' But Loki asked if he had a better idea. Alas, he had not.

"Loki disguised himself as Thor's maid, so he wouldn't feel so bad about being the only one wearing a gown and veil—which was necessary to hide his face. Together, the brothers traveled to Jötunheimr to be the guests of honor at Thyrmr's wedding." Ivarolf borrowed a scarf from an older woman in the crowd of spectators and draped it around his head as he marched in a circle around the warm, fiery hearth.

"The plan would not have worked, save for the fact jötnar are inherently dull-witted. Loki and Thor fooled them all, concocting excuses for the bride's odd manner. Finally, it was time for Thrymr to present his bride the promised gift—the hammer, Mjölnir, which he did."

Ivarolf pretended to grip a weapon's handle and raised his fist high. "Once Thor had his magic hammer, he threw off his disguise and bashed Thrymr over the head with it. He then swung Mjölnir with abandon at any giant in the room who opposed him, thus reclaiming his weapon and his place as guardian against the giants."

All cheered and clapped their hands. Ivarolf grinned and took a bow, and King Asbjorn's guests called out requests for the tales they wished to hear next.

Solveig was surprised to find she was enjoying herself. She knew in her core Ragna would wish it. Life did go on, even if it was different. However, Solveig was exceedingly tired, as she wasn't accustomed to the physical exertion she had been up to most of the day. That would change. She would mold and rework her body until it became what she demanded of it—or at least she would make what progress she could. *Thor had his hammer, but I shall have my sword.*

With the thought spurring her on, Solveig reached down and ruffled Mist's ears. "Come on, girl, time for bed." She excused herself, bade all a goodnight, and slipped away to her room to sleep.

26

Lagarfjord, Yeats, the day after Kai's return

Kai's homecoming had been a tremendous shock, as much to her as to everyone else. While everyone was overjoyed to see her, she recalled the pained expression on Tove's face long after everyone had gone home. She had focused her attention on Torsten and Leiknir, which was far easier to do than deal with her dear lover and friend—no, her *married* friend, who would no longer be her lover. Kai could imagine how Tove must have felt.

She thought I was dead, that I had taken her place for the slave market and then drowned at sea. Of course she was traumatized, and it makes sense she and Stigr would turn to each other for comfort. The three of them had been mates for years. *I just never imagined they would think I was dead. Didn't they know I'd find a way home?*

But Kai had to put it behind her now. Kjell had asked Haldor and Frigg to meet with them at his forge this morning. While she hadn't had time to tell all her stories, she had mentioned to him she had the ore. *I am excited about my sword,* she reminded herself as she strode through the thin layer of snow that had fallen during the night. Fall didn't last long and now, with the equinox far behind them, the daylight hours continued to shrink. *I wonder if I will have to wait until I meet all three conditions before Kjell forges it. Or maybe it just won't get its runes and blessing until then.*

She was glad for her new, warm cape, and with the unusual fur she drew many envious gazes on her way to the smith. *I'll need to go hunting often possible before the heavy snows arrive. Then Anika and Thora can help smoke the meat and I'll give them each a portion. I'll take the hides to the tannery because I'll want a new and still warmer coat and boots for winter. The ones Danika gave me are nice, but they're better suited for warm weather.*

Kjell's blacksmith's shop dominated a corner in the heart of Lagarfjord. A ribbon of smoke twirled from the top of the soot-stained stone chimney belonging to his impressive forge, complete with its attached bellows. Kjell, Haldor, and Frigg stood around a massive iron anvil and water vat in the center of a stoop connected to the main building of his shop. The A-frame roof was perpendicular to the main, steeply pitched top of the structure, presenting a partly open-air alcove where the smoldering work took place. A split-rail fence encompassing the small yard served to discourage animals from roaming into the potentially hazardous space. It was cluttered with barrels and crates of coal and charcoal, which could produce greater heat than a wood fire. One animal was always welcome there, though, and a fat, puffed-out orange cat and curious green eyes stared at Kai from her niche beside a corner support post.

"Did you bring it?" Kjell asked with a rare spark of enthusiasm in his gaze. Kai nodded and reached inside her cloak to pull out the blank hanging from its cord. He grinned. "Come inside."

Kjell ushered them through, and everyone took seats around a roughly hewn table. Heavy iron tongs, a short-handled shovel, a thick leather apron, and various styles of hammers hung on the plank walls, along with a few shields, axes, and other implements. A small, vent-sized window at one end let in light and fresh air, while several candles on the table afforded more illumination.

When Kjell held out his hand, Kai lifted the cord over her head and handed him her precious metal bar. His eyes gleamed as if they rested on a beautiful woman's form. "I can scarcely believe it. Tell me again how you came by this?"

"A child had fallen into a narrow crevice, and I was the only person around who was small enough to squeeze in and pull him out," Kai recounted. "It turned out the father—Bilhyryn's weaponsmith—was the only man in the area who could acquire the steel. His wife insisted he give it to me as a reward, but I think he was going to anyway."

"Yes, I can fashion you a superior sword with this," Kjell boasted. "But we shall add more. Even with the bog iron common in these parts, I've learned that infusing the weapon with bone ash increases its strength."

"I have brought a worthy specimen," Haldor said, and he placed a long bone on the table. "This is a femur from Sven Skull-Splitter, a famed warrior from my father's generation. After performing the proper ritual, I retrieved it from his burial mound. It will infuse the sword with his powerful spirit."

Kai marveled at the bone, and Kjell laid the piece of steel beside it. "I shall incinerate the bone and stir its ash into the molten steel ore you have supplied. I'll need to measure the breadth of your palm and the length of your arm to fashion the blade to your proportions, so it won't be too long and awkward for you to wield."

"But..." Kai hesitated. She wanted her sword, no doubt, yet she hadn't completed her tasks. "What about the other two conditions the gods laid out? I still must accomplish them."

She heard Frigg chuckle from behind her veil before her hand extended across the table to rest on Kai's. "You already have, dear."

Kai's jaw dropped. "When? How?"

"Little warrior," Haldor addressed her, catching her attention. "When you fought on the beach to win the right to take Tove's place among the captives, you, in fact, gave your life for hers."

"We knew it the instant you stepped into their boat," Kjell agreed. "Your unselfish nature spurred you to save my daughter by any means necessary, even sacrificing your own freedom."

"Thus, you met the second condition proving your strength of heart," Frigg explained.

"But I haven't returned from the dead," Kai protested.

Frigg responded with a gentle reminder. "Do you not recall how I told you the words of the gods should not always be interpreted exactly?"

"Believe me when I say you returned from the dead," Kjell assured her. "All reports stated the raiders' shipwreck left no survivors. One of our fishing vessels was assailed by only the edge of the storm, and the fisherman attested that never in his forty years had he encountered waves so high. We all believed you had perished, and we even held a funeral ceremony for you."

"Yes, Torsten said. Still..." Kai's words faltered as comprehension sneaked up on her.

"You have proven the favor of the gods rests on you," Haldor declared, "not only by surviving the storm but days adrift at sea. Then what do you do but continue to put yourself in harm's way to defend and rescue strangers? Such is the quality of honor and valor you demonstrate. You shall have your champion's sword, Kai. I'll carve on the runes and Frigg will bless it with her magic touch. Where it may take you is another matter, for those who would submit themselves to the fate of a champion often become as leaves in the wind, blown by the gods to where they are needed."

"You came to us with a dream of becoming a shieldmaiden," Frigg said in a sage tone, "yet I suspect such is not in your future, at least not in the way you may have envisioned it. I see a great battle coming, but not one fought within the shield wall, shoulder to shoulder with your fellows. It is like piercing a fog, and I can only catch a glimpse. Perhaps once you hold your finished sword, I may see it more clearly."

Kai was astonished, confounded, and erupted with such joy and excitement she actually bounced in her chair, countenance radiant. "Thank you! I, I... thank you!"

Kjell's mouth broadened into a grin. "You deserve this, Kai. It makes my heart glad to see it come to pass. Now, I must get started. The process will take at least a week. My goal is to craft the most excellent blade I've ever made. Oh, and Tove wishes to speak with you alone. She has gone off past the stream to the meadow where you pick blackberries. Don't let her tarry there too long, as winter is trying to announce itself."

While thoughts of Tove's marriage dampened her spirits, they were too buoyant to be quenched. Kai nodded. She wished for a moment alone with Tove too.

Kai strolled along the path out of town, past animal sheds and storehouses, until the buildings of Lagarfjord were but acorns clumped along the shore. The clouds overhead threatened more snow, and a chilly wind caught the edge of her cloak. There, seated on a fallen log near the perimeter of the forest, sat a frightened-looking young woman with her navy hood pulled over her light brown hair, hugging herself against the cold.

"Good morning, Tove," Kai greeted her as she approached. Tove glanced up with a haunted expression.

"I don't know what to say," she opened. "I couldn't sleep all night for thinking about you, trying to process everything. You're alive."

Kai sat beside her, and Tove threw herself into her arms, weeping.

"Listen to me," Kai instructed her as she caressed Tove's back. "You have nothing to feel guilty about. I wanted to take your place; I needed to take your place. It turned out to be pivotal to my destiny. I couldn't imagine losing you. I had to do everything in my feeble power to ensure your safety because—" Kai stopped to wonder why. "I love you," she repeated as she had freely done on other occasions, "and yet it was more than sentiment that fueled my actions. I wanted to prove myself worthy of some higher calling. I hope I would have done the same for anyone, but because I love you, it was easy."

"I thought you were dead." Tove lifted her head to peer into Kai's eyes. "We all thought you were dead."

A ghost of a smile crossed Kai's lips. "So I've been told—many times. Here is another thing for which you are blameless." She wiped away Tove's tears with a caress. "It's natural that you and Stigr turned to each other. The three of us have been best friends for years. You always wanted to marry and have a family—who better to choose than someone you know and are comfortable with? Thinking about making my way back to you was often the strength I needed to endure the hardship, and while part of me is disappointed, the news of your marriage was not entirely a surprise. I missed you, Tove. It felt like a constant ache in my side. Now..." As Tove's eyes welled up again, Kai leaned forward and kissed her forehead. "Now I will be happy for you."

"I missed you too. Kai, I feel so torn," Tove admitted. "You sacrificed everything for me, and I couldn't even wait a year. I was so lonely and grief-stricken. I loved you so much, but now I love Stigr, too; do you understand?"

Kai brushed back an errant lock of Tove's hair, studying the sincerity in her expression. "I do. And the odd fact that I am not more distraught over your marriage tells me many things. One is that true love isn't selfish, but only wishes happiness for its recipient. Another is that while I found endless joy and affection in our relationship, there is something else that means more to me."

"Your destiny?" Tove guessed. "I've always known how you longed to be a warrior, though no one took you seriously. You kept asking to be trained and were always brushed aside." Tove's tears stopped falling as she gazed into Kai's face. "Now they will no longer discount you."

Kai nodded, a gleam forming in her eyes. "Your father is crafting me a champion's sword like no other. I'm so excited and can't wait to hold it in my hand. The metal is strong and light—light enough I can swing it with ease. And I have you to thank."

"Me?" Tove started at her remark.

"Yes, you." Kai smiled and brushed a friendly kiss to Tove's parted lips. "If you were not so lovely and desirable, the raiders would not have wanted to take you back with them. And if you had not been my devoted companion, I may not have loved you enough to fight them to take your place. Without their ship carrying me south, I may never have found the Damascus steel, nor met the other requirements of the gods."

Tove peered at her in curiosity. "You never told me what those were."

With wonder in her heart at how events had unfolded, Kai confessed, "To give my life for another, and to return from the dead."

She kissed Tove's lips one last time, then rose, guiding her friend to her feet as well. "Kjell doesn't want you to stay out in this cold." She wrapped an arm around the taller woman and began a slow walk toward town. "Isn't it interesting how events we see as tragedies can sometimes work out for good?

You get the family you wanted, and I my hero's journey. It will be hard for me to see you with him for a while. Just know I will always love you and be your friend. Somewhere out there is a woman who doesn't want a husband, and I shall find her. Wish me luck?"

Tove turned and hugged Kai. "And I'll always love you, too, my valiant one. I do wish you luck, though I doubt you'll need it. I wish for all your dreams to come true."

27

Lagarfjord, two weeks later

Dressed in a hand-me-down brown gambeson and dusky woolen trousers, Kai danced along a cloud of elation as she trained with Jerrik. Strapped to her left arm was the shield Kjell had made for her, which was unlike any other warrior's. With a bit of the leftover Damascus steel, he had hammered out a thin, silver strip and fastened it into place around the wooden body of the rönd, with a matching shield boss in its center. He had engaged an artist to paint Yggdrasill in white over a sky-blue field, the Life Tree's branches reaching above the meridian and its roots stretching out below. It was such a thing of beauty, Kai almost hated to spar with it. In her right hand, she gripped Stinnr, her singular sword, inscribed with runes along its fuller groove.

Jerrik had introduced her to the spear and corrected some mistakes she made with the axe—the only hand-to-hand weapon with which Kai was familiar. He didn't need to instruct her in archery, as many considered her a master with a bow already, so most of their time together was spent on sword and rönd.

"Your shield is not only for blocking," the renowned warrior said. "While vital in that regard, you can also use it for offense." He demonstrated by pushing her off-balance with his rönd, then flipped it horizontal to the ground and thrust his sword underneath it. Kai, regaining her footing, hopped out of its reach.

"I see."

A few interested individuals had braved the icy drizzle to watch as Jerrik schooled Kai on King Freyrdan's training grounds inside his walled estate. While Kai hadn't caught a glimpse of the king, she was ever aware he could be watching. She did not wish to make a fool of herself with simple mistakes.

"And where you place your feet is at least as important as how you swing your blade," Jerrik continued the lesson. "Put your weight on your back foot for a defensive stance and on your lead foot for attack. And always stay on the move to keep your foe guessing. If you just stand there, you invite your opponent to kill you too easily."

"I'm nothing if not spry," she quipped in reply. It was true. While thrusts, chops, and slices with a sword were all new skills to her, Kai was extremely agile and abounded with energy.

"Also, because of your size—and this is not an insult, merely a fact—it is crucial to maintain a proper stance so you can brace with your thighs and feet." Jerrik performed a stance with his feet shoulder-width apart, leaning into his front leg with the heel of his back foot just off the ground. "Otherwise, an incidental swipe could knock you down. Turn your diminutive height to an advantage. It is pointless for you to try and strike your enemy's head or neck unless he is already down, whereas a deep cut to his thigh can prove fatal in minutes. Look for unprotected places low on his body—yes, even there," he remarked with a chuckle when Kai's gaze shifted to his groin. "Now, let's try again. This time, you play the aggressor."

Kai raised her shield, struck her stance, and danced her way closer to Jerrik. She led with a shield ram, followed by a slash toward his thigh. "Good," Jerrik called, then pushed back. At his pressure, Kai pivoted away from the thrust, spun on one foot, and jabbed at his back as his momentum drove him past her. She pulled her movement so it wouldn't actually hurt him, but he sensed the contact. "Now you are using your most valuable weapon of all—your brain!"

"Jerrik, Kai." Torsten tromped through puddles to where they sparred, interrupting the lesson.

"Greetings, Torsten," Jerrik replied, lowering his rönd and blade. "I won't keep her out in this weather much longer. There are indoor drills we can practice as well."

"Frigg wants to talk to Kai," his brother reported in a serious tone. "I'd like you to join us as well. She is in her hut with Haldor. Do you know where it is?"

Kai knew Frigg lived a short distance from town because the solitude away from other people's thoughts allowed her more clarity when communing with the gods and spirits, while Haldor kept residence in Freyrdan's great hall at the king's request. Her two acolytes, Yrsa and Madlen, used to share her dwelling, but she had not gotten new ones since the shipwreck.

"Yes," he confirmed. "I'll meet you there shortly."

When Kai fixed an anxious gaze on Torsten, he answered with a smile. "Do not worry. Come and clean up to meet with her."

The five of them sat on skins spread around the dirt floor of Frigg's thatch-roofed, one-room hut. The space was warmed by a friendly fire, and the völva's full attention rested on the petite young warrior-in-training in front of her.

"I have been given a vision," she began. "I believe it comes from Freya, yet it could be from my namesake, Frigga, wife of Odin. A woman of substance has called to the goddess for aid. To the west, across the towering mountains, in the land of Norvegr, a kingdom faces great peril, though all is not as it appears to be. The princess of Sogn, hailed for her matchless beauty, needs a champion to slay a giant. I believe the hero, Kai, is you."

Feeling suddenly too warm for comfort, Kai shed her distinctive mantle and swallowed in hesitation. "Me?"

"In the vision, I saw you with the princess, a stunning woman with unusually dark hair," Frigg shared. "Her clothing was a brilliant blue with a white fur wrap about her shoulders. You wore armor provided by Sogn's king and you held Stinnr in your hand to ensure your victory. Alternately, I was shown a different version of events, one in which a great calamity befell this land. In that vision, both the king and the princess were cut down by many spears, axes, and swords, and the woman of substance cried alone in her great hall."

"How could I matter so much?" Kai asked. "Can no one else defeat this jötunn? I will surely go and do my best, yet I find it overwhelming that my presence alone could account for such a divergent course of events."

Frigg lowered her veil so she could lock eyes with Kai. While Torsten and Jerrik maintained their composure, Kai was certain by the vibrations she sensed that they had never seen the seer's face before. Frigg reached across and took Kai's hand. Turning it over, she traced runes with her finger onto her palm.

"Nothing occurs in a void," Frigg said. "In the affairs of men as in nature, each tiny plant and creature plays its part. If the worm had not made the soil fertile, the tree could not have grown. If the tree hadn't grown, birds and animals could not have made their home in it. Without the tree, the man would have had no shade from the heat and no birds and animals to eat. He owes it all to the worm.

"Every step we take, each word uttered, reverberates through the nine realms, resulting in untold possibilities. For example, had you wandered into a different camp as a child and been found by someone other than Torsten, how different your life would be," she explained. "Had you thought to turn left instead of right, to travel north instead of south, you could have been pressed into servitude, abused, or even killed, yet here you are. Some say the Norn order our steps; in truth, they only weave a framework, whereas we retain the power to fill in the details. I cannot see exactly what it is you are to do in Norvegr, only the fact that your presence will make all the difference."

"Kai's training is not complete," Jerrik voiced his concern. "By the spring thaws, she should be ready to embark on this mission."

Frigg returned her veil to cover her head and face, considering his statement. "Spring will be too late. The journey itself will take a moon's time. Kai must leave at once."

"And travel a great distance in winter?" Torsten balked at the suggestion. "Ships are not sailing as many harbors along the route are iced in. You cannot expect her to venture overland in the freezing dark. I'll not have it!" He laid a firm hand on Kai's leg as if to pin her to the ground.

"Torsten." Kai turned to him with calm determination. "I do not believe the gods have spared me from every disaster only to call me into death's embrace in a snowstorm. If Frigg says I must leave now, I shall leave now."

Torsten lowered his chin and shook his head in dismay. "I just got you back. Who will teach Leiknir to hunt?"

Kai smiled, leaned in, and kissed his cheek. "He can already hunt; he only needs more practice. Don't worry. All will be well. Tell me honestly," she demanded, "if a beautiful princess called for your help, would you not drop everything and go?"

A dry laugh escaped his lips, but he could not bring himself to look at her.

Kjell broke the silence. "You saved my daughter, whom you loved. I believe you can do the same for the princess of Sogn."

"Norvegr." Jerrik rubbed his beard in thought. "Isn't that where Sigrid and Elyn were from?"

Haldor, who hadn't spoken, answered, "Indeed. And I can give you a map to show the way."

Excitement stirred in Kai's belly. She may not have completed her training, but a sense of urgency compelled her to leave her home and family once more and travel to a foreign land. With a gleam in her eyes, she said, "Show me."

Ten days later, the settlement of Gjermund

Torsten had given Kai a pony and insisted she ride it rather than walk the long distance, for which she was very thankful. Going by Haldor's map, she followed a westerly trail north of a fjord cutting deep into the land and north of several enormous lakes. Few people traveled in winter, but she had come across several hunters and one hearty merchant and his wagon, from whom she purchased bread and ale.

Having started out with traveling rations, Kai used her bow for fresh game when she happened upon it enroute. She was glad Anika had finished sewing a warm coat for her from the moose hide she had provided. With it, her new fur-lined boots and her lynx cloak, she had not suffered from the cold, even when she had encountered a few snowy days. The most problematic thing about the trek was the shadowy gloom of half-night that clung around her during the so-called daylight hours and the total darkness she rode in the rest of the time.

Kai had brought an oiled canvas and some rope to string up a tent to sleep in at night, so she didn't wake up covered in frost. Among her other packed items were her shield and weapons, a tinder box, an iron cooking pot, her drinking horn, a change of clothing, some personal women's items, and the little brass Valkyrie figure Thora had given her. Tove had kept it when Kai had sailed away with the raiders and she had returned it to her with a tearful hug, saying, "Let her keep you safe on your journey."

"After fewer than two weeks, you should arrive at Gjermund," Haldor had told her, "a trading town where the Swedes' land meets Norvegr. From that point, veer south and follow the coastline around until you reach Sogn, which should take about another two weeks."

The long solitary march granted Kai time to think about many things, not the least of which was the heartache of losing Tove. *She isn't lost,* she reminded herself. *Things are just different now. Besides, you always knew it would happen.*

She tried to focus her attention on other things and found herself musing about elves, dwarves, ogres, trolls, giants, and all the creatures of legend she had never seen. *I'll get to see a jötunn for sure this time, and likely battle it.* The prospect was as exciting as it was terrifying, but such imaginings occupied her mind so she wouldn't find herself crying over Tove.

I am going to do something important, help a kingdom in distress. This is my chance to prove even a little orphaned girl can realize her dreams. Sometimes the idea was too grand for Kai to get her head around: *I am going to slay a giant. Me! Or will I make a tremendous fool of myself?*

The smell of smoke and animal dung reached Kai around the same time she beheld the glow of light from the village ahead. Relief and excitement wrestled for first place among her emotions as she kicked her pony to move faster. *Haldor said they speak the same language here, only with a different sound to their voices. I have a few coins with which to restock my provisions. I hope they have a bathhouse with hot water,* she thought as she raced down the road into the town.

It wasn't even dinnertime yet, but it was already dark as the winter solstice neared. Torches lit the corners of buildings or perched from door posts as residents sloshed through slush to go about their business. Kai dismounted and led her pony through the streets, looking for a tavern or stable to spend the night. She was met with curious glances, and the townspeople gave her a wide berth. She approached a tall structure with barn doors and a signboard displaying a horseshoe symbol. Looping her reins around a post, she knocked. A huge, dirty fellow in a leather apron pulled it open a crack.

"Help ya?" he asked.

"Yes. I am traveling to Sogn on the west coast of Norvegr," Kai replied. "I am looking for board for myself and my horse overnight and a shop where I can buy some food."

"You have coins?" He narrowed his bushy brows at her.

"I do." When his gaze shifted to her sword, his eyebrows shot up in astonishment. Impulsively, Kai clamped a protective hand around her hilt.

"I see," he answered in a hesitant tone. "There is a stall you and your pony could share, and the bakery opens early in the morning. By the dock you'll find a general supplier."

"Thank you kindly." Kai smiled but did not release her grip on her pommel. The big man nodded and pulled open the barn door, allowing her and her horse to enter. Then he pointed to an empty stall.

"There's hay and oats in the bin," he said. "Water in the bucket."

"Is there a bathhouse?" she asked hopefully.

He eyed her speculatively for a moment before astonishment flashed across his face. "You're a girl!"

Kai was getting used to the reaction, given her penchant for wearing men's clothing and now having short hair. While most men in her land wore their hair long, some cut it or shaved their heads, and most did not boast strands as long as a woman's.

She nodded and unsaddled her sturdy little steed. "I am Kai of Yeats, daughter of Torsten the shipbuilder."

"And you travel to Sogn in winter—alone?" The stablemaster scooped oats into her pony's trough, as if he needed something to do other than gawk at her.

"Is it so remarkable?"

"Well, yes," the man answered. "Did you plan to secure a spot on a ship going northwest?"

Excitement stirred. "Is there one?"

"No," he replied. "And you cannot follow the usual route along the coast. It isn't safe."

That was unsettling. "I was told to follow the coast. What is wrong with it?"

"There is a war going on. Fools cannot even pause their hostilities until spring like decent folks," he explained. "We've had a fishing boat and three trading vessels confiscated by one kingdom or the other and no one is venturing that way anymore. Also, any caravan or merchant's wagon that's tried to use the roads has been attacked. And you are only a young woman alone—even if you carry a sword. You may as well postpone your trip."

A sense of uneasiness morphed into alarm, and Kai's heart thumped in her chest. "I can't postpone," she declared. "It's critical I reach Sogn soon. Isn't there another route, one which will avoid this vicious feuding?"

He shook his head and tossed two forkfuls of hay in front of her horse. "Well, over the mountains, but no one tries such a thing in winter."

"Would the general supplier have a map?" she asked, thinking if she knew where to go, she could make it.

This question, beyond all her others, proved too much for the stable master. "You can't be serious! Do you have a death wish?"

Kai smiled and placed a coin in his broad hand. "No. And you wouldn't believe the trials I've already survived. You never answered my question about a bathhouse."

"No." He considered her with a speculative gaze. "The alehouse serves pickled herring and a decent stew, and they have a basin for washing hands and face. There's a yard house out back. But you don't want to cross the mountains. The snows are extremely deep, and storms blow up out of nowhere. There are wolves and bears."

"The bears will be in hibernation and wolves don't often bother people who don't threaten them." Years of hunting had taught Kai much about life in the wild, and surely Norvegr's creatures didn't differ much from those on her side of the peninsula.

"You aren't afraid?" He assessed her once more. "No, you aren't. Adventurers frequent the alehouse. Mayhap one will have a map."

"Thank you."

With her pony settled, Kai walked to the alehouse, which was hard to miss. After several hours, she had gained a hearty meal, a satisfying drink, entertaining company, and a map showing the way to Sogn through the mountains, which bypassed the war zone. The hunter she spoke with said her horse wouldn't be able to handle the rough terrain, and she would find no food for him in the highlands, so Kai sold the pony to the stable master the next morning and packed what she could easily carry. With her shield strapped across her back and using her spear as a walking staff, she set off into the frigid unknown.

The going was not so hard at first. The weather started out calm and the grade gradual. However, by the third day, when Kai had moved into the higher elevations, her situation deteriorated. Gales blasted between peaks and down through the passes with tremendous force, and there were no trees for her to grab and hold onto. She was also beset by continual near-darkness.

At times, when following the map brought her into a lower pass, Kai encountered trees and had wood to build a fire, along with some shelter from the elements. Yet, climbing uphill was grueling; going downhill, treacherous; and plowing through deep snow, exhausting. It felt as if she was dragging huge stones tied to her legs, and every step proved an exercise of her will. When the snow wasn't falling, it was whirling around in the air, stinging her eyes and blurring her vision. In order to keep her spirits up, Kai often thought of Frigg's prophecy and the princess who needed her aid, imagining what Sogn would look like.

She had supplies of traveling food, but one clear day she shot a mountain goat and made a hot meal out of it. Unfortunately, a pack of wolves smelled her kill and surrounded Kai and her small fire. They stared at her with yellow eyes and paced menacingly in patterns while awaiting their chance to strike. She counted seven, though there could have been more. Hoping they would be content with the meat and leave her alone, she hurled the carcass and all her uneaten portions as far from her campsite as her arm would allow and stayed awake for hours feeding her fire. When she no longer detected their presence, Kai packed up her belongings and struck out again.

It was difficult for her to keep track of time when clouds blocked her view of the moon. Kai supposed it had been twelve days since departing Gjermund when she reached the highest pass on the map—the one nearest Gnóttdalr before descending into lower acclivities. As if rising from nowhere, a severe storm assailed the mountainside, gripping Kai in its vicious rage. The driving force of the wind blew her down, and the snow became so thick she could no longer plow through it. Her feet slipped, unable to gain purchase, and the icy blasts stung like a swarm of bees.

Kai realized she must find shelter, or she would perish, yet there was none to be found. Between the darkness and swirling snowflakes, she could barely see anything. She had just struggled to her feet when a powerful gust flattened her into a hole her body had formed in the snow. Lying there, catching her breath, Kai had an idea. She dug a short path to a nearby outcropping, and piled up snow from her hole, packing it into walls to block the wind. She had a tent, but if she tried to erect it, the canvas would surely blow away. Kai curled up in a ball under her cloak while the blizzard besieged her.

Although the meager shelter she had fashioned did some good, Kai had become so chilled to the bone that she wondered if this was where her journey would end. She had never known temperatures so frigid, or weather so inhospitable. Yeats has mountains, but she had never climbed them. They received snow in winter, yet nothing so deep. She had thought her mittens, fleece hood, winter clothing, and fur-lined boots would protect her, but they proved no match for the extreme cold.

I was supposed to follow the coastline to Sogn, she lamented as she hugged herself. It didn't stop her shivering. *If I only had a fire!*

"Freya?" Kai called into the maelstrom. "Why would you save my life on countless other occasions only to send me here to freeze to death?"

The only answer was the whistling of the wind.

Giving up was the sensible course of action... simply drifting off to sleep and never waking up. It would be painless. *I might rejoin my family that all died from a fever years ago. It wouldn't be so bad.* Kai couldn't stop shivering and had long ago lost feeling in her extremities. *I've enjoyed a good life, had adventures... I got my sword.* Kai wasn't exactly afraid, only sad. After all, she was young. She wasn't supposed to die yet. *I wonder if Torsten and the others will hold another funeral for me.*

Suddenly, she recalled Frigg's vision. The image of the beautiful, dark-haired princess in distress flashed into her mind, filling her with a renewed sense of urgency. *She needs me! Frigg said if I wasn't there to face the giant, the princess, her father, and many others would die. I can't give up!*

"Freya? Odin? Thor or Tyr?" Kai ventured a glance upward. "Whoever is listening, I need help. Please do not abandon me."

Closing her eyes to protect them from freezing, Kai imagined a big, roaring fire blazing in her snow hut to keep her warm. Despite the icy chill, the white flakes and wind, she kept visualizing lively flames popping, warming her hands, feet, and face, thawing out her frozen flesh and bones.

After some time had passed, Kai began to experience some reprieve. Her shivering ceased. She thought she smelled smoke, heard the crackling of tinder, and she opened her eyes. She had to blink them a few times, because there before her was a proper campfire, with orange flames dancing over sticks and logs. She felt its heat radiate toward her, and she was overcome with relief. It was a miracle, a gift from the gods to keep her alive and sustain her with hope.

Kai was entirely amazed and basked in the comforting heat. With a heart overflowing with gratitude, she called toward the heavens, "Thank you, thank you!"

She sat marveling at the sight in appreciation until slumber overtook her, and Kai fell asleep. That night she dreamed of the beautiful princess of Sogn. In the dream, she had fallen in love with the woman, who returned her feelings. The elation brought on by their affection stayed with Kai until she awoke, tingling with bliss.

She opened her eyes to daylight. The storm had subsided. Invigorated by the fact she had survived, she looked toward the spot where the fire had been. There was only snow. Scrambling up, Kai crawled over to investigate. There was no burnt wood, no ashes, no melted spots from the heat, no indication a blaze had ever been there.

I don't understand, she puzzled. *It was here.* She patted the icy ground. "It was here," she repeated aloud. In bafflement, Kai packed up her things and continued her trek according to the map. Confounded as she may be, she had to take advantage of the break in the weather.

The going was easier without the blizzard and the path's slope wasn't too steep. As she walked, Kai pondered what had actually transpired. She was left with two possibilities, each more fantastic than the other. *Either the gods provided a magical fire to protect me from perishing on the mountain, or the power of my own imagination concocted the illusion of blazing logs and my belief that it was real convinced me of its life-saving warmth.*

With several days' travel still ahead of her, Kai focused on the terrain and reaching Sogn—and on meeting the fair princess she had been sent to help.

28

Gnóttdalr, on the winter solstice

"Come, Solveig, we don't want to be late for the Yule activities," Ingrid called from her doorway.

Solveig had spent a month trying to strengthen her muscles and increase her endurance. While she had made progress, it was slowed for a week by her annual cough and by a nose that ran with mucus when it wasn't stuffed up. Her mother had treated her with the usual teas and steaming mint water, along with insisting she stay wrapped warm in bed for the first three days of her illness. The ritual aggravated Solveig, making her feel like a child; still, she appreciated her mother and understood rest was necessary for a speedy recovery. Now she was back to normal in time for the solstice celebration.

Throwing her warmest fur-embellished cloak around her shoulders, Solveig struck out with her mother in the dim light of midday. Outside the gates of the palisade, the whole town had gathered for Osmin's performance of the blót, on this occasion sacrificing the Yule goat to Odin, which they would later consume in the evening's feast.

After the endless words of ceremony, Osmin finally slit the goat's throat and drained its blood into a bowl. "To the end of darkness and the return of the sun!" he proclaimed.

"Now, good citizens of Gnóttdalr upon whom rests the favor of the gods, it is time for the lighting of the Yule wreath," Asbjorn announced. The selected spot for these festivities had a clear downhill path passing through a rocky meadow to the waters of the fjord. Today, the frozen earth was draped in a shallow coating of white, with a few deeper drifts. The slight snowfall was typical for this time of year on Norvegr's west coast, which was kept warmer than other locales due to the sea channels and air currents. Winters were long, rainy, and dark, and could be scattered with pockets of extreme cold, but altogether they were milder than those experienced farther east.

The townspeople's faces glowed with joyful anticipation as they parted to two sides, leaving a broad path between them. At the top of the hill, Baldr and Geirfinnr held a massive wheel taller than the king, which had been adorned with green boughs woven around its rim. Solveig knew they had doused the wreath in oil to ensure it would burn bright once lit.

Asbjorn, with Ingrid at his side, held a torch to the colossal wheel. "I light this wreath in hope and anticipation of the sun's return." No sooner than it was ablaze, the king's right-hand men gave the flaming ring a shove, and it spiraled downhill through the cheering assembly.

A man wove his way through the crowd wearing a false beard, long and white, and a hooded fur coat. He carried a sack on his back and leaned on a tall, gnarled walking stick.

"Old Man Winter!" cried a child. The man turned to the little girl, and Solveig saw he was Ove, the owner of the alehouse dressed in the costume. Everyone knew Odin liked to walk the world of men in disguise; Old Man Winter was one of them. Every winter solstice, the Allfather would ride across the night sky and visit their homes. Norse children would leave their shoes out by the hearth on the eve of the winter solstice with sugar and hay for Odin's eight-legged horse, Sleipnir.

Solveig had long ago figured out her parents took the hay and sugar and left treats in her and her siblings' shoes, but she thought it was an enjoyable tradition. Even though there were no children in her family now, a few warriors' little ones lived in the great hall. She knew Ingrid would ensure a toy found its way into every shoe tonight.

"When do the games begin?" Ove, or Old Man Winter, asked. "I may have prizes for the winners in my pack."

There were games for children, youths, and adults, most of which were designed around some skill required in combat. Skipping rope and three-legged races were popular with children, footraces and obstacle courses with youths, while axe throwing, spear hurling, archery, and feats of strength dominated the adult events. Women brought out their best basketry, weaving, and embroidery for the elders to judge and reward the ones deemed the finest quality. Solveig had competed in the Hnefatafl tournament for the past five years, winning the last three. She looked forward to the competition Brandt the Fox may give her. The old man had served her father as a great warrior in years past, but battle injuries and age had rendered his body no longer fit for combat.

"It is the curse of the most successful warriors," he had told her once. "If one wins all his battles, he grows so old he can no longer fight them. What then can he do to gain the glory of Valhalla?" She had often wondered about this quote, turning its paradox over in her mind.

As the dim light waned, people began venturing through the gates and into the great hall for more Yule customs. Solveig, who with her mother had been cheering for Baldr in the target events, shivered when a frigid blast caught her in its icy breath. Glancing up, she noticed the low clouds rolling in over the white-capped peaks and realized it was not only the hour that darkened the sky.

As if reading her mind, Ingrid said, "I suspect we are in for a mighty storm tonight. Asbjorn." She stepped over to him, clutching the front of her cloak. "We should bring the games to a quick close. A snowstorm is on the way."

Her father frowned at the uncooperative horizon. Solveig agreed with her mother. Most weather rolled in off the sea, but this wind blew down the mountain from their north—a sure sign of a blizzard. They had been spared for the past several winters and were due for one, but why did it have to come on the solstice?

"Very well," Asbjorn grumbled. "Final round!" His announcement was received with boos, hisses, and complaints, yet the contestants must have felt the shift in the weather too.

"We'll see you inside anon, Papa." Solveig bade him farewell, and she and Ingrid headed for their longhouse.

The Yule celebration continued inside, where musicians played lively tunes to the rhythm of drums. Holly boughs and mistletoe hung over the entry and a green fir towered under the peak of the rafters. Solveig and Ingrid, along with others in residence, had decorated the tree with tiny statues of the various gods, late apples tied on by their stems, and little wooden disks painted with animal figures, runes, or geometric designs. Children had fashioned ornaments of twigs tied together and looped with colorful ribbon or sprigs of holly berries. Delicious aromas filled the hall and the sacrificial goat—along with several more to accommodate the gathering—roasted on spits over the central hearth. Prominently displayed on the wall behind the king's table hung the Herlief memorial tapestry.

"What is the mistletoe for?" asked a little boy as he pointed up at the white berries mounted in a crown of their green leaves.

Ivarolf, the flame-haired storyteller, overheard him and rushed in with a theatrical explanation. A hush fell over the room as he started to speak. "Everyone has heard of Balder, Odin and Frigga's most favored son." Solveig and Ingrid stopped and turned to enjoy his tale.

"Balder, the god of beauty, light, purity, and joy, once had a dream foretelling his death," Ivarolf recounted in an ominous, mysterious manner. "When he told Frigga, she set out to ensure the dream would never come to pass. She secured pledges from every tree and plant, every beast and bird, every stone and mineral, the water and soil, everything she could find that they would not in any way harm her beloved son, and they agreed. But Loki, in his jealousy of Balder's popularity, discovered Frigga had overlooked one small, seemingly unimportant plant—mistletoe. Loki sought to exploit this one weakness but knew no one would willingly hurt Balder."

Though she knew the story by heart, Solveig hung on Ivarolf's every word. "Now the gods, realizing nothing could harm Balder, had made a game of throwing things at him and watching them bounce off. But one god, Hother, was blind and did not participate in the sport. Loki, who had carved a spear from a branch of mistletoe, came to him and said, 'Here, Hother,' and shoved the deadly weapon into his unsuspecting hand. 'I'll point you toward Balder and you can hurl this stick at him. That way, you will not be left out.' Hother, thinking it all in good fun, thrust the spear at Balder. All gasped in shock when it pierced his chest, killing him on the spot."

Children who had not heard the story started to cry, some reaching for their mothers. Ivarolf raised a hand and cocked his chin to let them know the story wasn't over yet. "The gods all fell to weeping and moaning in sorrow, except Loki. Then all the others knew he was to blame, not Hother. Loki scampered off to escape their wrath, while Frigga considered what could be done. The goddess traveled about Ásgarðr giving kisses to everyone who would lend their magic to help restore Balder to life. All agreed, except Loki, who was nowhere to be found. It turned out to be enough, and Balder was returned to life. Then all the gods made the mistletoe promise that it would never again do an uncharitable deed but would forever be consecrated to acts of happiness and usefulness. So, on this occasion of the shortest day of the year, we call on the mistletoe to keep its promise by blessing us with happiness and joy for the year to come."

Everyone clapped and cheered, and the musicians resumed their playing. Solveig turned her mouth to Ingrid's ear. "I recall a darker version of this story in which Loki prevents Balder's return from Hel. Balder, his horse, and his grieving widow were all burned on his ship as a funeral pyre. Which story includes the true ending?"

Ingrid considered her with wise brown eyes. "Which version do you prefer?"

A smirk formed on Solveig's lips. "Does truth exist, or is everything merely the way we wish it to be? I would choose a different ending for the story of Herlief and the Giant or Ragna and the Raiders, but my wishing it will not produce a different outcome."

"There are facts," Ingrid said, "and there is truth. However, they aren't always one and the same. We can believe our eyes, or we can believe our hearts. Each has its usefulness. Mortals will never learn all the answers, though I've found asking the right questions leads to knowledge. Odin sacrificed much to gain knowledge; would less be asked of us?"

"Mother, sometimes, I swear"—Solveig shook her head, emitting a frustrated chuckle—"you can be as aggravating as a völva with your riddles."

Ingrid winked and brushed a kiss to her cheek. "Let us get ready for the feast."

They had only taken a few steps when Osmin caught the room's attention for an announcement. "The Yule log!" He held up one end of a huge portion of oak trunk, with a brawny man securing the other. It had been cured for a year, and its bark was stripped off with large runes carved in it, pronouncing blessings for the return of spring. Together, they placed the hefty log into the firepit beneath the roasting meat. The joyful assembly cheered again.

The Yule feast was a grand success, despite most residents of the town needing to leave early because of the storm. Now the hour was late, and only those who slept in the great hall remained—as well as a young woman who had attracted Baldr's attention. They sat in a corner sipping mead and talking, eyes all aglow.

Erika, if I'm not mistaken, Solveig thought. *I wonder, will Papa allow Baldr to choose his own bride, or will he insist he wed some princess or other? It worked out nicely for Herlief because he fell in love with Jarl Bjorn's daughter, but Erika's father is a fisherman. Perhaps he just wishes for some warmth under his furs.* She wished him luck.

Outside the wind howled, blowing periodic dustings of snow under the grand double-doors which had been blocked with a beam to keep them closed. She could only guess at the storm's ferocity as the temperature inside the hall dropped. Geirfinnr lay on a bench passed out from merriment and drink, alongside a dozen other members of the king's guard. Her father and mother monopolized the Hnefatafl board. Solveig had won her match with the Fox, although it had been close.

It had been a good day, only now she felt the pangs of loneliness more profoundly than she had in weeks. Solveig was pushing up from the table when she heard a knock at the door. No, it must have been the wind. Who would be out in this blizzard?

Mist perked up and trotted to the center of the chamber. Solveig heard the tapping sound again and Mist barked. Asbjorn swiveled in his chair toward the entry and Baldr left the doll-eyed Erika to unbar the door. At first, he opened it only a crack. The wind whistled and snow swirled inside. Then, in astonishment, he threw it wide, hauled in a small fur-wrapped, icy bundle, and pushed the door shut. He secured the beam before turning back to the bundle.

"A traveler!" he exclaimed in disbelief. "Come, warm yourself by the fire," he offered the newcomer in a proper display of hospitality.

Curiosity led Solveig to cross the space and take a seat beside her parents, who were nearer the grand hearth. The shivery heap set a spear against the wall and settled on the firepit's stone rim, while Baldr removed an icy shield from the stranger's back and brushed off the frosty powder. Solveig had never seen one like it—a light shade of blue with an artistic rendering of Yggdrasil emblazoned across its breadth. Yet, the person who carried it was far too small to be a warrior. A child, perhaps?

"I seek the king of Sogn," a weak voice emerged from the depths of the traveler's cloak.

"You have found him," Solveig's father replied. "I am King Asbjorn Bloodaxe, and these are my son, Baldr; Ingrid, my wife; and my daughter Solveig. Welcome to my hall. Now tell us, who are you, and what in all the nine realms are you doing out on a night like this?"

The traveler peeled out of a fabulous cloak with a gorgeous, spotted fur adorning its shoulders to reveal not a child; not a man, but... Two intense blue eyes locked onto Solveig's as an expression of wonder lit the face of a woman—a tiny young woman with short, flaxen hair. She wore men's clothing, and a sword hilt protruded from a leather scabbard at her waist.

Solveig blinked. Her sight, poor as it was, should have been reliable from this short distance, but clearly it was not. She rose to her feet and took a few tentative steps toward the oddity. The traveler indeed possessed the smooth visage of a woman with a heart-shaped face and slender nose, though at the moment her creamy skin was chapped and reddened from the frost.

"I am Kai from Yeats, in the land of the Swedes," she replied. She pulled her gaze from Solveig long enough to remove her mittens and extend her hands toward the hot coals. "I had to push through the storm as Frigg said there was no time to waste."

"Frigg?" Asbjorn asked, crinkling his features in confusion.

"Frigg, my völva." This Kai from Yeats spoke with a foreign accent thicker than Troels' or his gothi's, yet its sound was much more pleasant to Solveig's ears. "We aren't certain if it was the goddess Frigga or Freya who actually sent me. I am so glad to have finally found you. The regular route was blocked by the warring kingdoms to the south, so I had to cross the mountains."

"You did what?" Asbjorn bellowed in disbelief.

Solveig found her tale just as astonishing, yet she did not sense the vibration of deception she had from Troels when he'd appeared. Mist went right up to Kai, sniffing her with friendly interest. The woman's face lit up as it had when they'd first locked gazes, and she sank her fingers into the elkhound's ruff and petted her head like she was her long-lost friend. Mist responded by licking her hand.

"I had to," Kai stated emphatically. "Time is of the essence, isn't it?"

Solveig continued to study the young woman guardedly, allowing her father to conduct the questioning. *She can't be older than me; shorter and thinner, to be sure. Yet she crossed the mountains alone in winter? She must be half-starved and frozen to the core. I wouldn't be surprised if she loses some toes.*

"Bodil," Ingrid called. "Bring food and mead to our guest at once."

"Thank you so much," Kai responded with a look of relief.

"You said you were sent to us by your völva," the king continued. "For what purpose?"

Kai's eyes widened, as if Asbjorn should know already. "To rid your kingdom of the giant, of course."

A bolt of shock passed through Solveig. She stared at the figure before her in utter disbelief and had to consciously close her mouth, which had fallen open at the woman's declaration.

"You mean word has traveled as far abroad as the land of the Swedes?" Ingrid inquired.

Bodil presented Kai with a plate of leftovers from the feast and a cup of mead scraped from the bottom of the bowl. "Thank you," she repeated to the servant before turning back to Solveig and her parents. "No. But Frigg, our seer, had a vision. She said a woman of substance prayed to the goddess for aid. Queen Ingrid, I suppose it was you."

Ingrid blinked and nodded, taking her husband's hand.

"A jötunn threatens your kingdom; isn't it true?" Kai's face paled with insecurity for the first time.

Asbjorn cleared his throat. "It killed my oldest son and many warriors."

"She said the king and princess," Kai continued, sliding an apprehensive glance to Solveig, "would be in grave peril if I didn't arrive before spring."

Solveig had heard enough. This entire story was ludicrous! She shot to her feet and threw her hands into the air. "Is this a joke? Or is it the gods who laugh at us? We require a mighty warrior, a champion, to slay a man-killing jötunn, and they send a little girl whose shield swallows her?" With indignation rising from her core, Solveig fired again. "You are no champion and no shieldmaiden. You insult us with your claim. We have already been mocked by one false hero, and several other good-intentioned warriors have set forth on the quest since his demise and never returned. See, Papa?" She whirled toward the king. "You make grand declarations promising my hand in marriage and every adventure-seeker in the Northland wishes for their turn to die. I'll have no part in this absurd discussion."

By this time, Solveig's temper had mounted into a tumult. *Besides, I want to be the one to save the kingdom! If this tiny person thinks she can succeed, surely so can I!*

Shooting a final glare at Kai, Solveig stormed out of the great hall to brood in private over the humiliation she was forced to endure at the hands of the fickle gods.

29

K ai's breath caught, and she felt a profound sense of remorse as she stared at the retreating form of the most beautiful woman she had ever laid eyes on. The blue gown and white fur wrap were right out of Frigg's vision. Every luscious curve of her figure, every silky strand of her deepest brown hair was perfection. Her chestnut eyes, first curious, then fiery, were mesmerizing in their vitality. The princess' fair face with its flawless complexion was like something from a vision... *And she hates me.* Kai felt the blow as surely as the time Bozidar had smacked her with the butt of his spear and sent her sailing through the air to land with a gut-wrenching thud. *She thinks I'm a joke.*

She should have been used to the reaction; she had received it all her life. Only now, she carried the magic sword. *Princess Solveig didn't see the sword!* Kai's spirits brightened. *Tomorrow, when she is in a better temperament, I'll show her my Stinnr and its runes, and she'll understand. Then she'll see me for who I am.*

"Please excuse my daughter," Ingrid said, snapping Kai's attention back to the present. "She has experienced grave loss in the past several months and is struggling emotionally." The queen, not impaired by age or childbearing, was also a beautiful woman, gracing a similar look and bearing as her daughter, though with hair not as dark.

"Yes," Kai responded in empathy. "Her brother and some of her friends, I gather. I am truly sorry about your family's suffering."

"Herlief was her older brother, whom she admired and was close to," Asbjorn explained. Kai sensed the pain in his voice and her heart went out to him.

"And Ragna," Ingrid added, and took in a deep breath. "Was a bold and skillful shieldmaiden who was highly placed in the chain of command. She was Solveig's dearest friend."

"I understand." Kai took a bite of her food and sipped the sweet mead, a treat not often afforded to one of her lowly station. "I also understand you must share her reluctance to believe me, even if you are more polite about it. I am accustomed to being discounted, yet I assure you I am up to the challenge."

"But to fight a giant?" The king shook his head.

After swallowing another delicious and welcomed bite, Kai stood and spread her arms, displaying her full size to his inspection. "Would you stand?"

King Asbjorn shrugged and pushed to his feet. Kai gazed up his impressive frame to a curious face mostly consumed by a wiry, burnished beard. "It is all a matter of perspective," she stated in humility. "Compared to me, *you* are a giant. You stand over a foot taller and must carry more than twice my weight, yet less than a year ago, I fought and defeated a foe just as large as you."

An incredulous laugh escaped his lips as a humorous gleam lit his gaze. He sat and motioned to her with an outstretched arm. "Pray tell, how?"

"With wit, ingenuity, and perseverance," Kai enumerated. "I had to save my friend. I suppose you could say it was an act of will on my part, but the point is, size is not all that matters in combat."

"I am aware," the king responded in consideration, "but the menace we face is no mere man. And adding to our troubles, our warring neighbors made off with most of our winter storehouses of meat and grain. I fear we cannot offer you such a meal for the duration of your stay."

Kai straightened, and her face gleamed with excitement. "No problem, my lord! I am a skilled hunter and well acquainted with foraging. I shall provide your table with whatever you require... except grain and cheese and such."

"A huntress, are you?" Ingrid scrutinized her with a sly smile.

"Oh, yes, my lady. I excel with a bow. And my sword," she remembered. Kai pulled it from her sheath and crossed the space to place it in the king's hands. "It is a champion's blade, is it not? Our best forger crafted it for me. See the runes our gothi inscribed?" She pointed to the etching as the king admired her

sharp, light blade. "And the völva blessed it with her seiðr." Kai waited on pins
and needles until King Asbjorn returned Stinnr to her waiting palms.

"This is a worthy blade indeed," he exclaimed. "It reminds me of Sigrid's
sword."

Kai's heart pounded in her chest. "Did you meet Sigrid the Valiant? Her sagas
are popular in my land, and I have admired her courage since my birth. Truly,
my lord, did you know her?"

"Sit and eat, Kai," Ingrid urged.

Obediently, Kai returned to her place by the fire and spooned beans into her
mouth, but her thirsty gaze never left the queen.

"Sigrid was my aunt by birth, and she and Elyn raised me from a child."

"So you are *that* Ingrid!" Kai exclaimed enthusiastically. "A woman of substance indeed!"

Ingrid's laugh was warm and endearing, and it set Kai at ease. Still, she longed
to hear stories of the famous shieldmaiden and her partner.

"You have a fine sword, a rare commodity, I must say," Baldr added, finally
joining the conversation. Kai glanced over her shoulder to spy the prince sitting
with a young woman. She supposed he could be her age, with fawn hair brushing his shoulders and a wispy beard springing along his jaw, "But a sword, no
matter how magnificent, cannot guarantee you victory."

"You are right, my prince," she agreed before turning back to Asbjorn and
Ingrid. "I am small of stature, yet great of heart. And there is one thing I have
proven I can do better than anyone—survive. When I was a child, my entire
family perished from some plague, yet I did not even fall ill. When I was captured
by raiders who wished to sell me as a thrall, their ship was crushed in a terrible
storm; I also survived days floating on a broken piece of mast to wash ashore.
Then again, when I crossed the Fille Fiell Mountains, buried in deep snow and
assailed by howling winds, I should have frozen to death, yet the gods took
pity on me, and I cheated the grave once more. I have stories you would scarce
believe, yet no amount of telling would convince you. However, if you allow me
to stay the winter and prove my worth to you, come spring, you'll trust me to
accomplish what the gods sent me to do."

King Asbjorn settled back in his chair, a drowsy look crossing his broad face. He nodded. "You may stay with my warriors here in the hall. Eat, drink, and train with them. Tell us your stories, and we'll share ours. Hunt in our forests and bring your game to the fire—only not until this storm passes," he added with an amused wink. "I would not be pleased if you get our hopes up only to catch your death in a blizzard."

"Yes, my lord," Kai eagerly replied. "Thank you. I won't disappoint you—either of you," she said with a glance to Ingrid.

Ingrid's gaze glimmered with humor. "See you don't, or I'll unleash my moody daughter on you."

Oh, please do! rushed through Kai's mind. *I will find a way to win her over tomorrow. Right now...*

As the king and queen departed the hall, she set her empty plate and cup aside and glanced around for a spot to lie down. "Over here." Baldr pointed to the only empty place on the hall's sleeping benches. She walked to where he stood and spread a blanket from her pack, placing the rest of the bundle at one end to lay her head on. "It was Ragna's place, when she wasn't with Solveig," he explained. "No one dared take the spot, but now it shall be yours."

Kai's eyes rounded. "I couldn't. Your sister is already angry with me."

"She'll get over it. I am heir, and I say you sleep here," he commanded.

Swallowing her apprehension, and too exhausted to argue the point, Kai crawled up, covered herself with her cape, and fell asleep in an instant.

She awoke the next morning to a disturbing sensation. Kai pried open an eye to see Solveig glaring at her from three feet away, arms crossed over her chest. Waves of fury flowed from her core with such intensity Kai feared she may spontaneously combust. "Baldr ordered me to sleep here," she managed in a weak defense. "I didn't mean to—"

Solveig spun on her heel and marched away. "You can eat if you want," she spat over her shoulder.

*W*hat impudence! Solveig seethed. She understood she hadn't behaved like a proper representative of the kingdom the night before and had been all set to exhibit a hospitable attitude toward their guest, until she found her sleeping on Ragna's bench. All right, perhaps Baldr had told her to lie there; it sounded like something her little brother would do. *He never understood about Ragna the way Herlief did.* And maybe the rest of the hall was full while the storm raged outside, but Kai should have slept on the floor. Everyone knew to leave Ragna's spot vacant... well, perhaps not a stranger, but ignorance was no excuse!

Solveig took her place at her father's table and scowled at the little warrior who was attempting to untangle herself from a cloak with all the grace of a newborn moose. It was an unusual garment, which someone had obviously made for her. And her distinctive shield. Probably had a weaponsmith for a relative. And a sword... now that was curious. It had to have been passed down to her from some ancestor. And why was her hair chopped off?

Despite Solveig's deepening scowl and predatory thoughts, she couldn't take her eyes off Kai. She was a curiosity, 'twas all. Solveig quickly found something else to pretend to focus on; the sleepy curiosity was stumbling their way.

"Good morning, Queen Ingrid, Princess Solveig," she greeted them in a groggy tone. She was kind of attractive, in a disheveled sort of way, but Solveig had already decided not to like her. "Could you please direct me to your yard house?"

"In this storm?" Ingrid exclaimed. The wind still howled, and Solveig shuddered to think what could greet them if someone ventured to open a door. "Nonsense," her mother declared. "There is a closet there," she pointed, "with a chamber pot and wash basin. We are all using it until the weather breaks."

"Thank you, my lady," Kai replied graciously in her rather pleasant accent. She bowed—bowed? Really?—then scurried into the closet as if it were a matter of life and death.

"I'm glad we have Kai with us for the rest of winter," Solveig's mother had the nerve to say. "With Sylvi gone, she will be of great help."

"I'd wager she can't weave or sew or do anything you imagine," Solveig muttered.

"She can hunt," Baldr proclaimed in triumph. "As soon as the blizzard subsides, I will go out with her and see if she's any good at it. She has a quality bow, and that sword—Solveig, did you see it?"

"Not yet," she grumbled, reaching for a handful of nuts and dried berries from the bowl. There would be no bread, no porridge, no cheese, no apples, nor any of the food they typically ate for winter breakfasts. Solveig could deal with it. After all, she wasn't some spoiled little rich girl who waited around for a man to rescue her. She was going to be a warrior. *Wait until Baldr sees my sword*, she thought.

Fiske brought a tray stacked with enough old traveling cakes for each person to have only one. "Bodil, can you pour the tea I made?" Ingrid asked.

"Not the pine needle infusion again," Asbjorn grumbled as he plopped into his chair.

"It contains vital nutrients," Ingrid replied in an offended manner. "You can't continue to consume ale as if it were water. Remember, we have no barley to brew more until next year's harvest."

Solveig had to cover her laughter with a hand at her father's appalled expression. "What? I hadn't thought of that. Hel take King Rundrandr and the raiders of Sygnafylke! It is bad enough we shan't have bread, but it is cruel to leave people without ale."

"I'm good with bees," Kai chimed in as she returned from the closet, appearing a bit more presentable. "If Baldr can show me where to find the hives, I'll collect more honey for mead. If you have a large enough store of dried fruits or berries, I know a recipe for wine you may enjoy."

Asbjorn lifted a hopeful gaze to Ingrid. She sighed. "Almost all the food we secured was raided and carried off at harvest time. There are the dried fruits and berries I had put in our personal pantry to nibble on over the winter, but not enough to make into wine."

"Actually, we import most of our wine, which makes it expensive," Baldr commented. "If you have the knowledge, please share it with us and we can try to produce some next summer."

"I'd be happy to," Kai replied. She stood at the far end of the table as if she were waiting for something, with an interrogative expression some might find endearing. Solveig turned her attention to the tasteless, petrified biscuit in her hand and frowned.

"Actually," Kai went on to say, "almost anything edible can be fermented into alcohol if you follow the right procedure. A goatherd in my village makes a potent drink out of the leftover whey from his cheese."

Her father's countenance brightened. "Have a seat at my table, Kai," he offered with a gesture. "Eat, drink the tea my wife brewed, and tell me more."

The girl slid in eagerly beside Geirfinnr and another warrior twice her size. *It's like she knows precisely how to ingratiate herself with my family,* Solveig moaned to herself. *While her humble charm may be more genuine than Troels' false one, it will work no better on me.* She ate her meal in silence, listening to the others converse with the odd Swede.

Even so, one thing about Kai interested Solveig; her curiosity insisted on seeing the woman's sword. *Is it heavy like my father's and brothers' swords?* she wondered. *And if so, how does that little thing lift it? She seems quite knowledgeable about alcoholic beverages; does she know as much about the forging of weapons?*

Solveig did not want to socialize with this woman, who seemed determined to insert herself into her family's inner circle, but as her mother had lectured her, "She's going to be with us for the winter, so you may as well try to get along."

After the table had been cleared, with the storm still raging without, Solveig ambled around until she ended up near where Kai sat, going through her small bag of belongings. A brass object caught the light of the fire and Solveig's eyes. "What is that?" she asked, packing as little interest as she could into the question.

The would-be warrior woman smiled up at her with a hopeful expression and handed the figurine to Solveig to examine. "It is a bronze Valkyrie, or perhaps a female warrior," she answered. "A friend from home gave it to me for luck. I find the craftsmanship superb, but I'm afraid I don't know who made it."

Solveig turned the sculpture over in her hands, marveling at its beauty. She had seen representations of a shieldmaiden before but did not have one of her own. "My mother made an embroidery of Sigrid and Elyn on silk. It hangs in her bedchamber," she commented.

"Could you tell me about them?" Kai looked at her with the innocent longing of a child.

No, she is nothing like Troels; no hidden agenda. Unlike the puffed-up bilker, she hadn't even mentioned a reward. Solveig dropped the statuette back into her hand. "It's a nice piece. You should hold on to it; perhaps it has brought you luck. I'll tell you about my grandmothers, but I'd like to see your sword. I behaved badly last night and left before you showed it to my family."

"Certainly." Kai seemed to jump at the chance to please Solveig. It was really quite sweet. "No apology is necessary, princess. The king and queen shared a little of what you have been through, and I promise to move my things to another spot. I'll not sleep on this bench again. It was never my intent to upset you."

Solveig wanted to roll her eyes at the woman's groveling, but she was practicing regal behavior.

"Here." Kai lifted the sword and placed it in Solveig's hands. "I named it Stinnr because Kjell, our blacksmith, declared it to be an unbreakable sword."

It was light and elegant, shorter than a standard weapon, yet lengthy enough to not be mistaken for a dagger. Runes were etched into its surface and Solveig read them aloud. "Óss, Odin's sign for wisdom. *Yr* the elk, for courage and protection. Týr, the god's symbol for honor and justice. *Peorð*, for mystery or magic?"

"Haldor said it was for feminine energy, although the rune can also have those meanings."

Solveig stopped and stared at the blade, the design of the pommel, the wrappings on the grip, the runes inscribed in the fuller. "No," she uttered in horror. "It can't be."

Panic rose in her gut and her hands shook. She shoved the sword back at Kai and clamped her jaw shut lest she give voice to words that should remain unspoken. It was the exact sword from her dream, the one she had watched strangers craft.

This was supposed to be mine! I dreamed this sword, and it was supposed to be mine. The fury filling her eyes caused Kai to shrink in disappointment. Solveig didn't care; she was more disheartened than this Swede could ever imagine. *I won't let her steal my right to defend my own kingdom!*

Solveig spun around and fled the hall.

30

Monstrous tentacles of defeat gripped Kai's soul, dragging it down a dark pit of despair as she watched Solveig storm off in a rage—again.

I can understand her thinking I was too little to be of any use and getting angry because I took her lost friend's bunk, but why did seeing my sword anger her so? I thought it would have the opposite effect. I just can't win. I wish I knew why she hates me.

Kai tried to make sense of Solveig's reaction to her. *Maybe it isn't just me. Perhaps the princess is just ill-tempered and doesn't like anyone. I built her up in my mind to be so wonderful and now I find she's just a shrew. Everyone back home liked me at least. And I crossed the Fille Fiell and almost froze to death for this?*

With a miserable sigh, Kai returned Stinnr to its scabbard and collected all her belongings. *At least she liked the little Valkyrie.*

"Where are you going?" asked a tall, muscular man with a tawny mane and full beard. From his attire, he had to be a warrior in the king's service.

"I have to find somewhere else to sleep for tonight, even if it is on the floor," she explained. "I'm Kai from Yeats, and I'll be spending the winter with you here in the hall—or at least staying until the storm subsides."

He took the bundle from her with a smile. "I'm Geirfinnr, and Baldr told me about you. I'm afraid I had passed out from the festivities when you arrived last night. Now, I think we can squeeze you in between me and Knud over here." He carried her pile of belongings down the bench to a spot nearer the door. "Did Solveig give you a hard time about taking Ragna's place?"

"Not exactly," Kai tried to avoid answering the question. "I just felt it wasn't appropriate. Her period of mourning hasn't ended, and I don't wish to offend anyone."

"Ragna was my friend, too," Geirfinnr said. He plopped onto the seat and patted it for Kai to join him. "You should have seen her in battle." A nostalgic glint shone in his eyes. "She was as tall as Baldr and nearly as strong. Fierce!" He laughed. "You didn't want to be on her bad side. She saved my life, you know, in that last battle."

"She sounds remarkable," Kai observed. "I wish I could have met her."

Geirfinnr's gaze sparkled at her. "She would have liked you—I'm sure of it. So Baldr says you're here to slay the giant."

Kai studied his neutral expression. "You aren't going to laugh?"

A corner of his mouth pulled up. "Should I? He said you have a hero's sword and have survived plenty of ordeals. But I faced the monster; I saw it kill Herlief and a score of others. The giant is real, and I've given the matter some thought. You seem to be just the right size to run around his legs and slice the main tendons at the back of his heels. If you did so, he would topple over, allowing the entire army to descend on him. Being a smaller target—and having such amazing luck—you could get close to him without being swatted away."

"It's a good idea," Kai concurred. "However, I need to see him for myself before I know exactly how to approach him best."

"The last 'hero' who claimed he would destroy the jötunn brought a powerful weapon with him," the brawny warrior said. "We still have it and a copy. We had more, but they were lost in our skirmish with the thieving brutes from Sygnafylke—the ones who killed Ragna and Troels. Troels was the supposed hero who negotiated the hand of the princess as payment for killing the giant." He laughed and slapped his leg. "You think Solveig doesn't like you? She couldn't stand him! Anyway, it's a huge crossbow called a scorpio. We might still want to use it."

"Fascinating." Kai enjoyed talking with Geirfinnr and was learning a lot. She wanted to discover more about Ragna and Troels, especially how close Solveig and Ragna had been as friends. Baldr had mentioned Ragna sometimes slept in Solveig's room. *Had they been like Tove and me?* But such wasn't something she could come out and ask this warrior. Instead, she said, "I'd love to see it and understand how it works."

"It's in a shed," Geirfinnr said. "I can show it to you when there isn't a gale blowing outside."

"Thank you. I'd appreciate it." Glancing around the big room, she noticed over a dozen people milling about, some eating their breakfast, others throwing dice or tossing a round sphere back and forth. Two women sat chatting while watching small children at play. Two other women worked at a loom in the far corner, and several men still snored under their furs.

"What does everyone do all winter here?" she ventured.

Geirfinnr shrugged. "This is unusual weather. Most days we can engage in outdoor activities, at least for several hours. There's much to do—more since the skunks from Sygnafylke made off with our stores." His disposition darkened. "Once we rid our countryside of the menacing jötunn, I'm advising King Asbjorn that we issue them some retribution."

"I understand," Kai empathized, "but he must consider carefully if it is worth the undertaking. Negotiating a peaceful resolution, some compensation their king could offer, would be preferable. Constant states of war prevent progress, and if both sides demand a life for a life, when would it ever end?"

"Do they not have wars where you come from?"

"They do indeed," Kai confirmed, "and I am well acquainted with the grief they cause. I always wanted to be trained as a warrior so I could protect my village or town, my family and friends. I can feel the emotions stirring in you, prompting you to exact revenge. I merely wonder if it is in your kingdom's best interest."

"Probably not," Geirfinnr admitted. "But it's in my best interest, just like paying back the ugly giant for killing my prince and my friend."

"Then I take it you plan to go with me to face it?"

Flashing her a wicked grin, he declared, "A sleuth of brown bears couldn't keep me away."

Kai busied herself for hours meeting the warriors who shared the great hall and their families. Outside, the storm showed no signs of abating. Remembering her ordeal crossing the mountains, she was exceedingly glad for the warmth and camaraderie she found in those four walls. It seemed the only person who avoided her was the one she most longed to connect with. Picking up bits and pieces of conversation and putting them together with what she had already learned, Kai deduced that the princess and the shieldmaiden had indeed engaged in a serious, passionate relationship and that Ragna's death had significantly impacted Solveig's behavior. The others presumed Solveig would move on and marry whatever champion disposed of the jötunn as the king had proclaimed, though now they wondered what would happen if Kai killed it.

If I kill the giant, King Asbjorn isn't going to give me, a woman, his daughter to wed, nor would I want it unless she did too, she thought. *I'm not here to win the princess's hand, but oh, if I could win her heart!*

S olveig had been driven to distraction by that ridiculous woman all day. She realized Kai was no imposter; she was worse—she was exactly who she said she was. She was humble and gracious, friendly to everyone, helped the young women with their children, and engaged with all the warriors. People laughed at some of her adventures and made sounds of amazement at others. On top of all, she showed a genuine interest in their stories as well.

Why does she have to be so... good? Solveig glowered. *She won't give me a legitimate reason to despise her. She even moved out of Ragna's space to one by the door where the cold air comes in.*

She sighed, disgusted with herself for so many reasons. *What made me think I could become a robust shieldmaiden? I never saw myself in the dream, only the sword. Why did I believe it was meant for me? All I wanted to do was... be on the outside who I am on the inside. Is it so impossible? I thought I would be the one to avenge Herlief, to rid the kingdom of the threat. I guess I was wrong.*

Then she recalled her mother's riddle: *There are facts, and there is truth. However, they are not always one and the same. Could it be the facts are against me while the truth says I can be whatever I desire?* It was something to consider.

The blizzard which had begun yesterday afternoon still howled. Solveig wondered when it would stop. She could only spend so much time in her room alone without becoming melancholy yet whenever she ventured into the main area of the longhouse, Kai was there making friends and talking in melodic tones with her exotic, sultry voice, her bright blue eyes dancing with delight at every common thing, her short hair bobbing about her chin. What was with that, anyway? Eventually, she would have to ask.

As the evening meal was being prepared, Solveig sat down at the small table with the Hnefatafl board. A good practice game was exactly what she needed to focus. She often played by herself now. She would operate both armies, attempting to invent new strategies or perfect old ones. About halfway through her second match, a hesitant voice sounded from behind her.

"Why are you playing by yourself?"

She recognized it at once and did not turn around. "To sharpen my skills. People don't often like to join me because I mostly win."

"I will play with you if you want company," Kai volunteered. "Losing doesn't bother me."

"What kind of statement is that? You don't care if you lose? What kind of warrior are you going to be—a dead one?" Solveig tossed a glance over her shoulder.

"Why do you hate me so much?"

And there she stood with sad eyes and a bewildered expression. She appeared even shorter with her shoulders slumped.

Solveig sighed and pivoted in her chair to face Kai. "I don't hate you. It's just... things have not gone the way I expected, and I'm having a tough time adjusting. It isn't your fault. Come. Sit." Regaining her stately manner, she turned back to the game table.

Kai slid into the seat across from her in hopeful anticipation. *What does she want from me?* Solveig wondered, yet she asked, "How often have you played?"

"Hnefatafl? Never. I saw a jarl engage in a match with our king's son once, but I come from a humble home, and we never had a set. If you'll refresh my memory on the rules, I'll give it a go," she declared optimistically.

Solveig stifled a laugh. *Of course, she doesn't know the game! That way, she has a good excuse for losing.* Maintaining a proper attitude, she showed Kai how the game was played. "You start out as attacker, as it is the easier team to operate. Do you think you understand how to move your pieces?"

Kai's intent gaze focused on the board, and she nodded. "I'm ready." She made her first move.

31

"What do you mean?" Kai moved her pawn before focusing her full attention on Solveig. Something resembling fear spread across the young woman's face.

"Nothing," Solveig responded with a shake of her head. "You wouldn't understand. Forget I said anything."

"You may think I am too insignificant to kill your giant," Kai admitted. "However, even you have to recognize I am not dull-witted. If you explain, I'll understand."

Solveig didn't want to pour out her heart to this stranger. She had no intention of making friends with her or displaying an ounce of weakness. *Why isn't dinner ready? I need a distraction.* Then she was struck by a surprising truth. Kai *would* understand. *I accused her of being a joke played on us by the gods. No one takes her seriously either. Everybody has underestimated her, yet here she is, defying all the nay-sayers.*

Solveig glanced at the board and moved her piece, paving the way for her king to safely reach his corner. She grappled with herself over whether to express her overwhelming feelings of frustration and self-doubt.

"Do not worry about it, princess," Kai suggested in a dispassionate tone, void of its previous anxiety. "If the topic causes you distress, there is no need to discuss it. I deeply appreciate you instructing me how to play Hnefatafl, only do not count on me to lose so easily in the future."

"Easily?" Solveig wondered at the little sprite. "You can't fathom how well you have performed at a game you are just learning. Next time you shall defend."

"So there will be a next time?" Kai's gaze sparkled at Solveig, whose heart turned a little flip. Why was that?

"Solveig, Baldr," Ingrid called. "Come now. The soup is hot, and we've roasted hazelnuts and pine nuts."

Now she calls me!

"There must be other games," Solveig assured her as she stood. "You are the best competition I've found thus far. Come and fill your bowl, and pray this storm ends soon."

T hat night, Kai lay on her sleeping bench under her furs and thought about Solveig. *She said she believed Stinnr should have been hers. I wonder what she meant, especially since it upset her when I asked.*

She rolled over, trying to get comfortable. The other women and children had gone to sleep, along with most of the warriors. Baldr, Solveig, and their parents had retired to their chambers, leaving a small group of soldiers gathered at a table in the far corner, making wagers on how many times they could toss a hazelnut into a cup three strides away without missing. Everyone had been limited to only one horn of ale, so nobody could enjoy their fill. However, the weather was enough to entice folks to slumber as the gale howled and frigid air seeped in under the doorway.

How did she even know about it? She acted surprised to see me when I first arrived. Kai puzzled this matter further before her thoughts drifted into more hazardous terrain. *She is so beautiful—and feisty, too. Headstrong, to be sure, but smart. Tove could never have mastered a game of strategy. And I find it hurts my heart to learn she lost her brother and her girlfriend, perhaps in a matter of months. And it must be unsettling to have the king offer her as a bride to whoever kills the giant. At least she won't have to worry about that anymore with me here.*

Kai shifted to her back again and stared up at dusky roof planks in the pale glow of firelight. *She almost smiled at me today, and she wants to play Hnefatafl with me again.* Contentment smothered in anticipation warmed Kai from the inside out, and she drifted to sleep through visions of Solveig's alluring smile.

The next day, the whistling gale had subsided. Kai stood by anxiously as Baldr and Geirfinnr unbarred the double doors and peeked outside. A small avalanche of powdery snow tumbled into the hall and behind it loomed a gloomy, gray sky. Thankfully, no additional snow fell.

"Knud, Caldervar, Ardmundr," Baldr called. Three sturdy warriors came to join him. "Get some shovels and clear the doorway while Geirfinnr and I go check on the horses. They'll require water and hay."

"What can I do to help?" Kai volunteered.

"You say you can hunt," Geirfinnr recalled with cheer. "I'd like more than watery soup for dinner tonight."

"Rabbits will be out after the snowstorm," Kai declared. "I can't guarantee enough for everyone here to have a whole one, but I'll do my best."

"Don't get lost," Baldr stressed.

Kai grinned. "I won't."

S olveig watched Kai launch out into the thick snow with the men, wearing her warm cape, a bow and quiver over her shoulders, much the same way Ragna used to do. *She's nothing like Ragna,* she thought. *And I won't get attached to her. She'll probably get herself killed at the earliest convenience.*

She retreated to her room in frustration. Solveig braced her palms to a bare spot on her wall and bowed forward until her head touched the planks. *I need to be doing something to help, demonstrating leadership, but I can't hunt or fight. Why couldn't the sword have been mine?* With a sigh, she pushed herself upright, noting the strain in her muscles as she did so. A curious thought sparked in her mind, and she leaned into the wall again. This time as she pressed herself erect, Solveig studied the effect on her arms, shoulders, and back. The slight burning sensation was not unlike what she had experienced moving her furniture about.

She repeated the action a few more times until it became difficult to accomplish, and a grin spanned her lips.

Here is something I can repeat throughout the day to strengthen my body without making noise or causing a commotion. Mama and Papa won't even notice. I will devise other exercises, too, like squatting to pick up a box from the floor and standing with it. Maybe I am not strong because I have been pampered too much. How do I know what my limbs can accomplish if I do not test them?

Solveig drove herself until she ached and was puffing hard, then she sat to catch her breath. A glance at her polished, reflective brass plate informed her she needed to brush her hair and dry her face before returning to the hall, or the others would know she had been up to something. Once her breathing was in check and she looked presentable, Solveig rejoined the others, determined to be useful.

"Baldr, how is it outside?" Asbjorn asked when her brother entered.

"Cold. Snow to my knees in most places, but calm," he reported. "We fed the ponies, broke the ice from their buckets and added some warmed water. Kai went hunting, so we'll find out if she's any good at it."

"The roofs to the yard house and a shed collapsed from the weight of the snow or force of the wind," Geirfinnr continued. "I'll take a team out to repair them right away."

"I should ride into town to check on the residents, see who is in need," Baldr suggested. "Someone's cottage or barn might have blown down."

Solveig broke in with resolve. "No. I'll ride into town to assess the situation there. Baldr can visit the outlying farms."

"Are you sure, Solveig?" her father asked with concern. "Baldr says the snows are deep."

"That may be, but a Fjording has long legs and can step through the drifts with relative ease. I am offering to perform the simpler of the two tasks," she explained. "Would you prefer I venture out into the countryside?"

"No," Asbjorn snapped.

"Papa, am I not your daughter?" She stepped close to him and lifted a hand to his thick upper arm. "I may not be able to patch roofs or shoot a deer, but

I can show concern for our citizens. I can assess damages, determine needs and priorities, and assign vigorous men to assist with repairs. Allow me to do what I can. Gnóttdalr is my town too."

His attitude softened, and he patted her hand with a nod. "Very well, but take an escort. Baldr, you, too. No one should be out in the dim light and deep snow alone."

"Yes, sir," both siblings replied.

Solveig and her burly attendant returned after dark, though the sky always remained so this time of year. Baldr was not back from his rounds yet, but the attention in the great hall seemed to surround a certain short, wheat-haired Swede and a pile of rabbits being cleaned, skewered, and hung over the fire. Even Mist sat mesmerized, tail swishing the floor as she waited for nibbles to be tossed her way.

"Look, princess!" enthused Ardmundr, one of the tough warriors who resided in the hall. "While we were clearing pathways of snow, Kai gathered all these rabbits for our dinner."

"Impressive," she replied without inflection. Kai threw a toothy grin over her shoulder at Solveig, who walked past them to where her parents sat. *I am not looking at her, not thinking about her, not being taken in by her skill at shooting small animals.* Ingrid was working on embroidering a silk ribbon meant to adorn a garment, while Asbjorn engaged in a discussion with Geirfinnr.

"I bring word from town," she said, sliding into a seat across the table from them. Fiske set a warm cup of liquid in front of her. "Thank you."

"What is it, dear?" Ingrid looked up and laid her craft aside.

"A dock is missing several planks," she began. "Two dwellings suffered severe destruction to their roofs and the people have moved in with neighbors for now. Other structures received minor damage, and I spoke with the woodcutters and carpenters. They are working on creating the boards needed for the repairs, which we should be able to start on tomorrow. But there are greater concerns."

"Let's hear them," Asbjorn declared, giving her his full attention.

"A small child and an old grandmother, both in the same home, died from coughs and fevers during the blizzard, and several other people showed signs of illness. I consulted the *grædari*, and we moved all the sick into one house where he is tending them. He says the cold is partly to blame, along with stale air from the huts being boarded shut for two days straight and the lack of proper nutrition. Osmin stopped by and performed some chants and blessings in case evil spirits were blown in by the storm."

"That *drittsekk* Rundrandr and his war," growled the king. He slammed a fist on the table and ground his teeth. "Taking off with our winter supplies to replenish what he lost or squandered fighting against Hördaland. I ought to send an envoy to King Geirmund and offer to join his side in the conflict once spring arrives. We could crush the thieving ratbag between us and retrieve what is rightfully ours."

"I am in favor, my lord," Geirfinnr proclaimed.

"To accomplish what?" Ingrid asked. "They will have eaten all the food by then. There'll be nothing to reclaim. More of our strong young men would die in retaliation for a few raids. Then Sygnafylke would exact revenge on us. When does it end?"

"And we are supposed to sit by and be walked over?" Asbjorn rounded on her.

"Their raiders killed Ragna," Solveig added in a hush, not wishing to engage in the argument, but wanting to make the single point that mattered to her. "Even so, we need to deal with the giant first."

Asbjorn sighed and scratched under his armpit. "Solveig's right. And before we can send an army to fight, we must be able to feed it. 'Twill be late summer or autumn when we can harvest gain again. It'll be too late for payback by then. Yet I'll consider sending a message to King Geirmund of Hördaland. Ingrid, you know I had no intention of interfering in our neighbors' affairs, but they attacked us. They stole our winter stores and now our most vulnerable people are at risk. Babies and elders," he grumbled. "Geirfinnr, I want you to select two reliable soldiers to ride to Jarl Anders in the south and Jarl Bjorn in the north to check on their food situations. I need to assess how all parts of the kingdom stand, and what has changed since their last reports two months ago. It is possible some towns and villages were not affected and still have plenty, or there may have been more damaging raids."

"Excuse me," sounded a small female voice with a foreign accent. "I understand the kingdom's grain stores are lacking, but have you considered kelp?"

Four sets of astonished eyes focused on Kai as if she had suggested they devour grass from a frozen meadow.

"You mean the bothersome seaweed that gets tangled in our oars when we row our longboats into infested waters?" Asbjorn asked incredulously.

Kai's face lit up as if she had struck gold. "Yes, the very same!"

32

The faces staring at her, mouths agape in incredulity, amused Kai. It was not an uncommon reaction whenever she mentioned kelp, but Anika had discovered its many uses in her culinary experimentation, of which Kai had been obliged to partake. During the summers away at the shipbuilding camp, they had often run out of rye and barley, requiring those preparing the food to be creative.

"Have you tasted the kelp, Kai?" Ingrid asked in a hopeful tone. Kai could see the intelligent queen's brain ticking inside her lovely head.

"I have, and I assure you, my lord, it is not grass," she directed to the king. "It can be served raw, in a salad, boiled, or added to a soup; however, the true value of the crop emerges in drying and preserving it. Dehydrated squares make for a satisfying, crunchy snack, but you can pulverize the dried plant into a powder and use it in all the same ways you would grain flour. Anika made a type of flatbread from it upon which she piled tasty sauces, cheese, and bits of meat, then baked it in a clay oven. If you don't like the salty flavor, soaking the leaves in fresh water for a day or two before draping it on the drying racks will help."

"I had no idea," Solveig said in curiosity.

"I recall something of this." Ingrid's face glowed with revelation. "Sigrid and Elyn told me stories when I was a girl about a bygone era, a time before theirs, in which a great calamity befell the land. Do you remember, Asbjorn?"

"I remember Sogn split into two kingdoms for a generation or more and the kings Grimolf and Tortryggr reunited it," he stated.

"Yes, it was before all that," the queen continued. "Darkness covered the earth and there was a year with no summer. Many starved or moved away and the leaders of Sogn turned to the sea for sustenance. They survived on resources from the ocean, which might indeed have included kelp. It seems to be quite versatile, causing me to wonder why people stopped harvesting it."

Asbjorn replied with a shrug, "Once the danger had passed, they returned to their ordinary customs and food traditions. Or else they did not care for the taste." He shifted an inquisitive gaze to Kai. "How difficult is it to collect and process?"

Kai swelled with the satisfaction of having more to contribute. "Torsten taught me to dive for kelp. I can gather boatfuls and teach any of your people who are good swimmers how. I also assisted Anika in drying the leaves and cooking with them."

Solveig frowned. "What good will this do us in the throes of winter? The water is too icy to go diving in. You'd catch your death."

"No, princess," Kai replied in confidence. "If I don't stay in the water too long at a time and can warm under blankets in the boat between dives, I can do it. Is there a fisherman who knows where your kelp beds are who could take me?"

"Yes." Kai twisted to see Baldr striding up behind her. "I know where to find it, too. The farmers have lost some of their livestock to the weather and are snowed in up to their rafters farther up the mountainside," he reported. "Two cottages require repairs, and I told them I would send workers and materials to aid them. One elderly man was killed when a branch fell on him. Three families have sick children. If Kai's idea of gathering kelp might help feed our people, Father, I would like to go out with her and the fisherman tomorrow. We should depart early enough to be in place by the time the sky lightens, but Kai, it will still be dark under the water if there is no bright sun. We could simply gather what floats on the surface."

"Only if you are sure it is fresh. It's better cut from the growing stem, but darkness isn't a problem. I can follow the kelp down to where the stalk is near the bottom and slice; it will float up and you and the fishermen can haul it into the boats."

"Very well," Asbjorn agreed. "Kai, if you find others willing to risk the frigid water, please teach them what to do, but don't take unnecessary risks. If you kill yourself collecting seaweed, who shall rid us of our giant?"

"I'll take care," she declared with a grin.

"Come with me," Baldr told her. "Let's go to the docks and get everything in order for tomorrow."

With Baldr and Kai off on their adventure in stupidity and her father overseeing all the able-bodied warriors assisting in cleanup and repairs from the storm, Solveig went with her mother to visit and bring solace to their sick subjects. Ingrid had a gift bag for each, including a jar of honey, a basket of nuts and dried berries, and an extra blanket.

Queen Ingrid was a wonderful example to follow, Solveig was realizing. She recalled every person's name in the hospice and sat to talk with them individually. Solveig wondered if that silly Swede would end up here, ill from diving into the frigid water. *Whatever is she thinking? And I actually believed she possessed a keen wit. She'll catch her death of cold and for what? Seaweed? Who will dare eat it?* Solveig decided her anxiety over Kai's health was unacceptable and tried to focus on comforting her citizens.

Before leaving, Ingrid spoke to the healer. "What else do you require for their care?"

"I am running low on yarrow and mugwort," he mentioned.

"I will bring you some from our personal stores," she replied. Solveig followed her mother's concerned gaze around the room, looking at those who lay coughing in their beds. "I will also send a tea mixture. Make sure to drop some of the honey in it once it's steeped."

"Very well, my lady. You are kind and generous."

While Solveig knew those words to be true, she hated to think anyone in leadership would behave otherwise toward their own sick residents.

Later in the day, while Solveig assisted her mother with meal planning, an excited young lad burst into the great hall. "The fishermen are back with the kelp. You should see it—it's *huge!*" he exclaimed before spinning on his heel and rushing back outside.

"Let's go take a look," Ingrid suggested to Solveig, reaching for her cloak.

Solveig grabbed hers, too, a knot clenching in her stomach. *It seems they are back safely; however, it doesn't mean Kai hasn't invited some dread lung disease into her freezing little body. She's so thin, no layers of fat to keep her organs warm. Baldr better have wrapped her in a warm, dry blanket and deposited her beside a blazing fire.* Then, as if to justify her concern, Solveig added, *If I cannot slay the jötunn, she must do it to save me from an undesirable marriage.*

Traipsing through slush under a gloomy sky, they arrived in town to find a crowd gathered around a community workstation, which had been established on a platform beneath a thatched roof. Melting snow dripped from its eaves, and the glow of a fire emanated from the center of the space occupied by Baldr, Kai, several fishermen, and an enormous deposit of brown kelp.

Kai, her short hair still damp, was enfolded in a blanket near the fire, pointing and issuing instructions to a group of eager men and women who hung long strings of flexible stems clothed in slender leaves over racks typically used to dry strips of venison or to smoke fish. "You may all take a pot full home to try raw or boiled," she offered. "It is indeed healthy and good to eat, but if you find it too salty, just soak it for a bit. While I think it tastes better fresh, dried portions can be stored for long periods of time and rehydrated in a bowl of water, nibbled dry, or pounded into flour."

"Can we bake bread with it?" a woman asked. "Won't it taste odd?"

"It turns out best when paired with traditional grain flour—a way to stretch what you have to last longer," Kai answered.

"It's slimy," noted a man hanging the stuff as he turned up his nose.

"A little, but you can wash and dry it," Kai replied with ease. "And if you boil it, you'll never notice. It's great served with mussels and clams or any seafood, really."

Ingrid stepped onto the platform to address the assembly. "The most important part is you can eat it." And she proceeded to relate the tale of the ancient disaster and how their ancestors had survived off the bounty of the North Sea.

While Ingrid distributed seaweed to the townspeople, Kai approached Solveig with an expectant look. "What do you think?"

It was an impressive amount of plant material for one day's work, and without their usual winter fare, it could make all the difference. "I'll taste this new food, and then I'll let you know."

"It isn't bad, just different."

Solveig turned her gaze to the petite, wet foreigner with her short hair and new knowledge. *Not bad, just different,* she considered. Suddenly, the odor of the sea filled her senses, and she waved a hand under her nose. "You smell like the ocean on a foul day."

Kai laughed. "The hazards of harvesting kelp. Does your town, perchance, have a bathhouse? I was sorely overdue even before diving today."

"You may use my bathing tub," Solveig offered before her brain had time to make excuses. She felt like kicking herself, but now that the words were out, she couldn't take them back.

"Oh, princess, how wonderful!" Kai bounced with excitement—or was she shivering from cold?

"Well, don't just stand there," Solveig ordered. "Get up to the longhouse at once. If you get sick and die, who will kill the giant?"

"Thank you!" The woman rushed ahead. Solveig followed and tried not to think about having a Swedish elf bathing in her tub.

She arrived home to find Kai sitting by the fire and she told Bodil to heat pots of water. "The water in the tub has been used a few times," she told Kai, "but it isn't very dirty. I'll have to have it drained once you're done, though. Come, I'll show you."

I hadn't planned for her to ever enter my private chamber, Solveig brooded as she opened the door for Kai. Yet she had no one to blame but herself. *What in Miðgarðr was I thinking? Mother! She's rubbing off on me.* Solveig wanted to kick herself. *Then again, she reeks of seawater, and who could abide such a distasteful smell all evening?*

"This is a fabulous room, princess," she responded in awe.

"Quit calling me 'princess,'" Solveig let out in an annoyed tone. "Everyone calls me Solveig, so you may as well too."

"I am honored, Solveig." The words escaped her lips like a prayer. "I'm sorry I'll ruin your water with my unpleasant odor."

"Don't worry about it. I prefer you wash them off and change the water than smelling you from across the great hall," Solveig said with as little humor as she could. "Now, use the tongs to place hot stones from the fire into the bath and Bodil will bring in a pot of hot water to add. There is soap and a drying sheet," she pointed out before turning to leave.

"Thank you." Solveig paused at the words but refused to look back. "You are very kind to me, and I appreciate it."

Kind? No. Practical.

"It is nothing," Solveig responded and left her to her bath.

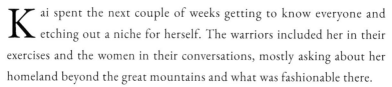

Kai spent the next couple of weeks getting to know everyone and etching out a niche for herself. The warriors included her in their exercises and the women in their conversations, mostly asking about her homeland beyond the great mountains and what was fashionable there.

When she was not socializing or teaching the women the various means of preparing kelp, Kai hunted. It seemed this was most needed as fresh meat was required daily for the king's hall and she was skilled with a bow. At first Baldr or Geirfinnr would accompany her so she didn't get lost in an unfamiliar forest, but they were needed at the great hall to help settle disputes between neighbors and to keep bored warriors from turning their weapons on each other.

That day, Kai was on her own, which was just fine unless she needed to drag a moose back to the longhouse. *It'd be mostly downhill. How hard could it be?*

She observed the signs in the forest as she walked up a gentle slope through tall firs and pines powdered in white. Although winter neared its peak and snow lay all around, there had been no other storm as severe as the one she had arrived in. A woodpecker hammered at a trunk and a squirrel scurried up a nearby tree. Then a fresh trail caught Kai's attention.

A quick examination told her a story. The footprints keeping to a narrow path were human, though they were not large enough to belong to one of the warriors. *Someone's youthful son out exploring?* she wondered and followed the trail.

Kai stalked the prints a short distance until she came upon a most unexpected sight. Ahead stood a tree with a solid low branch and—Kai shook her head and refocused just to be certain—Solveig was hanging on to it pulling herself up and down. A quick glance around told her she was alone, and that didn't seem right. The princess' back was to her, and Kai didn't want to frighten her, but she really wanted to know what she was doing out there.

She took a few more steps, entered the glade around the tree, and announced in a cheerful tone, "Good morning, Solveig. I see you know the game Leiknir and I used to play with Jerrik."

Solveig released the branch immediately and almost stumbled regaining her footing. She spun about with a stunned expression bordering on horror. "What are you doing following me?" she yelled.

Kai had kept approaching, but hearing the accusing sound in Solveig's voice, she stopped, worried about incurring even more of the princess' displeasure. "I wasn't following you," she answered. "I was out hunting, spotted small footprints and thought someone's lad may be getting into mischief out here alone in the woods. I swear I had no idea they were yours."

"Yes, well." Solveig smoothed her dress and looked away. "Go on and hunt then."

"There's nothing to be embarrassed about," Kai said, hoping to soothe her. "It's a great way to build one's strength."

"Why are you standing there gawking?" Kai shrank under Solveig's glare. She wasn't making the situation any better. Maybe she should just go, but...

Kai heard a sudden thrashing sound approaching from her left and instinctively moved between Solveig and the noise. In an instant, a black head with slicked-back ears, intense yellow eyes, and menacing teeth crashed through a bush. The wolf paused to snarl at them, and Kai realized it wasn't right. Sane wolves did not behave this way, nor did they foam at the mouth.

"Stay behind me," Kai whispered.

"I'm not afraid of a wolf," Solveig replied indignantly. "I've kept dogs all my life, some even bigger than that one."

"Yes, I'm certain you can take care of yourself, but look closer." Kai realized Solveig may not be able to make out the details she could. "It's gaunt with scraggly fur and foams at its mouth. It shows unusual signs of aggression and where is the rest of the pack? A lone wolf behaving like this must have the madness. I've seen it before. The disease can be passed to humans through a bite, or even a scratch, some say. I once knew a man who lost his mind and died of thirst after being bitten by a fox with these signs."

"What are you going to do?" Solveig's voice had grown concerned.

Kai thought quickly. *Using a sword, I run the risk of being scratched or bitten, but taking the bow off my shoulder and notching an arrow would take too long. The instant I move, it will attack.*

She drew Stinnr as quickly as a snake's strike and the mad animal leaped at her, claws and fangs bared. Kai drove her sword into the wolf's chest, and she jumped back, pushing Solveig with her while it thrashed on the ground. At least it was over swiftly. Kai pulled on a winter mitten before retrieving her sword to protect herself should it give a final jerk. Then she washed the blade with snow and pine needles so none of the blood remained.

S olveig was dumbfounded. It all happened so fast, and indeed, she hadn't seen the details pointing to madness in the wolf. For an instant, a thought flashed through her mind. *If I had been alone and had not seen it, had not known what was wrong, the wolf likely would have bitten me, and even if I fought it off, I could have caught the disease.*

Shifting her gaze from the body of the dead animal to Kai, she said, "Thank you."

"Oh, it was nothing," Kai replied casually. "I'm glad curiosity over those footprints got the better of me, though. Its body should be burned at once so the madness doesn't spread through the forest."

"Yes, of course." Then another worry wormed through Solveig's mind. "What are you going to tell people?"

"That I was out hunting, came upon a wolf with the madness, and killed it," she replied.

Solveig lowered her chin. "I mean about me being here."

"Oh? Were you here?" Kai asked in good humor. "Solveig, it's no one's business why you wish to sneak off to the forest to do pull-ups, and you were clearly upset when I saw you here. Truly, I do not wish to keep getting the wrong end of your anger. I think I'd rather wrestle a bear."

With a shake of her head, Solveig let out a little laugh. "You didn't hesitate. The instant you saw danger, you jumped in front of me. It wouldn't be an exaggeration to say you saved my life just now."

Kai shrugged and slid her now clean sword back into its scabbard. "It's what I do. But please, find somewhere safer, closer to home to work on your strength-building exercises. I'm not sure why it's a secret, but it's one you can trust me to keep."

Solveig watched Kai turn and walk off into the forest. She considered thanking her again for keeping quiet, but she hadn't kept the promise yet. She even thought of asking Kai to walk her home; that would be too embarrassing, though. After all, Solveig was training to be a warrior too. She needed to develop more independence, not to have a servant or a guard always at her side. *I'm relying on myself now,* she determined.

Then again, Kai hadn't laughed at her or chided her for being foolish. Nor did she run off and leave her to the diseased wolf. Come to think of it, she'd behaved exactly the way Solveig would have expected her to. Not that she would ever be sweet on the little Swede, but Solveig's opinion of her moved up a notch.

33

Over the next several weeks, Ingrid busied herself by learning everything about kelp and what could be done with it while still seeing to her regular duties. The men mostly praised the *víðir bjórr*, or "sea beer," as they had taken to calling the fermented, distilled beverage. Even though it contained no malt agent such as barley or hops, it made for a stronger alcohol. Dozens lined up at the boats each morning to go out harvesting with the promise they would be paid in víðir bjórr, and it gave them something to do.

The messengers had returned with reports from all six fylkes in Sogn. Raiders had not attacked the three to the north, and their jarls sent a dozen bags of grain and six barrels of ale from each of their storehouses to aid Gnóttdalr, Skalavik, and Hranafall, who had all suffered losses. Baldr had administered their distribution to the affected towns.

She also observed Kai. When she wasn't hunting or diving into icy waters teaching the fishermen how to harvest seaweed, the young woman trained in the yard with the other warriors. She proved exceptional with a bow and held her own with a sword, spear, or axe. While not as strong as Ragna had been—and displaying nothing near the power of the men—she was agile, gritty, and creative in a fight. Baldr had privately admitted he didn't know what to do with her if she wished to stay after the giant had been eliminated.

"Mother, she is an asset to both the kingdom and our household in so many ways, but I can't imagine putting her in a shield wall with the other warriors for battle," he confessed in dismay. "She can fight one-on-one but is too short and light to fit in with the army."

"Ragna was an exception," Ingrid had told him. "Usually, a shieldmaiden's role is to stay in the back and move to fill in holes where needed and to keep guard over your flanks. Could she accomplish that?"

"I suppose so," had come his contemplative reply. Still, they didn't know what Kai would want to do when her mission was complete. Ingrid would have guessed she would wish to return to her people if not for the look in her eyes when she beheld Solveig. A mother who had been raised by two mothers couldn't mistake such fervent admiration.

The delightful Swede endeavored to please everyone, especially Solveig, who mostly sought to avoid her. However, Ingrid's keen attention noticed more than where the newcomer cast her gaze. Her daughter had spent the past few weeks watching Kai from afar, even if she feigned indifference.

With the peak of winter upon them, Ingrid realized it would be two more months before her husband would send patrols in search of the giant. Though Kai had been with them a month already, it amazed her this petite woman with her extraordinary sword and tales to go with it could be the answer to her prayers.

Ingrid sat at the family's table at one end of the hall one evening, darning socks, when Solveig slipped in beside her, smelling of sweat. Her daughter had been acting peculiar lately, although the girl seemed to always behave strangely. She was nothing like her sister, Sylvi, who was easy to comprehend. Ingrid believed she was up to a secret caper yet wasn't ready to press the matter. Tonight, she would meddle in her daughter's affairs from a different direction.

"Kai is fitting in well, don't you think?" Ingrid asked. Across the room, the Swede was engaged in knife throwing with Baldr, Geirfinnr, and several other warriors, targeting the painted barrel top that hung on the wall.

"I suppose." Solveig's reply was curt, though Ingrid caught exactly where she focused her attention.

She sewed a few stitches. "The kelp isn't bad. In fact, the grædari has been using it in a soup to feed anyone who falls ill and says it hastens their recoveries."

"It's more palatable than I expected."

Ingrid watched her daughter sneak another glance at Kai when it was her turn to throw. "I especially enjoy the extra meat. When our stores were stolen, I feared we would run low, but she has proven her worth as a hunter."

"Yes, Mama, I get it." Solveig rounded on her in annoyance. "You wish to adopt her since she can do all the things I can't."

"Oh, no, Solveig." Ingrid set her darning aside and took her daughter's hands, drawing her full attention. "It isn't what I mean, and you know it. Why must you constantly compare yourself to others? You have so many fine qualities. You're intelligent, fiercely loyal, and an excellent leader. You excel at organization and planning, and this is all without mentioning your beauty."

"What good is beauty? Can it feed the people? Can it slay the jötunn?" Solveig puffed out a breath and shook her head. "I apologize. I'm trying to cope and finding it insurmountable some days."

"That is because you try to solve everything on your own," Ingrid soothed. "You need a friend, sweet daughter, someone you can talk to about what you are going through because you certainly don't confide in me. Do you remember the mischievous, gray-striped cat you loved so?"

"Loki?" Solveig's countenance lit up. "Of course I do. He was fabulous!"

"When he wandered off into the woods and never returned, you were devastated, inconsolable," she continued.

"Because I loved him and was so sad to lose him."

"You swore you would never love another living creature," Ingrid reminded her. "Then a few months later, you swooned over an adorable spotted kid goat and named her Freydis. She followed you everywhere, doing funny things to make you laugh."

"I made Papa promise she would only be for milk and cheese, never for the roasting spit," Solveig recounted fondly. "Anytime I was in a contrary mood, she could snap me out of it with her rampaging cuteness."

"And now you have Mist." Ingrid glanced down at the faithful elkhound curled around Solveig's feet. Lowering her voice to a disapproving growl, she added, "Who you spoil and allow on your bed when I instructed you not to."

Solveig offered her an apologetic look. "I needed her there." Then she straightened, shifting her attention to the cheers of the warriors who patted Kai on the back for some feat of skill she had missed seeing. "I know what you are doing," she stated dispassionately. "Pets and people are not the same. It was too hard on me to lose Ragna, Mother; I can't go through it again. Besides, nobody could ever replace her."

"No," Ingrid concurred. "They could not. Yet without risk, there is no reward. You need to develop a fresh relationship unlike the one you shared with Ragna. Sweet daughter, soften your heart. Allow yourself to feel anew. Think about what Ragna would want. Or do you believe she sits alone in Valhalla, pining over you?"

The thought struck Solveig like a blow to the chest. "No. She wouldn't be." She knew it was true. *Ragna is enjoying such a wonderful afterlife feasting, fighting, playing games, and exchanging stories, that she hasn't had time to miss me. She's probably wooed a Valkyrie by now and sleeps in her bed at night. It was an overwhelming joy to hear her say she loved me, but we no longer live in the same worlds. And she isn't waiting for me, as I have no hope of reaching Odin's hall of warriors.*

"I want you to be happy, Solveig," her mother said in a tender voice. "And I believe Ragna does too. It is natural to mourn the passing of those we love. Do you think I haven't cried at night for Herlief? He was my firstborn, a part of me who grew into an admirable man. He had just wed a lovely girl and then was ripped from our arms. Do I say I shall stop caring for my other children in fear I'll lose them one day as well? Do I harden my heart toward my husband to keep it from breaking should he pass before me? If you lock yourself so tightly behind the walls of your defense, you make yourself a prisoner to fear. What kind of life, then, are you left with?"

Solveig lowered her gaze and pulled her hands away to fold them in her lap. "I know your advice is wise and true, yet it isn't easy for me. I'm not blind to Kai's efforts to befriend me; I just don't want to be hurt again, and she appears so fragile."

Even if she didn't flinch to take on a mad wolf, she thought. Kai had been true to her word and never spoke about seeing her in the forest that day.

"Gerta, the milkmaid, is of hearty stock," her mother mentioned with an impish grin. "You should invite her up to play Hnefatafl sometime."

The ploy made Solveig laugh. "Gerta could both wrestle and drink Papa to the floor!" She shook her head, tears squirting from her eyes, glad she could release them in laughter rather than sorrow.

"And there is Geirfinnr," Ingrid added in a whisper. "He's not noble, but I believe your father would approve the match. He is a friend you could feel comfortable with." When Solveig started to speak, Ingrid raised a palm. "I know; you don't wish to wed a man. Have you considered that if Kai defeats the giant, you may not have to?"

"I've thought of little else since she arrived," Solveig confessed. However, she remained silent about her jealousy and desires to save the kingdom from calamity herself. "Then what happens when the next crisis arises, or Papa needs to forge a treaty? This talk about joining sides with Hördaland... Will he decide to use me as a pawn to wed some member of King Geirmund's family to seal the bargain? I can't stand it!" She kept her voice down, but it seethed with anxiety.

"Hush, child," her mother cautioned. "Don't borrow trouble or invent causes for concern where none exist. Your father is a fair man, and he loves you."

"I know." Solveig cast a glance around the hall to see what Kai was doing now. She didn't see her with the soldiers or the other women. *Could she have gone to sleep already?* Then she spotted a small person with flaxen hair sitting alone at the Hnefatafl board arranging the pieces. Since none beyond her family showed an interest in the game, she knew it had to be Kai. A softness fell over Solveig, and something urged her to join the little warrior. *Mayhap Mama is right; it wouldn't hurt to give her a chance.*

Excusing herself, Solveig glided across the room and lighted on a chair opposite Kai. "Plotting how to defeat me?" she asked in a curious tone.

"Precisely." Kai glanced up and flashed her a hopeful smile. "You said you'd like to play with me again, yet somehow, we never got around to it. I'm sorry I've been so busy."

"I'm not," Solveig declared as she helped place all the pawns in their starting positions. "We've been enjoying hearty meals because of your industry. Still, our rematch is past due. I believe you will be defending this game."

"Correct. How have you been?"

"I've had my moments, good and bad," she replied, giving honesty a try. "Overall, I trust I'm on the mend."

"I'm delighted to hear it," Kai remarked with cheer. "And I've managed to not get myself killed thus far."

A chuckle shook Solveig's belly. "And I am delighted to hear that. Now, I move first." Solveig and Kai took several turns in silence. Solveig discovered she wanted to know Kai better, beyond merely watching the woman interact with others, and one question had been uppermost in her mind all month. "Kai, how were you able to cross the Fille Fiell alone in winter?"

"It was the hardest thing I've ever done," Kai confessed, as she captured a pawn. "Climbing a mountain is fatiguing; walking through deep snow is exhausting. But combining the two…" She shook her head.

Solveig noticed her hair had grown some and now danced just above the top of her shoulders. "I can only imagine." She played her turn, then focused her full attention on Kai's tale.

Kai described the treacherous journey, the bitter winds, and the terrible storm during which she had all but given up. As Solveig listened, she was touched to hear that thoughts of her had inspired Kai to fight for her survival, even before they had ever met—if the story was true. Something in Kai's aspect convinced her it was. Then came an event beyond belief.

"I was balled up under my cloak," Kai told, "and kept thinking if I only had a fire. And when I opened my eyes, there it was. I could feel its warmth and was so overjoyed, yet the next morning, there was no sign the fire had ever been there.

The blizzard had ended, and I was alive, so it must have been a gift from the gods or a trick of my mind powerful enough to save me from freezing. Either way, I was extremely thankful."

Solveig was awestruck. Both scenarios seemed impossible, and yet Kai was there as proof she had crossed the mountains. "Magic." The word fell from her lips in skepticism. She had never experienced such magic, except for the dream about the sword. Could it have been real? But her vision had betrayed her.

"Frigg, the seer, taught me that in order to secure my destiny, I had to employ desire and belief," Kai related. "Both in equal and potent measures. While I have no doubt the gods can do as they please, I must wonder about the power of belief. Was the fire real or did my belief in it save my life?" Kai shook her head. "I honestly don't know, and mayhap never will. However, I can tell you I've never been more grateful of anything than when your brother opened the door to this great hall and let me inside."

Solveig pondered the possibilities. *Are we who we are because it is what we believe ourselves to be? And how far does the notion stretch? Are Ragna and Herlief in Valhalla enjoying Odin's table because they believed they would while in this life? I cannot imagine myself a bird and take flight as if I were; I would crash to the earth. And yet, Kai did not freeze.*

"I'm glad you didn't die, whether by the gods' intervention or a device of your own imagination," Solveig confessed. Then, to lighten the mood, she added, "Who else would I find to challenge me at Hnefatafl?"

Kai's smile at her declaration radiated with such intensity, it alone could have melted all the snow on the mountainside. A pang of guilt poked at Solveig. After making her move, she admitted another truth. "If I have been moody or impolite to you, it was probably from jealousy, for which I apologize."

Kai's hand stopped in midair, mouth gaping open, eyes rounded like an owl's. "Solveig, whatever for?"

Casting a glance over her shoulder to be sure nobody listened, Solveig confessed her hidden agenda in a hush. "I wanted to be the one to kill the giant and save the kingdom. Your sword appeared in my dream, and I foolishly thought it was to be mine. I've spent my life wishing for what I could never be, you see?"

Fixing her gaze on Kai, she stated, "I wanted to be like Sigrid and Elyn, only I wasn't strong or agile. I get dreadfully seasick and have a feeble constitution, not to mention I can't see farther than three feet in front of my face. And there you were, tall as a pixie, making all your dreams come true by what? Willpower and good luck? I was angry because the gods have never favored me the way they did you. This is not your doing and I appreciate you wanting to help. I just feel so… frustrated."

Laying her arm on the table, Kai considered Solveig with a look of compassion and incredulity twined together like strands of hair in a braid. "That's why you were practicing pull-ups in the woods that day. I didn't know you desired these things, but Solveig, when I look at you, I see beyond the most beautiful woman in all the nine realms. You are smart and tall and strong, a woman with authority who excels in so many arenas."

"Strong?" It was Solveig's turn to go wide-eyed. "And taller than you doesn't equal 'tall.'"

"Average height then, but yes—you are magnificent. Physical strength is only a trifle compared to the fortitude I witness in you. Think," Kai implored her passionately. "You lost your brother and your lover within months of each other, and still your focus is on saving your kingdom. Baldr says you were even willing to marry a man you despised if it meant ridding Sogn of the giant. You exhibit so much strength simply by facing your weaknesses and not letting them stop you from riding into town to make assessments or visit the sick, and I've seen you helping the other women who live in the hall when most princesses would sit about demanding they wait on her."

"Yes, well," Solveig protested. "None of that makes me fit for battle or adventuring."

"Frigg says heroes come in all types and sizes."

"Even the blind variety?" Solveig sighed, not wishing to raise her hopes only to have them dashed again.

Kai shrugged. "In the thick of it, you only see the foe pressing against your shield, anyway. Can you see me, make out the features of my face? An opponent you fight would be no farther away from you. Not every warrior is a marksman."

Solveig studied Kai—the pleasing symmetry of her face, her dazzling blue eyes, the angles of her chin and cheekbones, the curve of her nose. She examined her slender neck and the deep cut of the boy's tunic she wore. The muscles of her arms were lean and hard, her breasts beneath the wool of her garment smaller than her own, though firm and alluring. Before her sat a young woman who had defied the odds many times. *She thinks I'm strong. No one has ever said those words to me, even if she meant a strength of character rather than of body. And I am making my body more powerful, too. I wonder...*

"I see you, Kai," she uttered as her heart raced in her chest. "Will you do something for me?"

"Anything you ask," she replied.

Solveig glanced around again and leaned in close. "It must be another secret; nobody can know. Do you promise?"

"I vow by Odin's one eye to keep your confidence."

Satisfied, Solveig made her request. "Go to the armory without being seen and bring back two wooden practice swords. I wish you to teach me everything you know. I've watched you train but require hands-on experience. We'll need to arrange out-of-the-way places to meet and practice without others knowing what we are about. Would you do this for me?"

"On my oath, I wish to help you make your dreams come true." Kai's voice rang with such fervent sincerity, Solveig believed she would devise a means to pull the moon to the earth if she asked her to.

"No one has ever called me strong," she admitted in wonder. "Nobody."

The little nymph's face glowed. "You are, so believe it."

"Desire and belief, you say," Solveig mused aloud. "Thank you, Kai." Something tugged at Solveig, urging her to reach over and take Kai's hand, but she wasn't ready—not yet. She held her gaze for a little longer before returning her attention to the game. "Tomorrow we shall begin our covert training, and I expect you to provide excellent and varied excuses for your absences."

Kai flashed her a playful grin. "I can always tell them I'm off hunting or taking care of feminine matters. They never want to hear details about that."

Solveig let out a laugh. She had come to feel relaxed and at ease with Kai in a way she never had with Ragna. And while she still wished to be the hero who would save the kingdom, she no longer harbored jealousy or resentment toward the little Swede and her magnificent sword.

Mayhap Mama was right, she considered. *Life could be better with a friend.*

34

K ai felt as if she floated on a cloud everywhere she went for the next two
months. Solveig had finally let her in and even trusted her with treasured
secrets. She reveled in every new morsel she learned about the gorgeous woman
who had completely run away with her heart. She didn't care if she made a fool
of herself, as long as Solveig was pleased. And unlike the angry, bitter attitude
with which she had greeted Kai upon her arrival, Solveig truly seemed happier
now.

From time to time, Kai would catch Solveig glancing her way. Rather than
snap her head around and scurry off, the princess would allow her gaze to linger,
which encouraged Kai, lifting her soul on the wings of hope. She would flash a
smile at Solveig before returning to whatever activity she was engaged in to let
her know how pleased she was to no longer be the object of her scorn.

Kai typically rose early to set off on a hunt to earn her keep, though several
times a week as the weather permitted, she and Solveig sneaked off to train.
Sometimes they met at the hay barn or stable, and other times in the woods,
to escape prying eyes. Solveig lacked an instinct for sparring and was as clumsy
as she had predicted; however, she was a quick study and possessed a potent
desire to succeed. Therefore, she improved in a slow, steady fashion. Kai devised
a method of measuring her advancements in strength by tying buckets to both
ends of a staff and adding more rocks to them periodically for her student to
lift.

It wasn't a lack of grace, Kai decided, as Solveig excelled at dance without
stepping on anyone's feet or careening into them while frolicking about the

great hall. She had even pulled Kai out to dance with her once. That night, she could not sleep for the pleasure of reliving the encounter over and over, basking in bliss. No, she believed Solveig's difficulty lay in the paradigm imposed on the princess since her childhood. She had always been told she had no aptitude for combat; therefore, a faulty belief system hindered her progress. Maybe she had been ungainly as a child, but Solveig must have outgrown it, if watching her glide about the hall was any indication. Put a sword in her hand, though, and suddenly she couldn't remember she had feet.

Kai had not forgotten about Tove and the time they had shared together. Tove had been her first love, the one to awaken feelings in her common to young women that no man ever had. She wondered if she was pregnant by now and if Tove ever thought of her. But thinking about Tove made her sad because that door was closed to her. Kai preferred her feelings to remain positive, full of hope and anticipation of things to come, so she focused her mind on Solveig and their growing friendship. Sometimes Kai would stare at her reflection in Stinnr's blade and trace the runes with a finger, imagining all sorts of adventures the future might hold. At other times, she would close her eyes and picture Solveig's smile.

One night when the first signs of spring had made themselves known, Kai sat at the little table playing Hnefatafl with Solveig, as was their newly established routine. Kai loved all the time she got to spend with Solveig, which, between a couple of hours of training several days a week and gaming nights, had become quite regular. She adored seeing the princess smile, which was still a rare occurrence, and she loved her intense looks of resolve during their lessons. Solveig was determined, a quality Kai admired and related to. Despite her size, Kai possessed a natural aptitude for fighting that had allowed her to progress much more quickly... or mayhap she was not as good of an instructor as Jerrik had been. She hoped such was not the case.

Kai took her last move, capturing Solveig's king, thus ending the game.

"How did you do that?" Solveig exclaimed. She leaned forward, studying the board and remaining pawns. "This is twice you've beat me in as many weeks."

She blinked, then pinned Kai with a suspicious gaze. "Are you employing magic, perchance? Some seiðr dust brushed from your sword?"

Laughing, Kai shook her head. "No magic, just exploring new strategies. You still win the majority of our matches."

"Yes," Solveig mused as she sat back and scrutinized Kai with an amused expression. "Yet I suspect you have devised a way of distracting my attention with your lilting dialog and improbable storytelling. You expect me to believe you rode about on a goat as a child? And it went where you told it to?"

"Hilde was a fabulous goat, I'll have you know, much smarter than the average featherhead. And big, too," Kai responded cheerfully. "My parents had a large herd we raised in meadows away from town, and I was a small child. As far as I knew, everyone rode goats."

"It must have been hard to lose your whole family at once." Solveig's manner slid from playful to compassionate in a blink, and Kai sensed her sincerity.

"It was both distressing and terrifying, as I recall." Kai folded her hands on the table in front of her, realizing this was something Solveig would relate to. It was not a time for bravado but for vulnerability. "I was ten when a traveler stopped by. Mama and Papa offered him a meal and lodging for the night as is customary. I don't remember much about him. He was rather ordinary, but during the night a fever came upon him. He experienced chills and a cough, and I recall red blotches on his skin. Mama couldn't send him away in his condition, so she tried to care for him. Then my brother and papa got sick, too. I helped Mama and looked after the herd. The traveler died first. When Mama fell ill to the same symptoms, I did my best to follow her instructions, but by then I knew this plague could be fatal and I just remember being very scared. Papa said I needed to burn his body so the bad spirits wouldn't contaminate the ground, but his body was too heavy for me to move."

Pausing her tale, Kai emitted a dry laugh and flicked a gaze to Solveig. "We had a little harness for goats to pull a cart, and I hooked up two goats to him so they could drag his body to the pyre I built." She sighed. "Within three days, I was all alone."

"Kai, I am so sorry." A glance into Solveig's soulful brown eyes informed Kai of her genuine empathy. "I cannot imagine facing that at ten years old. What did you do?"

"This was the hardest part." Kai shifted her gaze to the gameboard and inhaled deeply. "Papa had said I had to burn the bodies to eradicate the source of the plague, which meant my mother, father, and brother, too. I think I spent an entire day sitting in shock, staring at them, trying to muster the fortitude to follow through with his command." Daring to look up into Solveig's face, she added, "I never understood why I didn't get sick too."

"It happens that way, sometimes." Solveig's voice was like a healing stream, rich with kindness and understanding. "I remember when Elyn became gravely ill, Mama and Sigrid tried everything. All the healers were brought in, and the gothi offered sacrifices. Elyn had only ever been true and generous, courageous and devoted, yet only she succumbed to the disease, though it plagued her much longer than three days—closer to three months. She just kept getting weaker, lost her appetite, but never her spirit. Sigrid kept saying she would get better and pull through. When she didn't..."

Solveig met Kai's gaze. "I'm a lot like her, you know. It sounds foolish, since I can't emulate her physical feats, and yet the desire burns within me. When Ragna didn't return, I was inconsolable as well, deep in denial, praying for her to show up safe and sound. But I had Baldr and Geirfinnr's testimony. At least she was granted the death she preferred: in battle with a sword in her hand. But I thought without her my life was over too. I couldn't be who I wished, so I tried to live vicariously through her, I think."

Solveig shifted in her seat and glanced at the wall, seeming embarrassed by her confession. Kai didn't want her to pull away. "I engaged in a bit of the same for a while," she quickly added. "Torsten, my adopted father, has a brother, Jerrik, who is a powerful and acclaimed fighter. I used to wish I was him. If I were Jerrik, I could slay the greatest dragon, sail to exciting ports, and really make a difference. But I was the smallest girl in my town, so I turned my desire to accomplish great things into helping whoever I could in whatever way I could. The only weapon I was allowed was a bow, so I practiced until I was better than anyone with it, and Torsten finally let start hunting. The forest became my friend, and I learned to listen to the animals and the trees."

"I must admit you are proficient as a hunter," Solveig said with a bright change in her voice. "And you have certainly helped me. Speaking of that, I think we're ready for stage two." A gleam shone in her eyes as she leaned forward with a whisper. "Tomorrow, bring me a real sword."

Kai's lips parted, and her brows drew together. "Are you sure?"

"Quite. Since I've learned the basics with a wooden prop, I must strengthen my arm by holding an actual weapon." When Kai said nothing, worry cropped up on Solveig's face. "Unless you think I'm not ready?"

Kai couldn't deny Solveig anything. Besides, she would be there to ensure she didn't hurt herself. "I will bring an iron sword from the armory, but you will begin with mine."

A brilliant smile lit Solveig's countenance, causing Kai's heart to leap. She clasped her hands together. "Oh, thank you!"

"You will need to be extra careful not to incur cuts during practice," Kai warned. "How would you explain that to your mother?" Solveig beamed and nodded.

Kai yearned to take the next step in building a relationship with Solveig but wasn't sure how. Perhaps a gift?

"Wait a moment," Kai requested as her breath caught in her throat. "Something to commemorate your advancement."

Leaping up, Kai scurried to the trunk at the side of her sleeping bench and dug around inside. Clutching an item, she raced back to her seat. She took a steadying breath and peered at Solveig's curious expression.

"What do you have there?"

"Something I want to give you," Kai replied. "Something befitting a woman warrior." She held out her bronze Valkyrie figurine and placed it on Solveig's side of the table facing her. "In honor of you graduating from toys to a real blade."

Solveig picked up the statue to examine it with a look of wonder on her face. "Kai, I can't accept this. It was a gift to you. It's... the only thing you own, besides weapons."

As she started to hand it back, Kai flew into a panic. *She can't be rejecting my gift! Is it too soon? Did I misread the progress in our relationship? Her fondness for me?*

Kai reached out to stop her, covering Solveig's hand with the figure and holding it still. She sensed the warmth of Solveig's skin, and a tingle passed through her at the simple touch. Though perfectly innocent, the contact held an intimate quality for Kai, and she wished to linger in it.

"Please. She has brought me good luck. I hope she'll do the same for you. Besides, didn't your mother teach you how to accept a gift with grace and gratitude?" she added with a touch of humor to lighten the mood. Reluctantly, she drew back her fingers and waited.

Solveig studied her for a moment, then nodded. "Very well," she replied. "I suppose I could hold on to her for us for a while. Besides, we wouldn't want her to be stolen from your chest as all kinds of disreputable people frequent the great hall when there is food or drink to be had. She'll be safe in my room and can keep watch from there. However, I retain the right to give her back to you at a later date if I deem you require a boost in good fortune."

A thrill danced in Kai's heart, and she smiled in relief. "There now! That wasn't so hard."

Solveig sat on the edge of her bed brushing her long tresses per her nightly ritual, but this time her gaze rested on a hand-sized bronze image of a woman in armor, holding a shield and sword. She wore a helmet with a sturdy nosepiece, and her long hair flowed from beneath it. The artist had accentuated her breasts and hips to ensure everyone knew it did not represent a man.

That could be me, Solveig thought. *I wonder what possessed Kai to give it to me.* A divergent line of thought answered in her head, *You know perfectly well she is infatuated with you.*

She pursed her lips, and her brows furrowed. *She'll get over it soon enough. It is one thing to allow myself a casual friend, someone I can stand to have around so I'm not always alone; entertaining the idea of another close relationship is out of the question.*

Yet Solveig recalled several conversations that had veered uncomfortably close to the border of intimacy, such as the one this evening involving Kai's family and she and Ragna. A week before they had engaged in a lengthy philosophical discourse on the gods and fate versus free will. She was surprised to discover how similar their beliefs on the matter were, considering most people she knew fell squarely into the fate camp, thus ridding themselves of personal responsibility.

It also had occurred to her that she and Kai had battled both the odds and others' perceptions of them their whole lives, which pushed the Swede up a notch on Solveig's admiration scale. Kai always had a story to relate and seemed to intuitively know when to shift topics to keep her attention and good humor, yet Solveig refused to admit the little warrior's company made her happier than anyone's she could recall. *It's just nice to have a companion, and she is comfortable to be around,* she would tell herself. *I'm not, nor will I ever be, enamored with her. She's useful,* she conceded. *Where else would I find someone to instruct me and supervise my practice with a sword? Someone who would be so patient and encouraging when I am so inept? Who would praise my every tiny achievement as if it 'twere a milestone? She is...*

Solveig set down her brush and picked up the Valkyrie. She traced the grooves and studied the figure's face, feeling its weight in her hand, the smoothness of the metal. "She's one of a kind," she whispered aloud, referring to both the gift and giver. "The only item she possessed, and she gave it to me. I should think of something to give her."

As she glanced about her room, a voice screamed in her head. *NO! You can't do that. It will only encourage her. You've sworn not to love again, and if you start exchanging gifts, admiring this woman, picturing her adorable grin and spunky attitude as you lie down at night, you'll be right back where you started—able to have your heart broken again. Just let it go. She doesn't expect a return gift.*

What would she do with it, anyway? Like you said, someone who wanders in would probably steal it.

Taking her cue that it was time for sleep, Mist hopped up on the bed, turned several circles, then settled beside Solveig and laid her head on her lap. She peered up with an expressive look of interest, then stretched up to sniff the bronze piece. Curiosity met, she licked her mistress' hand, lay down again, and let out a humph. Solveig acknowledged her with a rub behind the ears, glad for her steadfast company.

With a deflated sigh, she set the figurine back on her nightstand beside the candle. She stared at it for a while, trying to settle her conflicting emotions. One thing was for certain: she could be excited about handling an actual sword tomorrow void of internal contradictions. With the thought in mind, a satisfied smile crossed her lips, and Solveig blew out the light.

35

The next day, as the first buds appeared at the tips of twigs and the warmth of a spring sun coaxed hibernating creatures back to life, Kai met Solveig in a little valley behind a hedge of trees over a rise from the king's palisade. She placed Stinnr in the princess's hand.

"You will notice many differences between a steel blade and a wooden one," she explained. "The weight, balance, and the vibrations when it strikes something, for instance. You should start with my sword because it is light, and I'll wield this old iron thing."

Solveig whirled the weapon around, getting a feel for it before they began the lesson.

"Do everything the way we practiced, only try not to cut my arm off or skewer me, please," Kai added with a wink. "Remember, it would leave you without an instructor."

"I have no intention of damaging you, my dear," Solveig quipped.

Kai raised the old sword to a ready position, trying her best not to glow. *She said, 'My dear'!* Ripples of joy cascaded through her, and it took all her effort to remain focused on giving instruction. "Now, block my strikes like we practiced and don't forget to move your feet," she said. She threw clumsy swipes and chops with the unfamiliar weapon, doing so slowly enough to give Solveig the opportunity to react. This time, iron clinked against steel as they went through their moves. "Not bad," Kai praised her.

"This sword isn't much heavier than the wooden one," Solveig marveled. "Though I see what you mean about the vibrations, and yours is so heavy when it hits mine, it's hard for me to hold the blocks and push it away."

"Even if you had a Damascus steel blade, most soldiers you'll face will bear weighty iron ones like this." Kai lowered her weapon and stepped back. "Don't you have an old sword of Sigrid's? I'm sure it would be just as elegant as Stinnr."

Solveig let her sword arm fall and rubbed her shoulder absently as she shook her head, a look of regret on her face. "No. She took it with her on her quest to find Bifröst." Then her expression lit up with eagerness. "But Elyn's should still be here somewhere. When we are ready, I'll ask Mother to give it to me. Herlief and Baldr received their own ancestral blades from Papa's side of the family. Oh, Kai, why didn't I think of it before?"

Bounding the few steps between them, Solveig grabbed Kai in an exuberant hug with her free arm. "Now, my turn to make the advances!"

Color rose in Kai's cheeks, and she hoped Solveig was too distracted to notice. It was her first hug from the princess, and Kai wished it had lasted longer. Still, the touch, no matter how brief, filled her with such joy and delight, she was certain it had exposed her feelings for Solveig. However, if she'd noticed, it didn't show.

"Remember to lead with your right foot and put your hip into your swings and thrusts," Kai reminded her. As she blocked, she assessed Solveig's progress. Once she had thought of Elyn's sword, she'd displayed more confidence since the beginning of the lesson today. They trained until Kai had determined Solveig was too tired to continue, though the princess protested.

"Look," Kai demanded as she plucked Stinnr from Solveig's hand. "If you hadn't worn gloves, you'd have blisters by now. How would you explain them to your mother? And what excuse will you offer for being away all afternoon?"

Solveig flashed a wicked grin. "I can tell Mother you took me for an early spring stroll to point out where baby animals will be born while I instructed you on the herbs we gather for medicines. She'll think we just went off to be alone together."

Kai's heart raced, and her palms started to sweat. "Is that what you and Ragna used to do?" She regretted the question at once, worried it might upset Solveig to talk about the slain shieldmaiden. To Kai's surprise, Solveig's face remained bright as they took slow, meandering steps toward the king's compound overlooking Gnóttdalr.

"At first," she admitted with a soft smile. "Before I was ready for my family to know about us. Ragna saw other women, and men, too, but then…"

"I'm sorry, Solveig." Kai lowered her chin, unable to look at her. "I shouldn't have said anything. It's none of my business."

"It's all right."

Kai felt Solveig take her hand, and it sent a thrill up her arm. "Ragna isn't sitting around Valhalla pining for me." It was a magical moment Kai would never forget. She doubted the woman would ever return the intensity of affection that inspired Kai's every breath, but at least they had become friends. She could be content with that.

From the instant she had heard of the princess in the distant land who needed her help, Kai had fantasized about her; however, when she'd seen her that Yuletide night, she was captivated. She had tried not to let it show in her every word and glance, but that proved too burdensome and false. Kai was who she was. It mattered not if Solveig never returned her affections; she would give her life for her as readily as she had for Tove. She hadn't liked being ignored those first few weeks, yet she understood. And now, she strolled along hand in hand with the most extraordinary woman she had ever met.

Once in sight of the fence around the longhouse yard, the two parted ways, Kai handling both swords. She joined Baldr and Geirfinnr to spar, apologizing for finding no game in the forest, though she wasn't certain they believed her. Her arm was glad to have Stinnr this time, instead of the heavy iron blade, and she swung it with greater ease.

A little while later, Ingrid called out the back door, "Come get cleaned up for dinner now; it's almost dark." Kai wished she had other clothes for the banquet chamber and scented bathwater or oils, so she could make herself more desirable to Solveig. She had been granted other baths since the first one in the princess' room, so she wasn't too dirty. Parting ways with the men, she stopped by the yard house and then washed her hands and face in a rain barrel. Kai smoothed her fingers through her hair and brushed down her tan tunic before entering the great hall, hoping she at least looked presentable.

"Are we in for a story?" she asked Geirfinnr when she spotted the red-haired Ivarolf flitting about.

"I hope so," the brawny warrior replied. He slapped a rough hand on her shoulder. "His tales are the best. You know, you're turning out all right. Ever since you invented víðir bjórr, saving us from the curse of constant sobriety, I'm starting to believe the gods really sent you."

With a jovial grin, he gave her shoulder a shake and struck off to join his friends. She glanced around the chamber until she spied Solveig at her table with Baldr and the rest of her family. They were joined by a couple of warriors, the town's healer, and a fellow dressed as a traveling merchant, whose conversation drew their attention.

Kai loaded her plate and drew a horn of víðir bjórr from the vat, then took them to sit on her bench. Two weeks ago, Solveig had requested she move back to the place that had been Ragna's, claiming she didn't want her so near the door. Kai liked that spot, as it put her closer to the king's table, which she supposed made it easier for Solveig to see her—another thought to keep her warm at night. She had been invited to Asbjorn's table a few times, but it was often filled with higher-ranked warriors, visiting dignitaries, and other important people, as it was tonight.

It didn't bother Kai to be excluded from the king's table; after all, she hadn't killed the giant yet. She took pleasure in the knowledge Solveig would engage her in a Hnefatafl game later, where they could talk privately, sharing experiences and feelings as they had the night before while sharpening their wits. For now, she sneaked secret glances toward Solveig and was encouraged to occasionally catch her doing the same.

As Kai wondered what topic they would explore after dinner, the scouts Knud and Caldervar rushed in. "We have found the monster's lair!" Knud exclaimed.

S olveig's attention shot to the scouts in an instant, and her heart raced. The moment of truth had arrived, but would she dare follow through with her plan? *I'm not ready.* Apprehension seized her soul.

"It has moved closer," Caldervar expounded once he had the hall's attention. "Less than a day's ride to the southeast, in a cave along the ridge."

"And you saw it?" Asbjorn demanded.

"With our very eyes," Knud swore.

"We must prepare," Solveig's father announced with determination.

Ingrid touched his arm. "How does Arvid, the gothi, fare? I wish to ask questions of him before anyone leaves to face the jötunn."

"You don't believe his tricks, do you, Mother?" Solveig asked. Disgusting memories of the pretentious Troels and loathsome Arvid's deception flashed across her mind.

"No, dear," Ingrid replied. "But since he was injured so severely and has taken all winter to heal, we haven't had a chance to question him thoroughly. I'm certain he knows more about this beast than he has revealed."

Solveig's temper settled, and she nodded to her mother. "Geirfinnr," Ingrid called. "Would you go check on Arvid? If he is able, bring him here. If not—"

"I'll go to him for interrogation," Asbjorn completed her thought. "Now, Kai, what are your intentions?"

Kai was already on her feet, standing beside the scouts. "I'll be the first to approach the giant. Geirfinnr, Baldr, and I have worked on several strategies to deal with him and can determine which is best once we have inspected the terrain."

"We decided to select the smallest possible number of warriors," Baldr, who sat to the king's right, stated, "to avoid unnecessary loss of life."

"That makes no sense," Asbjorn retorted. "We shall take the entire army!"

"And leave the capital undefended?" Baldr objected. "Something has been wrong with this situation all year."

"Yes, and the last time you went after the giant, your party was attacked by raiders from Sygnafylke," Asbjorn noted. "I don't believe it was a coincidence, either."

"Troels was not from Jutland," Solveig insisted. "He didn't talk like a Dane. He could have been a spy sent by King Rundrandr the Wolf."

"I agree he had false intentions," Ingrid said. "However, if he was working with Sygnafylke, why did their soldiers kill him?"

"Mistaken identity?" Solveig suggested.

"We don't require an army to dispatch the jötunn," Kai assured them. "Yet if this unfriendly neighbor poses a threat, more than the three of us shall be required to ward them off."

While the company tossed various ideas back and forth, Solveig worked up the nerve to defy them all. *How far will I get? Will Papa hogtie me and set guards to stop me? Am I really only a frail woman with poor vision? No. Kai has taught me to fight, and I have increased my strength. I haven't even fallen ill in several months. I am the descendant of legendary heroes with their legacy to fill. I shall not be relegated to obscurity. As Kai displayed unyielding courage when caught in the blizzard's teeth on the mountain, so must I defy the gale which roils against me.* Steeling her nerves, Solveig repeated to herself, *Desire and belief. I can do this. I will seize my destiny, too!*

No decisions had been reached by the time Geirfinnr returned, escorting Arvid and Osmin into the hall.

"Osmin, thank you for joining us," Ingrid greeted the gothi. "You have shown great hospitality caring for our injured guest this winter. Arvid, I'm glad to see your strength returning."

"He hasn't fully recovered," Osmin said as he helped Arvid onto a bench at the king's table.

"Arvid." Asbjorn fixed him with a grave look. He folded his hands before him, sitting straight, shoulders back, chest broad, solid as an oak. "My scouts have discovered the new location of the giant. I demand the truth, the whole truth, or so help me, I'll carve you up and feed you to the beast."

A hush fell over the chamber. The king was often gruff, but Solveig had never witnessed her father acting so fearsome. Arvid shrank back, guilty eyes darting about the hall. He coughed and shivered. Osmin laid a hand on his arm. "Answer honestly and all will be well."

"W-what do you wish to know?" the old man stuttered.

"Troels was not from Vendill, was he?" Ingrid asked. "He was no Dane."

"I..." The gothi opened his palms in front of him. "I don't know where he was from."

"And you?" Asbjorn's tone rolled like thunder trapped inside a jar. "From whence do you hail? Why do you not serve your king?"

"I've heard the rumors of war and you're likely to find out, so I'll answer the best I can," Arvid agreed. "I once served King Geirmund in Hördaland but fell from his favor."

"You were cast out?" Osmin asked in surprise.

Arvid lowered his head. "It isn't something a person speaks about. Some gothi travel, others serve in a temple or at court. None says, 'Listen to me because my king didn't.'"

"Why did he dismiss you?" Asbjorn demanded. "Were you banished?"

Solveig paid close attention. She understood the implications of banishment, a punishment equivalent to execution.

"I was banned from practicing my craft in Hördaland, not banished entirely."

"What about the jötunn?" Solveig asked. "How did you become involved with Troels?"

"Troels and I met in Sygnafylke, though he claimed to be a Dane," Arvid avowed. "He said he was embarking on a quest and needed my aid."

"So, the demonstration with the runes was to convince my father Troels was genuine and not a fraud," Solveig pressed.

Arvid's gaze fell, and he nodded.

"Then how did you know where to find the giant?" Ingrid inquired.

"Troels already knew where it was, only by the time we came here, built the scorpiones, and returned with your warriors, it had abandoned the cave and moved elsewhere."

The gothi's testimony made sense, although Solveig believed he was still hiding something. Her parents pressured him with more questions until Ingrid decided it was enough for the time being.

"We'll put him in a wagon and carry him with us," Baldr announced, a grave expression covering his youthful face. "He knows more about this and could be useful. Kai, Geirfinnr, we must be ready to depart at first light. Father, we shall take an escort of ten warriors to keep watch for a Sygnafylke trap and leave the rest to protect the city. Is there anything else?"

"Yes." Solveig rose and strode around the table to stand beside Kai. "I am going with them."

36

"You what?" Asbjorn bellowed as he bolted up from his seat. "You'll do no such—"

"Herlief may have been your son, but he was my older brother," Solveig retorted. Every muscle tensed and she steeled herself, standing her ground. "All my life I've been told what I cannot do; no more! I spent the winter building my strength, and I asked Kai to train me in secret."

"Ah." Ingrid's visage blossomed with recognition of her daughter's subterfuge.

Solveig pressed on, not wishing to give her father a chance to object. "I'll prove to you I can make the journey." Glancing around the room, she spied a gangly youth who had been training with the warriors. "Dagfinn," she called, pointing at him. Summoning her most commanding tone, she ordered him to come and sit. "I will show you all."

Taking the seat across from the young man with peach fuzz on his face who matched her height and weight, Solveig slammed her elbow on the table and angled her open palm toward him. "I've watched the men of this longhouse engage in contests of strength. There's one you call arm wrestling. Dagfinn, will you accept my challenge?"

"Solveig, this is absurd," her father chided her. "Don't embarrass yourself, child."

"And you, do not talk down to me," she shot back to everyone's shock.

The lad hesitated and glanced at the king for permission. Asbjorn scrunched his brows, pursed his lips, and waved dismissively at them before plopping down again.

"I'll try not to hurt you, Princess Solveig," Dagfinn promised.

Solveig stared dangerously at him and tightened her grip around his hand. "And I'll do the same."

Though her words received a scattering of chuckles, most in the hall were too stunned to make a sound. Solveig remembered the technique Kai had taught her. *Do not rely on your arm; rather put your entire body in the contest. A woman's strength lies in her legs and hips, so use them. Start from your toes and push the energy up your calves and thighs, into your core and shoulder, and only then into your arm. Use your neck and head; every pound of your weight must create the force you apply. If possible, pull your opponent's arm toward you instead of trying to push it over.* She braced her right foot and began the cascade of power.

Solveig had chosen a seat from which she could see Kai. She glanced at her while bearing into her move. It was as if she could feel the confident vibrations radiating from the unlikely warrior, bolstering her strength and assurance. Solveig focused her mind on one thing—victory. She pushed and pulled with taut muscles, bringing her opponent's arm down gradually. The young man's tendons tightened, and he gritted his teeth with a groan. Solveig was vaguely aware of cheers and bets being laid, yet they did not distract her. Kai had told her the only way for a woman to beat a man at this contest was to do so quickly. Noting Dagfinn's strain as the back of his fist bent toward the wooden planks, she discharged a last, intense burst of energy, pouring the power of every inch of her body into the action. A gasp arose as she slapped his hand to the table.

"I win!" She released the surprised and probably embarrassed youth's fist and pushed to her feet. "Thank you, Dagfinn, for a worthy, hard-fought bout. Now Papa, I realize this young man is neither you nor Geirfinnr, but I hope I've demonstrated I am not the weakling you have always believed me to be."

"Solveig, it isn't a matter of weakness," he huffed out in dismay.

She saw Ingrid lean over and whisper in Baldr's ear. He nodded and left the table for their private rooms. It piqued Solveig's curiosity, though she was busy trying to persuade the king.

"And Kai has been teaching me to fight with a sword, spear, and axe, how to use a shield and to be vigilant and aware of my surroundings," she continued. "And before you blame her, I ordered her to obey and keep it a secret until the day I revealed what I've been about. Did you notice my increased energy and how I haven't come down with a season-changing sickness recently? I may have been useless as a youth, but I've grown into myself now. And besides, I have every right to be included in all aspects of governing Sogn, including defending it from dangerous invaders."

Solveig turned and raised open hands to the room, seeking support from others. "Do I not engage in all other activities of leadership? Haven't I dedicated myself to the betterment of our kingdom? When have you witnessed apathy from me? Or sloth? Or self-indulgence? Am I not an honorable woman?"

"You are," Asbjorn concurred in tense frustration. "No one thinks you dishonorable, little dove. Yet there are many ways to serve other than combat. Be content to follow your mother's example."

"She will never be satisfied with my life, husband," Ingrid said as Baldr returned, dragging a large chest along the floor behind him.

The assembly watched as he rounded the table and stopped in front of Solveig, where he dropped the end with a loud thud. Dust puffed from the top of the trunk and her heart caught in her throat as she wondered what lay inside.

"Oh, Ingrid!" Asbjorn moaned and covered his face with a wide palm. "Don't you understand I only wish to keep her safe?"

"I know full well how you love your daughter and strive to protect her," Ingrid replied. "Look at her, Asbjorn. She is a grown woman and has seen twenty-three winters. She has a mind and will of her own, dreams and ambitions we have stifled, and yes, with the best of intentions. But how long can a bird remain in its nest? And what is that bird's purpose in life if it is never allowed to fly?"

The king regarded Ingrid with a troubled gaze. A hush fell in the chamber as he tapped his thick fingers on the table. "And what if the monster kills her like it did Herlief?"

"I will never let that happen," Kai declared with conviction as she stepped to Solveig's side. "Trust me when I say Solveig's safety is my primary concern. However, I am also concerned with seeing her fulfill her dreams and aspirations. King Asbjorn, Queen Ingrid," she continued, impassioned in her speech, "I grew up hearing songs and sagas repeated about Sigrid and Elyn, the mighty shieldmaidens from Norvegr, and the tales inspired me beyond imagining. One day, skalds shall recount the time Princess Solveig and her bodyguard, Kai, rid the kingdom of a dangerous and meddlesome jötunn. Baldr will have a place in this story, as well as many of his own, but please, my lord, do not deny her this. Solveig was born to be a hero, a formidable woman with a valiant legacy to uphold. The gods did not allow a plague or slave traders or a shipwreck or a frigid trek over mountains in winter to stop me from accomplishing my destiny; they won't stand in the way of Solveig's. Will you?"

All eyes shifted to the king, and Solveig held her breath. Kai's words were the most glorious she had ever heard spoken and, in that moment, she wanted to kiss her—give her the fearsome, bold, impassioned kiss she deserved for her advocacy and devotion.

"Humph!" He rubbed a finger down the side of his nose before raising his palms in surrender. "If it means so much to you, Solveig, fine. You can go. But I'm coming too! I'll not send any more of my children off to die while I remain behind these walls in safety. Ardmundr, clean and polish my armor; sharpen my sword and spear. I will see this giant for myself."

Amazed voices sounded around the hall, and Solveig detected the triumph on her mother's face. "Here," Baldr said, then opened the trunk.

Solveig blinked to be sure her eyes did not deceive her. She bent down and lifted out Elyn's sword, protected in its scabbard for a decade. She felt Kai near her as she peered in. Underneath it lay Elyn's steel-studded blue armor, with matching bracers and greaves.

"I believe it will fit you perfectly." Ingrid had joined them, and her voice touched Solveig's soul with wonderful delight. "She was about your size."

As she studied the chest's contents, she spied a silver helmet with its distinctive cheek and nose guards, webbed leather lining, and a chinstrap. Solveig was in awe. Her grandmother had worn this into battle, on her adventures, and she herself would don it on the morrow.

"At the bottom are some old things of Sigrid's from when she was twelve or thirteen," Ingrid continued. "Kai, I believe they will fit you. I can't have the two of you rushing into the jaws of danger ill-prepared, now can I?"

"Oh, Mama!" Solveig threw her arms around the queen. She kissed her cheek as a tear formed. "Thank you so much! I can do this. I swear you won't mourn my death, only celebrate our victory."

"I pray you are right," Ingrid exhaled with deep emotion. "But I must let you be you." Releasing the embrace, she peered around Solveig to Kai. "I believe you'll allow no harm to come to my daughter as long as you live, although to be honest, I must wonder how long that will be. You are a worthy soul, Kai of Yeats. Now, go slay a jötunn."

Solveig hugged and thanked her father between his barking orders to everyone, assured Baldr she wouldn't be in the way, and beamed at Geirfinnr's congratulations for her courage. As their plans for the morning solidified, Solveig asked Kai to take the opposite handle of the trunk and help her carry it to her room. Once inside, she lit several candles, stirred the firepit, and latched the door. Then she turned to the woman to whom she owed all this newfound spirit.

Kai remained in a corner, glancing nervously about, biting her lower lip. She lifted hesitant eyes as blue as a robin's egg to hers. The nervous expression caused a flutter in Solveig's stomach, and she suddenly noticed how warm the room had become. *She is so adorable; why didn't I see it before?*

"Thank you, Kai," she began, "for your support and for everything you've done to make this happen. What you said today ... you made my heart sing."

"I only told the truth," Kai replied.

Solveig took a step closer, an amused look on her face. "Skalds will recount my tale? I was born to be a hero?"

"All true, every word," Kai stated without a hint of humor.

Now Solveig was near enough to smell her, to feel her breath, to sense her very heartbeat. Her gaze played over Kai, and she realized she was falling for her. The only questions that remained: should she allow it of herself again, and on the eve of battle? No. She should bid Kai goodnight and show her out. Recently, though, Solveig had paid little attention to what she should do and much to what she desired to do.

She ran her fingers through Kai's short, silky strands, which barely brushed her shoulders. Her hair was straight, fine, and delicate, not as thick and voluminous as her full-bodied tresses, though it was as pleasing to the touch as it was to the eye. "You are ... amazing."

Solveig's fingertips traced the lines and curves she had been studying for weeks, from Kai's hair to her face. Every inch was satiny smooth.

As if Kai could read her mind, she said, "Your mother's cream has done wonders for my chapped skin. Please thank her for me."

Solveig grazed her thumb across Kai's lips, which had so often smiled at her. She felt the tenuous breath she then took, a response that both amused and aroused Solveig. A taste would help her decide what should come next, so she leaned in and kissed Kai. *Stimulating.* Kai responded with languid warmth, matching each flick of her tongue.

When she pulled back, Solveig examined Kai, who wore a blissful expression, eyes closed, swaying as if she was a bit dizzy, and a satisfied smile bloomed on Solveig's face. "Stay with me tonight, for tomorrow, either we march to glory, or we leave this earth and all its trappings behind."

Kai's lids fluttered open. "I'll stay if you want me to."

"Good." A tingle of nervous doubt suddenly shot through Solveig. It was obvious Kai doted on her, but what about when their mission was over? Surely, she would return to her homeland, and then what?

She fiddled with Kai's hair before stepping away. "Don't expect too much. I want you to have a comfortable night before we ride out in the morning. It'll be an early start and we both need to be rested."

"True." Kai's voice sounded so disappointed.

"This is the side of the bed I sleep on," Solveig said, motioning to the left. "Please remove your boots and trousers and take that side."

While Kai followed her instructions, Solveig slipped off her strap dress and smock, leaving on her white linen chemise to crawl under the covers.

"Thank you for inviting me to sleep in comfort." Kai folded back the blanket, lay in her spot, and pulled it over her. "Do you want me to blow out the candle?"

There was another on Solveig's side and a low glow from the fire, now banked low in the hearth. "Sure, if you like."

While Kai snuffed out the taper, a whine sounded at Solveig's feet. She had forgotten about Mist and her comfy nightly ritual. "Not tonight," she said in a forceful tone. "Guard the door." Her loyal companion obeyed with a whimper, her tail drooping in disappointment.

"You have such a wonderful dog," Kai commented before rolling onto her side, facing away from Solveig. She seemed oddly shy; then again, Solveig realized she had been giving her mixed messages—not on purpose, but rather because she was confused herself.

Leaving her candle burning, she nestled up to Kai and pressed her torso to her back, draping an arm around her tiny waist. "Mist is a joy," she said.

As are you, she thought.

Though Kai didn't speak, Solveig knew she was awake and probably as excited and apprehensive as she about what the next day would bring. She edged her head closer, inhaling Kai's scent, allowing herself to feel the satisfaction and comfort her nearness brought, luxuriating in the warmth of her body. As she lay cuddling Kai beneath the blanket, a singular sensation formed in Solveig's core, like a tiny seed unfurling its sprout under the soil. As it pushed forth, it spread through her like a fast-growing vine, overtaking one part of her after another until it had consumed her in glorious revelation.

Solveig savored the novel awareness, marveling in its unfamiliar facets, until she glowed with unimaginable elation over an experience she had never had before. Holding Kai made her feel powerful.

She had known pleasure and ecstasy in this bed with Ragna, who had been taller, heavier, and stronger than she was, but the shieldmaiden had been the mighty one. Kai was not weak or helpless by any means. She was a tough, tenacious woman who never shrank from a challenge, no matter how great, and yet she was like a soft rabbit in her embrace. The euphoria of invincibility surged through Solveig, and she liked it. Exhaling, she sensed the vibrations radiating from her heart to fill the room with an overwhelming energy she could not contain. In an instant, she knew what she wanted.

Solveig reached down with her fingers and worked them under Kai's tunic, then returned her hand to her firm stomach, only this time with no fabric in the way. "I want to touch you, to feel your skin under my fingertips. Is it all right with you?"

"Yes," came a breathy utterance. "Your touch is like seiðr to me."

A smile of wonder curved Solveig's lips, and she snuggled closer to brush kisses on Kai's neck. "You inspire me," she breathed into Kai's ear before tracing its contour with her tongue. She sensed the need rising in her core, screaming at her to embrace the wild abandonment. Her hand crept higher to cup Kai's palm-sized breast. Subtle, silky, and still firm, it felt like kneading dough before letting it rise. When she brushed her forefinger over the nipple; it stood erect in a bumpy ring of stimulation, which compounded her monumental longing even more.

"You ..." Kai's words caught in her throat, and she swallowed them.

Solveig grinned as she felt the shiver pass through the woman's body at her command. This impression of potency was intoxicating, and Solveig had no interest in fighting it, only in riding it through to its conclusion. "This tunic has to go," she said. Kai turned on her back and glanced over at Solveig with a delirious expression.

"If you say so," she managed, then assisted Solveig in removing it.

Solveig raked a greedy gaze down her sleek, toned body, then paused in confusion. "You don't have any warrior tattoos."

"No, I don't. I had only begun my training when Frigg received her vision and I was sent to you," she said. "And Jerrik wasn't sure King Freyrdan would let me join his fighters."

"Well, that oversight can be easily remedied," Solveig declared. "Now, off with those *brais* so I may enjoy all of you."

Kai dropped the undergarment off the side of the bed and gazed at Solveig in wonder. "Is this a dream? Do you really want me? Because I dreamed of being with you so many nights as I lay alone in the hall."

"We shall see if it's a dream," Solveig quipped. She straddled Kai, took her wrists, and pinned them to the pillow on either side of her head. Then her mouth went to work on Kai's outstretched body, from navel to sensuous, thirsty lips. Kai's moans and whimpers drove Solveig's desire more urgently.

"Do not move," she commanded, releasing Kai's hands to yank off her own under-gown and toss it aside. Reclaiming Kai's wrists, she slid over her captive in tantalizing fashion before assaulting her throat with a needy mouth, leaving a passion mark as evidence.

"Kai," Solveig whispered, hovering above her. She gazed into dreamy eyes that compelled her to confess the truth. "You make me feel so many things—things I never felt."

"I haven't even touched you yet," Kai responded in astonishment. "You seem to enjoy torturing me, though."

"You'll get your turn," Solveig promised with a smile of pleasure. Then she dove back in to plunder and stake claim over her newly conquered territory.

37

"How do I look?"

Kai gazed upon the most magnificent sight she had ever beheld—Solveig wearing Elyn's distinctive blue armor. The small steel disks sewn into the gambeson glistened like moonbeams on waves while the fabric hugged her curves like a lover's caress. The matching greaves and bracers made her look formidable. Just looking at her stirred Kai beyond words.

Last night had been the single most amazing experience of her life. She had believed the kisses and intimate touches she had shared with Tove were feminine sexual activity, and they had been enjoyable; Solveig, however, had introduced her to an ocean of pleasures she never knew existed, schooling her in advanced techniques of orgasmic delight that left her body humming. Taking cues from the master, she had apparently sent Solveig on her own intense flight of ecstasy—or at least, such had been her goal. *All those people who think her fragile have never spent a night in her bed,* she thought. Solveig possessed the energy of a hare, the instincts of a wolf, and the stamina of a racehorse, not to mention the acute attention to detail and tender touch of a princess.

As long as Kai had loved Solveig from afar, she had faced no fear of loss, as the entire relationship had only existed in her mind. But now, even the hint of losing Solveig's affections terrified her. *Was it only for one night? An 'in case we die' thing?*

Kai banished the thought. "On my oath," she stated, "you are as spectacular as any of Odin's Valkyries."

Solveig beamed at her. "Sigrid's old attire appears to fit you," she said. Kai glanced down at the breastplate atop a gray gambeson and black leather leggings pulled above her hips. A broad matching waistband of thicker rawhide provided added protection for her midsection.

"Here, turn around and let me tighten the straps," Solveig said. Kai complied, sucking in a breath when the princess tugged on her breastplate. It was embarrassing to think a twelve- or thirteen-year-old Sigrid had been larger than her full-grown self. "There."

Pivoting, Kai faced Solveig, swimming in her eyes, battling the urge to pull her back onto the bed. Instead, she lifted the helmet from the trunk and handed it to her.

"No," Solveig stated with concern. "You should wear it, as you will face the gravest danger."

Kai shook her head. "It is more important that you return unharmed."

"More important to whom?" Solveig retorted.

"To everyone," Kai assured her and pushed the helmet into her hands. "Besides, I've never worn a helmet before, and I fear it would get in my way. It's probably too big for me anyway, so please." She stroked Solveig's cheek and brushed a kiss to her lips. "Now, my hair is still too short to braid, yet long enough to fall in my eyes. I would appreciate if you had something I could tie it back with."

Solveig set down the helmet and nodded. "I suppose I should do the same. Could you assist me?"

"Certainly."

She took the beaded leather twine Solveig gave her, pulled back her hair, and tied it. With great pleasure, she stepped behind the princess and ran her fingers through her luxurious strands. She recalled doing so last night while taking breathers between bouts of lovemaking.

As Kai plaited her hair, Solveig asked, "What do you expect will happen when we get there?"

"I cannot guess," Kai admitted.

"Whatever happens, I want you to know something." Solveig hesitated and Kai braided in silence, anticipation whirling through her empty stomach. "You have given me the most marvelous gift possible."

Confused, Kai asked, "The little warrior figure?"

"No," came a gentle rebuttal. Solveig turned in her arms and slid her hands across Kai's shoulders. "You make me feel strong."

A soft smile touched Kai's lips. "You've always been strong. I believe in you, Solveig."

"You do." She kissed her. "No one else ever has, you see? I didn't even believe in myself until you came and showed me impossible things weren't so impossible after all. I still can't see well, but I feel confident like never before, as if all my imperfections didn't matter."

"They don't. We will face this challenge together, and everyone shall remember your valor. But promise me this." Kai pinned her with a commanding look and took her cheeks between her palms. "When fighting ensues, do not stray from my side. Stay near so I can protect your back and your flanks. Your father and brother may forget you are with them, but I shall be focused on safeguarding you. Swear it."

"I swear, Kai, only if you vow to spare half your focus for safeguarding yourself. I'll be exceedingly displeased if you are killed. Understood?"

Displaying a grin of relief, Kai nodded. "Understood."

Solveig graced her with one more kiss, then stepped away. "It's time."

The party rode out at dawn's first light. The scouts who knew the way took the lead, followed by King Asbjorn and Baldr, Kai and Solveig, Geirfinnr, and the other volunteers, sixteen in all. A wagon carrying the two huge crossbows and the recovering Arvid brought up the rear. Asbjorn had left a larger troop of warriors to defend Gnóttdalr in case the giant was part of a Sygnafylke plot. Though they traveled as swiftly as they could, they didn't reach the location of the cave until the afternoon.

"It's just ahead," Knud announced, pulling his pony to a halt. "Past this stand of trees. See the cliff there?" He pointed to a slab of rock looming up from the slope of the mountain.

Asbjorn nodded and took a drink from his water bag.

Caldervar continued. "The cave is in the crag. There is an open area of rough ground about the size of a hog pen in front of the opening. Not a lot of room to maneuver."

"Let me scout the terrain across from the entrance to find a suitable spot to place the scorpio," Baldr suggested.

"Yes, and I'll creep up to the clearing to see if the giant is about," Kai added.

"Good," King Asbjorn concurred. "The rest of us will wait here. Dismount, everyone," he commanded. "Take a quick break and remain quiet."

Kai exchanged a glance with Solveig and handed her the pony's reins. "I'll not be long," she promised in a hushed tone, before striding away from the team.

With Stinnr hanging from her belt and her shield looped over her back, Kai picked her way through the brush like a fox, disturbing nothing. After crossing a distance no farther than between the king's longhouse and the docks, she discovered the trees thinned, and an open space appeared before her. She crouched behind the last bush and surveyed the area. The crack in the stony cliff towered at more than twice her height with a breadth equal to her arm span. A small trail of smoke puffed from the opening while more seeped out from a crack higher in the rocks. He was in there, or someone with a fire was at least.

Not seeing or hearing anyone, she crept out from behind the scrub and took steady steps toward the cave. Identifying a pungent stench of urine, she veered to where the vegetation met the cliff wall and found a stagnant pool. *His version of a yard house, I presume.* She was uncertain of how acute a jötunn's sense of smell was, though she supposed approaching from this angle would hide her scent from even the keenest bear's nose.

Detecting movement from the corner of her eye, Kai glanced over to see Baldr scoping out the area across from the fissure. He nodded to her, and she edged her way to the mouth of the cavern. Crouching to make herself smaller and closer to the ground, she peeked inside. A few old bones lay near the aperture and a low light glowed from farther in. She could hear faint shuffling noises and a grunt before she saw a looming dark silhouette cast on a shadowy stone wall.

Kai pulled away and gave Baldr a silent nod, then crept back to the cover of the thicket and to the waiting party.

"I didn't get a clear view of it, but something big that knows how to build a fire is in the cave," Kai reported. "It seems to be alone."

Baldr joined them. "We can bring a scorpio along a narrow animal path. I found a stone large enough to set it on opposite the cavern opening," he stated. "The wagon and horses should stay here, though, as the noise would alert the giant of our approach."

Asbjorn nodded. "Geirfinnr, help Baldr carry the weapon, and Knud, haul the bolts."

The warrior who had survived the first encounter with the monster stood motionless, peering at the king, looking terror stricken. He swallowed and his axe hand quivered. "Y-yes, my lord."

"Is there a problem?" Baldr asked, conveying concern rather than accusation in his tone.

"No, no problem." He grabbed one of his hands with the other to calm it. "I just recall... I fought it before, is all. I shall carry the bolts and not falter."

Geirfinnr laid a firm hand on the frightened man's shoulder. "Aye, Knud. I've done battle with the beast as well, witnessed the same horrors as you. Do you think I have not sweated in the night, awoken by the screams of our friends? All is well."

Knud nodded, and Geirfinnr gave him a pat, then left with Baldr to retrieve the weapon.

"I suggest a couple stay with Arvid and the wagon," Kai advised the king, "while the rest set up in an arc behind the scrub line. When everyone is in place, I'll lure it out."

"I should be the one to face him," Asbjorn declared. "He killed my son."

"Yes, my lord, only you are nearly a giant yourself," Kai reasoned. "He will see you, feel threatened, and attack, whereas I will not seem dangerous. I may not even register as human to him, just a little wood sprite or mountain vættir for him to chase away."

With a sigh, he agreed. "Very well. Lure him out."

Feeling Solveig take her arm, Kai shifted her gaze to the princess. "You should stand with Baldr at the scorpio. It will give you the clearest view, and he'll be there to guard you while I'm in the clearing. Once I maneuver the jötunn into the line of fire, he'll pull the lever. The bolt should deliver a grave wound. I will then dash about and cut the ligaments at the back of his legs so he topples over. At that point, everyone shall rush in and strike their blows."

"It is a sound plan," Asbjorn concurred.

"Be careful he doesn't fall on you," Solveig commanded.

Kai offered her a grin. "Not a chance! I'm much swifter than a clunky old giant."

"In that case..." Solveig surprised Kai, her father, and the entire company by planting a kiss on her lips in front of them all. "Let's do this."

Once the colossal weapon and all the warriors were in place, Kai wandered up to the cave entrance as if she was out for an early spring stroll. She pretended to be witless, so her presence wouldn't put the giant on guard.

"Oh, look, a lovely grotto!" she sang out in a melodious voice she imagined might belong to a wood elf. "Let me see if someone is home."

She tossed a small stone in ahead of her, the sound of which echoed about the cavern. Then she strolled out of the afternoon sunlight into the smoky gloom of the unknown. The entryway towered above her yet was relatively narrow until the channel opened into a wide chamber. In its midst smoldered the fire and what she beheld rising from a thick log-bench was unbelievable.

Kai's heart raced, and her breath caught in her chest. She looked up, up, and up to a being with long legs and massive feet. The top of her head barely reached the rope belt tied around a tunic fashioned from animal skins. An enormous hand scooped up a rock and hurled it at her as a gravelly voice bellowed something that sounded like, "Go away!"

Though she couldn't get a good look at him in the poor lighting, she could tell he was hunched like very old people often were, causing her to wonder about the creature's age. Knowing she would have a better view outside, she called, "Come and get me!"

After scrambling a few steps, Kai spun around to see if he was following, but he was starting to sit. *Odd. Why isn't he attacking me?* "Hey, giant!" she shouted and stomped back toward his inner lair. "I am a mighty warrior here to slay you. Come out and fight!"

He resumed his looming posture and stared at her. Then she could have sworn he laughed. A jötunn laughing at her! Kai rolled her eyes and shook her head. "You too? I'm serious." The gruff chuckling noise sounded louder, making Kai angry. She was tired of being laughed at. With a quick scan of the cave, she spotted a gigantic spear. Its headpiece appeared to be a sword lashed onto a staff the width and length of a small tree trunk. Kai rushed over, snatched it up with both hands—it must have weighed more than a longship's oar—and ran out into the light. "Is this yours?" she taunted. "If you want it, come and take it from me!"

She heard the stomping of his feet as he strode after her. "Mine!"

Kai trotted into the center of the clearing and turned around to wait for him. When he emerged, he raised a platter-sized hand to shade the sun from his eyes. Now she could get a proper look at the giant, and an uneasy realization struck her. She moved closer to him, just to be sure, as she gazed at the black and red leathery skin of his misshapen face.

"Move, Kai!" Baldr called. "You're blocking my shot."

"Wait!" She spun to face the others, holding up the spear and standing her ground. In a slow, nonthreatening motion, she pivoted toward the humongous figure behind her. She laid the oversized weapon on the ground and, in a tone of recognition and compassion, said, "I see you."

Shock filled the giant's eyes, and he fled back into his hollow.

38

olveig's jaw dropped as she stood motionless beside Baldr and the scorpio, which was cocked and ready to deliver its crippling blow. While she could not make out a single detail, she easily recognized the fuzzy giant looming over Kai at twice her height. Her lover had waltzed into his lair, teased and taunted him into position, and then ... it fled from her?

"Why did you do that?" Baldr yelled in a rare display of emotion. "I had him and you blocked my shot!"

Kai dashed over to them with a look of wonder. Asbjorn stepped up behind Solveig, and the five of them, including Geirfinnr, stared at her, awaiting an answer.

"Because we need to make sure we are doing the right thing," she declared with conviction. "He may be unusually tall, but this is no escaped miscreant from Jötunheimr. He is a man, a human being."

"But his grisly appearance?" Geirfinnr queried in disbelief. "I saw it up close, and 'twas that of a monster."

"Listen to me," Kai implored him. "Frigg, my völva from Yeats, suffered severe burns to her face, half of it anyway. The heat and flames left her skin scorched red and black with disfiguring scars just like his, only this fellow's are worse. They consume his entire face and neck and probably more areas covered by his clothing. He talked to me, in our language," she expounded with passion. "Not only did he refrain from attacking me, but he acted afraid—of me! Geirfinnr, are you certain this is the same 'giant' you fought before? I don't want us exacting retribution on the wrong person."

"I'm pretty sure," he answered, then glanced at the shadowy cave entrance. He took in a deep breath, swallowed, and nodded. "I am almost completely certain this is the same behemoth, yet I admit, his behavior is inconsistent. Mayhap he has grown weak from a lack of food."

"Jötunn or man, it makes no difference," her father barked. "He killed Herlief and dozens more, terrorized our land, and presents an ongoing threat. He must die."

"Before doing something which cannot be undone, we should interrogate Arvid again," Solveig advised. "There's more he hasn't told us. Herlief and the others were slaughtered before he and Troels appeared on our doorstep, yet have we received any testimonies of violent attacks since then? Force Arvid to tell us everything."

"I suppose my vengeance can wait a few more minutes for knowledge's sake." Asbjorn sighed and shoved his sword back into its sheath. "Stand down!" he called to the others. "Let's uncover it all."

Solveig fell in beside Kai as they marched behind her father and Baldr, while Geirfinnr stayed with the weapon to guard them against a surprise attack by the giant. "A man, truly?" she whispered.

Kai nodded with assurance. "As human as you or me."

Recalling her suspicion when none had believed the early reports, much less how nobody in living memory had ever seen a jötunn, Solveig was willing to believe Kai's assessment. "Then why is he so enormous? Even I could see how he towered over you."

"I don't know," she replied quietly.

Upon reaching the horses and cart, Kai hopped into the back, where Arvid rested, surrounded by pillows and blankets. Exerting more effort, Solveig climbed in after her, and they took seats flanking him. Asbjorn rambled up to the side of the wagon beside Arvid and drew his dagger, regarding him with an icy glare.

"You lied to us," he growled.

"No, my lord!" The frail old gothi shook as his eyes darted among their faces.

"Then you omitted many parts of the story," Kai stated. "For he who dwells in the cave is a larger-than-average man who was disfigured in a fire. He may have lost his sanity, but not his humanity."

"My lord!" he cried, swinging to face the king. "It was Troels, not me."

"Do not shift blame on one who isn't here to speak on his own behalf," Baldr commanded.

"My son and warriors were killed in your scheme," Asbjorn uttered in a low, dangerous hiss. He flashed his blade before Arvid's terror-stricken eyes, scrutinizing him with scorn. "I can torture the information out of you if it's what you prefer."

"No, wait!" Arvid moaned. "I am too old to endure torture. If I tell you all, will you swear to make my death quick?"

Solveig exchanged a nervous glance with Kai. She understood part of a king's duty was to mete out justice, which included punishing wrongdoers, but she had never witnessed an execution herself. Their law did not equate killing someone in a fair fight with murder, nor condemn retaliation against a man who had injured, stole from, or insulted another. However, cowardly acts of subterfuge and unjust schemes to gain wealth and power at the expense of unsuspecting victims were serious crimes demanding weighty penalties.

"If you swear by Thor's hammer your testimony is true, I'll grant you a swift death, should your actions warrant it," Asbjorn vowed, returning his knife to his belt.

"I swear."

"Let's start with the obvious," Asbjorn proceeded. "Is the creature human, and does he have a name?"

"He is, my lord," Arvid confessed. He withered like a sail that had lost the wind and slumped into his pillows. "His name is Gudrun."

Solveig stared at the frail imposter of a holy man and worked to quiet the rage churning in her gut. "What happened to him?" she demanded. "What did you and Troels do?"

"Troels was a duper, albeit one with charm and a sturdy frame," Arvid began. "He moved around from town to town, and the first time I met him,

I recognized what he was about. He offered to cut me in for my silence. Then four years ago, after King Geirmund expelled me from Hördaland, our paths crossed again. He couldn't wait to show me the asset he had recently acquired. He wished me to help mold the young man into what he needed for his scheme."

"Young?" Kai asked in surprise. "How young?"

"Certainly no older than you, mayhap younger," Arvid replied, flitting a glance in her direction. "Troels found him after a tragic mistake on the part of the boy's parents. You see, something was dreadfully wrong with their son: he didn't stop growing. By the time he hit puberty, his head scraped the roof of their hut. All their neighbors were afraid of him, and they claimed he was slow-witted as well. Gudrun's father was a tanner, and villagers stopped bringing their skins to him and started spreading rumors about a jötunn impregnating his wife. Their other children suffered ridicule as well, and their entire standing in the community was under threat, so, they arrived at an unsavory decision."

Arvid shook his head and wiped a hand down his face, pausing to inhale a shuddering breath. "He used certain oils and extracts in his tanning process that are poisonous if consumed, and he gave them to his wife, who poured them into the boy's soup, hoping it would do the job quickly without unnecessary pain. He convulsed and crumpled to the floor after eating it, and believing he was dead, they dragged his body outside onto a pile of sticks and straw they had prepared. Then they poured oil over him and lit the fire."

"Only he wasn't dead," Kai interjected.

"No." Arvid's gaze fell to a spot in the wagon. "The pain from the blaze must have awoken him, and Gudrun leaped up and ran away. Troels was in their village at the time and was sparked by a fiendish idea. He promised the boy's parents he would take care of the problem for a small fee, then he captured the frightened lad and enslaved him."

Solveig felt sick to her stomach. "You mean Gudrun's parents tried to poison him and burn him alive, all because he was different? A little too tall, not quite as bright as other youngsters?"

"You must consider the implications, sister," Baldr said. "They were likely afraid for their own lives and worried about what kind of future such an unusual child might have. When a baby is born with a severe deformity, isn't it put out on the ice or left in the forest to save it from a life of misery?"

"This is different," she countered. "He had already seen, what, fourteen winters?" she asked with a glance at Arvid, who merely shrugged. "I'm certainly glad nobody decided to finish me off for having poor eyesight or Kai for being too short. No one is perfect."

"You both present compelling arguments," Asbjorn admitted, "yet I want Arvid to continue. Tell us what Troels did to him and how you fit in."

Arvid slumped further, as if he might collapse entirely. "Troels' plan was to convince people that Gudrun was a vicious giant, frighten them, then swoop in to the rescue—for a fee. Each time I employed my runes trick as a sign from the gods, and he required half of his payment in advance. We would then strike out to 'kill' the giant, collect Gudrun, and move to a different village."

"But how did the two of you control such a large, powerful man?" Asbjorn asked.

"We ..." Arvid hung his head.

"You tortured him," Baldr inserted with disgust. "You inflicted pain, deprived him of food and water, required him to perform exactly to your specifications or else."

Arvid nodded.

"Then what changed?" Solveig charged.

"A year ago, we ran the charade in Sygnafylke, except the jarl insisted on coming and bringing his warriors to assist Troels. He couldn't allow them to kill his most important asset, so I was to set traps and conjure noxious smoke to meet them when they entered the cave. He got Gudrun to massacre the soldiers by convincing him they were demons from another realm, there to drag him to Hel. Then he was so impressed by how well the young man performed—" Arvid sighed and rubbed his temple—"he wanted him to do it again. Troels said it made for a more urgent plight than simply having a jötunn who attacked livestock and knocked over huts."

"And you were complicit!" Solveig snapped. "You helped him torture and deceive this oddity of nature and used him as a weapon to kill other people. That's ... evil!"

"You gave your word to grant me a quick death," Arvid reminded the king.

"One thing I don't understand," Asbjorn said with furrowed brows. "Baldr and two longboats of warriors accompanied you and Troels on the ill-fated quest to kill the giant. Was it your intent for Gudrun to destroy them all?"

"No." Arvid squirmed and glanced at Solveig. "We staged the first slaughter during which Herlief and the others were killed to get your attention, to secure your resolve to hunt down and punish the man we'd convinced you was a jötunn. Troels didn't anticipate how ... humanly Gudrun would react. He became uncooperative, despite everything we did to control him. He threw fits and cried over all the dead warriors. Troels had heard word of King Asbjorn's beautiful, unwed daughter, and that sparked a new plan in his twisted mind. Instead of absconding with your silver, he fully intended to marry Princess Solveig and position himself to take your throne, either before or after your passing, my lord. He indeed wished the army along to help kill Gudrun, but this time we were attacked. Troels excelled at pretending to be a hero, but honestly, Princess Solveig makes a better fighter."

"Why didn't you confess all this when Osmin graciously invited you into his home and spent countless hours seeing to your well-being?" Solveig pressed. "Here we were, nursing you back to health while you held all this treachery inside you. If Gudrun had wished, he could have killed Kai or all of us, only without you and Troels pulling his strings, he's just a hurt, confused young man who's been told he is a monster. Have you no shame? Do you not care what the gods will think of you? Do you not fear Helheim?"

Arvid lifted his chin and looked straight into Solveig's fiery gaze. "There is no Helheim. There are no jötnar, elves, dwarves, or trolls; no nine realms; no gods. It's all a lie. We are but dust who shall return to dust. Life is meaningless. So, no, I do not care about things that don't exist."

"You have lost your faith," Kai observed. "A man who once served the gods."

"Which is how I know they are false," he snapped. "My prayers were never answered, my sacrifices not honored. There's no magic in the runes, no spirits to guide us. When I needed them most, no gods granted me aid." Bitterness filled his tone and resentment darkened his countenance.

Baldr cocked his head at the former gothi. "Perhaps when they recognized your dark heart, they merely turned their backs on you."

Silence fell over the group for a long moment. A horse nearby snorted and pawed the earth, impatiently waiting for something to happen, and the sun hung lower in the sky.

Breaking the stillness, Kai ventured, "What do we do now?"

39

The king exchanged a glance with Baldr while a hive of bees buzzed around Kai's stomach. It was the most horrifying tale, and it left them with a moral dilemma of their own. Should they execute an individual who had committed terrible acts under the compulsion of a man already dead? And then there was Arvid, who was complicit in Troels' cruel scheme and had no doubt performed his fair share of atrocities against poor Gudrun. She had been sent to slay a monster, but it had turned out the true monster wasn't the misshapen giant after all.

"He might have been compelled, but it was Gudrun who crushed Herlief like a nut," Baldr pointed out.

Though it may not have been her place, Kai spoke out. "My lord, Gudrun had been tortured and his mind filled with lies. Then he was attacked by an army with spears and swords. Wouldn't anyone have fought to defend himself? Wouldn't you if you were surrounded by angry men bent on slaughtering you? I do not pretend to know the best course of action, but we should think carefully before doing something irreversible."

"I would like to talk with Gudrun," Solveig declared. "I would like to hear his side of the matter."

"Such is fair," Asbjorn determined. Then he bore into Arvid with a seething glare. "We'll deal with you directly."

Hand in hand, Kai and Solveig followed the king and Baldr until they reached Geirfinnr and the oversized crossbow, which was still cocked and pointed at the cave opening.

"He hasn't stirred," Geirfinnr announced, and Baldr told him what had transpired.

"Kai, can you persuade him to come out again?" Asbjorn asked. "I don't think it wise for us to all enter his domain."

"I believe so," she answered and scampered across the clearing.

With a calm coolness that belied her nerves, Kai entered the young man's den. "May I come in, Gudrun?"

He sat on the log with his head in his hands and grumbled in barely recognizable words, "Go away."

"My name is Kai," she said in a friendly fashion as she inched closer. "We have captured Arvid and Troels was killed by raiders last fall. There's nobody to hurt you now."

"I hurt," he uttered. "Hurt all the time."

Kai's heart was pricked by his forlorn tone. She sat on the far end of his log, appearing very small. "We are alike, you and I."

Gudrun's head shot up in surprise, and a sound akin to laughter rumbled in his throat. "Are not."

"We are," she repeated. "I stopped growing too soon and now I'm smaller than all the boys and girls my age. You didn't stop growing, only got taller and taller. People didn't understand. They weren't afraid of me, for what harm could a tiny person do? But they were afraid of you. That's why people hurt you."

"No," he replied in despair, lowering his chin and turning away. "I'm a monster."

"You are no such thing!" Kai proclaimed with conviction. "Troels and Arvid are monsters, your parents were monsters, but you are a man—just an extremely large one."

"You are pretty. I am ugly. We're not alike."

Kai examined Gudrun's burn-scarred face. It appeared his nose had been melted, giving it an unnatural, shrunken shape. The left side of his mouth was pulled back, like a piece of patched fabric that had shrunk, causing his lips to remain open, constantly exposing his teeth and gums. *He said he hurt all the time. It can't be comfortable and must cause his mouth to feel dry. It also explains why it is difficult for him to speak.* She supposed people who saw him, who didn't know what had happened, would turn away in horror and disgust. *Men always attack those who are different and whom they don't understand.*

He shot her a glance, then turned his back, lifting his arms to hide. "Go away!"

"Gudrun, look at me," she ordered. He lowered one arm and peeked in her direction. Holding his gaze, she spoke in a gentle tone. "You are not a monster. My king is out there, and he wishes to speak with you."

Though she noticed his face had lost its ability to show expressions, his eyes grew sorrowful before he turned away. "He wants to kill me. I should let him."

"Right now, he only wants to talk. I'll be honest," she said. "We don't know what to do about you, but King Asbjorn is a fair and just man, not like Troels. He wished to hear your side of the story. Notice no one attacked you the first time you came out. Will you trust me?" Kai stood and held out an open hand toward his gigantic frame.

"I'm scared," he admitted. "Gudrun doesn't want to hurt people. I don't want them to see me and hate me."

"Don't be afraid. I will protect you." Kai realized the absurdity of her claim. A tiny woman protecting a giant? Yet she supposed it may be just the catalyst to spur him to move.

His gruff, rumbling laugh sounded, and he shook his head. "I'll go. Only Kai has ever been kind to Gudrun." He extended a rough hand toward her, and Kai latched onto it, his words enough to break her heart. Then she led him out into the waning light.

Solveig paced nervously, waiting for Kai to return. "We shouldn't have let her go in there by herself," she muttered. "What's taking her so long?"

"Be patient, Solveig," her father told her. "We've heard no battle noise, nor cries for help. Remember, consulting Gudrun was your idea."

"I know," she scowled.

"Kai is quick and resourceful," Baldr added. "If the negotiations go poorly, she can easily outrun him."

"I suppose." The scuffle of feet sounded in Solveig's ears, and she snapped her attention to the dark spot on the cliff face, seeing two figures emerging.

"See? Here they come," Asbjorn declared with relief.

Solveig wasn't certain what she saw. She was so overjoyed it included a seemingly unharmed Kai that she broke through the brush ahead of the others, advancing toward the pair with a sense of uneasy anticipation.

At her approach, the gigantic man stopped and threw an arm over his face, cowering. Kai held fast to his other hand with both of hers, using all her wee weight to anchor Gudrun in place. "A Valkyrie!" he exclaimed in terror.

"No, no, Gudrun," Kai coaxed him. "It is only Princess Solveig. She will not hurt you. She is my friend."

"Do not shrink away, Gudrun," Solveig begged. She halted her advance, in awe of Kai holding his enormous hand. She looked like a tot clinging to her father. The giant could have easily tossed her aside, yet Kai appeared to be the one in charge. "We know what Troels and Arvid did to you. What they did was wrong."

She was aware of her father behind her, then Baldr and Geirfinnr at her sides.

"I am called Asbjorn Bloodaxe, King of Sogn," her father announced in a formal, yet not over-severe, manner. "We have matters to discuss. Will you sit with us like a civilized man and talk?"

Solveig was close enough now to see why everyone had thought Gudrun was a monster. She had never encountered a human so tall or with such oversized limbs. He would have been taller except for the hunch in his back. Tufts of scraggly hair protruded from a head proportional to the size of his body, and though he tried to hide his face, she distinguished its grotesque features. It was difficult not to stare, as people are always mesmerized by horrific sights, if only for their novelty. Still, her heart was pricked with compassion for one who had only experienced pain and rejection in this life—even if he had killed her brother.

Solveig took slow, nonthreatening steps until she arrived at Kai's side. She laid a hand over Kai's, where it rested, gripping Gudrun's, and slid a finger over his rough skin. "Sit with us," she requested.

With a slight nod, Gudrun consented. It was with a groan and extreme effort he lowered his stiff, aching body to the ground and crossed his legs in front of himself. "Did I kill some of your people? I'm sorry," he said, lowering his chin against his chest.

Solveig and the others sat in a circle on the ground around him while Kai stayed close to his side to keep him calm. "Yes," Asbjorn replied. "My friend Jarl Anders' son and my son, Herlief, along with scores of our warriors."

"They came to hurt me, to kill me," he responded in a mournful pout. "Master and the wizard killed the ones who entered the cave and others in their camp, but they told me I had to kill the warriors. Master said they would boil me in a pot and Hel would carry my soul to the depths of Helheim forever if I didn't. But..." Suddenly, he balled his hands into fists and pounded them against his disfigured face.

"Stop it!" Kai commanded. "What are you doing?"

Gudrun rocked and wailed. "Why did I obey Master? I was afraid. I'm a coward! Master and the wizard hurt me if I disobeyed. Why did I have to be so big and ugly?"

A tear of pity formed in Solveig's eye, and she glanced at the others.

"It wasn't the gods, but ignorant, selfish men who abused you," Kai declared. "Men who can't tolerate anyone who doesn't fit their expectations."

Relaxing his tense muscles, Gudrun caught the king's gaze. "Kill me. I always ache. I can't show my face. Everyone hates me. I hurt inside. I've done bad things and don't belong anywhere."

Pricked with sorrow, Solveig scooted beside her father and touched his arm. "Papa?" she whispered questioningly.

He patted her hand and spoke softly to her alone. "Do you remember when my favorite pony broke his leg? He was suffering and couldn't walk. It would never heal properly."

"I remember you said you had to put him down because it was the most merciful thing to do, but Gudrun isn't a horse. Punish Arvid instead."

"Arvid will get what he deserves; however, Gudrun has asked it of me, child. Look at him." Asbjorn glanced toward the hulk sitting beside Kai, his head and shoulders drooped. "There's no place for him in our world. It is a kinder act to send him on his way."

While her mind accepted his words as true, her heart was burdened. "We won't get Herlief back, nor Ragna, nor any of the others. Regardless," she sighed, "you are king, Papa, and I support your judgment."

Asbjorn sat up straight and addressed Gudrun in a noble style. "How would you prefer it to be done?"

"You are the leader. I killed your son," he answered gravely. "If I lie down, can you cut off my head in one blow?"

Solveig watched her father study the gigantic man. He pushed to his feet, and everyone except Kai followed. "I believe so. I have a robust arm and a powerful back. If I put my all into the strike, and you don't move, I can sever your neck instantly without pain. It is an honorable death. You may hold your spear in your right hand and die as a warrior. Then it'll be up to the gods to determine your fate. Is this what you wish?"

Tears streamed from Gudrun's eyes, and he nodded. "You're a worthy king. I don't deserve your kindness."

"Are you sure?" Kai asked. Solveig could see how she struggled not to cry.

"I'm tired," he sighed.

"Then I'll get your spear for you." Kai scrambled up and trotted to where the weapon lay. By the time she returned with it, Gudrun rested on his stomach on the rough ground with his head on a broad stone. She placed the handle in his right hand, and he curled his fingers around it.

With a glance, Solveig saw all the others had gathered, except the two left guarding Arvid and the horses. It was a somber moment when Asbjorn drew his sword. Kai had moved beside her now, and Solveig turned her face into her shoulder, grateful to feel her arms envelop her.

"It is all right," Kai whispered and held her close.

Suddenly, a rider galloped into the clearing, and Solveig's eyes shot open to see him jerk his mount to a skidding stop. "My lord! Soldiers from Sygnafylke! Gnóttdalr is under attack!"

40

K ing Asbjorn froze in mid-swing and pivoted to face the messenger, shock consuming his features.

"What!" he bellowed. "Why, that conniving, treacherous snake, Rundrandr! I knew we should have forged a treaty with Hördaland against him. Children, this is what happens when a ruler doesn't retaliate swiftly and decisively. If I hadn't been in mourning for Herlief—" A look of wrathful resolve flashed in his eyes.

"Everyone, to the horses," he commanded in a strong voice. "We must make all haste to save the kingdom. Baldr, assign men to ride to Jarls Anders and Bjorn, as they are closest. See if they have been attacked also, and if not, enlist their aid. If the Wolf wants war, he shall have it!"

"Papa, wait a moment!" A sudden thought occurred to Solveig, and she rushed to kneel beside Gudrun, who still lay prone, awaiting his execution. "You reside in my kingdom, so that makes me your princess," she told him. "You owe me a debt for killing my brother, and you will pay it. Only then shall the king grant your request."

Gudrun rolled on his side and peered at her in confusion. "What must I do?"

"I know you said you were tired of killing people, but my kingdom has been attacked," she explained. "You can redeem yourself of your crimes if you will be our champion and fight with us against the interlopers."

"Redeem myself?" he asked hesitantly. "Me, a champion?"

"Yes!" Kai exclaimed. "If I can be a hero, you can be a champion. We must protect the princess. It is our duty."

Gudrun sat up and turned a tentative gaze to Asbjorn. "Yes, yes," the king agreed. "We could use your help, only hurry." Turning his back, he and the warriors raced toward their horses.

"Can you run?" Solveig asked as the giant pushed to his feet. She noticed he wore crude shoes and leg bindings. "You are much too big for one of our ponies."

"I run fast," he answered. "Help the beautiful princess."

Solveig beamed at Kai, took her hand, and together they dashed away, with Gudrun following.

E ven though the troop rode at a gallop, night overtook them, and they arrived to see a town lit up by burning fires under a moonlit sky. Solveig's heart tightened in her chest and a righteous resolve flooded her body. Those who had attacked Gnóttdalr would pay.

"Dismount!" Asbjorn called, and she slid from her pony, panting and lathered in foam. "Geirfinnr, Caldervar, spread out and find them. Everyone else, with me."

Leaving the horses, Solveig marched alongside Kai, behind her father and brother, down a road past a blazing barn. A distressed sheep bleated to find its flock, accompanied by the crackle of burning wood. A woman draped in a brown shawl dashed out from a fish-cleaning hut.

"My lord, thank all the gods!" she cried. "They descended on us like wolves and wounded my husband." Her eyes grew wide as soup bowls, and she let out a blood-curling shriek of terror before fainting.

It seems Gudrun has caught up to us. Solveig smiled.

"My lord!" Geirfinnr called. "They've laid siege to the king's compound. The guards have been able to keep them out, but their numbers are great."

"How many?" Asbjorn queried.

Caldervar joined them, huffing. "I estimate a hundred or more."

"We are fourteen men, two shieldmaidens, and a giant," Baldr stated. "Add in our soldiers in the fortress and we shall crush the forces of Sygnafylke."

"Prepare your weapons and shields," Asbjorn commanded. "Gudrun, are you ready to redeem yourself, to be the princess' champion?"

The colossal man waved his enormous spear. "Aye!"

"You are now a valued member of our army," Baldr stated. "We'll approach up the road from town and form a shield wall. When their soldiers attack us, you must run behind them, tossing warriors about. It isn't essential for you to kill them, only to terrify them. Do you vow to do so?"

"I do. I will help Kai and the princess," he promised, then lumbered off to take his position away from the road.

"This is it," Asbjorn declared with steel intensity. "Follow me."

Silently, they marched up the hill from town toward the torch-lit bailey. Solveig's left arm was wound through her shield strap. She gripped its handle firmly, clasping Elyn's proven sword in her right fist. Doubt and a tingle of fear wiggled through her. *What if I'm not good enough? What if I make mistakes? What if people get hurt or killed defending me? I've never been in a battle before.*

"Here's what you do," Kai whispered, and her steadfast voice dispelled the worrisome thoughts. "You will be like a dragon's scale, an integral part of the shield wall. Keep your rönd pressed to mine and Baldr's, as you'll be between us. Brace yourself with your legs, especially your back-right foot, and put your left shoulder into your shield. When they push in, dig for your power, for it surges through your veins. Jab with your spear to injure or back them away. If Baldr and I move, step with us. If we stand, do not give ground. It is a battle of wills as much as force."

"I understand," she answered, and tried to swallow her apprehension.

"If the shield wall breaks, or if we are instructed to spread out, you may wish to switch to your sword," Kai added. "We spent much more time practicing sword fighting and you have an awesome blade. Solveig." Kai looked at her and a warm sensation washed over Solveig. "I know you can do this. You are absolutely amazing, and there is nothing you can't accomplish."

Appreciation for Kai swelled in Solveig, enhancing her strength and determination. She almost let a confession of love slip from her lips, but this was not
the time or circumstance for such sentiment. She nodded and flashed an assured
grin. "The same goes for you, my remarkable elf."

"Shield wall!" shouted her father with full authority. The warriors assumed
their positions while Solveig steadied her nerves.

*Desire and belief, Kai says. I desire to win this battle and stay alive doing it. So,
what—I must believe it will happen? But how?* Solveig wondered. *Kai envisioned
a fire, and it kept her warm. I see myself holding her in my bed. Her hair has grown
long, and we have been enjoying pleasures. She offers to take me on an adventure
at sea and I'm excited to go with her. For this to be made real, we must win and
not die.*

Solveig tucked the desired vision into her mind and focused all her strength
of body, mind, and spirit into holding her ground as the warriors of Sygnafylke
crashed against her rönd with greater force than she could have imagined.

K ai held her position and jabbed with her spear. She felt the blade slide off
a foe's greaves, pulled back, and plunged it in again. With her eyes flicking
between Solveig and her own feet and legs, Kai leaned every ounce of her meager
weight into her shield, countering her opponent's assault. She knew what to do
from training exercises with Baldr and the others, as bouts of push and thrust
were regular practice, yet this was her first experience in an actual battle, the first
time other people's lives depended on her.

She delivered another jab, feeling her blade slice through flesh. A cry rang
out amid the din of huffs, grunts, and insults. This grappling continued, and
sometimes Kai would gain a step, other times lose one. She had just started
wondering what had happened to Gudrun, if mayhap he had run away, when
her ears detected unmistakable screams of terror and disbelief.

"A giant!" a man screeched. "Run for your lives!"

"Hold your positions!" bellowed another. But Kai sensed the give in her adversary's force and pressed her advantage. Baldr and Solveig picked their way forward, step by step, as well.

More shouts, then the wails of a man followed by the clatter of him landing atop his fellow warriors. "Go away!" bellowed Gudrun's gruff, indistinct words.

Sygnafylke's line broke into chaos. "Attack!" Asbjorn shouted.

The gate opened, and troops from inside the palisade poured out at their enemy's rear while their shield wall separated into individual fighters. Kai plunged her spear into a disoriented man's side and released it, drawing Stinnr. She glanced at Solveig, who simply dropped her lance and ripped Elyn's sword from its scabbard. She nodded at Kai, and they moved forward as one.

Some invaders fled, others engaged them in single combat, but most focused their attention on Gudrun.

"King Asbjorn," called a frantic voice. "Why are your warriors not fighting the jötunn?"

"Join with us against the monster!" cried another.

"He fights on our side," Asbjorn retorted with glee as he sliced through a foe's shield with his mighty axe. The man tossed the splinters aside and blocked the king's next blow with an iron sword. Asbjorn hooked his axe-head over the fellow's blade, rotated his wrist, and sent it hurling away. His return blow cleaved the attacker in half.

Kai returned her focus to the enemy opposite her. He swung his axe, and she ducked, sweeping his calves with her sword. She drew her blade into his muscle, cutting sinews with its sharp edge, and he stumbled with a desperate cry. She spun to Solveig's flank, blocking a burly invader's path. He slammed down at her with his heavy weapon, but she flung up her rönd. The force of his blow shoved her to one knee, whence she skewered his foot with Stinnr. Sliding out from under him, she positioned herself at Solveig's side once more.

Her heart soared to witness the princess holding her own in combat. She kept her shield up, moved her feet, and whirled her sword with precision. Nor was Solveig shy to pierce an opponent's body with her steel as she battled like a true shieldmaiden. Together, they defeated two more invaders before Syg-nafylke's leader called for a retreat.

"Chase the cowardly mares back to their ships!" Asbjorn bellowed. Kai caught her breath as she watched the king, Baldr, Geirfinnr, and dozens of other warriors run after the fleeing enemies.

With a glance at Solveig, she asked, "Are you all right?"

"Excellent!" Solveig panted and lowered her shield to let her arm rest, a gleam of triumph in her expression. "Invigorated! Did you see how we chased them away? Kai, at first, I was afraid I wouldn't measure up, but ..." She sucked in more air, grinning in amazement. "You encouraged me, and I did it. By all the gods, I did it! I may be confined to my bed tomorrow, but I have never felt so alive. I helped save my home. Papa will insist on meeting with King Rundrandr, or more likely formally join forces with King Geirmund, and we'll have our work cut out for us, repairing the damaged and destroyed buildings and tending to all the wounded. Soon it'll be planting time, and we have no seed grain. Papa will have to trade for some. Oh, Kai, this is wonderful! Did you see me? I didn't fall back. I did what you taught me, and held my ground!"

In her exuberance, Solveig released her shield and wrapped Kai in a joyful hug. Relishing the attention, Kai enveloped her in a firm embrace. "You were magnificent! I'm so proud of you, yet I knew you could do it. Isn't it what I told you all along?"

"I couldn't have done it without you," Solveig gushed. "And that's the truth."

"I doubt any of us could have done it without Gudrun," Kai added. At once, a troubling thought struck her. "Where is he?"

Both women stepped out of their embrace and scanned the battlefield.

"Gudrun!" Kai called. There was no answer. "We must search for him." Kai clasped Solveig's hand to lead her, knowing it would be hard for her to navigate in the dark. The noise of their army pursuing the intruders to the shore had grown more distant, so Kai listened as she and Solveig maneuvered around the dead and injured from both sides. "Gudrun, where are you?"

They passed a swath of Sygnafylkers fanned out on the ground, some writhing in pain, others lying still. "We will see to you once our wounded have been treated," Solveig told them as they pressed on.

Spotting an unusually large figure ahead, Kai pointed. "There." Kai and Solveig moved faster until they arrived at the place where Gudrun had crumpled.

"You are hurt!" she said as she released Solveig's hand and leaned over him, checking the wounds. There were so many. Spears, arrows, axes, and swords protruded from his body, which was coated in blood. Instinctively, Kai and Solveig began pulling the offending weapons from his flesh. He moaned in pain and drew in a rattling breath.

"Enemies gone?" he uttered.

"Yes." Solveig kneeled by his head and brushed his matted hair with a gloved hand. "You were our champion tonight," she praised him. "Their numbers were too great. Without your help, we wouldn't have prevailed. Thank you, Gudrun."

"Please," he begged. "End my pain."

When Kai plucked out the last shaft she could see, Gudrun rolled onto his back, staring up at them with agony arising from his soul. The only others around were a few men from the king's longhouse bearing the wounded in to be treated. Asbjorn, Baldr, and the other warriors were chasing away their enemies, leaving only Solveig and herself. She glanced at Solveig, who shook her head and lowered her chin.

"You proved yourself a friend, Gudrun. You were courageous, not a coward at all. Frigg says heroes come in all sizes. Remember that," Kai charged him. Scanning the ground, she spotted his spear and brought it to the young man, placing it in his hands. Solveig stepped back as Kai unsheathed her blade. "My arms are not as powerful as King Asbjorn's," she confessed, "but I have a magic sword. This is Stinnr, forged of Damascus steel, infused with the bones of a great warrior, inscribed with mystic runes, and blessed with a völva's seiðr. With this sword, I can end your suffering. I pray it sends you to Valhalla, for you are a fearsome foe in combat. In Ásgarðr your face will be normal again, and you'll eat and drink with the gods. Are you ready?"

"Thank you, Kai," he managed between labored breaths. "Ready."

Pride in Gudrun mingled with the heaviness of heart she felt at her duty, yet he was dying. This was for the best. Kai raised Stinnr with both hands and slammed the razor-sharp edge across his throat. Relief washed through her to see the deed accomplished in a single strike. She stood for an instant, peering down at his lifeless body and damaged face. "How cruel men can be," she murmured.

Solveig's arms reached around her and tugged her against her breast. "And how kind." She rested her chin on Kai's shoulder. "If you hadn't come, Kai, this poor boy would never have experienced kindness, even if it was for a only moment."

She felt Solveig's comforting kisses on her cheek and sank into her, closing her eyes.

"What was it your Frigg predicted?" Solveig's voice took on a curious quality. "If you didn't come to help us, the king and the princess would be cut down by many spears, axes, and swords, and the woman of substance would cry alone in her great hall. Kai, think!" She gave Kai a squeeze from behind. "If you hadn't been with us today and seen the giant for who and what he was and stayed Baldr's hand on the weapon, we would have killed him earlier—although I likely wouldn't have been there, for without you building my confidence I'd still be sitting alone in my misery. However, our enemies would have attacked, as they did today. They outnumbered us, even after my father's troop arrived from the mountainside. Our forces would have been crushed without Gudrun's aid and the terror he instilled in their warriors. If not for you, we would have unknowingly destroyed our only hope of victory. You saved Sogn, just as your völva foretold, only it wasn't by the might of your sword, but rather by the power of your compassion."

"Kingdom or not, my life has changed for the better by having you in it."

41

A week later

Kai felt privileged to sit beside Solveig at the king's table for a special occasion. She drew many amazed gazes from the crowd as tales of the battle had been greatly exaggerated. The latest version declared the brave little Swede had single-handedly slain the ferocious jötunn with her magic sword, Stinnr. Her protests and efforts to set the record straight were all ignored.

With a bashful smile, she looked at Solveig. She looked particularly stunning in her sunshine dress. Her hair was down, adorned with a flower. The princess was ever graceful and attentive to those gathered around the table. Admiring her, Kai was grateful Ingrid had offered her a spring-green gown Sylvi had outgrown, which she had donned that evening, wanting to look nice for Solveig.

Jarl Anders and Jarl Bjorn were present along with King Geirmund's representative from Hördaland, as the king was busy stripping the defeated Rundrandr the Wolf of his title, wealth, and land. King Asbjorn, being a man of his word, had granted Arvid's request and accorded him a swift death. None objected nor rose to the disgraced gothi's defense, though many gathered to stare in astonishment when Gudrun's broken body was laid upon a pyre and sped on its way to the afterlife.

Solveig had introduced Kai to Sylvi, who had returned with Karina and her brother, Harald, a cheerful young man who doted on her. They'd also joined the king's table, which had been lengthened to accommodate the significant number of dignitaries. Kai must have seemed shy, fading out of conversation, although it was because her mind insisted on replaying the happenings of the week.

On the night of the battle, Ingrid had met them at the door with tearful hugs before rushing off to help the healer tend to the wounded men. Kai and Solveig had been drained, physically and emotionally, by the events of the day, and had fallen into Solveig's bed exhausted. When they'd awoken the next morning, duty had demanded their constant attention. There were repairs to make, the injured to treat, bodies to be buried, and storehouses to be replenished. Even the supply of dried kelp had been destroyed in the attack. Kai spent most of her days hunting to provide enough meat. Spring was not the best season for it, as she wished to avoid killing mothers with babies who would perish without them.

While she had still enjoyed Solveig's company at night, they hadn't a chance to engage in any personal conversations, which made Kai nervous. Now that her mission was complete, and things were getting back to normal, where was her place? Would Solveig wish her to stay? If so, in what capacity?

I need to tell her how I feel, she thought, *even if it means I meet with rejection. How can I consider myself courageous if I can't do a simple thing like declaring my love?*

But she is a king's daughter, she argued with herself. *She will be expected to wed a prince or a jarl and have many children, even if she continues in her role as defender of the realm. I'm just an orphan from a foreign land.*

Everyone laughed at a joke she hadn't heard, and Kai took a bite of her meal. She noticed Solveig purposely dropping a morsel of venison for Mist, who sat expectantly by her feet.

"Hear, hear!" Asbjorn stood, drawing everyone's attention. He lifted his chalice and said, "To our honored guests, bold warriors, and fierce shieldmaidens!"

Everyone raised their horns and cups. "Skoll!"

After swallowing a gulp, he proposed another toast. "To our fallen comrades who feast in Odin's hall this night!"

"Skoll!"

Kai drank in salute and remembered Gudrun.

"And now," Asbjorn announced, "we have another reason to celebrate. Jarl Bjorn and I have talked, and it seems his worthy son Harald is smitten with my Sylvi." Smiling faces beamed as hushed comments trickled through the crowded hall. "And she has wholeheartedly agreed to be his bride!"

The assembly cheered, and Solveig laid a hand on Kai's arm. "See how happy she looks?" she said. "I am so glad my sister wishes for this match. Since Herlief died, it is another way our families can be joined. She will keep her dear friend Karina as a sister-in-law."

"They both seem elated," Kai agreed, glancing at the glow on the couple's faces.

"Now you just need to find mates for Baldr and Solveig," someone called out from the back of the hall.

The suggestion pierced Kai's soul as she was forced to consider Solveig could still be married off to a man not of her choosing. She recalled King Asbjorn had announced he would give his daughter's hand to whoever killed the giant. *That was me.* She swallowed the words, too afraid to say them in the hall. Taking breaths to steady her nerves, she stared at a spot on the table.

"Didn't the little Swede kill the jötunn?" asked a dinner guest.

"As it turns out, there was no giant," Asbjorn declared. "Just an abnormally tall man who had been burned in a fire and coerced into a deceitful plot to steal my throne. He was our ally, in the end."

"Papa."

Kai swallowed a lump when Solveig called to him, wondering what she would say.

"Yes, dear?" He and Ingrid shifted their attention to her.

"I must point out that Kai did exactly what she came to do," Solveig proclaimed. "She persuaded Gudrun to join us, and when he suffered mortal wounds, 'twas she who struck the killing blow. So, in a manner of speaking, Kai indeed killed the giant, thus meeting the terms of your bargain."

Asbjorn's expression waffled between dismay and consternation. "Now, see here, Solveig—"

"My lord," Kai spoke out. "I could have done nothing without Solveig. She deserves equal credit for ending the threat and saving the kingdom from ruin. I propose you make a vow before these witnesses saying Solveig has earned the right to wed whomever she wishes, or not to marry at all if it is her choice."

Ingrid beamed, Solveig gripped Kai's arm tighter in expectation, and Asbjorn sighed, rolling his eyes. He twirled his empty hand in the air while draining his cup. "Very well. I declare my daughter Solveig may do exactly as she pleases where the topic of marriage is concerned from this day forward. I shan't interfere."

Some people laughed, others cheered, and most appeared quite content.

Solveig's expression radiated joy and appreciation as she turned it on Kai. "Thank you," she whispered. "Kai to the rescue again."

"It was only fair." Kai dared to hope Solveig would choose her, despite her multitude of shortcomings.

It seemed the feast would last forever. Solveig had enjoyed a few frolicking dances with Kai, as well as one with Geirfinnr and another with her future brother-in-law, Harald. But it had been a long week, and her energy reserves were extremely low.

Kai didn't claim the right to marry me, she pondered. *Was it because no precedence exists for such an arrangement or because she doesn't want me in that way? Is she about to leave, return to Yeats? I need answers.*

When the musician's song ended, Ivarolf hopped onto the platform and raised his hands. "Who is eager for a story?" The crowd cheered, and those who had been dancing competed for seats.

Solveig caught Kai's sleeve. "I'm ready to retire to my chamber. Would you like to join me?"

"Yes." Her brilliant eyes sparkled, and Solveig supposed she was looking forward to another night of pleasures. Only Solveig had determined she wanted more. She wanted her to stay.

Mist remained in the hall, still hopeful more food would need to be scarfed up from the floor, no doubt. Inside, Solveig latched her door and turned to Kai. After a much-needed and luxurious kiss, she retreated and tried to settle her anxiety. "You look nice in Sylvi's dress."

Kai answered with an infectious smile. "I'm glad you think so. I'm always wearing worn-out trousers and grungy tunics. I wanted you to see a different side of me for a change."

She seems as nervous as I feel, Solveig thought. *I must get to the point.* "I was wondering..." By then she had wandered to the far end of her bed, several feet away from Kai. Glancing up, she noticed Kai's eager expression. *She probably thinks I'm about to propose a new pleasure game. Oh, Odin's beard—just ask, already!*

"What happens now? I mean, with us? I suppose you wish to return to Yeats to your family and friends, to tell your völva what happened. You'll want to go home, right?"

Kai's countenance fell, and her excited eyes dulled in disappointment. "Is that what you want me to do?"

"It's not up to me, Kai," Solveig said. "You have to decide these things for yourself."

"Oh." Kai crumpled to sit at the foot of the bed. "I suppose I need to go back to let them all know I'm still alive." She let out a dry chuckle. "I wouldn't want them conducting another funeral for me. But..." She peered up at Solveig with longing in her eyes. "I had really hoped you and your father could find a place for me here. I know I'm a foreigner, yet ... I thought people liked me, that I was an asset."

"Kai, you are; we do." Solveig scooted around to sit beside her, still uncertain how to proceed. "I'm not saying I want you to go; I just won't force you to stay."

Kai took her hands and focused every ounce of her energy on her. "There's something I need to tell you. You may think it silly, and it's all right if you do. But the truth is, I love you, Solveig. I was struck with a powerful attraction when I first saw you, though you clearly didn't feel the same way. Then, over the winter, you gave me a chance, and we became friends. I know I'm not a tall, powerfully built shieldmaiden like Ragna was, and I'm not from a noble household, nor do I have two coins to rub together. But what I do have, everything I am, is devoted to you. If you don't want me to stay—"

"I do!" Solveig blurted out. Gently grabbing Kai by the back of the neck, she pulled her into a passionate kiss, affirming her own affection. She wished the kiss would never end. *She loves me!*

Upon her body's mutinous demand for air, she retreated an inch yet kept her trembling lips as close as she could and still speak. "More than anything, I wish for you to stay with me. I love you, too. Can't you tell? And for your information, I've decided I like being the larger, more physically imposing member of the pair." She flicked her lashes at Kai playfully and added another kiss to the mix.

"Really?" An adorable, excited expression returned to Kai's face, and her smile could have lit a gigantic cavern.

"Here's the thing, my love," Solveig stated earnestly. "You and I will never be Sigrid and Elyn. We can't fight epic battles, wrestle bears, or ride on whales' backs. But we *can* be Solveig and Kai. We can have our own adventures, ones that don't require great height or perfect eyesight, where our brains and hearts will matter more than the power of our sword arms to settle conflicts. The skalds shall tell our stories one day, and even if they don't, just having you in my life is enough.

"Kai, there is one feat greater than fulfilling one's destiny—helping another step into theirs. You did that for me, and I love you so very much." Solveig's fingers trailed through Kai's silky hair, creating a sensation she had grown to enjoy a great deal. Confidence surged through her as her sultry voice delivered an ardent proposal. "I'd like to spend the rest of my life showing you just how delighted you make me feel."

Kai's eyes twinkled, and the corners of her mouth turned up in a mischievous grin. "Is that so? Then I have an idea for our first adventure. It involves you, me, and this enormous bed."

Solveig laughed, pulled Kai close, and dove in for another kiss ... and all the glorious explorations to follow.

EPILOGUE

Summer, 691 AD

S olveig stood at the bow of the longboat with her arms wrapped around Kai, who steadied them both with a hand against the dragon figurehead. She'd proudly donned the blue armor that had once belonged to her grandmother, with her historic sword strapped to her belt. Kai had taught her several techniques to prevent or dispel her seasickness, which, to her elation, had worked wonders.

"What do you see?" Kai called over her shoulder.

Water slapped the planks of the ship, and a westerly breeze filled the sail, allowing the crew to take a break from rowing.

"I see a vast expanse of ocean—lots and lots of water." Solveig laughed. "And a fair number of clouds drifting about the sky. Over to our port, I can make out dark shadows which are the coastline and the mountains rising from it. And I see the dolphins riding our bow. It's amazing how they escort our vessel like Njord's ambassadors. Papa always says they are a sign of good fortune."

"They are," Kai agreed.

Solveig radiated with a mixture of expectation and satisfaction, the tingle of excitement invigorating every part of her being. This was the life she had longed for, and she couldn't imagine anyone other than Kai to share it with. It may only be a trading venture, but she was going to see foreign lands, magnificent sights, and there could be danger: a storm on the waves, a sea monster, hostile raiders. In that moment, Solveig was confident she and Kai could take on the world together.

The past several months had been a paradise, as she and Kai had gotten to know each other better. Their skills and temperaments complemented one another, making them excellent partners, and there was no denying the pleasures the pair shared in bed.

Solveig's father had come to terms with her lifestyle choice and accepted Kai into the family. Her mother was busy planning Sylvi's wedding, which they had promised to return in time for when the leaves would begin to fall. Baldr had stepped up as heir to become the king's right-hand man, learning what he had to master to rule one day—and how to breed Fjordings.

"I know you are excited to be going to visit your home." A few strands escaped Solveig's braid and blew in her face as they cut through the waves. She lifted a hand to brush them aside, then returned her arm to encompass Kai's waist. Kai looked magnificent in Sigrid's old armor and leggings. Her hair was long enough to plait now, but Kai kept it in a single tail. Solveig liked it, as it seemed to fit her style and personality.

"I can't wait for you to meet Torsten and Leiknir," she replied enthusiastically. "And especially Frigg. We'll have to stop by Lagarfjord and Bàtrgørð because I don't know who will be where."

"I know I'll love all of them," Solveig agreed.

"And it's a good thing we brought plenty of merchandise to exchange, for we'll be stopping by Truso on the southern shore of the sea. My friend Gavril is a merchant who loves to trade for Norse products. I'm sure he'll have silks and trinkets you'll like."

"I'm certain he will." Solveig gave Kai's firm stomach a little squeeze and brushed a kiss to her cheek. "I really look forward to seeing Uppsala. Mother and Papa went when I was small and told me such grand stories. Now I'll get to see it for myself."

"You will not forget it, I promise," Kai vowed. "We should be home from our voyage in plenty of time to organize the harvest. It was fortunate the northern jarls could spare some seed grain."

"Indeed. By next year our food stocks will have returned to pre-raid levels," Solveig predicted. "And while some may wish to keep seaweed in their diets, I doubt the demand will remain high once they have their traditional foods in ample supply. I, for one, will not miss drinking víðir bjórr!"

They both laughed, and Kai shook her head. "It was rather odd tasting."

"Odd? It was disgusting. The men only drank it because it delivered a potent kick."

"Well, I am not a qualified brewer," Kai admitted. "I may have gotten the recipe wrong."

"Regardless, you got so many things right, my love," Solveig cooed. She gazed out over the sea, breathed in the salty air, and reveled in the flow of the breeze. Here she was on her first real adventure with an amazing woman who made her feel invincible. She wondered about the dolphins, the gods, and the fortunes of humans. Most of all, she wondered about the mystery of belief and the power of love.

"I'm glad you think so," Kai answered. "I'm positive of one thing I got right: you."

She turned and tipped her lips to meet Solveig's in a kiss that she gladly returned. Beneath the saltiness of the sea brine, she could taste Kai's sweetness. And so, they rode the waves into the rising sun, into a future of many voyages and challenges to come. Whether enjoying a wildflower field of summer or surviving the desolation of winter, they trusted their love would forever bring them victory.

If you enjoyed Legacy of the Valiant, you'll want to read the other Tales from Norvegr.

MORE BOOKS BY EDALE LANE

Tales from Norvegr
Sigrid and Elyn: A Tale from Norvegr
https://www.amazon.com/dp/B0B5W48342
Legacy of the Valiant: A Tale from Norvegr
https://www.amazon.com/dp/B0BZK7Y655
War and Solace: A Tale from Norvegr
https://www.amazon.com/dp/B0CGP4WVYP
Jorunn, Shieldmaiden of Hárfell (prequel to The Long Winter of Miðgarðr)
https://dl.bookfunnel.com/bpowqyeg4j
The Long Winter of Miðgarðr
https://www.amazon.com/dp/B0DKP2MWD2
Viking Quest
https://www.amazon.com/dp/B097NTZVPC

The Lessons in Murder Series
Meeting over Murder
https://www.amazon.com/dp/B0B7R69R7B
Skimming around Murder
https://www.amazon.com/dp/B0B9R6FJWL
New Year in Murder
https://www.amazon.com/dp/B0BDQSPT6L
Heart of Murder
https://www.amazon.com/dp/B0BQQS57FY

Reprise in Murder
https://www.amazon.com/dp/B0C2YDKLSB
Homecoming in Murder
https://www.amazon.com/dp/B0C7M2VKSH
Queen of Murder
https://www.amazon.com/dp/B0CKRYLNSW
Cold in Murder
https://www.amazon.com/dp/B0CSXMBJLJ
Foreseen in Murder
https://www.amazon.com/dp/B0D3G5JMLP
Matrimony in Murder
https://www.amazon.com/dp/B0DDJY4JXY

SapphicLover69
https://www.amazon.com/dp/B0DCZRW2K

Daring Duplicity: The Wellington Mysteries, Vol.1
https://www.amazon.com/dp/B09QDTF9YN
Perilous Passages: The Wellington Mysteries, Vol. 2
https://www.amazon.com/dp/B0B16FWN63
Daunting Dilemmas: The Wellington Mysteries, Vol. 3
https://www.amazon.com/dp/B0BMDQ8TLC

Atlantis, Land of Dreams
https://www.amazon.com/dp/B0D7TB52CG

Heart of Sherwood
https://www.amazon.com/dp/B07W4M3R5L
Walks with Spirits
https://www.amazon.com/dp/B09VBGQF27/

The Night Flyer Series

Merchants of Milan, book one
https://www.amazon.com/dp/B083H6WNKD
Secrets of Milan, book two
https://www.amazon.com/dp/B088HFM7Q5
Chaos in Milan, book three
https://www.amazon.com/dp/B08Q7H6DFX
Missing in Milan, book four
https://www.amazon.com/dp/B09CNXF1CX
Shadows over Milan, book five
https://www.amazon.com/dp/B09KF53VTZ

Visit My Website:
https://www.authoredalelane.com
Follow me on Goodreads (Don't forget to leave a quick review!)
https://www.goodreads.com/author/show/15264354.Edale_Lane
Follow me on BookBub:
https://www.bookbub.com/profile/edale-lane
Newsletter sign-up link:
https://bit.ly/3qkGn95

ABOUT THE AUTHOR

Edale Lane is an Amazon Best-selling author and winner of Rainbow, Lesfic Bard, and Imaginarium Awards. Her sapphic historical fiction and mystery stories feature women leading the action and entice readers with likable characters, engaging storytelling, and vivid world-creation.

Lane (whose legal name is Melodie Romeo) holds a bachelor's degree in music education, a master's in history, and taught school for 24 years before embarking on an adventure driving an 18-wheeler over-the-road. She is a mother of two, Grammy of three, and a doggy mom. A native of Vicksburg, MS, Lane now lives her dream of being a full-time author in beautiful Chilliwack, BC, with her long-time life partner.

Enjoy free e-books and other promotional offerings while staying up to date with what Edale Lane is writing next when you sign up for her newsletter.

https://bit.ly/3qkGn95

Made in the USA
Monee, IL
16 November 2024

70313206R00179